Dear Reader,

Those of you who read my books know that these days I write contemporary romantic thrillers as Jayne Ann Krentz, historical romantic suspense as Amanda Quick and futuristics as Jayne Castle. At the start of my career, however, I wrote classic, battle-of-the-sexes-style romance using both my Krentz name and the pen name Stephanie James. This volume contains one or more stories from that time.

I want to take this opportunity to thank all of you— new readers as well as those who have been with me from the start. I appreciate your interest in my books.

Sincerely,

Jayne Ann Krentz

JAYNE ANN KRENTZ

WRITING AS STEPHANIE JAMES

DANGEROUS GAMES

HQN™

ISBN-13: 978-0-373-77320-6
ISBN-10:   0-373-77320-X

DANGEROUS GAMES

Copyright © 2008 by Harlequin Books S.A.

The publisher acknowledges the copyright holder of the individual works as follows:

THE DEVIL TO PAY
Copyright © 1985 by Jayne Ann Krentz

WIZARD
Copyright © 1985 by Jayne Ann Krentz

CONTENTS

THE DEVIL TO PAY

For Suzanne,
a good friend on the same path.
WRITE ON!

CHAPTER ONE

SHE COULDN'T SHAKE THE FEELING that she was being watched.

Emelina Stratton paused, her hand on the knob of the back door of the deserted beach house, and nervously swung the flashlight in an arc. It barely pierced the gathering fog. She had about ten feet of visibility, and even that would soon be gone. There was nothing to be seen in the writhing shadows that clung to the lonely stretch of beach.

It was only her all too-vivid imagination at work again, she told herself resolutely. Lively enough on an average day, her imagination was running wild under the present circumstances.

Getting a grip on herself, she tossed the long, heavy braid of chestnut hair back over one shoulder and tried the doorknob. Locked. Of course it would be locked. It had been too much to hope that Leighton would have been so careless as to leave the door conveniently open. She wiggled the knob fruitlessly for a few seconds and then gave up. It would have to be one of the windows. Would she dare to break one and pray that Leighton would assume it was only an act of vandalism by some young kids?

The sensation of being under observation returned again as Emelina started down the back steps. Once again she cast an uneasy glance around the dark, foggy beach.

Several yards away a light surf lapped almost gently at the rocky Oregon shoreline. Above the soft sound of the waves she could hear nothing alarming. But the unconscious response of her body to impending danger grew stronger, lifting the delicate hairs on the nape of her neck and sending small shivers along each nerve ending.

Nothing moved in the surrounding shadows. Emelina rubbed her hands along her arms. It was cold here at midnight on the Oregon coast. The close-fitting black sweater she had worn wasn't nearly enough protection from the bite of the fog-shrouded air. Pity. It had looked exactly right for a commando mission.

Damn her imagination! It was a poor companion on a job like this. Perhaps professional burglars got along in their chosen profession precisely because they lacked the ability to dream up such vivid images of disaster! Emelina couldn't believe that anyone would attempt this sort of thing on a regular basis if he or she had to put up with all these nerve-wracking imaginings!

As she tested the window frame she told herself for the hundredth time that there was very little likelihood of anyone else's being around this quiet strip of beach at this hour. The fog was thickening by the minute, which should deter the average midnight stroller, even if there were any such living in the quiet little coastal village nearby. There were a couple of other houses behind Leighton's, all deserted at this time of year. There were also a few cottages up on the bluff overlooking the beach. They were inhabited. In fact, Emelina was living in one of them, herself, but as far as she could tell, everyone else was in bed for the night. "Early to bed, early to rise" seemed to be a local motto. They rolled the streets up early in town.

The window didn't budge an inch.

"Damn!"

With the short exclamation of disgust, Emelina stepped back and swung around to search for a likely looking rock. She went utterly still at sight of the pair who had materialized out of the fog behind her.

"Oh, my God!" The words were a whisper of sound as she sucked in a sharp, frightened breath. Instinctively her startled gaze went first to the Doberman before shifting to its master.

The sleek black-and-tan dog didn't move. It sat quietly on its haunches, watching her intently. The small, sensitive ears were pricked alertly, and the unhuman, dark gaze never wavered.

Slowly, unwillingly, Emelina lifted her eyes to the dark, dangerous man who stood beside the dog. It struck Emelina in that moment that Julian Colter was as quietly lethal looking as his Doberman. It was the first time she had seen either of them at this range however, and up close the flashlight's beam revealed that the man radiated a more subtle element of menace than the beast. For in addition to the somehow graceful threat of power he seemed to share with the dog, Julian Colter wore an aura of command. He was clearly master of both the Doberman and himself.

"Good evening." The soft, gravelly voice drew Emelina's nerves taut. She felt as if she had just stepped into a Dracula film and was being introduced to the count, himself. "If you're looking for a place to spend the night, I can offer far better accommodations than you'll find in that deserted house."

I'll bet, Emelina thought grimly. Could she outrun him? She swallowed with difficulty. Even if that were a possibility, and she sincerely doubted it, common sense warned her that no one could outrun the Doberman. Did Colter recognize her? Had he seen her occasionally from a distance just as she'd seen him during the past week? What the hell was he doing down here on this beach at this hour?

"No." Emelina chewed on her very dry lower lip and tried again, jamming her free hand into the front pocket of her black denim jeans in an effort to hide the fact that it was trembling. "No, I wasn't looking for a place to sleep." Had he mistaken her for a passing hitchhiker looking for a convenient bed for the night? Good. Maybe he hadn't recognized her. "I... I was just out for a walk."

"A walk." Julian Colter took a pace closer, ignoring the flashlight's glare. The Doberman followed. The gathering fog swirled around them both. "It's a rather unusual hour for a walk, isn't it?" he inquired with grave politeness.

In the harsh glow of the light she held in her hand Emelina could barely make out his features. But she could see enough to tell that his gaze was almost totally unreadable. "You seem to be out doing the same thing," she pointed out with bravado.

"Ah, yes," he agreed with a faint, very polite inclination of his head. A brief flash of white betrayed the smallest of amused smiles. "But, then, I have a reason to be out here on the beach at midnight."

"You...you do?" Emelina gnawed on her lip. Had she unwittingly interrupted a dangerous rendezvous?

"Ummm. I was following you."

"What?" For an instant sheer outrage combined with Emelina's fear. "*Following* me! You had no right to do that! Following me! Whatever for?"

"Well, there isn't a whole lot to do in this village, as you may or may not have noticed," he murmured with mild apology. "You interest me."

"Good God! I'm not hanging around this godforsaken place for the sole purpose of providing you with a little entertainment!"

"I realize that. Which brings up the intriguing question of what you are doing around this place, doesn't it? Why don't you come back to the cottage with Xerxes and me and we'll talk about that little matter over a glass of brandy. It's getting chilly down here, don't you think?"

The dog got to his feet at the sound of his name and glanced up expectantly at his master. Emelina stared at both of them and thought again about running. "No," she whispered. "That's impossible. I have no wish to go to your place with you, Mr. Colter!"

The shark's smile came and went again. "I see you know my name. That gives you something of an advantage, I'm afraid. I don't know yours."

"Good," Emelina retorted unthinkingly.

He appeared mildly regretful. "Come along, night lady. I feel in the need of a few answers before I go to sleep."

He took a step closer and Emelina lost her nerve completely. In blind panic she turned and fled back along the beach. It was not the smartest move she could have made. The shoreline was rocky and uneven, and with the swirling fog she could barely see five feet in front of her.

But she ran, recklessly, heedlessly, as if Dracula and his pet werewolf were on her heels. Emelina didn't see any other choice in that moment except flight. She knew what the townspeople were saying about Julian Colter, and memory of their low-voiced speculation was more than enough to send her fleeing.

The werewolf caught up with her first. There had been no shouted warnings to stop, no sharp, menacing bark.

Neither man nor beast had wasted time and effort on such deterrents. They had both pursued silently, having no intention of allowing her to escape.

The Doberman appeared out of the fog at Emelina's side, running easily, his mouth open and laughing in the fitful moonlight. Emelina swung around and braced herself for the attack, her hands in front of her.

But the dog didn't attack. He came to a halt, too, sitting on his haunches and smiling up at her. Belatedly, Emelina realized that he thought it was all a game. He hadn't been ordered to attack. The Doberman had simply followed when she'd started running, enjoying the night race.

She was staring at the animal when its owner stepped out of the mist. If Julian Colter had been running, there was no evidence to document the fact. Even as Emelina dragged in a harsh breath she realized that the man looked no more strained than the dog.

"If you take him running like that very often, you'll have a friend for life." Colter smiled, indicating the Doberman. "He loves a good race." Then, before she could prepare herself, he reached out and took hold of Emelina's arm. "But it's not really a good night for running, is it? Let's go back to the cottage. Come on, Xerxes," he added, glancing down at the dog.

Emelina found herself going along as obediently, if not as willingly, as Xerxes. There really wasn't much choice. Strong fingers were locked around her upper arm now, not yet painful but full of the promise of unshakable will. Julian Colter was after some answers tonight, and now nothing was going to stand in his way.

Desperately Emelina tried to marshal her thoughts. She had to come up with a convincing tale or she was only going to dig the grave deeper than ever. Grave. What a horrible image. She gritted her teeth and cursed her own imagination again.

"Do you have a name, night lady?"

There was no point lying about it, she supposed. "Emelina. Emelina Stratton." The words came out sullenly, masking the fear she felt.

"Emelina. I like that. I'll call you Emmy. You don't have to be afraid of me, Emmy," he added surprisingly.

"I'm not. At least, no more than I would be afraid of any man who accosted me on the beach at midnight!" she exclaimed with a great depth of feeling.

Colter nodded understandingly as he guided her up the path to the bluff overlooking the beach. "I only want a few answers, Emmy."

"Why? What business is it of yours what I do at midnight?"

"I told you, you interest me. You arrive a week ago, all alone, and take a cottage that's not more than a short block from my own. It's the middle of winter, which is not a popular time for tourists in this part of the country. You spend your days keeping watch on that deserted beach house and then one night I see you making your way down the street toward the beach path. I find you about to commit an act of breaking and entering at midnight. I ask myself what anyone would hope to find worth stealing in that old place and I ask myself why a woman like you would come here in the middle of winter to carry out such an act. And I can't seem to come up with any answers. So Xerxes and I decided we'd just follow along tonight and ask you. Simple, hmmm?"

"Too simple. This is none of your business, Mr. Colter, I guarantee it. It has nothing whatsoever to do with you." Emelina shuddered as she thought about what she had overheard concerning this man.

Mafia, the waitress in the cafe had confided to the diner in the next booth only that morning as Emelina had sipped coffee. *Probably hiding out while things cool down back East.*

The waitress, Emelina knew, was not alone in her analysis. *Syndicate type,* the clerk at the grocery store had decided when the person in the checkout line ahead of Emelina had mentioned Colter's name. A high-level Mob boss who had found it convenient to take a winter vacation on the Oregon coast.

Whatever the truth, there was no doubt Julian Colter had managed to incite a great deal of speculation among the villagers. He kept to himself, was chillingly polite when he found it necessary to deal with a clerk or a salesperson in town, and went everywhere with the Doberman. Everyone knew Dobermans were savage beasts, trained for attack and bred for ferocity. As far as the townspeople were concerned, the dog was a fitting companion for the man.

Emelina risked a slanting, sideways glance at the man who walked by her side, holding her captive. It was true. There were certain similarities between man and dog. She shivered. She'd only seen Julian Colter from a distance until tonight. Now, the impression the villagers had formed was easy to understand. Emelina saw nothing to make her doubt their conclusions about his profession.

There was a harsh ruthlessness in the unhandsome profile. The hawklike nose and aggressive jawline were etched with power. The damp air had left the pelt of coal black hair looking darker than ever in the mist-refracted moonlight. There was iron at the temples, a gray that would be spreading more quickly through the black hair as the man neared forty.

Forty probably wasn't far off for him, Emelina decided uncharitably. If forced to name his age, she would have said thirty-eight or thirty-nine. She would also have said that, in terms of experience, Julian Colter was probably a good deal older. Judging by the grimly hewn lines at the edges of his mouth and the detached, cynical expression in his dark eyes, Colter had gained his experience the rough way.

The rest of him was hard and lean, but beneath the dark trousers and heavy leather jacket he wore, his body moved with a masculine grace that seemed to echo the dog's. Lethal, yet somehow beautiful in its own fashion. Emelina gnawed worriedly on her lip as they started up the path to the top of the bluff. Was he carrying a gun under that leather jacket? What was her best course of action now? Somehow she had to convince him that she was no threat to him.

For that could be the only reason he had bothered to follow her tonight, she decided with sudden inspiration. A Mafia chieftain who was hiding out under an assumed name in a lonely coastal fishing village would naturally be suspicious of another stranger in town. Yes, that was the explanation for Julian Colter's interest in her. Almost idly she found herself wondering what his real name was and then promptly decided that it was best if she didn't find out.

Xerxes bounded ahead to the top of the cliff and stopped to wait for the two humans. When they finally arrived he turned and trotted toward the nearest weathered cottage. He waited again on the doorstep as Julian silently dug out his keys and fitted them into the lock.

"Probably no need to lock one's doors around this neighborhood, but some habits are hard to break, aren't they?" Julian drawled, shoving open the door for his unwilling guest. "Besides, with all these strangers roaming around at night…"

Xerxes delicately pushed his nose under Emelina's hand as if he were urging her inside. Emelina jumped at the sudden contact.

"It's all right. I think Xerxes likes you," Julian murmured, prodding her gently over the threshold.

"How can you tell?" she muttered resentfully, snatching her hand away from the dog's sleek head.

"Well, he hasn't torn your throat out yet, has he?"

Emelina stared at the brief grin Julian tossed in her direction as he switched on a light. "Your sense of humor leaves something to be desired," she told him with a shudder. Automatically she moved toward the remnants of a fire which still flickered warmly on the hearth across the room.

"Sorry. I don't get much chance to practice it. My sense of humor, I mean." He watched her as she nervously crossed the bare wooden floor. The cottage was typical of the weather-beaten houses that dotted the hills overlooking the ocean. Sparsely furnished with old throw rugs, overstuffed and somewhat tattered furniture, it had, nevertheless, a surprisingly pleasant atmosphere of crumbling comfort, especially with the fire blazing in the fireplace. "I'll get you a brandy. It's damn cold out there, and you aren't wearing anything other than a thin sweater."

Emelina said nothing. She could hardly explain that she'd been concerned with freedom of movement and hadn't wanted to be dragged down by a heavy jacket in case it was necessary to run or hide. She kept her narrowed, wary gaze on the fire as Julian moved about the small kitchen, pouring brandy. She was aware of his cool assessment.

She also was well aware of what he saw as his night-dark gaze roved over her. The long, chestnut braid hung down the center of her back, pulling the rich length of hair away from her face to reveal an ordinary set of features. At least, Emelina had always thought of them as ordinary. Large, faintly slanted hazel eyes that were neither blue nor green dominated the otherwise unimpressive line of a firm nose and a soft mouth. She was thirty-one years old.

Taken independently there was nothing remarkable about the individual features, but together they comprised an expressive, deeply individual face which reflected the personality of the woman behind the blue-green eyes. No discerning person looking at Emelina would have doubted the underlying intelligence or the imaginative curiosity and awareness that were such strong elements of her nature. It was a face that could easily reflect laughter or dismay or any of a number of emotions. Those who knew her well were convinced that the hazel eyes sometimes changed color when those emotions were especially intense.

When she glanced in a mirror Emelina told herself there was a look of good health about her features. A look that was all too robustly repeated in the rounded curves of her very feminine frame. Emelina could have cheerfully done with a little less of that healthy appearance, she had often decided. The black denims fit rather snugly over a softly rounded derriere, and the black sweater outlined full breasts. She found herself wishing she'd worn a bra. But, then, she hadn't exactly expected to run into anyone else this evening!

"Feeling more comfortable?" Julian inquired politely as he returned to the living room and handed her a brandy. Xerxes had settled down on the small rug in front of the fireplace, sharing the warmth with Emelina.

"Yes, thank you." Reluctantly Emelina took a sip of the brandy and tried to think how one made casual conversation with a Mob boss. Somehow she must convince him that, whatever his business was here, hers was entirely unconnected!

"Sit down, Emmy." Julian sounded as if he were retasting her name. He indicated a fat, comfortable chair behind her. Emelina sank down into it slowly, wishing she could think of some alternative. He took the faded chair across from her and propped his feet up on the hassock. Across the rim of his brandy glass, his dark eyes met hers. "Now take your time and tell me why that old house interests you so."

"It has nothing to do with you," she assured him earnestly. At least there had been no gun visible when he'd removed the dark leather jacket, she thought in relief. "I couldn't sleep and just decided to go for an evening stroll."

"At midnight?" he inquired with gentle skepticism.

"I like to walk on the beach at midnight!"

"In nothing but a light sweater and jeans?"

"Mr. Colter, I don't know why you should be so interested in my nocturnal habits," she retorted a little desperately. "I give you my word they have absolutely nothing at all to do with you!"

"Perhaps that is a little matter which could be altered," he suggested easily.

"I beg your pardon?" Emelina stared at him, totally at a loss.

"That was a subtle masculine pass, Emmy," he explained dryly, mouth crooking with genuine amusement as he viewed her frown. "Apparently a little too subtle, since it seems to have gone straight over your head. I'm surprised at you. You look like a reasonably intelligent woman, and you're certainly old enough to recognize innuendoes, subtle or otherwise."

Emelina finally realized what he was saying and to her chagrin flushed a deep, rosy shade. "Believe me, Mr. Colter, I have no intention of combining my nocturnal habits with yours! I thought we were discussing something much more serious than…than whatever it is you're trying to discuss." She got to her feet, ignoring Xerxes, who lifted his head and watched her alertly. "If you went to the trouble of following me and dragging me back here just to suggest we spend the night together, you've wasted your time and that of your dog! I am not the least bit interested!"

"Because you're in town on business?"

"Exactly. Good night, Mr. Colter. I'll see myself home." Perhaps if she moved quickly enough she could outbluff him. Xerxes, however, reached the door ahead of her and sat in front of it looking extremely hopeful. It was enough to bring Emelina to a full stop. She didn't trust the Doberman any more than she trusted his master. That hopeful look was probably reflecting the dog's inner wish to have an excuse to go for her throat. Slowly she turned around to glare at Julian, who continued to sprawl in his chair.

For a moment silence hung in the room. None of the three moved. Julian was clearly not going to call off the dog. He simply sat quietly and sipped at the brandy, his eyes never leaving her. Xerxes waited behind her.

Helplessly, her mind full of vivid images of a Doberman's attack, Emelina drifted back to her chair and picked up her glass of brandy. It was becoming increasingly obvious that she wasn't going anywhere until Julian Colter had his answers. But if it was answers he wanted, why had he bothered with the small pass? It occurred to Emelina that if there was one thing more dangerous than a Mafia boss, it might be a bored Mafia boss on vacation.

"Would you like a little more brandy?" Julian finally inquired politely.

"No, thank you." Emelina sat stiffly in her chair and focused on the fire. She didn't like his quiet intimidation, but she didn't have the faintest idea of how to get out from under it. Unless simply telling the truth might do the trick. "Mr. Colter, this is all very complicated and it doesn't concern you."

"Julian," he corrected softly.

"Julian." Emelina's frown deepened. "If I tell you why I was down on the beach tonight, will you call off your dog?"

Xerxes, as if sensing he was the subject of discussion, paced over to her chair and thrust his head into her lap. Emelina recoiled slightly.

"I don't think my dog wants to be called off," Julian observed pleasantly. "He likes you."

"Perhaps you'd better explain to him that I'm basically a cat person," Emelina suggested wryly as she hesitantly touched the animal's neck. Xerxes's ears twitched.

"Xerxes doesn't worry about the competition. He knows he can take what he wants."

Emelina glanced up sharply. "Are you trying to tell me that you and Xerxes share a similar philosophical approach to life?" she challenged, somewhat surprised by her own dash of boldness.

"I simply made a statement about my dog, Emmy. Don't read too much into it."

Emelina sighed, focusing on the problem she was facing. Unconsciously her fingers began to rub Xerxes behind the ears. "That house on the beach belongs to someone I know, Julian."

"Go on."

"He's not a very nice person." Julian probably understood people like Eric Leighton, she realized. "The man who owns it is blackmailing my brother."

"Blackmailing your brother!" His astonishment appeared genuine, and Emelina wondered briefly at it. Blackmail and related endeavors must be old hat to a man like this. "Whatever it was I expected to hear, it wasn't that. Please go on with the tale, Emmy."

She shrugged, trying to appear casual about the whole

thing. "There isn't much more to tell. I'm here to see if I can find out anything that will help my brother get Leighton off his back."

"Leighton presumably being the owner of that beach house?"

"That's right. Now if you don't mind…"

"Relax, Emmy," Julian advised gently. "You're not going anywhere just yet. You must realize you've opened a whole can of worms."

"None of this involves you!" she insisted. "Not unless…unless…" She broke off in sudden shock and swung her stricken eyes to his face.

"Unless I'm mixed up with Leighton? Is that what's worrying you now?"

She swallowed. "Leighton's always been a loner," she breathed. "I can't see him working for you or anyone else. I can see him having a partner, but I don't see *you* in that role."

Julian arched one black brow. "I can assure you he's not working for me."

Emelina sagged a little with relief. What a horrible mess that would have been! Dazed by the near miss, she sank back against the chair's cushion, her fingers still massaging the sensitive area behind Xerxes's ears. The dog shouldered a little closer and his eyes closed. A temporarily contented werewolf. "Well, that's really all there is to it. I'm hoping to find something useful around that house of his. Something my brother can use."

Julian eyed her consideringly. "Why isn't your brother the one keeping tabs on the house?"

"We don't want Leighton to become suspicious. My brother lives in Seattle. He works for a large corporation there. If he were simply to disappear for a few weeks to come down here and keep watch on the house, someone would be bound to notice and then Leighton might find out."

"And you, on the other hand, are free to disappear from your social milieu for several weeks?" he drawled. "There's no one back home wondering where the hell you've disappeared to?"

"Writers are expected to need time to themselves," Emelina told him proudly.

"You're a writer?"

"That's correct," she snapped.

He paused a moment and then asked carefully, "Have you written anything I might have had occasion to read?"

"I doubt it."

"What have you published?" Julian persisted.

"Well, I haven't actually been published yet," she confided in a little rush. "But I'm working on it. I have two manuscripts out to publishers right now, in fact! I'm trying to create a category that's a cross between romance fiction and science fiction."

"Is there, uh, much of a market for that sort of thing?" he asked delicately.

"No," Emelina admitted morosely.

"I see." There was a wealth of meaning behind the simple words, and Emelina ground her teeth a little savagely. She'd heard too many people say those particular words in exactly that manner. An unpublished writer was often the object of much pity, condescension and gentle scorn. One of these days, she vowed silently for the millionth time, things will be different.

"Is there anything else you'd care to know about this evening, Julian?" she inquired far too sweetly.

"Yes, as a matter of fact, I am curious about one other thing," he smiled. "Whose idea was it?"

"What idea?"

"The idea of coming down here to keep watch on that beach house?"

"Mine. Why?" she muttered.

The shark's smile broadened, and Julian's dark eyes flickered briefly with genuine amusement. "I just wondered."

"I get the feeling you're not taking all this too seriously, which is just fine with me," Emelina ground out emphatically. "May I please go home now?"

"If you don't mind, I do have one or two other questions."

Emelina closed her eyes in silent dismay. The overly polite words were tantamount to a command to stay where she was. "What else would you like to know?"

"If you're still awaiting discovery back in New York, how are you managing to eat in the meantime?"

Her eyes flew open. "Why in the world should that matter to you?"

"I am cursed with this insatiable curiosity where you're concerned," he apologized humbly. "As I keep pointing out to you, there simply isn't very much to interest me around this burg."

"Well, don't think you're going to amuse yourself with me!"

He inclined his head in acknowledgment of the statement and then sat waiting with a patience that annoyed Emelina. Unable to resist the silent pressure, she answered him gruffly. "I work in a bookstore in Portland."

"Ah."

"What's that supposed to mean? Ah?" she demanded aggressively.

"It means, ah, you're not being supported by anyone while you hone your writing skills," he explained smoothly.

"Of course not! For heaven's sake! I'm thirty-one years

old and quite capable of supporting myself. I have been doing so for a long time!" she stated proudly.

"Not sinking further and further into debt while you live on the expectation of huge advances from the publishing world, hmmm?" he teased lightly.

Emelina's eyes blazed with sudden fury. "I am not in debt! I make it a point never to get into debt! I pay my bills, Mr. Colter. Every last one of them."

He blinked lazily in response to her unexpected vehemence. It wasn't his fault, she realized belatedly. Julian Colter could hardly know about her own personal history, which included an irresponsible father who had left a mountain of debts behind when he'd been killed in a stock-car crash and a handsome, graduate-student husband who had left a huge pile of student loans and related bills to pay when he'd run off with a classmate. No one who didn't know her background could understand the importance to Emelina of being free of debt. She sighed inwardly, wishing she hadn't overreacted to the comment Julian had made.

"Okay," he said agreeably. "So you're a would-be writer who pays her bills. And it was your idea to come to the coast to keep an eye on this beach house. You claim your brother is being blackmailed...."

"He is!"

"And you're running around at midnight in the middle of winter looking for evidence to use against the black-mailer," Julian concluded. "Quite a tale, Emmy."

"You don't believe me?" she whispered. Her hand paused on Xerxes's neck, and the dog opened one eye reproachfully.

"The funny part is, I think I do." Julian smiled. "It's probably a little too crazy to be anything other than the truth."

Emelina let out her breath in relief. "In that case, I'd ap-preciate it if you'd let me go home now. As you can see, none of this has anything to do with you. It's just a coincidence that we happened to wind up on the same beach together, Julian," she ended deliberately in case he'd missed the point. "I really have no interest at all in whatever reason you have for being here in the same town."

"I'm crushed. No interest in me at all?"

Once more Emelina surged to her feet. Xerxes nudged her leg with his nose, protesting the change in position, but she ignored him. He didn't seem quite so dangerous now that she'd spent fifteen minutes stroking his ears. "Good night, Julian. I'm sorry you had to go to the bother of ruining both of our evenings!"

Dog and man followed her to the door. "I'll take you home, Emmy."

"That's not necessary," she protested quickly.

"I would be guilty of the worst possible manners if I were to send you out into the night alone." He pulled the leather jacket out of the closet and draped it around her shoulders. Then he reached for a heavy sweater for himself and politely opened the door.

Outside the fog swirled in thick white sheets. Emelina could barely see a foot in front of her face. Xerxes trotted outside as if it were broad daylight.

"I'll get a flashlight," Julian said, opening another cupboard. "Good thing you're only a block away, isn't it? Of course, you're welcome to spend the night, if you'd rather not venture out into this soup."

"No, no, I'll be fine."

"I was afraid you'd say that." His mouth lifted in wry humor. "Let's go."

Once outside it wasn't quite as bad as it had seemed. They made their way slowly along the street, which lacked anything as sophisticated as a sidewalk, until they arrived at the run-down picket fence that surrounded Emelina's cottage. At the door, Emelina turned and made a bid to dismiss her unwanted escort.

"Thank you very much, Julian. As you can see there was absolutely no need to trouble yourself this evening. Now that you've had the answers to your questions, I hope you'll leave me alone so that we can both go our separate ways."

He eyed her as if she were displaying a distressing amount of stupidity. "But you've hardly begun to answer my questions, Emmy," he corrected softly. "Surely you must see that. We have a great deal more to discuss, you and I. But it is getting late and I agree it's time you were home. Tomorrow, however, I think we will pick up this conversation where we left off."

"But I answered your questions!" she gasped furiously.

"Emmy, you only whetted my interest."

"But, Julian!"

He leaned forward and stopped her protest by brushing his mouth ever so lightly against her own. It was the gentlest of warnings, but Emelina got the message immediately. She shut up, stepped inside her door and slammed it closed behind her. She was trembling with reaction to the events of the evening and the hint of threat which had been left behind on her lips. Belatedly she realized she was still wearing Colter's jacket.

A little awkwardly she stepped away from the door, aware of the warmth of the leather and the way it carried a trace of Julian's scent. Quickly she shrugged out of it, alarmed by the strangely intimate sensation.

Outside in the thickening fog Julian made his way slowly back to the cottage he was renting. Xerxes paced faithfully at his heels, and Julian called to him softly.

"Good boy, Xerxes. Good boy." He paused and then

murmured, "What did you think of her, pal?" The dog laughed silently up at him. "You liked her, didn't you? She's scared of you, though. She's scared of both of us. Probably heard all the talk in town. I wonder what she's really doing here on the coast. That story she told was pretty wild. On the other hand, I didn't get the feeling she was lying." Julian shook his head. "Interesting, isn't she? Intriguing."

He reached the cottage door and let himself and the dog inside, wondering if the woman had been telling him the truth. Had she really been out on the beach in the middle of the night doing undercover work to help her brother out of a blackmail jam? The astonishing part was that he could almost believe the ridiculous tale. There was something about the way she met his eyes, something about the way her rounded little chin lifted when she challenged him. She had the spirit and, he had a hunch, the imagination to get herself into trouble.

How many women of his acquaintance would undertake an exotic task such as she claimed to have set herself for the sake of helping a man, even a relative? Most of the ones he knew would have dissolved into hysterics at the notion of blackmail and probably not a single one would have found themselves on a deserted beach at midnight attempting a bit of breaking and entering.

Most of the people Julian Colter had encountered in his life didn't take loyalty to another human being to that extreme. The possibility that he might have come across a woman who saw nothing wrong in that sort of outmoded loyalty was more than intriguing.

It kept Julian awake for a good portion of what remained of the night.

CHAPTER TWO

As a writer, Emelina told herself very early the next morning, she should take the attitude that every experience was grist for the mill. But as she tugged on a pair of jeans and reached for an emerald-green velour sweater she found it difficult to view the experiences of the previous evening with the sort of objectivity required in order to use them in a story.

The memory of Julian Colter materializing out of the fog along with his Doberman still sent chills down her spine. It would be a while before she could write about that experience with a steady hand at the typewriter!

Still, she reminded herself resolutely as she tied the laces of her canvas shoes and reached for Colter's leather jacket, which was lying on the end of the couch, there was always the possibility of using that scene on the beach in some future novel. Yes, she would tuck it away in the back of her mind, and someday she might find it very useful.

Letting herself outside into the nippy morning air, Emelina draped the leather jacket across her arm and started down the narrow street to the cottage at the other end. She had awakened with the knowledge that she wanted Julian Colter's jacket out of her house as soon as possible.

Emelina couldn't explain her reaction to the intimacy implied by the jacket's presence in her cottage, but she couldn't ignore it, either. She wished she'd thought to return it to its owner the previous evening.

But Julian's brief, warning kiss had driven every thought from her mind except getting behind the safety of her own door. Emelina sighed and walked a little more quickly as she neared Julian's cottage. She could only hope Colter wasn't an early riser. Her plan was simple. She would leave the jacket hanging on the front doorknob and then leave without announcing her presence.

Unfortunately for the simplicity of her plan, Xerxes did prove to be an early riser. She heard his sharp, questioning bark as she slung the leather jacket over the knob. Before she could get off the front porch, the door opened.

Xerxes came bounding out, apparently enormously pleased to see her again. Julian stood in the doorway and watched his dog's greeting with calm amusement.

"Down, Xerxes," Emelina muttered, cautiously patting the dog's head as she stood with one foot on the bottom porch step. "That's a good boy. Down!" Having a Doberman trying to pounce on one was enough to make anyone a trifle anxious, she decided. Then she glanced up at Julian and decided that in this case the dog's owner was a source of greater anxiety.

"Good morning, Emmy. You're just in time for a cup of coffee."

"No!" she said instinctively, trying to edge down the path. "I mean, no thank you," she amended, remembering her manners. "I was just on my way into town for coffee. Thank you very much. I only stopped by to return your jacket."

Julian glanced down at the garment draped over the doorknob. "So I see. Well, since I now have a jacket, I think I'll come into town with you and buy you that cup of coffee. Come on, Xerxes. Back in the house. You'll get your morning walk a little later."

Xerxes looked wistfully at Emelina, who was astonished that a Doberman could assume such an expression, and then he loped obediently up the steps and back into the cottage. Julian closed the door on him and reached for his jacket.

"There's really no need to accompany me," Emelina began, racking her brain for a way out of the unexpected date. "I go into town every morning for coffee. It's quite safe and I'm used to it!"

"I know," Julian agreed gently, zipping up the jacket as he came down the steps. "I've seen you. I've been looking for an excuse to invite myself along, and this morning I have one, don't I?"

Emelina's eyes narrowed as she regarded him resentfully. "What excuse?" she challenged.

"Why, that we're more or less conspirators," he replied ingenuously, dark eyes laughing down at her as he fell into step beside her. "After finding you down on the beach last night trying to search that house I feel *involved*."

She shot him a skeptical glance. "You're not involved and you know it. You're just bored and looking for a way to amuse yourself. You said as much last night!"

"Lucky for me you came along, hmmm? This morning I think I would like to hear the rest of the story, Emmy."

"What do you mean, the rest of the story? I told you what you wanted to know last night!" she protested. Angrily she glared straight ahead as they walked along the edge of the road into the quiet village. How was she going to get free of this dangerous man? Why on earth had he latched onto her like this?

"There are one or two details still missing," he explained easily.

"Such as?"

"Such as *why* your brother is being blackmailed."

Emelina's expressive mouth firmed. "That's none of your business."

He slanted her a cool glance. "Convince me," he ordered succinctly.

Her eyes widened in renewed nervousness. "I told you last night this has nothing to do with you," she whispered. Was he still thinking that somehow she was a threat to him? A Syndicate chief hiding out was bound to be more than normally suspicious, she realized unhappily.

"Like I said, convince me." Julian pushed open the door of the coffee shop and ushered her into the pleasant, bustling warmth.

As he guided her toward a vacant booth Emelina felt the curious looks of the other patrons, most of them locals. A wave of new uneasiness assailed her as she slid reluctantly into the booth. There was no doubt but that the village folk would begin speculating at once on the fact that the single lady vacationer in town was having coffee with the mysterious Mob boss. Damn! Things were going from bad to worse in a hurry.

Julian seemed oblivious to the stares and muttered comments, but as she eyed him while he quietly ordered coffee, it occurred to Emelina that he undoubtedly knew very well what was being said around him. He was simply too arrogant to give a damn. Mafia types were undoubtedly *very* arrogant. Emelina winced at the thought and tried to tell herself that someday this would all make a really great manuscript.

"So let's hear it, Emmy. Why is your brother being blackmailed?"

She drew in her breath as the coffee arrived, poured a great deal of cream into her cup and decided the only chance of escape with a man like this was the truth.

People like him would know at once if one were lying. She shivered.

"My brother is a very brilliant, very fast-rising executive with a large multinational conglomerate," she began in a tight voice. "He is in line for a vice-presidency and an important transfer to San Francisco."

Julian nodded, saying nothing as he sipped the steaming brew. His dark gaze never left her face.

"Eric Leighton appeared out of nowhere about a month ago. He had once been a...a close friend of my brother's."

"Some friend," Julian observed mildly, "to resort to blackmail."

"Yes." The single word of agreement was dragged from Emelina.

"But that's the thing about close friends and...others," Julian went on thoughtfully, "they often can't be trusted. Loyalty is a very rare commodity in this world."

"You ought to know," Emelina retorted without pausing to think.

He arched one brow.

"I mean, in your line of work and all. You've probably learned the hard way that you can't trust everyone," Emelina explained hurriedly, wishing she'd kept her mouth shut.

"About your brother," he prompted coolly.

"Yes, well, Leighton used to be very close to my brother and a handful of others. They were all friends in college, you see," she said carefully. "My brother was not always on the fast track to the executive suite, I'm afraid. At one time he was out to change the world. The quick way."

"Ah, I think I'm beginning to get a glimmering of understanding."

"Keith was very committed to his beliefs," she went on, edging her way closer to the core of the matter.

"In other words he was a flaming radical in college, out to change the world."

"Something like that," she admitted and then said loyally, "He believed in what he was doing at the time. He was very dedicated!"

"But he's since changed his mind?"

"Well, like everyone else, he's grown up and decided that the world can't be changed overnight. He's a very dynamic, hard-working person, and he has a lot of natural ability. The corporate world turned out to be a sphere in which he does very well. But he works for a very conservative, very staid company."

"And his bosses wouldn't look so kindly on him if they knew about his radical past?"

Emelina shook her head sadly. "And Eric Leighton, who hasn't done very well at all since he dropped out of college a few years ago, has decided he wants some of the success of his friends who have made it in the establishment. He's set up a very neat blackmailing scheme. For a price he'll keep his mouth shut about my brother's past."

"How did your brother react when Leighton approached him?"

Emelina lifted one shoulder. "Oh, he was all set to call in the cops and blow the whole thing wide open. But I convinced him that in the end he would suffer because Leighton was sure to make a point of exposing Keith's past to the world. I thought there might be another way to handle it. We know Leighton was involved with drugs in college. It was no secret at the time. My brother and I think he's probably still making a living by smuggling drugs or some related activity. We know he's never had a real job or tried to fit into society. Keith remembered that Leighton had once had a house on the Oregon coast. It was left to him by his parents. Leighton used to say it would make a good place to wait out the 'revolution.'"

"Which never came," Julian put in with a smile.

"Anyhow, Keith checked quietly with someone in the office of the local county recorder and found out that the house on the beach was still registered to Leighton. It occurred to me that it might be worth watching for a while. If he's involved in other illegal activities besides blackmailing old friends, there's a possibility he's using this secluded beach house for some aspect of his work."

"So you volunteered to come down here and spend a few weeks keeping the place under surveillance, is that it?" Julian asked, stirring his coffee absently.

"Something like that," Emelina confessed. She chewed her lip in a gesture characteristic of all her anxious moments. "Doesn't that sound like a logical sort of plan?" Nothing like getting advice from an expert, she told herself, watching him with a hopeful expression.

"Not particularly," Julian retorted, his mouth twisting wryly. "I think your brother had the right idea initially."

"Calling in the cops?" she exclaimed, shocked. "You think that was a good idea?" She couldn't imagine someone in Julian's line of work thinking it was ever a good idea to call in the police!

"They have their uses," he told her dryly, eyes narrowing.

"Well, it's out of the question. It would ruin my brother's career!"

"Blackmailers never go away, Emmy. You must have heard that by now. They'll go on bleeding a victim for as long as they can get away with it. You have to call the bluff."

"It's not a bluff," she whispered fiercely. "My brother's past, if it were known, would put his career in jeopardy. You don't understand how conservative his firm is! Oh, he probably wouldn't be fired or anything, but his superiors would almost surely lose interest in paving his way to the top. They would decide that basically he wasn't really their kind! Most of them came out of prestigious schools and were very careful to steer clear of campus political movements. They wouldn't *understand!*"

"You sound very concerned about your brother's welfare," Julian observed mildly.

"I am! He's my brother!"

"Your older brother or your younger brother?"

"My younger brother. He's twenty-nine, two years younger than me."

"Which is why he apparently let you talk him into this wild scheme to trap Leighton. He may be a fast-rising corporate man, but he's still a younger brother, with a younger brother's mentality, I suppose."

"What's that supposed to mean?" she demanded furiously.

"Only that he's accustomed to being bossed around by his older sister," Julian chuckled.

"You know nothing about my family or my relationship to my brother!"

Julian shook his head. "I know that, crazy as your plan undoubtedly is, you seem to mean well by it. You're determined to protect Keith, aren't you?"

"Well, of course, I am! He's my brother!" She stared at him, baffled that he should even make such an obvious statement.

Julian smiled. "Okay, I'll help you."

"You'll *what?*"

"Keep your voice down. Do you want everyone in town to know what you're doing?" he cautioned briefly.

Emelina tried to recover from her shock and force her mind to think in a rational fashion. Julian Colter's help was the very last thing she wanted. Help from a mysterious Syndicate boss would carry a very high price tag, indeed! "Thanks, but no thanks, Mr. Colter," she told him heatedly. "I prefer to handle this on my own."

"This kind of surveillance works better with two people."

She blinked. "It does?"

"Oh, definitely. Besides, my cottage is much closer to Leighton's house than yours is. It will be easier and less obvious if I handle part of the job of watching it."

For the life of her she couldn't read his expression. Emelina sat very still, running his logic through her head. He had a point, she told herself in consternation. And there was no doubt Julian Colter probably knew a great deal more about this sort of thing than she did. Then she shook her head, clearing away the deceptive reasoning. She must remember exactly who this man was and how very dangerous he could be. "Thank you, Julian," she said very formally, "but I don't want your help."

"Not even for your brother's sake?" he murmured.

She flinched. "It's just that I don't think it will be necessary to have outside assistance on this project. I'm perfectly capable of handling it by myself."

"Forgive me for saying this, Emmy," he drawled, "but I have the impression that while your plan has the merit of having been born of a vivid imagination, it might be lacking in one or two practical aspects. You don't really have any experience in this sort of thing, do you?"

"Well, no, but I don't see why it should be so difficult!"

"Look at the mess you got into last night. What if I had been Leighton?"

That shook her a little. "You weren't, so I don't see that it matters!" she managed staunchly.

He gave her a wry glance. "You're afraid to let me help, aren't you?"

"Frankly, yes."

"Why?"

Emelina clenched her teeth, striving for a polite response to the outrageous question. He must be very well aware of why she didn't want his help! "This is a personal matter and I don't want to involve strangers," she finally mumbled, not quite meeting his eyes.

"You've already involved me by telling me the whole story," he pointed out.

"For which I could kick myself," she groaned morosely.

He gave her a level look. "I didn't exactly give you much choice."

"No, you certainly didn't," she agreed. "Are you always this overbearing and intimidating?"

"Goes with the territory," he explained dryly.

Emelina shut her eyes briefly in dismay. "Yes, I suppose it does."

"Well?" he pushed with a hint of challenge.

"Well, what?" She glared at him. "Am I going to accept your too-generous offer? Not on your life!"

"Not even for the sake of your brother?" he murmured insinuatingly. "Doesn't your loyalty to him extend as far as engaging the best available expert?"

Emelina surged to her feet, aware that she was being pressured, and furious at the man in the booth for applying the pressure. Her eyes went almost green as she leaned over the table, palms planted firmly on the Formica. "I will say this one more time, Julian Colter," she hissed through her teeth. "I do not want your help. I don't need your help. This is my business and I will attend to it. I have no intention of finding myself under any obligation to someone like you. Have I made myself perfectly clear?"

Julian watched her over the rim of his coffee cup. His face was set and hard, and his dark eyes were pools of un- fathomable danger. "Very clear."

"Good, I'm glad we understand each other!" Emelina straightened and turned on her heel, anxious to leave him far behind. But Julian's voice caught her just as she was about to stride toward the door.

"Keep in mind, Emmy, that whatever your fears about me, I'm the one man in the neighborhood who might be able to really help your brother."

Emelina shoved open the cafe door, violently aware of the eyes of the local people following her out into the street. They couldn't have overheard Julian's last remark, of course, but they were bound to be deeply curious about her relationship to the mystery man in their presence.

Damn! Damn! Damn! What a disastrous turn of events! Head down, hands shoved into the pockets of her jeans, Emelina berated herself during the entire walk back to her cottage.

No one but a fool would deliberately get herself in debt to a man like Julian Colter! In debt to the Syndicate? The Mob? The Mafia? Whatever the proper term was, she sure as hell didn't need that kind of trouble!

Visions of movies and books she had read on the subject leaped into her mind. Newspaper stories of famous person- alities who had found themselves obligated to an under- world figure haunted her as she let herself back into the cottage. Her vivid imagination found no end to the fright- ening images it could conjure from such material.

And then she thought of her brother. Keith had agreed to let her watch the Leighton house for a few weeks, but if at the end of that time nothing happened that could be useful in a fight against Eric Leighton, he was determined to turn the whole thing over to the authorities and let the chips fall where they might.

Emelina muttered another string of rather explicit oaths as she considered the damage that could be done to her brother's flourishing career if his past was brought up and used to embarrass him publicly. Her brother might be disgusted enough with Leighton to take his chances, but Emelina couldn't bear the thought of seeing everything he had worked for during the past few years go down the drain.

Keith deserved his success, and she was going to see that it wasn't ruined by a vicious, scheming blackmailer like Eric Leighton! Emelina began to pace the floor as she considered her options. Brow furrowed, she beat a steady path between the front window of the old cottage and the kitchen counter. She *had* to get something on Leighton. And she only had a few weeks in which to do it. Keith would take matters into his own hands if she didn't accomplish something quickly. It had been all she could do to convince him to let her try her own plan.

But there had been absolutely nothing to see during the past week. She had kept an earnest vigil, but unfortunately Julian Colter was right. It was impossible for one person to keep a round-the-clock surveillance project going.

Julian Colter. Why did the one person who offered help have to be *him?*

She was on the point of cursing her bad luck when Emelina happened to remember the expressions on the faces of the other diners in the coffee shop that morning. She had known exactly what was passing through their minds and she had a hunch Julian knew, as well. What was it like going through life drawing that kind of attention?

Well, it was his own fault. He shouldn't have chosen his particular line of work if he didn't care to cause such comment! Then again, perhaps he hadn't chosen it. Maybe it was something you were born into. Perhaps Julian had never had any real choice in the matter.

Her mind drifted off along that tangent for a while longer as she tried to picture a young Julian growing up as the heir apparent in a crime family. Distractedly she shook herself free of her musings and returned to the problem at hand. Julian Colter's life work was definitely not her concern.

Yet every time she reached the turnaround point on the floor in front of the bay window overlooking the ocean, Emelina found her mind returning to the subject of Julian Colter. He could help her. If anyone could, it would be he. Instinctively she was more certain of that than she had been of just about anything else in her life.

In debt to a man like that? What was she thinking of? Emelina Stratton knew what it meant to be in debt, but she'd never been involved in that sort of obligation!

Out of sheer desperation she grabbed her notepad and threw herself down on the lumpy couch in an effort to take her mind off her problem by focusing on her writing. After all, she had promised herself that in between trips to check on Leighton's house, she would do some real work here on the coast.

It was a pointless exercise. Her active imagination simply would not concentrate on the characters of her space gothic. It insisted on returning to the subject of the man in the cottage at the end of her street. And to the problem of helping her brother.

Julian Colter would probably know how to go about solving her brother's problem.

That one inescapable fact kept returning to tease and tug

and cajole. Yes, he would know what to do, but what price would she wind up paying? She would have to make it absolutely clear that if she did accept his help, *she* was the one under an obligation to pay the tab, not her brother. Could one make deals like that with people like Colter? Would he honor his side of the bargain and hold only her responsible?

She could always ask him, couldn't she?

Emelina threw down her pen in a gesture of self-disgust. What was the matter with her? How could she even think of running such risks?

For her brother's sake, of course. Keith was closer to her than anyone else in the world. She rarely saw her beautiful but flighty mother, who had remarried and was happily living in luxury on the East Coast. Her father had disappeared during her junior year in college, leaving behind all those debts. Her marriage had been a disaster. Through it all Keith had been her friend as well as her brother.

What it all boiled down to was the simple fact that she would do anything she had to do in order to help him. And when she looked at the matter in its simplest terms, Emelina decided shortly after sunset that evening, the options narrowed considerably.

She needed the best available help, and she knew where to get it. There was no reason to hesitate any longer. Squaring her shoulders, Emelina dragged a striped Hudson Bay blanket-coat out of the closet and belted it on. Resolutely she turned up the high collar and pulled open the door of the cottage. She really had no choice.

The walk up the street was one of the longest Emelina had ever undertaken. It lasted forever and yet all too soon she was walking up the path to the slightly tilted porch of Julian's cottage.

Xerxes was aware of her before she could knock even once. She heard his expectant little whine and braced herself for his cheerful assault when the door opened.

"Ah, Emmy," Julian said, a wealth of satisfaction in his voice as he stood on the threshold and took in the sight of her standing on his front step. "I had a feeling you wouldn't disappoint me."

Emelina was too busy fending off Xerxes to get a good look at Julian's face but she thought she caught a trace of satisfaction in his eyes as well as his voice and didn't quite know what to make of it.

"Down, Xerxes," she ordered gruffly as the sleek dog danced around her. He shoved his head under her hand, and she was more or less obligated to pat him. The long pink tongue came out to thank her. "I've come to talk to you about…about my problem," she said to Julian as she hastily wiped her hand on her jacket.

"I assumed as much. Come in, Emmy. Have you eaten?"

"No, but I'm not really hungry," she assured him quickly.

"If you are going to accept my help, you might as well accept my food," he pointed out with unassailable logic. "And perhaps a drink, too, I think," he added as he shut the door behind her.

Emelina had a moment of panic as the door closed and she found herself trapped in the room with him. She made a frantic grab for her fortitude and nodded once. "Yes, I think I could use the drink."

Xerxes draped himself contentedly by the fire after seeing Emelina into the old stuffed chair she had used the previous evening. Silence reigned in the room until Emelina found a glass of deep red Zinfandel pressed into her hand. She took a long sip and then met Julian's eyes as he sat down across from her.

"There's just one thing," she stated very carefully. He gave her a politely inquiring look. "My brother is not a part of this deal. I'm the one making the arrangement with you."

"I understand," Julian said very gently.

Emelina would have given a lot of money in that moment to have had the gift of reading minds. What the devil was he thinking? "I am the only one who will be required to repay your offer of help," she clarified, feeling as if she were digging her own grave.

He inclined his head in acknowledgment.

"Can I trust you?" she whispered.

"You can trust me." It was a quiet statement of fact, and Emelina found herself believing him. There was no real reason to do so, yet she did. Perhaps men like this really did have their own code of honor. He saw her watching him and lifted his glass in salute. "To our bargain, Emmy Stratton."

They sipped the solemn toast in silence. For a long moment there was only the crackle of the fire on the hearth and the pounding of Emelina's pulse as she absorbed the impact of what she had done. She couldn't seem to take her eyes off Julian's face. He was the personification of the devil, she told herself. Or perhaps it was Dracula he personified. Legend had it that such creatures could be strangely attractive to a woman.

Emelina's breath stopped for a split second as she realized just what she had been thinking. *Oh, no,* she screamed silently, *surely I'm not going to find myself in that kind of quicksand!* Her eyes widened. Attracted to Julian Colter? Never!

"What are you thinking, Emmy?"

"That when you sup with the devil you need a very long spoon," she replied with utter honesty. The old advice had

never seemed so apropos. Getting close to Julian Colter
was an excellent way to get one's fingers burned. Badly.

A strange little smile played at the edge of his hard mouth
as he regarded her. "Since I want you to share my supper
with me, I shall go and see just how long a spoon I can find,"
he murmured, rising lithely from the depths of the old chair.

Emelina was left to stare into the flames and wish she
could have bitten out her tongue before speaking.

When Julian returned to the living room it was with a
platter of sandwiches, two bowls of heated soup and a
small salad. The speed with which it arrived made Emelina
realize that it must have been ready before she had knocked
on his door.

"You were expecting me?" she inquired rather dryly,
helping herself to a cheese and lettuce sandwich, even
though she hadn't planned on accepting his food.

"Let's just say I was hoping you'd show up this evening."

They ate slowly, saying little. Emelina found the flames
on the hearth unusually fascinating, and Julian seemed to
think the same of her tightly drawn profile. Neither of
them was inclined to go back to the business at hand.

"You're scared to death of me, aren't you, Emmy?"
Julian said at last as they finished off the sandwiches.

"Hardly," she found the gumption to retort. She
flicked a crust of bread in Xerxes's direction. "I'm just
naturally cautious!"

He laughed at that, surprising her. It was the first time
she'd heard him give way to humor to such an extent. It was
at her expense, of course, she reminded herself crossly.
Xerxes downed the bread crust and licked his chops politely.

"I don't think you're cautious at all, Emelina Stratton.
·Not when you're out to protect your brother. Would you
offer that same loyalty to a lover, I wonder?"

"What?" Her head came up quickly as she stared at him in astonishment. The expression on his face held her absolutely still. She saw the deep, masculine curiosity and the restrained flicker of desire that had invaded the compelling dark eyes, and every instinct she possessed came abruptly to life. The result was a chaos of emotion and crossed signals that left her easy prey.

Julian Colter reached across the short space that divided them and tugged her effortlessly into his lap.

CHAPTER THREE

"YOU'VE ALREADY FOUND the courage to dine with the devil," Julian whispered deeply, his mouth hovering above hers. "Let's see if you have the courage to let him kiss you."

Emelina lay cradled across his thighs, one of his arms locked warmly around her. She was fiercely aware of a hypnotizing wonder. The attraction she had briefly recognized earlier in the evening was very real. *My God,* she thought bleakly, *why does it have to be with this man?*

Before she could summon the protest she knew she ought to make, Julian's hand lifted to frame the side of her face and hold her still for his kiss. She was aware of the heat of his fingers alongside her cheek and then came the far more intimate heat of his mouth.

How could a kiss be at once marauding and persuasive? Demanding, yet coaxing? How could a man like this kiss a woman as if she were an infinitely valuable and precious creature? Where Emelina expected rough aggression she received sensual insistence. Where she expected dominance she received warm inducement.

The dichotomy was spellbinding. Emelina closed her eyes, not daring to move as his lips teased hers. She felt his fingers slide upward into her braided hair, pressing her head close to his shoulder. Then came the tip of his tongue outlining her trembling mouth. Gently, insistently, persuasively, that tongue moved, his lips nibbling at hers until, with a soft little moan, Emelina succumbed to the sensual demand and allowed him into her warmth.

She felt rather than heard the growl deep in his throat as he hungrily invaded the territory she had ceded. The fingers in her hair began to thread and twist until she was vaguely aware that her braid had been undone. Beneath the searching impact of his kiss she stirred at last, instinctively seeking safety when it was far too late.

As if sensing her belated wariness, Julian deepened the embrace, filling her mouth with the provocative taste of his own. When her hand fluttered anxiously to his shoulder he released his grip on her hair to catch her fingers and guide them up to the coal darkness of his own heavy pelt. When he released them her hands were somehow entwined in the depths of his hair.

"Emmy, sweet Emmy. Don't be afraid of me. Give me what I want. You're so intriguing, so soft…" The words came lingeringly, persuasively as he reluctantly broke the contact of their mouths to seek the line of her throat.

"Julian, Julian, *please*." But in that moment Emelina couldn't have said what it was she wanted from him. Her eyelids were squeezed tightly shut as if to block out the strange reality of what was happening and her amber-gold nails scored the nape of his strong neck.

"I've been watching you for days," he breathed huskily, his palm sliding down her throat to her shoulder. "Wondering about you, speculating, playing guessing games with myself. The closer I get, the more you intrigue me."

"It's only that you're bored out here in the middle of nowhere," she began, but he interrupted her with rough certainty.

"Hush, Emmy, you don't know what you're talking

about." And then his hand trailed boldly downward to the curve of her full breast and closed over it with a possessiveness that should have annoyed her violently.

Emelina couldn't find the scathing protest she needed. Instead she gasped softly and turned her face into his shoulder, pressing close to the comfort of the wool plaid shirt he wore. Her fingers at the nape of his neck clenched almost convulsively and she heard his sigh of masculine pleasure.

"A man could lose himself in your softness, Emmy," he growled as if he half resented, half longed for exactly that fate. Gently he explored the shape of her, and she sensed his growing impatience at the resistance offered by the bra she wore beneath her velour top.

Slowly his hand released her and drifted farther downward until he found the hem of the emerald sweater. Emelina flinched as he slid his fingers inside and discovered the warmth of her skin.

When he felt her start of uncertainty Julian tightened his hold, urging her closer. She was suddenly aware of the hardness of his thighs beneath her, felt the gathering male tension in his body. Once again Emelina told herself she must break free of the seductive web he was weaving, but just as she found the strength to try pulling back, he found the clasp of her bra and released it.

In the next moment the weight of her breast was filling his hand, and Emelina moaned again, this time with the desire that was springing to life in her loins. What was it that attracted her to a man like this? How on earth could a dangerous devil like Julian Colter overwhelm the defenses that had stood for years?

When his thumb grazed over a nipple, coaxing it forth, a melting warmth began to flow through her veins. She knew herself capable of a reasonable level of affection, but she had never though of herself as a particularly sensual woman. There had never been a man who could quicken her senses this way. The casual approach her husband had taken to sex had left her disappointed and unenthusiastic about the intimate embrace. Since the end of her marriage, it had been an easy matter to keep her physical relationships with men on a safe level. She had not even been tempted to allow a man into her bed.

But, then, she hadn't known real temptation, Emelina realized suddenly. This was the genuine article. This pulsating, beckoning, melting sensation Julian was creating in her. *This* was real temptation. The danger in Julian Colter lay not only in his profession, but in the incredible effect he had on her.

"No," Emelina finally managed in a rasping, throaty voice as she tried to resist what was happening. "Julian, please stop."

"But I want you so, sweet Emmy. I need you tonight. Can't you feel the need in me? Be generous with me." He circled the now-firm bud of her nipple with the tip of one finger while his lips moved along her throat. His voice poured over her senses like warm honey.

"Julian, I can't," she whispered achingly.

"You feel so good under my hands. How can I let you go?" The hand on her breast shifted at last and flattened boldly against the soft curve of her stomach. He raised his head and sealed her mouth once more with his own as if to forestall the protest she would make when he began fumbling with the fastening of her jeans.

Emelina did attempt a protest. She stiffened immediately as the intimacy of the gentle assault made itself known. She must not let him go any further. She mustn't. But the cry was locked forever in her throat as his tongue filled her mouth. Then his fingers were undoing the zipper of her jeans and stroking the nylon of her panties.

Panic finally rose within her, overriding the sensual glow created by his touch. Emelina planted her hands on his chest and shoved, breaking the contact between them at last. The effort left her breathless, her heart pounding.

"No, Julian. Stop it. I don't want any more of this."

He stilled, his dark eyes assessing her wary hazel gaze and the trembling curve of her softened mouth. "Is this the limit of your courage, then?" he teased gently.

"Definitely," she retorted as stoutly as possible. He didn't seem angry, she thought in silent relief. Perhaps he would be manageable after all. Was the devil ever really manageable, though? Or did he simply choose to appear that way on occasion when it suited him?

"I think you underestimate yourself, Emmy," Julian murmured, bending his head to brush his lips lightly across her forehead.

"Let me go, Julian."

"Is that really what you want me to do?"

"Yes," she whispered. "I want to go home."

"And I want to keep you here all night."

"You can't!"

He hesitated a long moment and Emelina wondered desperately what he was thinking. She sensed his own inner conflict and wondered at it. It was difficult to imagine a man like this being torn by conflicting emotions. There was a wistfulness in his expression that abruptly reminded her of Xerxes. Sleek, lethal creatures such as these two had no business looking wistful!

"All right, Emmy, I'll take you home."

She hid her astonishment at the surprisingly easy victory, wriggling quickly off his lap as he released her.

Hastily, turning her back to him, she adjusted her clothing and tried to tame the wild mane of her chestnut hair which tumbled now in disarray.

"Emmy?" She didn't turn around. "Emmy, there's no one else, is there?"

It was more a statement of fact than a question. Emelina tightened her lips, wondering if she could pull off a quick lie. It would be best if he thought that there was someone else. There might be some measure of safety in having him believe that. "Believe it or not, I do have a rather active social life," she began flippantly, fastening her jeans.

He was on his feet and suddenly very close behind her. His arms came around her waist and his face buried itself in her hair. "Emmy? Please don't tease me or lie to me. Just tell me the truth."

Her mouth went quite dry with a nameless fear. Why should she worry about telling the truth to a man like this? On the other hand, she wasn't a very good liar. His arms tightened, pulling her back against his still-aroused body. Emelina took the warning at face value.

"No," she got out huskily. "There's no one else. Not anymore."

"There was once?" he persisted gently.

"I'm divorced," she declared starkly.

"So am I."

"Oh." She wasn't quite sure what to say next.

"Which leaves us both free, doesn't it?"

Emelina was silent, mentally searching for a way out of the trap.

"Doesn't it, Emmy?"

"What are you trying to do?" she demanded bitterly. "Make me acknowledge that somehow because I don't currently have a lover, I'm fair game?"

He spun her around at that and suddenly, for the first time, Emelina saw anger in his night-dark gaze. It froze her to the spot, sending a chill down her spine.

"I was simply making an observation," Julian ground out slowly. "The fact that both of us are free is going to make things easier, but if you did happen to have a current lover, it wouldn't have made any real difference. I'd still want you and I would still do my best to make you want me. Do you understand?"

"Yes, I most certainly do," she flung back recklessly. "You're saying you'd still consider me fair game whether or not I had commitments elsewhere! Of all the arrogant, unethical, contemptible…"

The anger went out of his eyes to be replaced by rueful amusement as Julian firmly silenced her with a palm across her mouth. Above the edge of his hand her eyes continued to berate him, but he only shook his head. "Please, Emmy, that's enough for tonight. You'll hurt my feelings!"

"Hah!" she muttered scornfully as he removed his hand. "I doubt that you have many feelings other than…than the kind you just exhibited while you were kissing me," she concluded a little lamely.

"You mean other than sexual feelings?" he suggested helpfully. "Well, I will admit to those." He glanced down at the still-taut outline of his own body, and Emelina was horrified to find her glance automatically following his. Hurriedly she wrenched her eyes away from the sight of his hardened frame and turned to stare fixedly into the flames of the fire. "But I do have other kinds of feelings, too, Emmy," he added softly.

"I think I'd like to go home now," she stated remotely.

"Very well." Without further protest he collected his jacket and hers and whistled to Xerxes. "Let's go."

Julian saw her politely to her door and waited until he'd heard her lock it before he reluctantly started back to his own cottage with Xerxes at his heels. He was wryly aware of the steady ache in his lower body. Emelina would never know how close he had come to overriding all her nervous objections tonight. He'd wanted her. Very badly. Julian set his teeth as the night breeze off the ocean caught his hair and chilled him.

Perhaps the chill would calm his tight body, he decided moodily. With luck it would have the same effect as a cold shower. Damn it, but it had been a long time since he'd wanted a woman this suddenly, this positively. His hands curved unconsciously as he remembered the soft roundness of her breast and thigh.

He knew what it meant to desire a woman physically, but he was rapidly coming to realize that what he wanted from Emelina Stratton amounted to something much more complicated than physical satisfaction. Face it, he told himself grimly, he wanted a large chunk of that loyalty she was prepared to give someone she loved. He wanted to know what it was like to have a woman who was loyal to him completely. A woman who would stand with him against the world if need be. A woman who would give herself completely to him.

Now he had struck a bargain with a woman who seemed quite prepared to honor her end of it. What would she do when he called in the tab? Would she really pay the price he was beginning to think he would demand? Would she repay him with the loyalty and honor and faithfulness he craved?

God! He was turning fanciful as he neared forty, Julian decided in mocking self-disgust. Had he come to this isolated place only to suffer through a midlife crisis? What was the matter with him? Emelina Stratton owed him nothing at all. At least, not yet.

And even if he could manage to ensure that she was in his debt, how could he also ensure that she would repay him in the way he wanted?

Well, first things first. Step number one was to seal the bargain as thoroughly as possible. She had only allowed herself to risk getting this close to him because she thought he might be able to help her get her brother out of the blackmailing mess. He'd better see what he could do about that little detail!

When Xerxes automatically trotted toward the path leading up to the cottage, Julian whistled him back onto the road and together they walked to the edge of the bluff to stare down at the empty beach house which belonged to Eric Leighton.

For a long moment Julian stood there, the leather collar of his jacket turned up around his neck, his hands buried in the fleece-lined pockets. Broodingly he considered the house and the story Emelina had told him. He no longer doubted her tale, but there was every reason to doubt her wild plan of keeping an eye on Leighton's beach house. His woman had one hell of a vivid imagination, Julian decided, his mouth twisting indulgently.

His woman. The words rang through his head as he realized how right they sounded.

"I'd better give her the feeling I'm working on this ridiculous project," he muttered to Xerxes, who glanced up inquiringly. "Tomorrow night we'll take her back down to that beach house and have a look inside. There probably won't be any great clues lying around on the floor, but at least she'll think I'm making some effort to carry out my end of the deal."

And it was vital that she believe he could be trusted to honor his end of the bargain, Julian thought as he turned back toward his own cottage. He wanted her thoroughly committed to him.

The memory of his inner satisfaction earlier that evening when he'd opened his door to find her on his front step returned as Julian slid into bed sometime later. He lay back against the pillow, his arms behind his head, and stared up at the ceiling. He'd been right to try to lure her with an offer of help. Her loyalty to her brother was deep enough to make her strike the bargain.

There was a certain mental satisfaction in seeing the progress of his plans, but that didn't altogether compensate for the physical dissatisfaction of his body, Julian realized grimly. He went to sleep wanting Emelina in his bed.

Emelina did her best to throw off the aftereffects of Julian's lovemaking, but the next morning she felt curiously hungover. There was a new restlessness in her that had nothing to do with the task she had undertaken for her brother. *Why did it have to be Julian Colter who had done this to her?*

Gloomily she made a pot of coffee and sat in front of her window, drinking it. There was no point rehashing the events of the preceding evening. She'd spent half the night doing exactly that. What was the matter with her? She had made a bargain with the man, but she certainly didn't want to feel this compelling, uneasy attraction to him. Matters were dangerous enough as they stood!

She heard Xerxes before she heard the knock on her door. The cheerful yip of the Doberman made her grimace. That dog was as bad as his master. He seemed determined to make her like him. Emelina didn't care for Doberman pinschers any more than she cared for mobsters!

"Oh, good morning, Julian," she managed weakly as she opened the door. His eyes went accusingly to the cup of coffee in her hand.

"Xerxes and I didn't see you go by on your way into town for your usual morning cup of coffee."

"Er, that's because I decided to have it here instead." She could hardly tell him she hadn't wanted to risk walking past his house and having him join her once more. Emelina thought of the staring eyes yesterday morning in the cafe and winced.

"Do you make good coffee?" Julian asked unabashedly. Emelina could have groaned aloud. "No," she tried hopefully. It didn't daunt him.

"Well, I'm not too fussy." He waited expectantly.

"Will you have a cup?" she asked in resignation.

"Thought you'd never ask." He was striding inside, ordering Xerxes to lie down on the hearth rug, before she could blink an eye. "Actually, I came by to ask if you'd like to go with me tonight when I walk down to Leighton's house to have a look around," he went on conversationally as he settled into the overstuffed chair by the window.

"Oh, yes!" For the first time that morning Emelina knew a burst of genuine enthusiasm. "When are we going?" She quickly poured out his coffee.

"Around sunset, I think, so we won't have to use flashlights. They might draw attention if someone should happen to notice the light in a vacant house." He accepted the mug she handed to him and sipped cautiously. His eyes narrowed as he swallowed. "You were right," he told her dryly.

Her brow went up as she sank into the seat across from him. "About my coffee? I warned you." She took another taste of her powerful brew.

"I can see why you've been walking into town for a cup every morning!"

"If you don't like my coffee, you're free to leave," Emelina pointed out testily.

"I wouldn't think of being so rude," he retorted manfully. "But tomorrow morning you must allow me to take you back into town or make a pot myself!"

For some reason Emelina's sense of humor asserted itself. "Love me, love my coffee," she taunted lightly, blue-green eyes laughing at him.

"I thought the phrase was 'love me, love my dog,'" he tossed back easily, but there was a gleam in his eyes.

"Not a chance." She flicked a wary glance at the quiet Doberman. "Dogs like that weren't made to be loved." Emelina's momentary humor faded as she continued to stare at Xerxes, who lifted his head to stare back. "They're bred for savagery. Trained to be guard dogs, sometimes killers."

"I don't think you fully understand Xerxes. Or me."

Whatever Emelina might have said to that was fore-stalled by Xerxes, who, aware that attention was on him, got lithely to his feet and padded across the room to thrust his head into Emelina's lap. Intelligent brown eyes met hers pleadingly. There wasn't anything she could do except re-luctantly pat the animal.

"If I learned to tolerate your coffee, could you learn to tolerate my dog?" Julian inquired a little too softly, watching her intently.

"We've already struck one bargain between us, Julian. Let's leave it at that." Emelina downed the last of her own coffee and leaped to her feet to get some more.

He didn't stay long. Perhaps he was afraid of wearing out his welcome, Emelina thought dully as she watched

Julian and the Doberman head back down the street. She ought to be happy to see the last of him for the day, but somehow when he left her cottage he managed to take the excitement and warmth out of the old place. It was an excitement and warmth he had brought with him, she realized with an uncomfortable sense of wonder.

When Julian returned it was almost sunset. He was wearing a pair of jeans and an old flannel shirt and he'd left Xerxes behind. "I don't think we'll be needing him," he told Emelina as she came down the step to meet him. "He'd only be in the way on a venture like this. Besides, he'd probably leave paw prints in the dust on the floor." He scanned her jeans and close-fitting sweater approvingly.

"What about us? Won't we leave tracks, too?" Emelina walked quickly beside him, frowning intently into the distance.

"We'll be careful. With any luck the place will be furnished with a lot of old throw rugs like our cottages are. They won't show footprints. I hope."

Emelina chewed on her lower lip. "Julian, do you think it's safe to be doing this?"

"Safer than it was for you to be doing it alone at midnight!" he growled feelingly. "You were an idiot to go down there alone that night, you know," he continued matter-of-factly. "Anyone could have spotted your flashlight and followed you!"

"Someone did," she pointed out wryly.

He shot her a quick glance. "Be grateful it was I," he told her repressively.

She had the distinct impression she had managed to annoy Julian. For some perverse reason that thought served to lift her spirits. Or perhaps it was only anticipation of the approaching adventure. "Have you burgled many houses,

Julian?" she asked chattily as they started down the path to the beach.

"We're not going to burglarize the place. We're only going to search it," he muttered.

"There's a difference?"

"About ten years in prison!"

"Have you ever been to prison, Julian?"

"No, I have not! Good grief, woman. You have a rather low opinion of me, don't you?" he complained half under his breath.

"I was just curious."

"Well, that's something, I suppose. Better to have you curious than indifferent." Before she could think of a response to that line, he was drawing her around to the side of the house that faced the ocean. "Now, I don't think anyone up on the bluff can see us, even if there happens to be someone looking this way," he explained, surveying the window with a critical eye.

"Can you open the window without breaking it?"

"It doesn't look very well latched. Pretty old. It will probably give with the right amount of pressure."

"Like everything else in your world?" she asked quietly.

He turned slowly, his dark glance cool and intimidating. With elaborate casualness he folded his arms and leaned back against the side of the weathered house. Quite suddenly Emelina wondered if she might have transgressed too far with that last thoughtless crack. As she always did when she was nervous, she chewed on her lower lip, her hazel eyes going almost green.

"Unless you'd like some real pressure applied to your nicely rounded backside, Emelina Stratton, you'd better control your new-found urge to provoke me."

Emelina blinked. Was that what she was trying to do?

Provoke him? Perhaps. It was a small method of retaliating for this damn bargain he'd foisted on her. Or had she suddenly discovered an inexplicable desire to taunt him for other reasons?

"I'll behave, Julian," she drawled with syrupy politeness. "I didn't realize you were so easily offended."

He straightened away from the side of the house and turned back to the project of prying open the old window frame. "I'm not easily offended. It's just that I have the distinct feeling I'd better draw some lines or you'll be running roughshod over me!"

"Coward," she couldn't resist mumbling.

The window opened eventually under protest. Emelina felt her sense of excitement build rapidly as Julian went in first and then helped her over the ledge. As she stood gazing around at the shadowy interior of Eric Leighton's beach cottage, Emelina's first reaction was one of dismay.

"It looks like your cottage or mine!" she complained. Indeed, it contained the same sort of tattered and worn furniture, the same faded rugs and had the same weathered look as all the other beach houses.

"Well, what did you expect? A pile of cocaine sitting on the hearth waiting to be shipped out?" Julian asked calmly, stepping from rug to rug as he made his way toward the kitchen.

"Something like that, at least!" she retorted, glaring at his back.

His mouth crooked wryly. "Stay on the rugs and let's have a look around. I'll take the kitchen. You can start on the bedrooms."

There was only one bedroom and it contained nothing but a slanting bed and a chipped dresser. Emelina searched carefully and diligently, and when she was finished Julian went through the room, himself. They did each of the small rooms in the same fashion, but it soon became obvious that nothing in the nature of startling evidence was going to come to light.

"What about loose floorboards or secret safes in the walls?" Emelina demanded forty-five minutes later as she carefully tugged open a hall cupboard.

"What about them?" Julian growled, turning to see what she might find in the cupboard. "Do you want me to pry up every floorboard?"

"I suppose not," she sighed, frowning at the collection of neatly folded brown paper bags stacked on the bottom shelf of the cupboard. "Looks like Leighton is the compulsively thrifty type who saves all his paper bags."

"Yeah?" Curious, Julian came to stand behind her as they stood staring into the cupboard. "I wonder why?" He reached down to flip through them.

"Some people are that way." She shrugged. "You know the kind. They save every plastic bag from the produce department and fold every paper bag they take home from the store. Also, Leighton was into saving trees for a while, as I recall. He and Keith were rabid on the subject of environmentalism for a time."

"Did you ever actually meet Leighton?"

"Once or twice." Emelina lifted one shoulder. "There's nothing all that memorable about him. He lacked the charisma it takes to make it as a truly successful radical leader, and he tried to make up for it in other ways."

"Like dealing dope?" Julian murmured.

"It made him a big man on campus for a while. Gave him a feeling of importance. Keith began drawing away from him after he realized the direction Leighton was going."

"Your brother wasn't part of the drug scene?" Julian drawled.

"Absolutely not!" Emelina defended her brother hotly. "He was into health foods and meditation, not drugs!"

Julian looked at her wonderingly. "This brother of yours, I take it, has never done anything wrong?"

"Nothing *really* wrong," she emphasized firmly.

"Uh huh. But he's still nervous about what Leighton could use to blackmail him? There must have been something, Emmy."

"I told you, his present employer just wouldn't understand about the protest rallies and the radical politics and some of the other stuff. He never did anything wrong, Julian, he just lived a very unconventional lifestyle. That's all! But it would be enough to embarrass him now." There were the six months Keith had spent in that crazy commune, for example, she thought fleetingly. She could just imagine how that would go down with Keith's sixty-year-old mentor in the corporate offices!

"I get the feeling you'd stick by Keith even if it turned out he had gotten into something he shouldn't have," Julian said.

"Anyone can make a mistake, Julian," she admonished. "Which is not to say my brother made any really serious ones," she added quickly.

"I give up," he said with a half smile. "It's clear you'd defend him regardless of what he did or didn't do." Julian shut the cupboard door on the stack of folded paper bags. "Come on, it's getting dark. We'd better get out of here."

"But we haven't found anything."

"It was an off chance that we would, honey," he soothed. "Surely you realized that? Even if Leighton were using this place for illegal purposes he wouldn't be likely to leave evidence behind."

"I was so hoping to find something, though. I guess all we can do now is keep an eye on the place for the next few weeks and see if anything suspicious happens."

"Yes," he agreed, not looking at her. "I suppose that's one thing we should do."

"What else?" she asked eagerly as they climbed back out the window and Julian checked to make sure no obvious hand prints remained on the frame.

"Well, I could make a few inquiries."

"I see." Visions of Julian putting the far-reaching tentacles of his Mafia contacts into operation made her shudder involuntarily. It was frightening dealing with this kind of power. She must keep reminding herself just what she had gotten into by making the bargain with him. Sometimes, such as during the past hour, she almost forgot. He seemed so very *human.*

Julian saw the distant speculation in her eyes as they started toward the path to the bluff. He could just imagine the images her active imagination was conjuring up now. But there was one point he wanted to make before he saw her back inside her own cottage and returned to his lonely bed. His mouth hardened as he tried to find the words.

"You realize," he stated coolly, "that we're partners in crime now?"

She frowned. "What are you talking about?"

"We just illegally entered and searched that house. It's private property, Emelina. We had no right to be in Leighton's beach place."

"So?" She moved uneasily ahead of him to climb the path.

"So, I just want you to realize how involved you're getting in something that is not exactly legal."

"Are you trying to tell me we're following the same trail as Bonny and Clyde?" she tried to say flippantly.

"I hope we'll come to a better end than they did," he retorted dryly.

Belatedly Emelina remembered that in the legend of Bonny and Clyde the two outlaws hadn't lived long. They had died as violently as they had lived. "I shall rely on your professionalism to keep us out of serious danger, Julian," she told him bracingly.

"You're missing the point, Emmy," he said bluntly as he took her arm to start down the street. "I'm trying to make you see that we're more or less committed to see this through together now. By breaking into that house with me, you helped seal our bargain a little more thoroughly. Do you understand?"

She pulled her arm out of his grasp, coming to a halt to stare up at him in surprise. "Did you think that I'd try to wriggle out of our deal?" she demanded proudly. "Is that the real reason you took me with you this evening? So I'd commit an illegal act with your assistance and feel committed to our bargain? You're a very devious man, Julian Colter, but for your information, you outfinessed yourself. I have no intention of backing out of our arrangement. I was *committed* to this project before you ever came along, remember?"

He watched her face in the disappearing light. "I want you to realize that you're committed to me, not just the project."

She drew away from him, her nerves on edge. "Don't you think I'm aware of that? I know what I've done by accepting your offer of help, Julian," she whispered tightly. "I always pay my debts. You don't have to worry. I'll make good on the tab when you present it."

Emelina turned and fled toward her cottage.

CHAPTER FOUR

IT WAS XERXES WHO CAUGHT Emelina as she tried to sneak into the village for coffee the next morning. She groaned softly to herself as the black-and-tan dog gave a joyful yip of greeting and bounded down from the front step where he'd been sitting. A quick glance assured Emelina that Julian was not in sight, so she spoke hurriedly to the enthusiastic animal.

"Down, boy! Go back. Back to the house. Do you hear me?" She tried to speak gruffly and to infuse her tone with command, but Xerxes seemed to miss the point. He whined and put his head in the neighborhood of her hand, looking up at her with that wistful glance that seemed so out of place on both him and his master.

"Back, Xerxes!" she tried again, but when he wriggled his ears suggestively she sighed and scratched them for him.

Julian's voice broke into the small scene, and Emelina whirled to see him topping the crest of the bluff. He'd been down on the beach near Leighton's house apparently. Xerxes must have beaten him back to the cottage. "It doesn't work if you give him mixed signals," he told her in mild amusement. "You have to be firm. Telling him to go back to the house while you're petting him at the same time only confuses him."

"He doesn't look confused," she noted dryly, glancing

back down at the dog. Xerxes made an excellent excuse not to study Julian in the morning light. The wind-tossed dark hair with its iron-gray strands, the lithe, strong figure cloaked in jeans and the familiar leather jacket, looked too appealing to her this morning. The last thing she wanted to do, Emelina reminded herself nervously, was find Julian Colter appealing.

"He's not confused, because he knows which signal is the more important one, I guess," Julian decided as he reached the pair. "Being petted is bound to outrank being ordered away from you."

"Silly dog," she muttered, "why don't you go find some stranger to attack?"

"Personally, I'm grateful to him," Julian drawled. "If he hadn't stopped you out here on the road, you would have gone right on into town without me, wouldn't you?"

"With any luck," Emelina agreed under her breath.

"Shame on you. And after giving me your word you'd allow me to buy you decent coffee this morning."

"Did I?" Emelina flushed guiltily, trying to remember the conversation. "I don't recall giving you my word on the subject," she said slowly.

"Well, it was definitely implied," Julian said briskly before quietly ordering Xerxes back to the house. "Come on, Xerxes. Inside. You're delaying my morning coffee."

Emelina frowned. Damn it, she hadn't implied anything of the kind as she recalled. But it was too late to argue. Julian was already falling into step beside her and there was really no alternative except to agree to his company. He would be even more difficult to send back to the house than Xerxes had been!

"What were you doing down at Leighton's house?" she inquired abruptly as they approached the cafe.

"Just thought I'd take another look around. Something's bothering me and I can't put my finger on it."

Emelina glanced up quickly. "What is it that's bothering you?"

"I'm not sure. The feeling I got about that cottage. Something doesn't fit." Julian smiled at her as he opened the cafe door. "Don't worry about it. I'm the one who's supposed to do the worrying, remember?"

The covert glances and the instant of speculative silence that greeted Emelina as she walked into the cozy coffee shop beside Julian raised the hair on the nape of her neck. Yesterday her response to the curiosity and questions around her had been a distinct uneasiness, tinged with embarrassment. This morning, for some reason, her reaction was one of haughty anger. Unconsciously she straightened her shoulders and lifted her chin in subtle challenge as she walked beside Julian to an empty booth.

Who the hell did these people think they were to be so rude? Julian wasn't bothering them. Whatever his profession may have been, here on the Oregon coast he was just another vacationer. Besides, she had made a pact with him. Like it or not, that seemed to put her in his corner, Emelina realized as she took her seat.

"Stop glaring at that fisherman at the counter," Julian advised gently as the waitress approached.

"He's staring at you."

"So?"

"So, it's rude! He has no business staring at you!" she hissed.

"He's curious," Julian explained offhandedly and then turned to give their order to an equally curious waitress.

Emelina sat back against the cushion and watched Julian's harshly carved profile as he dealt with the waitress. "Doesn't it bother you?" she finally asked hesitantly as the waitress disappeared. "The curiosity and the speculation, I mean?"

"Not particularly. I don't much care what these people think about me."

"You're so arrogant," she murmured, moving her head in a gesture of outright wonder. "You wouldn't bother to explain yourself to these people even if you were the president of a bank instead of a…" Her voice trailed off rather abruptly, and Emelina turned a rather fiery shade of red.

"Instead of what, Emmy?" he prompted, dark eyes amused.

"Never mind," she retorted aggressively. "How long are you going to stay here on the coast, Julian?" Anything to change the conversation!

"I haven't decided."

Which probably meant he didn't know how long it would take until it was safe to go back to his regular haunts, Emelina thought knowingly. "Where do you come from, Julian?"

"Arizona."

Emelina nodded morosely. She'd heard rumors about the underworld figures who had moved to the Sunbelt.

"Any other questions?" Julian inquired politely as the coffee arrived.

Since she was unable to think of any "safe" questions, Emelina shook her head and gulped hot coffee. Her eyes followed the waitress vengefully.

"You can stop glaring at the waitress," Julian advised dryly.

"She's talking about you to that fishing person." Emelina kept on glaring at the woman until the waitress realized she was under unfriendly scrutiny and, flushing slightly in embarrassment, went to pour coffee at the end of the counter.

"Let her talk. What are you thinking of doing? Racing over there and beating both of them up because they're speculating about me?"

"It's not funny, Julian."

He shrugged, apparently unconvinced. "Can I ask you a few questions now?" he went on with exaggerated civility.

"Like what?"

"Like why you're not married any longer," he said calmly, astonishing her.

"That's a very personal question!"

He shrugged again. And waited. There was a quality about his waiting that made Emelina shift uneasily in her seat. This man could be intimidating without half trying, she thought resentfully. "Julian, the only thing I got out of my marriage was a pile of debts that had to be paid off. It is not a subject I like to discuss, especially with strangers!"

"I'm hardly a stranger, am I?" The glance he gave her was a little like the kind she was beginning to expect from Xerxes. Why she bothered to respond to either creature was totally mystifying. "What sort of debts?" he pressed.

"My husband had taken out a lot of loans to cover his expenses in college and graduate school. He had expensive tastes," she added, remembering the Corvette and the handsome clothes. "When he left me, I had to drop out of college to pay off his bills." She grimaced and turned to stare out the window. "It seems like I've spent half my life paying off debts!"

"Who else saddled you with them?"

"My father was always overextended," she murmured, remembering her laughing, good-natured, horribly irresponsible parent. "It finally got to be too much, even for him, so he pulled a disappearing act a few years ago and left Keith and me to pick up the pieces. My mother is very much like him in temperament. Fortunately she's remarried into money!" She swung her head back to find Julian studying her. "I have excellent credit references, Julian," she told him with a trace of bitterness. "You don't have to worry that I won't pay you."

"Even though what I ask for won't have anything to do with cash?" He continued to watch her with that steady, assessing glance.

"Could we talk about something else?" she pleaded.

"If you like."

"Why aren't you still married, Julian?" she dared, feeling that he owed her some personal history in exchange for the background information he'd pried out of her.

"My wife ran off with another man," he explained very simply.

"I see." She wished she'd resisted the urge to ask.

"The other man was once my best friend and business partner," he continued roughly.

"Oh, Julian!" Eyes widening with dismay, Emelina stared at him. "How awful for you! No wonder you're so concerned about...about..."

"About loyalty and commitment?" he filled in for her. "Yes."

"What happened to them?"

"My ex-wife and my ex-friend? Why do you ask?"

Emelina glanced away. "I just wondered. It occurred to me that you might have felt, er, vengeful."

"I did. For a while."

She wondered if he'd taken steps to carry out some terrible Mafia-style revenge. Her mind fashioned an almost unlimited series of possibilities based on several violent books she had read. She decided not to ask any further questions on the subject. "I was going to pick up some groceries and my mail," she went on deliberately, seeking a way to draw the intimate discussion to an end.

Julian nodded, setting down his cup. "Good idea. I'm having my mail forwarded here, too. But I have an alternative suggestion as far as the groceries are concerned."

"What's that?"

"Let's choose them together. We can have dinner at my place tonight."

Emelina knew a command when she heard one, and somehow she couldn't seem to summon the strength of purpose to ignore it. "All right."

"Is your coffee a sample of your culinary talents?" he teased as they rose from the table.

"If you're worried about being stuck with all the cooking, you needn't be," she retorted hotly. "I make a really terrific chicken curry!"

"Sold. Let's go find us a chicken."

As they started out of the restaurant, Emelina felt the curious stares drilling into Julian once more, and this time an unreasoning defensiveness took hold of her emotions. Damn it, whatever Julian was, it didn't concern these people! What right did they have to talk about him behind his back and eye him so rudely?

Pinning the nearest offender with a narrowed, challenging gaze, Emelina took a step closer to Julian and slid her arm under his. The small gesture couldn't possibly have been lost on the villagers. Emelina was definitely signaling where her alliance lay. Her chin lifted defiantly.

Julian glanced at her arm in surprise before crushing it against his side with a suddenness that suggested he was afraid she'd change her mind. Thus entwined, they made their exit from the cafe.

They walked in thoughtful silence up the street to the

grocery store. Emelina didn't know how to ask for her arm back, and Julian appeared to have no intention of releasing it voluntarily.

Emelina could have cheerfully kicked herself. Why had she followed the impulse to take a stupid stand like this in front of the people in the cafe? Julian Colter didn't need anyone's assistance. He was the last one to be concerned about what the others thought!

"I'll have the butcher bone some chicken breasts," Julian offered as they entered the store at the end of the block.

"Okay, I'll see if they carry anything as exotic as chutney here," Emelina said quickly, grateful for the release of her arm. "Meet you at the checkout counter." She hurried down a far aisle, seeking a momentary escape more than she sought chutney.

It was something of an accident that she stumbled into a small row of bottles full of the spicy condiment at the end of the aisle. Perhaps it was some sort of strange omen, she decided, picking up a bottle and heading for the spice rack nearby to search for curry powder.

What she discovered at the spice rack, however, was the middle-aged woman who, along with her husband, owned the grocery store.

"Oh, good morning, Emelina. I saw you come into the store a few minutes ago."

Emelina eyed the almost militant look in the older woman's eyes and cringed inwardly. Now what? "Good morning, Mrs. Johnston. How are you today? I'm looking for curry powder."

"Got some right here." Mildred Johnston reached for the small can and handed it to her. "Came in with that Julian Colter, didn't you?"

"Uh, yes, as a matter of fact, I did," Emelina mumbled,

trying to back away. Mildred Johnston was an acknowledged source of prime information among the local gossips. Emelina had realized that much two days after she'd arrived in town and begun doing her grocery shopping at Johnston's Market.

"Heard you had coffee with him the other morning, too, dear," Mildred went on determinedly.

"Yes."

"You want to be careful about who you strike up a friendship with, Emelina. You don't know anything about Colter, do you?"

"Well…"

Mildred leaned closer. "They say he's in the Syndicate."

"Really?" Emelina asked weakly.

"If I were you, dear, I wouldn't get too friendly with him," Mildred Johnston murmured knowingly. "Bad news. Oh, he's kind of interesting, I'll grant you that, but a nice young woman such as yourself wouldn't want to get involved with someone in the Mob! Why, his name isn't even Colter!"

"It isn't?" Emelina felt the same stirring of rebellion she'd experienced a few minutes earlier in the coffee shop.

"I doubt it. Colter is probably an alias. He's hiding out while things cool down back East, you see. Take my advice, Emelina. Steer clear of him." Mildred concluded her small lecture with an admonishing nod.

The words came out before Emelina could stop them. "Mrs. Johnston," she began icily, "if I ever decide I need your advice concerning my friends, I'll ask for it. For your information, Julian Colter is a friend of mine. We're working together on a project and I trust him implicitly. At least I know he's not going to gossip about me behind my back and that's more than I can say for ninety-five percent of the rest of this town! Furthermore, I am not a nice *young* woman, I'm thirty-one years old. Old enough to make up my own mind about who I will have for a *friend.* You might want to take into consideration one other thing, Mrs. Johnston. If you're so convinced Julian is Mafia, you probably ought to guard your tongue, hadn't you? He might grow a little impatient with small-town gossip. And there's no telling how he might decide to put an end to it!" Emelina finished with relish.

Mildred Johnston stared at her, stunned. "You don't think he'd…he'd…" She began awkwardly, only to let the horrified sentence trail off as her gaze went past Emelina to the man who had appeared from the next aisle and was now standing behind her.

Emelina whipped around in time to see Julian smiling blandly at a stricken Mrs. Johnston. "Oh, there you are, Julian. Did you get the chicken? I have everything else we need except for the flaked coconut. I think it's toward the front of the store. Shall we go?" Head high, she led the way toward the checkout counter. Julian obediently followed, leaving Mildred Johnston staring.

He didn't say anything at all until he picked up the paper bag full of groceries from a very silent clerk and left the store with Emelina. Then he murmured quietly, "Throwing your weight around a bit with the locals, Emelina?"

She heard the amusement in his voice and glowered. "It was your weight I was throwing around. I don't like the way people stare and gossip about you, Julian. But I think Mildred Johnston will be a little more careful what she says from now on!" she concluded in grim satisfaction.

"I doubt it," he chuckled. "Although she may be a little more careful who she says it to. You can be quite intimidating, Emmy."

"She deserved it."

"Now it's you and me against the world, hmmm?" he questioned lightly as he led her into the post-office building.

Emelina contented herself with anxiously chewing on her lower lip. Was that the way matters were shaping up between her and Julian? She had the distinct impression that she was edging over an invisible line which, if she crossed it completely, would somehow place her squarely in Julian's camp. If she wasn't very careful, she would find herself committed to more than just repaying a debt. It was a sobering thought.

The package that awaited her in the post office was even more sobering, however, although Emelina accepted it with the sigh of resignation with which she had greeted a lot of other packages just like it.

"From New York?" Julian inquired curiously, glancing at the return address label. "From a publisher?"

"A rejected manuscript," Emelina muttered, collecting it and the rest of her mail. "I'm used to them."

Julian's brow furrowed. "What will you do with it now?"

"Send it out to another publisher," she groaned as they started down the post office steps.

There was a pause and then Julian asked gently, "May I read it first?"

Emelina shook her head vigorously. "Absolutely not! No one reads my manuscripts except faceless editors in New York who send impersonal rejection notices! I don't even allow Keith to read my work! I have a policy of not showing my manuscripts to anyone who's not in a position to buy them."

"You're afraid of a face-to-face discussion about your work?"

"Terrified of it," she agreed firmly. "It's much too

personal at this point. I can't explain it. I just know I haven't got the courage to allow anyone to read my work. Maybe I'm afraid they'll laugh or tell me I'm wasting my time. Or maybe I'm afraid they'll lie and tell me it's good when it really isn't. I only know it would be a waste of time, because I intend to keep trying to write, anyway. So why subject myself to unwanted criticism?"

"I see your point," he agreed slowly. "But I'd still like to read something you've written."

"Not a chance," she informed him brusquely. "What time shall I come by for dinner tonight, Julian?"

"You do have a way of changing the subject, don't you?"

"Six o'clock?" she prompted determinedly.

"That will be fine. Why don't you come inside while I unpack these groceries now, though? You can say hello to Xerxes again. Did you have breakfast?"

"Oh, yes…and no, thanks, I don't think I want to see Xerxes again. I'll come by this evening, Julian."

"I'd like you to come in now," he told her coolly. "How about another cup of coffee?"

"That's quite all right, I really don't want any more, thanks."

"I insist," he murmured, his gritty voice lowering to an even softer note. "After all, we seem to be friends, now, right?"

"Julian, I want to get this manuscript ready to mail off again, and there were some chores I was going to do around the cottage…." But he already had the cottage door open, and Xerxes was leaping outside to greet them both. Before Emelina knew what had happened, she was standing in Julian's kitchen, watching as he unpacked the grocery sack.

"I have some wine I brought with me," she ventured,

deciding to be civil. "I'll bring it along tonight." Absently she patted Xerxes.

"Excellent." He nodded approvingly as he opened the refrigerator and placed the chicken on a shelf. "Emmy," he began as he drew the last item out of the paper bag, "about what happened this morning at the coffee shop and later in the grocery store…"

Emelina was bracing herself for a return to that awkward subject when she realized he had stopped talking and was staring thoughtfully into the brown paper bag. "What's the matter, Julian?"

"The receipt's in the bottom of the bag," he noted slowly.

"It usually is," she retorted in mild annoyance. Why should that matter?

"Yes," he agreed even more slowly, still looking into the sack, "it is. The receipt usually falls to the bottom of the bag and gets tossed out with it. Or folded up and stored in a closet," he added carefully.

Emelina's eyes narrowed. "Folded up and stored in a closet? You mean in a closet like the one down in Leighton's beach house?"

"Ummm." Slowly Julian crushed the paper bag in his hand, but not before he had withdrawn the receipt. "Receipts are dated, Emmy."

Emelina found herself gnawing on her lower lip as she locked eyes with a suddenly very serious-looking Julian. Her mind clicked quickly as her imagination took hold. "You mean that if we went through those paper bags stored in Leighton's closet we might find some dated receipts?"

"It's a possibility. And since those paper bags were probably transporting groceries Leighton knew he'd need while he stayed at the cottage…"

"We might be able to see when he was last here?"

"If we had enough receipts," Julian observed quietly, "we might even be able to see if there were some sort of pattern to his visits. If they occurred on a regular basis. Want to go have a look this evening around sunset?"

Emelina's eyes sparkled with new excitement. "Why don't we go now? No one would notice!"

"Someone might," he contradicted firmly. "We'll go later when we stand a better chance of finding the coast clear!"

"Oh, Julian," she protested disgustedly.

"You wanted my professional expertise in this matter, remember? It's no good buying advice if you're not going to follow it. Sit down, Emmy, while I give you a lesson in how to make really first class coffee!"

EMELINA'S SECOND ADVENTURE in breaking and entering, or *prying open* and entering, as she insisted on calling it, took place at dusk. This time she and Julian wasted no time before climbing through the window and heading for the hall closet where Eric Leighton had stored his paper bags.

It took only a few tries to demonstrate that Julian's idea had merit. There were receipts in the bottoms of several of the grocery sacks. Hastily they collected all they could find, refolded the bags and hurried back out the window.

"We're getting pretty good at this," Emelina noted gleefully as she climbed the path ahead of Julian clutching a handful of grocery receipts.

"Thinking of giving up writing for a life of crime?"

"This is not exactly a crime, Julian! Leighton's the criminal, not us."

"Keep reminding me," he begged.

Instantly Emelina felt a bit contrite. Perhaps Julian did not like to think of his chosen profession while he was on vacation or hiding out. All kinds of businessmen needed time away from the job, she supposed. "I'm sorry I'm making you work while you're supposed to be on vacation, Julian," she said as they topped the rise and walked to the cottage.

"Don't worry about it. I'm going to be well paid for my efforts, remember?"

That kept her quiet all the way through the chicken curry, a salad and a bottle of Chablis. This time it was Julian who wished he'd kept his mouth shut. He much preferred her lively conversation, he realized unhappily as they cleared the table. He should have resisted the desire to remind her yet again of the debt that lay between them.

It was his own insecurity about being able to collect on that debt that prompted him to keep referring to it, he thought as he stoked the fire in the fireplace and poured out two brandies. Talk about a shot in the dark! The odds of learning anything useful from those receipts on the coffee table were pitifully bad. Of course, there were always those "inquiries" he planned to set in action soon.

"Let's see what we've got here," he said briskly, seating himself on the rug in front of the hearth and spreading out the receipts. "You keep track of the dates I read off, okay?"

"Okay." Some of Emelina's enthusiasm returned as she contemplated the pile of papers on the floor in front of Julian. Eagerly she picked up a pad and pencil and began to jot down dates as he read them to her.

Julian was the more astonished of the two when a pattern did, indeed, begin to emerge. Emelina, he guessed, had been expecting an important finding, but he had been considerably more doubtful. The relief he experienced as the pattern began to come together was much more than he would have expected under the circumstances.

"I don't know yet what we can make of it or how much stock we should put in it, but there's definitely a similarity about all these dates. They all fall on or about the twenty-eighth of the month, don't they?" he said at last, scanning the notes Emelina had taken.

She nodded. "All at the end of the month. Julian, we're coming up on another month's end. Next Wednesday will be the twenty-eighth of this month!" Her hazel eyes were vivid with anticipation and excitement.

Julian glanced up and saw the glow in her blue-green gaze and something in him hardened. "Is this what it takes to make you look at me like that?" he heard himself whisper harshly. "A few clues about Eric Leighton?"

He sensed her tremor of awareness and knew she realized how the atmosphere in the room had abruptly shifted from the excitement of a hunt for clues to the excitement of a far more sensual sort of hunt. It had happened so suddenly that she didn't know how to handle it. Julian was grimly aware of the fact that he wasn't feeling much like a gentleman tonight. He wanted her too badly to give her the time she needed to deal with the violent shift in the mood of the evening. Every masculine instinct he possessed was urging him to move quickly before she thought of a way to escape.

"Julian…" she began hesitantly, her fingers tightening on the pencil in her hand. "Julian, I don't think we should…" She broke off again, her teeth nibbling uncertainly on her lower lip.

"Come here and let me taste that sweet mouth," Julian rasped softly, reaching for her. "I'll be a lot gentler on it than you are!"

With a rising surge of anticipation and desire, he eased her onto her back against the old rug, sprawling across her rounded curves with aggressive delight. She felt so *good* beneath him. So warm and soft and exactly right.

Slowly, lingeringly, he lowered his mouth to sample the

lower lip she had been abusing with her teeth. On a husky groan of need, he took the full, inviting shape of it delicately between his own teeth and nipped with sensual demand.

Beneath him he felt her body stir. Julian's carefully leashed passion began to flare into blazing life. How could he possibly stop himself tonight?

He wanted his sweet Emmy with every fiber of his being. Tonight he would see to it that their bargain was sealed on yet another level.

CHAPTER FIVE

EMELINA FELT AS IF SHE'D been inundated by the wave of masculine desire that swept over her. She'd known an unusual level of response the last time Julian had taken her in his arms, but tonight it was as if he were intent on overwhelming her senses, rather than testing them.

The fact that he was succeeding at the task was a measure of how far she had gone along the road to commitment, because Emelina knew herself well enough to know she could not allow a physical bonding without an emotional and mental sense of commitment.

But even as Julian's body sought to master hers, leaving her fewer and fewer options as the seconds ticked past, Emelina's head whirled with chaotic questions. How could she be feeling this kind of commitment to this kind of man? Whatever bond existed between them should extend no further than the tie of indebtedness. God knew that chain was going to be bad enough to live with! How could she even be tempted to explore the physical commitment?

Even as she lectured herself with fierce desperation, though, Emelina realized the questions were rapidly becoming academic. Something in her did not want to fight this man. Long-submerged feminine instincts urged her to please him, and she was woman enough to recognize that on some primitive level she actually wanted to add another link to the strange chain that bound them together.

It was wrong. Crazy, foolish and impossibly dangerous. Yet as Julian's teeth probed with exquisite tenderness along her lower lip, Emelina found herself remembering the odd desire to protect and defend him that had overcome her earlier that day. The sense of wariness she had always felt around him remained, but it was now tempered by the demands of the pact they had made. For better or worse she was on his side of the fence until the debt had been repaid.

"Emmy, you make my blood hot, do you know that, sweetheart? Just watching you these past few days has made me feel too warm, too restless, too much in need. I want you to know the same kinds of sensations. I want you to want me so badly you'll give yourself to me completely. Let me make love to you, sweet Emmy."

Let him make love to her? The question was how could she possibly stop him? Emelina moaned, the small sound lost in his mouth as he covered her lips completely with his own. She felt a delightful tingle of anticipation and marveled at it. Quite suddenly she didn't want to think about the ramifications of what she was doing. Her instincts cried out for the full commitment.

"Julian, oh, Julian," she breathed as he slowly freed her mouth to explore the line of her throat. Her palms lifted to curve around his shoulders, testing the strength there. She could feel the hardness in his body and knew the extent of his arousal. It was intoxicating.

"Your body was made for mine," he growled, burying his lips in her throat as he slowly found the first button of her shirt. "There's something just right about it. Full and round and soft and unbelievably sexy!"

"If that's a nice way of saying I'm plump," she managed

shakily, "I think I resent it!" The soft banter amazed her. Could this really be her daring to tease at a time like this?

"It's a way of saying you're perfect. Just what I need," Julian contradicted and then he drove his tongue between her parted lips as he found the second button of her shirt.

Emelina was so fascinated by the sensual rhythm he created that she barely noticed the complete removal of her garment until Julian's palm moved lightly over her nipple. Then she gasped aloud and writhed against him, trying instinctively to get closer.

Julian muttered something low and urgent and roughly exciting as she moved beneath his touch. His body grew even heavier on hers, crushing her softness deeply into the faded rug.

Sensation piled on top of sensation, but the dominant one was Emelina's growing desire to give Julian what he seemed to crave. Her body cried out to satisfy. It cried out, too, with an unexpected wish to be satisfied. She stirred at the realization, pushing her breast more firmly into his hand. When his thumb stroked erotically around the budding nipple she sighed with pleasure.

"Julian, I should stop you. I know I should stop you. Why can't I?" she asked wonderingly.

"There's nothing you could do tonight to halt me. Don't think about it, Emmy. Don't even think about it," he repeated with masterful assurance. As if to reinforce his words, Julian transferred his mouth to the tips of her breasts, using his teeth there with the same delicate deliberation as he had used on her lip. Emelina trembled and her leg, which still lay free of his weight, flexed at the knee. It was as if all the nerves and muscles in her body were slowly tightening. The feeling was at once delicious and a little unnerving.

"Touch me, sweetheart," Julian growled hoarsely. "Please touch me."

How could she deny him? Emelina's fingers moved through his hair and down to the nape of his neck, slipping inside the collar. There she kneaded the smooth band of muscle, glorying in the tremor that went through him.

Provoked by her accomplishment to further daring, she flattened her palms against his chest and drew them down to the first button of his shirt. Julian lifted his weight from her far enough to allow Emelina to unbutton it. When her fingers became increasingly awkward, he grew ruefully impatient and sat up to finish the task himself.

She lay on the rug looking up at him in the firelight and wondered at her own reactions. When Julian tossed the shirt aside and met her eyes, she immediately forgot the pulsing tautness in her own body and concentrated fully on his.

"You're so beautiful," she breathed, reaching out to lace her fingers through the crisp hair of his chest. "Like Xerxes."

His dark eyes burned over her as his mouth twisted in wry humor. "Like my dog? Thanks!"

"Sleek and strong and…" She broke off, not wanting to say the rest.

"And what?"

Emelina decided she ought to have guessed he would make her finish the sentence. "And a little frightening," she concluded honestly.

"Are you frightened of me, Emmy?" Slowly he stretched out beside her, his hand roving across her midsection to the fastening of her jeans. His gaze held her still as he began to remove the last of her garments.

"Sometimes." Her mouth had gone very dry, and her lower body felt too hot, too tense. What was wrong with her?

"Don't be. As long as I know I can trust you, you have

no reason to fear me, sweet Emmy." He lowered his head and brushed her lips fleetingly. Then Julian slid his hands beneath the waistband of her jeans and pushed them down over her hips. Before Emelina could decide if she wanted matters to go that far, they already had. She lay nude on the hearth rug, her chestnut hair fanned out beneath her, hazel eyes watching him from beneath half-closed lashes.

In the firelight their bodies glowed almost golden. Emelina knew a fierce desire to see the rest of Julian's hard length. She wanted to see all of him painted with that golden glow.

"You're growing very bold," he teased gently as she found the zipper of his denims. "It's about time!"

Embarrassed, Emelina made to draw back her hand, but he caught her wrist and placed it firmly back where it had been. Encouraged, she slowly undressed him. The aggressive, aroused state of his body made her suck in her breath.

"Now touch me some more," he begged. "God, your fingers feel good on my skin!" All the while he stroked her thigh, weaving patterns on the soft curve that seemed to heighten the gathering tension in her. When he moved those patterns to the inside of her leg she moaned aloud and buried her face against his shoulder.

"Do you like that, Emmy?" he whispered, working his hand upward along the satin softness of her inner thigh. "Am I pleasing you, honey?"

"Oh, yes," she breathed and thought how kind he was to worry about whether or not he was pleasing her. Her ex-husband had never been overly concerned with the subject, assuming that if she didn't get whatever she needed out of the marital embrace, it was her own fault. Emelina found herself filled with such gratitude for Julian's concern that she wriggled closer on the rug and hesitantly reached down to feel the muscled slope of his leg. It was rough with hair and excitingly different from her own.

She tried to please him the way he was pleasing her, stroking and caressing closer and closer to the waiting hardness of him. But when she hesitated too long to take him intimately into her hand, Julian groaned and pushed himself against her palm, demanding the sensual touch.

As if the feel of her hands on his aroused body was something he had been anticipating for a very long time, Julian pressed himself closer. He slid his palm between Emelina's legs and under her rounded buttocks, using his thumb with erotic sensitivity on the flowering heart of her desire. Emelina was put totally off balance by the exquisitely erotic sensations that flooded through her limbs.

"Julian! Oh, my God, Julian! I feel so...so..." She couldn't find the words. The sensation was pleasurable, but it was also distracting. She forgot her wish to caress him as perfectly as he was caressing her. Emelina forgot everything for a moment except the warm, melting honey that was coursing in her veins. She wanted more of it; wanted to follow the path that beckoned as it never had before in her life. Nothing mattered now except learning at last what real satisfaction could mean.

Blindly Emelina groped for Julian's shoulders, tugging him close. Her legs separated invitingly and the hard tips of her breasts taunted him.

"Emmy," he rasped, obeying her feminine summons. "Emmy, I want you so!"

He shifted, raising himself over her. With a surge of power Julian fit himself between her thighs, entering the moist satin folds of her with a blunt impact that took away Emelina's breath.

The shock of his possession seemed to clear her mind

for an instant, wiping out the strange, restless striving for satisfaction that had been driving her. As her body absorbed the solid strength of him Emelina came back to reality.

The important thing was to please Julian. She wanted that far more than she wanted to taste the ultimate passion. She wanted Julian to be happy.

When he nipped at her throat with gentle savagery and began to drive himself into her with a passionate cadence of growing desire, Emelina wrapped him tightly in her arms, arching her hips willingly to meet his.

"Yes, sweetheart," he grated fiercely, "give yourself to me. I need you so!"

Emelina obeyed, her whole being focused on satisfying him. She sensed that he wanted her to melt completely. Julian needed to know that she couldn't resist his lovemaking. Emelina bent all her energy on giving him what he sought. Her hands flattened against the planes of his back and her legs held him tightly as she clung to him, whispering the words she sensed he wanted to hear.

She tried to gauge the pace of his arousal, wanting to time herself perfectly for him. It was so important that he be satisfied! Aware of the steady hardening of his body and the muscled tension beneath her hands, she decided the moment had arrived for him.

Willingly, eager to provide exactly the response he wanted from her, Emelina threw herself into imitating what she felt must be a close semblance of the passionate convulsion that took hold of a woman at the completion of lovemaking. She sank her nails carefully into the firelit skin of his shoulders, tensed her lower body as tightly as possible and whispered his name over and over again in breathless abandon.

Emelina knew it must be an excellent reproduction of

the real emotion because on the few occasions when she'd tried to please her ex-husband with it, he had been egotistically satisfied with the effect.

But instead of following her performance with his own genuine burst of masculine satisfaction, Julian went still above her. Emelina opened her eyes in confusion, aware of his hardness within her. What was wrong? she thought frantically. Wasn't he pleased? Why didn't he react the way men were supposed to react at times like this? Had she failed to satisfy him? Emelina knew a surge of fear at the thought. She had wanted so much for him to be satisfied!

"If you've finished with the theatrical performance, perhaps we could go on to the real thing?" In the firelight, Julian's features were drawn and taut with controlled passion and something else, something very close to anger.

All at once Emelina felt very vulnerable. He hadn't been fooled for an instant. Helplessly, hazel eyes wide and pleading, she looked up into his face. What could a woman say in a situation such as this?

"Julian…" She caught her breath, aware of the hard length of his frame covering hers so completely. "Julian, I'm sorry. I can't. I mean, I never have been able to and I…I…only wanted to please you." The words came out in a sad little rush, and Julian's eyes blazed with dark fire.

"Shut up, my sweet Emmy and follow me."

His mouth came down on hers and his hips arched deliberately. Emelina gave up. She had done her best and had failed. Now she could only cling to him while he headed down strange paths that she had never fully investigated. She only hoped he wouldn't be too terribly disappointed if she failed to follow completely.

With the burden of trying to satisfy him off her mind, Emelina found herself concentrating on her own emotions.

What were those flickering embers that were beginning to heat her loins and sent shivers down her spine? Where did this strange tension really lead?

Julian made love to her as if she were his whole world. He used his hands and his lips to tease and torment her as Emelina had never been teased and tormented before in her life. She abandoned herself to the incredible experience, no longer worrying about anything other than the thrilling pleasure that was rippling through her in waves.

She moved beneath him now, not with calculated thought, but with unconscious demand. Her nails sank into his skin again, but this time they nearly drew blood. Her legs wrapped him close, but this time she squeezed him with every ounce of her feminine strength, not fully appreciating just how strong she was.

"Julian!" The cry was a command and a plea as Emelina's head arched backward over his arm and her eyes shut tightly against the invading desire.

"Hold me, Emmy. Hold me as if you'll never let me go!" Julian ordered roughly, his fingers sliding down between their bodies to find the tangled, moist thicket between her legs. There he did something that seemed to send Emelina over the edge of an invisible cliff.

In that final moment she couldn't even breathe his name. She had no breath left. The tension within her uncoiled in a flashing, electrical current of energy that convulsed every nerve and muscle in her body. She clung to the man above her as if he were the only refuge in the storm racking her soft frame. She was barely aware of the fierce unleashing of his own satisfaction. Dimly she heard her name being harshly called and then she collapsed beneath him, certain she would never be able to move again.

It was Julian who moved first, but not for some time.

Emelina came drowsily out of her timeless, dreamless state as he reluctantly drew away from her body and rolled to one side. When she turned her head on the rug to look at him from beneath her heavy lashes she found him watching her with a grim satisfaction.

"Don't ever, ever lie to me, Emmy," he grated softly, moving his fingers absently through the chestnut-brown tresses tangled around her head. "Not verbally or physically. You'll never get away with it. Trying to lie to me is the one sure way to make me very angry. I want only honesty from you, do you understand?"

In spite of the warm aftermath of pleasure, Emelina knew an abrupt shiver of chilling uncertainty. "I'm sorry, Julian. I only wanted to please you. I didn't think I was capable of…of finding out what it was really like and I knew you wouldn't be satisfied unless you thought you had pleased me so I…I tried to act pleased. Oh, I don't know how to explain," she mumbled, turning her head aside so that she no longer had to meet his eyes.

He caught her chin on the edge of his hand and raised her head again. This time she saw the tenderness in his eyes. "You sweet idiot. You're a creature of passion and excitement, don't you know that?"

"No," she retorted baldly. "I don't!"

"Well, you are and from now on I'm going to be the only man who has the right to put you in touch with that side of yourself. Is that very clear?" He traced the outline of her lips with his thumb.

Emelina felt too vulnerable and confused to argue. She could only stare at him, searching for an explanation of what was happening. Julian saw the grave questions in her face and leaned forward to brush his mouth against hers. "And if you ever pull a stunt like that fake act of passion again, I guarantee I will stop right where we are and turn you over my knee. By the time I've finished paddling your charming derriere you will be unable to think of playing any more games!"

Desperately she struggled for a way of responding to the indulgent gleam in his eyes. "That sounds kind of kinky."

His amusement exploded into outright laughter as Julian gathered her close. "It is," he assured her. "Very kinky. I wouldn't dream of suggesting it if you weren't such a wild little witch in bed!" Then he drew his hand along her thigh and began teasing her mouth with his own. Emelina felt his amusement changing into another emotion.

"Julian?" she questioned softly as the first faint ripples of excitement began stirring in the pit of her stomach.

"You apparently have a lot to learn about making love, sweetheart, and considering your advancing age, I don't think we'd better waste any time."

"Oh," she said quickly, without pausing to think, "I've always heard that women are at their best as they go into their thirties."

"Show me," he invited.

When Emelina awoke the next time it was morning and she was lying in Julian's bed, not on the hearth rug. It wasn't the sunlight filtering through a cloudy sky that opened her eyes, nor was it another passionate advance from the man sprawled next to her. It was a cold, damp nose being thrust into her palm.

Xerxes watched her intently, his dark head resting on the bed. The expectant, faintly wistful expression on his face was enough to make Emelina groan and bury her own head back under a pillow.

Xerxes took more forceful action. He nudged her again with his nose and Emelina heard a tiny sound emanating from far back in his throat. Was Xerxes growling at her? That thought was enough to bring her wide awake. She stared at the dog suspiciously as she clutched the sheet to her naked breasts. As far as Emelina was concerned, there was probably a great similarity between dog and master. She fully expected either one of them to resort to intimidation if they didn't achieve their objectives through more polite methods.

Xerxes looked up at her with a satisfied expression. He was making progress.

"He wants out," Julian yawned beside her. "It appears you've been elected for the duty. I can see there are some terrific fringe benefits to having you in my bed. Why don't you run along and let Xerxes out and then practice making coffee the way I showed you the other day?"

Emelina frowned severely into his blandly innocent face, a part of her far too aware of the fact that he was as naked as she was under the sheet. "I am not going to get into the habit of waiting on you and your dog!" Heaven help her! She wasn't going to get into the habit of waking up in his bed, either, she added grimly to herself. Even if doing so meant rediscovering a passionate side of her nature she hadn't dreamed existed. Some discoveries involved far too much risk.

Xerxes made that faintly menacing sound in the back of his throat again and Emelina snapped her head back to glare at him.

"I think you'd better get moving," Julian drawled behind her. "He sounds like he's getting impatient. And I could sure use that cup of coffee."

"I've told you, I'm not going to be a dogsbody for either of you!" she sniffed defiantly.

This time it was Julian who growled, a small, intimidating sound which belied the lazy humor in his dark eyes. Emelina wasn't up to dealing with two intimidating males on that particular morning. She snatched the quilt off the end of the bed and, wrapping it awkwardly around herself, stalked off to obey Xerxes's summons.

Julian watched her leave the room, his eyes following her with a curious mixture of amusement, remembered passion and possessiveness. Then he flung himself back against the pillows and contemplated his new future.

He would have to tread cautiously now. There was no doubt that he had rushed her into bed last night against his better judgment, but how could he have resisted staking the intimate claim? She was so exactly right for him, and Julian frankly acknowledged to himself that he had acted out of a very primitive fear of losing her. All his instincts bade him chain her as thoroughly as possible. And the bonds of passion seemed, to his male mind, yet another way of tying her to him.

His mouth curved slightly as he recalled the satisfying heat of Emelina's desire once it had been unleashed. Damn it, he really would paddle her nicely rounded rear end if she ever pulled that bit of fakery again! Her ex-husband must have been a complete fool to let her get away with that. He hadn't known what he was missing. Which was just as well, Julian assured himself complacently. He didn't want to think about the problems he would have encountered if he'd met Emelina and found her to be a happily married woman! She belonged to him.

Julian sighed and threw back the sheet, his bare feet hitting the wooden floor with a thud. He shook his head ruefully as he felt a twinge of desire just at the thought of Emmy Stratton in his arms. At his age he ought to have a little more self-control! With any other woman he would have had plenty of control, he realized as he headed toward the cold bathroom and switched on the electric wall heater. But Emmy was different. Emmy made him go a little crazy.

Which only made it all the more imperative that he employ some caution. The trap he was setting had to be as tight as possible. He didn't want to take any unnecessary risks.

Last night had probably been inevitable, Julian decided practically as he stepped under the shower. But he'd seen the wariness in her eyes this morning when she had awakened, and he knew that Emelina wasn't yet ready to agree to spend all her nights in his bed.

Which was only fair, Julian thought grimly. After all, he still had his side of the bargain to carry out.

"Here's your coffee. Take it or leave it," Emelina announced as she boldly walked into the bathroom and handed the mug around the edge of the curtain. Assign her to make coffee, would he?

The mug was taken from her hand but she wasn't given a chance to withdraw her fingers. Julian caught hold of her wrist and held her as he cautiously sipped the brew she had created.

"I don't think you were paying attention when I gave you that lesson," he finally declared consideringly. "This is pretty awful."

On the other side of the curtain Emelina smiled with defiant satisfaction. "I'm a slow learner."

"Not in every subject," he drawled, pushing aside the curtain to regard her as she stood still draped with the quilt. Her hair was tousled and she looked very inviting to his eyes. Deliberately he set down his coffee mug and used his free hand to unwrap her.

"Julian, no!" she protested, slapping at his fingers. Hastily she averted her eyes from his strong, naked length.

"Hush, sweetheart," he soothed in a deeply hypnotic

growl. "I'm only going to help you get ready to face the new day." Gently he yanked her into the shower stall.

It was a long time later before Emelina sat down to breakfast across from Julian. Her mood was a precarious one, compounded of wariness and a feeling of commitment that made her deeply uneasy. A part of her wasn't at all sure she liked what had happened to her last night. It left her feeling strangely trapped. Another part of her was beginning to welcome the bonds closing in around her. That realization was the cause of her wariness. Being attracted to Julian Colter was frightening.

"About the dates on those receipts," Julian began calmly as he poured syrup over a stack of buckwheat pancakes.

"Yes, what are we going to do?" Emelina was more than a little grateful for the neutral topic.

"If there's anything to your crazy theory that Leighton is using his beach house for illegal activities, then we are led to the conclusion that those activities seem to be on a schedule. Whatever is happening is happening at the end of month."

"That makes sense, doesn't it? Shipments of any kind, legal or illegal, normally get made on schedule."

"Emmy," he sighed, "I hope you realize how very unlikely it is that anything remotely resembling illegal activity will take place at that beach house next week."

"We have to find out, Julian! This could be the break I've been looking for!"

"Okay, okay. We'll find out. I just want you to be prepared for disappointment," he advised steadily.

"I will be," she agreed too readily, not at all prepared for any such thing.

He looked at her. "I also want you to remember that if I help you find out what is or is not going on at Leighton's cottage, I've completed my end of the bargain."

Emelina swallowed an oversized bite of pancake and nodded mutely. "You don't have to remind me," she finally managed in a small voice.

He groaned and reached across the table to cover her hand with his. "I'm sorry, honey. I should have known I didn't have to remind you. After all, you always pay your debts, don't you?"

"Yes," she whispered and attacked her pancakes.

Julian allowed her to return to her own cottage after breakfast without an argument, which rather surprised Emelina. "What are you going to do this morning?" she found herself asking as she stood on his front step patting Xerxes goodbye.

"Make a couple of phone calls."

"To whom?"

"Someone who works for me. Run along, Emmy. I'll drop by for lunch. Don't bother trying to make me any coffee. I'll bring my own."

"Giving up so easily on training me?" she dared, smiling at him.

"Not at all. I just don't believe in trying to teach you too many things at once. I've decided to concentrate my energies in more productive areas at the moment. Areas in which you show a marked aptitude. We'll return to the coffee problem at a later date."

Emelina hurried down the steps and up the street to her cottage, her face warm and flushed under the impact of his too-knowing gaze. It was like falling into quicksand, this sensation of being bound more and more tightly to a man. She'd never experienced anything like it in her entire life, and she didn't know how to fight it.

Of all the men in the world, why did she have to find herself in this situation with someone like Julian Colter?

Why couldn't she have found someone safe and traditional and nonthreatening?

Emelina tried to take a firm grip on her emotions as the morning passed. Somehow she was going to have to find a way to handle this crazy mess. It was bad enough that she was in debt to the man. She simply must not let the attraction she felt for him carry her over into the bottomless pit of love.

She happened to be glancing out the window an hour later when she saw Julian walk out of his cottage with Xerxes at his heels. Together they headed toward town. To find a phone booth? The summer cottages didn't have such amenities. Who was Julian going to call? Emelina shuddered to think of the sort of person one called in a situation like this! In an effort to take her mind off thoughts of Mafia henchmen she curled into a chair by the window and went to work on her latest plot. For some vague reason the hero she was describing began to take on marked similarities to Julian Colter.

Julian showed up as promised for lunch. He was carrying a thermos of coffee under his arm, and Xerxes tagged along at his side. The three of them ate in an atmosphere of comfortable familiarity, which amazed Emelina when she thought about it. But when Julian volunteered no information about the person or persons he had contacted that morning, she could contain her curiosity no longer.

"Well?" Emelina demanded, pouring out the thermos of coffee. "Did you get everything taken care of with that phone call?"

"Cardellini will be along this afternoon," Julian said mildly, lounging back in his chair.

"Who's Cardellini?"

"I told you. Someone who works for me."

"Yes, but what does he actually do for you?" Good lord! Why was she pressing the issue? Did she really want to know?

"He handles security matters for me," Julian explained gently. There was a cool gleam in his dark eyes that dared her to ask any more questions.

"I see," Emelina said weakly and concentrated on her coffee.

Cardellini did, indeed, arrive that afternoon. Emelina looked out her window, chewing nervously on her lower lip as the long black Lincoln Continental halted in front of Julian's cottage. A young, grim-faced man with dark hair and a pinstripe suit climbed out of the car and greeted Xerxes with a familiar pat on the head. Emelina could have sworn there was a faint bulge under the jacket to his suit, the sort of bulge made by a shoulder holster. Lovely, she thought unhappily. All her imaginings about Julian Colter's lifestyle were turning out to have a strong basis in reality.

She let the curtain fall back into place and lifted her chin with inner resolution. She had known what Julian was when she made the bargain. There was no sense letting herself get upset now. Her main goal was to stop Eric Leighton, and Julian Colter showed every sign of being able to handle the matter.

And if she was going to be a part of this, she might as well go the whole route, she added, grabbing her jacket from the closet and letting herself out the door. After all, she was *committed!*

Determinedly she paced down the street and up the steps to Julian's front door, where Xerxes greeted her cheerfully. The door, itself, however, was opened by the young man with the grim face, and Emelina had a moment's doubt as she stood looking at Julian's employee.

"I'm Emelina Stratton," she announced boldly.

"Let her in, Joe. That's the lady in charge of this little operation." Julian's voice came from the kitchen. "She's just in time to watch a professional make a perfect cup of coffee."

Joe Cardellini nodded gravely and stepped back. Emelina sidled hastily around him and glanced into the kitchen in search of Julian. "Hello, Julian, I just thought I'd drop by for a moment," she began quickly, watching as he measured coffee into a pot.

He cast her a sidelong glance. "You mean you thought you'd see how the plans were going, hmmm? Meet Joe Cardellini. He's the man who will get you your evidence, if there's any to be had."

Very politely Emelina shook the hand of the quiet young man in the pinstripe suit. She noticed that he was still wearing the jacket, and was grateful. It would have been difficult to carry on a normal conversation with a man wearing a gun in a shoulder holster. She'd rather not have to look at it.

"How do you do, Mr. Cardellini."

"Miss Stratton." He nodded formally. There was quiet reserve in young Joe's face. A reserve that spoke of a little too much of the wrong sort of experience, as far as Emelina was concerned. Then she realized that there was even more of that sort of look in Julian's features. How was it she was coming to overlook it in her lover's face?

Her lover. Hastily Emelina plunged into conversation. "What are you going to do down at the cottage, Joe?" she asked in what she hoped was a chatty fashion.

"Plant some listening devices and record whatever is going to happen next Wednesday or Thursday," he explained calmly.

"Oh." Emelina frowned and behind her Julian chuckled.

"What did you think he was going to do, lie in wait for Leighton on the beach and gun him down when he appeared next week? This is the modern age, Emmy. We do things scientifically, utilizing the best of modern technology. You want evidence? We'll get you evidence."

"Thank you," she mumbled humbly, not looking at either man.

"You're welcome," Julian drawled. He switched on the coffeepot before finishing his sentence. "The gunning down part will come later, if necessary."

Emelina flinched. "If necessary?" she squeaked.

"If we can't get sufficient evidence on Leighton to call him off your brother, we'll have to resort to other, more elemental techniques, won't we?" Julian smiled blandly.

CHAPTER SIX

"DON'T TEASE HER, BOSS." It was Cardellini who responded first to Julian's outrageous words. "There's no need to go upsetting her like that. You'll just make her nervous." His serious gaze moved sympathetically over Emelina's taut face.

"She's been nervous around me from the start," Julian said dryly. "Don't worry about her, Joe. She knows what she's getting into. And so do I. Why don't you run along and take a look at the Leighton place."

"Yes, sir." Properly rebuked and sent about his business, Joe Cardellini quietly let himself outside.

Emelina's eyes narrowed. "He was only trying to be polite. You didn't have to dismiss him like a…a servant!"

"He works for me. For the salary that young man receives he can take a few orders. How I treat him isn't his real problem, anyway."

"What is?" she demanded suspiciously.

"How you treat him is what will determine whether or not he gets to keep his cushy job."

Emelina's mouth fell open in astonishment. "How I treat him! I've only just met the man!"

"Ummm. And already he's leaping to your defense. Steer clear of him, Emmy, or I'll fire him." Julian calmly reached for two cups and saucers.

"That's utterly ridiculous and you know it! It's insane! What in the world is the matter with you?"

"I have this little problem with possessiveness. Want some good coffee?"

"No, thank you!" she flung back. "As Mr. Cardellini has observed, I'm already a little nervous. Getting more so by the minute, too!" She stalked to the window, giving him her back.

She didn't hear him cross the room, but suddenly he was standing very quietly behind her. When he reached around her to push a steaming mug into her fingers Emelina knew it was a peace offering, and she couldn't quite stifle the small smile that tugged at her expressive mouth.

"Are you laughing at me?" he asked, his lips against her hair.

She shook her head. "It's just that you remind me so much of Xerxes on occasion. When you put that coffee cup in my hand it reminded me of the way Xerxes shoves his head under my palm when he wants to be petted." She shook her head ruefully. "What am I going to do with the two of you?"

"Pet us." His fingers lifted to stroke the nape of her neck under the fall of chestnut hair and Emelina shivered.

"Are you trying to apologize for accusing me of seducing poor Joe?" she demanded, refusing to be placated.

"Maybe," he sighed. "I'm not used to apologizing, Emmy."

"Try it," she ordered succinctly.

She heard him draw in his breath before saying levelly, "I'm sorry, Emmy. I shouldn't have jumped down your throat like that for no reason."

"No, you shouldn't have," she agreed caustically.

"It's just that I'm a bit sensitive on the subject."

"You have no right to be!" she gasped, still staring out the window.

"You can say that? After last night?" The fingers at the nape of her neck moved caressingly. Emelina shifted restlessly, stepping just out of reach.

"What happened last night doesn't give you any rights, Julian," she whispered. Her fingers clenched into a small fist at her side as she realized that she was lying. Somehow it had given him rights. She didn't like it; didn't want to have to deal with it, but Emelina knew that the sensation of commitment she felt this morning was stronger than ever. She silently gritted her teeth and wondered if she'd gone out of her mind. Nobody but a lunatic would get involved in a mess like this!

"I don't think you really believe what you're saying, sweetheart. I think you know I'm not going to let you go to another man now that I've made you mine," Julian whispered heavily. "But you don't have to panic at this particular point. I'll try not to rush you."

"I can't tell you how that relieves my mind!" she snapped, spinning around to face him with one hand on her hip. Hazel eyes snapped fire as she glared at him. "I'll try to avoid a case of hysterics over the matter."

His eyes slitted briefly as he took a sip of his coffee. "Do that. I can't abide hysterical females."

"Choosy, aren't you?"

"Very. Now, having exhausted that argument, I suggest we go on to another topic. I was going to suggest we have dinner at a little restaurant up the coast tonight. We'll have to use your car, since I don't have one here."

"Are you going to include Joe in the invitation?" she demanded saucily.

"The issue doesn't arise. Joe will be gone by this afternoon. He won't be back until I call him back."

"And when will that be?" she challenged morosely.

"As soon as I think there might be something to hear on the tapes he's rigging up at Leighton's house. Now stop trying to provoke me, honey. We've got another four days to kill together before we see whether or not anything momentous is going to happen around the twenty-eighth."

"If you think I'm going to hang around so you won't perish of boredom..." she began seethingly, only to be interrupted as he took one step forward and removed the cup from her hand. The next thing Emelina knew she was being soundly kissed. All the passionate memories of the previous night were reawakened by that kiss, and it silenced her more effectively than anything else would have done. When Julian withdrew they were both breathing a little too quickly.

He rested his forehead lightly on hers and muttered huskily, "About tonight."

"Yes?"

"The invitation is only for dinner. Not bed."

Emelina didn't know whether to be relieved or disappointed. In the end relief won out. Or so she told herself.

She was still telling herself the same thing four days later on the twenty-eighth. Julian had been with her almost constantly, but he had made no further move to take her to bed. She went for long walks on the beach with him and Xerxes and occasionally into town for coffee and the mail. The trips into the village gave her some small satisfaction: the overt staring and low whispers had ceased. Word had apparently spread that Mr. Colter preferred not to be the subject of open speculation. And no one made any further move to warn Emelina that she was mixing with bad company.

"You've got them all terrorized, honey," Julian observed

as they headed back to the cottage on the fourth day. "Notice how polite everyone was?"

"You mean you've got them all terrorized. All I did was point out the risk they were running. Julian, doesn't it bother you, having people talk about you like that?"

"Not particularly. I came here for rest and isolation. My reputation seems to have bought me a lot of both. Other than a few low-voiced remarks, no one has bothered me," he pointed out easily.

"Except me," Emelina noted dryly. "I've really put a dent in your plans for rest and isolation, haven't I?"

"You," he said softly, "have made the whole trip worthwhile."

Emelina met the warm look in his eyes and took her courage in both hands.

"Julian, exactly why are you here in Oregon taking a vacation?" She waited for the answer, her heart beating anxiously. Did she really want to hear that he was hiding out or that he was resting from the rigors of a Mob war? Worse than that, did she want to hear that he was a target for some competitor?

"I was trying to escape the pressures of business," he told her mildly.

Which told her absolutely nothing, she thought, and then decided she was grateful not to hear the whole truth. Hastily she changed the subject. "Well, today is the twenty-eighth, Julian. Maybe tonight we'll find out something incriminating about Eric Leighton," she said brightly.

"Maybe."

"You sound skeptical."

"Honey, I've told you from the start that this scheme of yours is nothing if not harebrained. It has the merit of being highly imaginative but…"

"But you don't think we're going to get anything useful out of it? Why did you go to all the trouble of having Joe set those hidden microphones, then?" she asked.

"Because I always try to carry out my end of a bargain. Just as you do," he replied simply.

By the time Julian had walked Emelina back to her cottage later that evening there was still no sign of any activity around the Leighton beach house. Julian had allowed her a quick glance from the top of the bluff just to reassure her that she wasn't missing anything.

"Emmy, if anything at all happens down at that house tonight, we'll get it on tape. You're not to go near the place on your own, do you understand?" he lectured firmly as they drew to a halt on her doorstep.

"I hear you, Julian," she sighed.

"Don't worry," he said with a lopsided grin, "you're not going to miss anything. Just stay put until morning. And think about me," he added, pulling her into his arms.

Thinking about Julian Colter had occupied a major portion of her nights lately, Emelina decided in disgust as he released her after a quick, hard kiss. He had been as good as his word. There had been no attempt to rush her back into bed since their one night together. Emelina wondered at his patience, but she didn't dare question it aloud. Besides, if she were going to question anyone's motives, it should be her own! She was the one who seemed to be bothered by a curiously incomplete feeling as she lay alone in her bed at night.

Relieved, damn it! That was what she was, *relieved,* not lonely!

Xerxes nudged her for a farewell pat and then Emelina watched the two lethal-looking males walk back down the road. Was Julian right? Would tonight prove nothing? What would she do then? She had been counting so much on her wild plan bearing fruit. If this didn't work out, another way would have to be found to protect Keith.

Julian seemed willing to go the next step for her. With a faint shudder, Emelina let the curtain drop back into place and headed for bed. She'd think about alternatives only if her initial scheme didn't work. No sense borrowing trouble. She was far enough in debt as it was.

That thought kept her awake for the next two hours. Being in debt to a man like Julian Colter would be enough to keep anyone awake, she finally decided, tossing back the covers with a restless movement and padding out into the kitchen to see what might be in the refrigerator.

There was enough moonlight to make it unnecessary to turn on the kitchen light, so Emelina was standing in the dark, munching on a cracker spread with cream cheese when she saw the taillights of a car in the distance.

Someone was driving toward the beach. To be specific, someone was driving toward Eric Leighton's beach house. The remainder of the cracker and cream cheese went down awkwardly as adrenaline began flowing through her veins. Something was going to happen tonight after all! She had been right!

Hastily she choked down the cracker and sped to the bedroom to find her jeans. Dressing in the dark she yanked on a pair of tennis shoes, the denims and the black pullover sweater she'd worn the night Julian had discovered her at the Leighton cottage. She had to know what was happening.

Julian's warning not to go near the place was brushed aside as Emelina let herself out the front door of her cottage and started toward the bluff. The excitement of knowing her plan was working pushed everything else out of her mind.

Sticking to the shadows of the silent cottages, Emelina

slipped along the street until she was hurrying past Julian's house. For a moment she was afraid she would hear Xerxes's familiar greeting, but all was quiet in the moonlight. The lights were out in the house as she went past.

At the edge of the bluff she lowered herself onto her stomach and wriggled closer to peer down at the beach below. She had been right. The car she had spotted earlier was taking the long way down to the house, following the graveled road that came from the far end of the beach. Shivering with the cold of the damp night air, Emelina watched with her heart in her throat. Would Eric Leighton be in that car?

The vehicle pulled to a halt in back of the cottage and a man about the age of her brother climbed out. Emelina stared, trying to remember exactly what Leighton looked like. It had to be he. Who else would possibly be arriving at this place at this time of night? The man was carrying a paper sack in one hand and a suitcase in the other.

Frustrated at being unable to ascertain what was happening, Emelina inched forward along the bluff. If she were very careful, she could crawl unseen down the path once the man below had disappeared inside the cottage. When the door closed behind him and a light came on inside the old house she took a deep breath and, crouching low, began to edge down the bluff to the beach.

What could be going on down there? Why wasn't anyone else around? What was in the suitcase? The questions nagged at Emelina all the way to the foot of the bluff where she sought cover behind a rocky outcropping. She was lucky the stretch of beach was not open and sandy with no cover. The rocks along the edge of the cliff provided plenty of shelter.

But being closer wasn't providing any answers. No one

else arrived and nothing at all seemed to be happening in the beach house. Emelina risked crawling across an unprotected stretch of ground to get to a larger rock that was nearer the house.

There she huddled, running her hands up and down her arms in an effort to ward off the cold while she surveyed the beach cottage. Why the devil hadn't she thought to fling on a jacket? She was going to freeze if she had to wait very long.

That thought had just flickered through her mind when the faintest of sounds behind her made her forget completely about the chill in the air. Instinctively she whirled, knowing there was someone in the shadows.

She moved too slowly. Before she could turn halfway, a hard palm was slapped across her mouth and Emelina was being borne down into the sand at the base of the rock. A man sprawled across her, his arms holding her securely.

"Shut up and stop struggling, you little fool!" Julian's voice was a fierce, grating whisper of sound in her ear.

Instantly Emelina went still, largely out of sheer relief. Carefully Julian removed his hand and sat up slowly, pulling her back against him. "Don't make a sound," he murmured.

Emelina struggled for the breath that had been knocked out of her, nodding mutely. The warmth of his body was very welcome and she huddled close. With one arm wrapped around her, Julian edged toward the side of the protective rock and glanced toward the house.

"Damn!" The single word was uttered with quiet force. "We're trapped here now. There's a boat coming in to shore."

Emelina tried to peek around the corner of the rock. "A boat?"

"Hush. I mean it, Emmy. Not a word out of you until we're safe back at my cottage. Believe me, I'll give you reason enough to yell then! I told you not to come down here tonight! How did you dare to disobey me like this? My God, woman, I'm going to wear the hide off your sweet butt with my belt!"

When Emelina started to protest he clapped his hand over her mouth again and ordered her to be silent. Damn it, she thought furiously, who the hell did he think he was? This was all her idea. Her plan, her scheme, not his! She had a right to follow the action.

Above her, Julian swore soundlessly and inched her close to the cold sand, half covering her with his warmth. From Emelina's point of view, however, things had improved. She now had a partially obstructed view of the beach. There was a boat being rowed in to shore and Eric Leighton—it *had* to be Leighton—was casually walking down the steps of the cottage to meet the two figures who sat in the boat.

As soon as the small craft was beached, all three figures started back toward the house. Emelina caught traces of the low-voiced conversation as they passed within several feet of the rock behind which she and Julian were hiding.

"Geez, it's cold out here tonight. You got some coffee, Leighton?"

"Yeah, I picked some up on the way. You always complain about the cold, Dan. Even during the middle of summer, you bitch about it!"

"Ah, well," the third man opined philosophically, "considering the profit involved in these little trips, I, for one, am willing to get a little chilled while making the run."

"Everything on schedule?" Leighton asked crisply.

"Oh, yeah. Charlie's sitting out on the cruiser tonight, waiting for us to get back with the shipment."

"Charlie? What happened to the usual guy?" Emelina could hear Leighton's concern.

"Got picked up for indulging in a joint at a gay bar last week." The man gave a crack of laughter. "Can you believe it? Two years of running the hard stuff up and down this coast without a hitch and the poor joker gets busted for grass!"

"The cops were probably looking for an excuse to close down the bar he was in and he had the bad luck to be there on the wrong night," the second man decided. "It's okay, though. He'll be back on the run next month."

The remainder of the conversation was lost as the three men moved up the rickety porch steps and into the cottage. After what seemed an eternity Emelina dared to wriggle a little beneath Julian's enveloping weight.

"You're heavy," she whispered.

"Tough. Lie still."

"But they're inside the house now. They can't possibly see us."

"We have no way of knowing how long they'll stay there. We could be halfway up the path when they decide to head back for the beach. We'd be sitting ducks." Julian shifted slightly, drawing her more closely to him. "We're stuck here for the duration. I swear, Emelina, when this is all over I'm going to take measures to make sure you can't sit down comfortably for a week!"

"You're overreacting," she accused.

"I'm being amazingly calm under the circumstances! When I woke up and realized Xerxes was pacing the house, whimpering to get out, I knew something was wrong. I got dressed and went over to your place. As soon as I realized you weren't there I knew where to come looking." His hand on her waist tightened menacingly. "I just want you to know, Emmy Stratton, that what I'm going to do to you when we get out of this mess will undoubtedly hurt you a great deal more than it does me!"

"You can just stop threatening me," she grumbled furiously. "No one asked you to come looking. I was doing fine on my own down here."

Above her she heard a strangled oath as Julian fought to control his temper. Before he could say anything coherent, however, the door to Leighton's cottage opened again and the three men emerged. The two who were heading for the small boat were still sipping coffee from foam cups, and one of them carried the suitcase Leighton had brought with him.

"Take it easy," Leighton said casually. "I'll see you next month."

The other two nodded, and a few minutes later Leighton was giving the boat a shove to wrench it free of the sand. He stood watching as the small craft disappeared around a jutting cliff and then he walked quickly back toward the cottage. A few minutes later the lights inside the house were turned off and Leighton was in his car, driving back up the road to the top of the bluff.

"Okay, Miss Secret Agent of the Year, let's go." Julian heaved himself to his feet, locking his fingers around one of Emelina's wrists. She was yanked up beside him and led toward the narrow path without a word.

It wasn't until they reached the top of the bluff that Emelina managed to catch her breath. Then she broke into excited speech, her face aglow with the triumph she was feeling. "It worked, Julian! We know for certain now that Leighton's using the cottage for drug dealing or something. I can't wait to tell Keith. All he'll have to do is confront Eric with the facts and the man won't dare try to continue blackmailing him. What Keith has on Leighton will be a lot more dangerous than what Leighton has on my brother!"

"You think it's going to be that easy?" Julian growled roughly as he hauled her toward the cottage. "You think a man like Eric Leighton is going to tolerate the fact that your brother has an idea of what's going on once a month down there on that beach? You're a fool, lady. If your brother tries to reverse the blackmail, he's very liable to wind up very dead!"

The blood drained from Emelina's features. When Julian stepped inside the door and turned on the light, it was to see a very stricken woman staring back at him. Her hazel eyes wide with sudden fear, she stood stock-still in the middle of the cottage living room.

Ruthlessly he shoved aside the urge to enclose her in his arms and offer comfort. "It's about time you had a healthy dose of fear," he rasped, shoving his hands into his jeans pockets and planting his feet wide apart as he confronted her implacably. "This isn't a game, Emmy. I'll admit I was surprised to see Leighton actually make an appearance down there tonight. I'll give you full marks for your intuition and your imagination. But you get a big zip for intelligent reasoning. You could have gotten yourself in a hell of a lot of trouble out there on that beach. What do you think Leighton and his friends would have done if they'd discovered you?"

"I was very careful, Julian!"

"You were very stupid," he corrected grimly.

"Stop yelling at me, Julian! It was my plan. I had every right to see if it was working!"

"I gave you orders to stay away from that house tonight. You gave me your word on the matter."

"I did not," she flared. "You asked me if I understood your orders and I said I did. I didn't promise to obey them."

"You've got a hell of a lot of nerve splitting hairs like that," he snapped.

Emelina blinked, beginning to realize just how angry he really was. Her teeth sank unconsciously into her lower lip as she began looking for ways to placate the devil. "Look, Julian, I'm sorry you were so worried, but everything worked out all right. There was no harm done, and we know now that Leighton really is up to something on the twenty-eighth of each month. I really appreciate your help in setting up my trap, and that was a positive brainstorm you had regarding the receipts in the bottom of the grocery bags. Without that clue we might have wasted weeks of watching and waiting. But there's no need to be so angry now. Everything is fine. We're on top of the situation at last, and Keith and I can take it from here."

He stared at her incredulously. "Forget it, Emmy. You're not going to soothe me the way you would Xerxes, with soft words and a few pats on the head!"

The dog in question lifted his ears inquiringly as he watched the two humans across the room. When they continued to ignore him, however, he went back to dozing quietly.

"I'm not trying to soothe you," Emelina stormed. "I'm trying to reason with you!"

"I'm not in a mood to listen to your convoluted reasoning. I'm in a mood to paddle the daylights out of you. It seems like the only way to make my point this evening!"

Emelina took an instinctive step backward, abruptly aware of how close he was to carrying out his threat. "Julian, don't you dare touch me!"

He took a purposeful step forward. "Don't you know better than to dare the devil, Emmy?" he drawled with heavy menace. "I'm damn well going to touch you. I'm going to teach you a lesson you won't soon forget, lady. From now on, when I give you an order you're going to obey it."

Emelina's nerve broke. There were times in a woman's life when discretion truly was the better part of valor.

Emelina turned and fled through the front door of the cottage, wrenching it open and sailing over the threshold before she even stopped to think. Through the open door behind her Xerxes bounded happily, more than willing to participate in this new game, even if it was nearly one o'clock in the morning. After him came Julian.

Run from him, would she? Julian thought furiously as he leaped down the steps in pursuit. Didn't she realize she belonged to him now? If he wanted to chew her out for disobeying his orders, he damn well would do exactly that! If he wanted to rage at her for scaring him senseless, he had every right! She had come close to getting herself killed, and she deserved to pay for the hell she had put him through.

He saw her run up the street toward her cottage, Xerxes dancing at her heels. In the moonlight Emelina's hair flew out behind her, and her rounded flanks seemed to taunt him. Julian realized he wanted to do a hell of a lot more than pound that sexy bottom of hers. After he'd driven home the lesson he intended to teach her, he wanted to make love to Emelina until she cried out for mercy. Let her run. It would only make the final reckoning all the more gratifying.

Steadily he closed the distance between them, grimly aware that the chase was sending a surge of pure masculine heat through his veins. There was something primitive and satisfying about running down one's woman in the moonlight, Julian acknowledged. The elemental chase cut through all the layers of civilization and put matters on a very basic level. He felt strangely exhilarated and fiercely determined to win the contest of wills.

Then he was upon her. She made a small, half-strangled

sound of protest as his arm closed around her waist and dragged her to a halt in the middle of the road. Xerxes paused, glancing up questioningly. Was the game over already?

"Julian!" Emelina gasped, struggling for air. "Let me go! Put me down this instant!"

He ignored her demand, spinning her around instead and stooping briefly to throw her across his shoulder. He was aware of her confusion and disorientation as she desperately tried to catch her breath. Julian locked her firmly in place, aware of the full curve of her thigh under his hand. It was rapidly becoming a toss-up as to which he would do first: turn her over his knee or make love to her. He contemplated the two alternatives all the way back to the cottage.

Emelina experienced a combination of outrage and fear that left her as breathless as the short, panicked run. Desperately she doubled her small hand into a fist and pounded fruitlessly on his back. He seemed utterly impervious to the assault. When she tried to struggle, he slapped her smartly across her derriere.

"You might as well settle down and behave yourself because you're not going to get free," Julian growled as he mounted the steps to his cottage and kicked open the door.

Something about the way he used his booted foot on the door brought home to Emelina just what state of mind Julian was in. The masculine aggression in him was very evident. He was aroused, both with anger and with another emotion. She swallowed uneasily and realized just how highly charged the situation really was.

Julian didn't pause as he carried her over the threshold. Without hesitation he strode down the short hall to the bedroom. Bending, he dumped Emelina unceremoniously into the center of the old bed. As she sprawled there, he straightened, his hands on his hips, and stood surveying his captive with satisfaction and anticipation.

Emelina watched him with grave uncertainty. She was still outraged at his actions, but she vaguely realized that she wasn't exactly afraid of him. At least, not in the literal sense. Julian Colter was aroused and affronted and highly displeased with her this evening, but she knew with sure feminine instinct that he wouldn't ever hurt her in any serious way. She had known that from the moment he had caught up with her and tossed her over his shoulder. Even in his aggressive mood, there had been a certain care about the way he had handled her. A man intent on physically hurting a woman would not have touched her the way Julian had.

All of which did not mean that the next few minutes were going to be very comfortable. There was no escaping the fact that Julian was far from being placated.

"Please, Julian, try to calm down and be reasonable," she began carefully, scooting backward across the old bedspread. "I'm sorry I annoyed you tonight, but if you'll just take a moment to think it out, you'll realize I had every right to keep an eye on Leighton's place this evening."

He contemplated her with narrowed eyes as he raised his fingers and coolly began undoing the buttons of his flannel shirt. "I've been asking myself all the way back to the cottage whether I ought to beat you or make love to you until you can't move. I think I've finally made up my mind."

Emelina's eyes widened nervously, and she inched a little farther toward the opposite side of the bed. The direction in which she was retreating was a dead end, however, because the bed was shoved up against the wall on the far side.

"Julian, this is a time for talk. S-sex isn't an answer in a situation like this," she tried to say rationally. "We have a-a slight misunderstanding between us, I'll grant you. I can certainly see your point of view," she added quickly as he slung his shirt across the room and dropped his hands to the fastening of his jeans. Then she drew in her breath sharply as he kicked off his shoes and stepped out of the denims. In a few short seconds he was totally naked. She could only stare in stricken fascination at his aroused and predatory body.

"Come here, Emmy," he commanded far too softly. "Come here and tell me about our slight misunderstanding. Let me make my point of view even clearer."

Her eyes moved helplessly across the dark, curling hair of his chest, down to the strength in his thighs before she tried once more to meet his gleaming eyes.

"Julian, sex never solves anything!" she squeaked.

"I disagree," he murmured, putting one knee on the bed. "I think it's going to afford me a great deal of satisfaction. And if it doesn't, I can still try my other alternative."

"Beating me? Julian, you wouldn't dare!"

He merely smiled. It was the sort of smile she could imagine Xerxes giving a victim before he launched himself for the *coup de grace*. In that moment Emelina knew that she didn't stand a chance of deflecting Julian from his intent.

"Come here, my sweet Emmy," he growled huskily. "I'm going to ride you tonight until you don't have the energy left to try running from me again."

Emelina sucked in her breath and scrambled out of reach until she was up against the wall, figuratively and literally. "Damn it, Julian, I won't let you intimidate me!"

He didn't bother with any more words. Julian's dark eyes went almost black as he reached for his woman with the determined arrogance of a man who intends to take what belongs to him.

CHAPTER SEVEN

IT WAS EMELINA'S ANKLES that Julian grabbed. He manacled them with an unshakable grip that was surprisingly gentle and then he tugged her toward him across the bed. As he pulled her close he used his grip on her slender ankles to part her legs until she was lying helplessly sprawled before him. Kneeling between her jeans-clad thighs, Julian looked down at her with lambent fire in his eyes.

"Did you think I'd let you get away from me, sweetheart?" Slowly, with infinite promise, he lowered himself along the length of her. His fiercely masculine nakedness burned through the fabric of her clothing as he let her know the full weight of him.

Emelina tried to shift beneath the erotically crushing force of his body and found herself unable to move. He lay blatantly between her legs, framing her face with his rough palms. Emelina told herself she wasn't really afraid, just a little wary because of the aggressive way he had chased her down and hauled her back to the cottage.

"You can be awfully arrogant, Julian," she accused on a husky note. She watched his taut features from beneath half-lowered lashes, aware of the hardness of his legs as he stretched between her thighs. Her pulse, already quickened because of the chase, was now racing with the stirring of passion. "Arrogant and uncivilized."

"You bring out the primitive in me," he drawled, nuzzling the curve of her throat. "And if we're going to trade insults, I could make a few unflattering remarks about your brains, or lack thereof! Don't ever, ever take a chance like you did tonight. Do you hear me, Emmy?"

"It was my plan and my neck I was risking," she pointed out cautiously, wondering just how much she really meant to him. It occurred to her that his concern went beyond what she would have expected. How much did he truly care for her?

"Your pretty neck belongs to me, remember? I have first claim on it until you pay off your debt!"

Emelina's eyes widened in renewed outrage. "The *debt!* Is that all you're worried about? That I survive long enough to pay you? Why, you selfish bastard! If you think you can drag me into bed after making a statement like that, you're out of your mind!"

"Emmy, Emmy," he soothed on an astonishing note of indulgent humor. "You know damn well you're in my bed because I want you here and because I can make you want to be here. Forget about the debt for now and make love to me."

He silenced her further protests with a heavy, drugging kiss that merged the warmth of their mouths. He forced the intimate taste of himself on her until she was intoxicated with the essence of him. Julian continued to hold her face still for his kiss, while he anchored her body with his.

With an unconscious sigh of surrender, Emelina softened beneath him. This was the man who could unleash the passion within her. This was the man whose touch she had been craving for the past few days. Never before in her life had she truly craved the feel of a man's hands on her body. And this was the man she instinctively wanted to protect even though he was probably the last person on earth to need her poor defense.

Her fingers lifted to thread through the darkness of his silvered hair, and her legs closed restlessly around his naked thighs. Emelina knew in that moment that she was where she wanted to be. Why should she go on resisting the irresistible?

"Ah, Emmy, you're so warm and soft and perfect," Julian growled as he felt her response. "I would chase you across the face of the earth, let alone down a short street. I need you in my bed."

"Yes, Julian, oh, *yes!*" She squirmed beneath him as the tingling awareness in her loins began to escalate. His thrusting manhood was pressed sensually against her, and she longed to have him undress her completely. The passion which flared between them seemed to spring to life so easily! For her all it really took was his touch and the knowledge that he wanted her.

"Do you need me the same way?" he whispered provokingly. The tone of his deep voice told her he knew full well that she was rapidly becoming lost in the maze of physical response.

"Please, Julian."

"Tell me about it," he breathed as his fingers went to the hem of the black pullover and slipped underneath the fabric to find her breast. "I want to hear you say the words."

"I want you, Julian. You must know how much!" She trembled as he rasped her nipple gently with the palm of his hand, and her fingers raked along his bare shoulders.

"I want to hear you tell me exactly how much. What do you feel when I touch you like this?" he persisted, taking the budding tip of her breast between thumb and forefinger.

Emelina's head shifted restlessly on the bedspread, and her eyes closed tightly as the delicious sensations rippled through her body. "You make me *ache,* Julian. I never knew what it was like to really ache with need until I met you."

He groaned as she spoke the words with passionate honesty. Then he lifted her briefly against him and pulled the top over her head. Casting the garment onto the floor, Julian lowered her back down onto the bedspread and crushed her bare breasts with his chest. His eyes burned over her face as she sucked in air.

"Oh, my God, Julian…"

"I can feel your nipples," he breathed tightly. "Like hard little berries pressing into me." Then he lowered himself along the length of her until he was tasting those same berries with his damp, velvet tongue.

When Emelina was beginning to think she would go mad from the tantalizing effects of his lovemaking he suddenly pulled away from her, moving back to a kneeling position between her legs. She opened her lashes slightly to find him watching her with passionate intensity.

"Julian?"

"Finish undressing yourself for me, honey," he commanded in a throaty growl. "Unfasten your jeans and take them off for me. I want to watch you as you get ready to go to bed with me."

Emelina hesitated, suddenly shy. She wasn't at all sure her fingers would function properly under the impact of that dark gaze. It was easier to let him take the initiative when it came to doing away with her clothing. To undress herself seemed yet another act of commitment; a gesture of acceptance.

But hadn't she already accepted him as a lover? What was the point of stalling now? Slowly her hands went to the fastening of her jeans.

"Don't stare at me so," she begged, her fingers trembling as they began to lower the zipper. "You're making me nervous!"

"You're making me a little crazy," he retorted, the corner of his mouth kicking upward as he moved back a bit to give her room. When she awkwardly slid the jeans to her ankles and let them drop off the edge of the bed Julian reached out to touch the vulnerable inside of her thigh with a feathering action that made her moan his name in soft pleading. Provocatively she held out her arms to him, urging him close once more.

"Your panties," he reminded her, letting his fingertips stray to the center of the scrap of nylon, which was all that remained of her clothing.

"You're a beast!" But already she was lifting her hips against his hand, wanting more of his touch.

"I'm only a man who wants you very badly. And I think you want me too. I can feel the hot mist of you, sweetheart. You're such a passionate little creature. My God, Emmy. Take off your panties for me!"

Under the impetus of that command, coupled as it was with the incredible desire in his eyes, Emelina, her fingers trembling more than ever, managed to remove the last of her clothing.

"My sweet Emmy." With a muttered, half-savage exclamation of need, Julian came back to her, sliding aggressively into the warmth that waited for him at the juncture of her soft thighs.

Emelina gasped aloud as he possessed her with the urgent force of a man who can wait no longer for his woman. She clung to him, seeking the hard strength he offered with undisguised need.

Slowly Julian set a heated rhythm that tautened the mysterious tension within her until Emelina thought she would burst. She listened to the arousing, exciting words he grated against the skin of her throat and in the throes of her hunger, whispered many of them back to him. They seemed to provoke him as much as they did her.

"Hold on tight, honey," he rasped as he sensed the approaching rapids in the turbulent stream of their lovemaking. "Just hold tight and let it happen!"

Emelina gave herself up to the ecstasy he provided, unaware of the half-moons her nails left in his shoulders or of the way her thighs enclosed him so tightly he thought he might never be free. When she stiffened beneath him, Julian managed to raise his head far enough to watch the flow of emotions across her face. Then he was pulled into the torrent with her, unable to hold back any longer.

He watched her float back to reality in his arms, smoothing a strand of chestnut-colored hair back from her face as she opened her eyes to meet his gaze. "This is where you belong, Emmy. Here in my arms. Don't try to run away from me again. I'll only come after you."

"Will you, Julian?"

What was she thinking? Probably that he was incredibly arrogant to make such a statement. Julian sighed. She had no way of knowing how far he was prepared to go to make his words the truth. What would she say when he told her what he'd decided to demand as her part of their bargain? Would she argue and accuse and then agree because she was a woman who always paid her debts? Or would she try to run away rather than face the sentence he intended to impose?

No, thought Julian in deep satisfaction. She wouldn't run. She might be furious, perhaps even fiercely resentful of the situation in which she found herself, but his Emmy would pay her debt.

He could bank on it.

"You look very pleased with yourself, Julian Colter," she observed, arching one brow as she stared up at him from the curve of his arm.

"I am," he said simply, bending down to kiss the tip of her nose. "And it's all your fault."

"Is it?"

"Ummm. I always like it when I can make my point in such a satisfying manner." He grinned, the lazy pleasure in his eyes completely unhidden.

"You do it this way a lot?" she asked with an attempt at flippancy.

The grin was wiped from his face and replaced with a narrowed stare. "What do you think?"

For some reason Emelina found herself taking the question very seriously. "I don't think so," she said slowly. "I don't think you would use sex to control a woman. Not in the final analysis."

He regarded her interestedly. "Why not?"

"Because it's not a dependable weapon and you're so-phisticated enough to realize it. You know that the loyalty and commitment you want from a woman can't be bought with sex."

"You're very philosophical this evening," he grated. "You're also right. I take great pleasure in being able to make you melt in my arms, but, unfortunately, I know you wouldn't obey me or stay with me or even spend any time with me just because you like what I can do for you in bed." He sounded disgusted at not being able to wield that par-ticular weapon.

"You'd rather I'd promise to do anything you said just because you're good in bed?" she dared to tease.

"It would make things simpler."

"It would also make me a rather shallow creature.

Someone at the mercy of her own passions," Emelina pointed out coolly.

"Instead of which, you are at the mercy of your own concept of integrity, aren't you?" he threw back enigmatically.

"What's that supposed to mean?"

He stroked her with slow intent. "Someday soon I will explain. Go to sleep, Emmy. In the morning we have to talk about what happens next."

Emelina yawned obediently, suddenly very tired. "About Leighton and his gang?"

"And about your brother. He has a right to know what's happening down here. What happens next should be up to him."

"You have a plan to suggest to him?" she queried sleepily.

"I'll tell you all about it in the morning." Tucking her into the shape of his body, Julian urged her wordlessly to sleep. But long after she had quieted in the curve of his arms he lay awake in the darkness, thinking about what she had said. Emelina was right. He knew better than to try to control her with sex. It would never work. Did she have any inkling of just how he did plan to control her? Probably not. As far as he could tell she hadn't thought beyond the present. Julian stared at the shadows on the ceiling and thought about the risk he was planning to take. He couldn't bear to contemplate the prospect of failure.

THE FIRST WORDS JULIAN spoke to her the next morning took Emelina by surprise. She was dutifully handing him a cup of coffee while he showered when he said, "We'll leave for Seattle this afternoon. As soon as Joe gets here and plays those tapes for us."

"Seattle! Today?"

"Emmy, I hate to tell you this, but your coffee is not improving. I don't think you're trying."

"Perhaps I haven't enough incentive to try harder." She grinned into the mirror as she ran his comb through her hair.

"I might have let you off the hook last night for disobeying me, but don't count on my overlooking your lack of effort in coffeemaking too long," he threatened. "This brew of yours really is a beating offense!"

"I hadn't noticed that you let me go scot-free last night," she complained, stretching her deliciously sore muscles. She was wearing his toweling robe and in the mirror she looked all soft and fluffy. Emelina had never thought of herself that way before, and she wasn't sure the notion pleased her now. Deliberately she grimaced into the steamy mirror, baring her teeth like Xerxes.

"What the hell are you doing? Making faces at yourself?"

She snapped her head around to find him watching her while he sipped the coffee. "I was trying to regain some of the feistiness that you crushed last night with your macho manners!"

He grinned his slashing pirate's grin. "With very little prompting I could be persuaded to carry you back into the bedroom and crush it some more. It springs back so nicely."

"Is that a sexual innuendo?" she demanded.

"Yeah. Want me to explain it to you?"

"No, thanks. Tell me why we're going to Seattle," she ordered with a sniff of disdain.

"I want to talk to your brother."

"Why, Julian?" This time there was a serious note in her voice, and she turned to meet his gaze worriedly.

"I told you last night. He has a right to be consulted about what happens next. He's got a couple of alternatives."

Emelina tapped the comb on the sink rim while she thought about that. "I don't think so, Julian."

He lifted one black brow in lazy inquiry. "Emmy, you know as well as I do that you don't have the right to make this kind of decision for him," he said very gently.

"I know. I agree that it's up to Keith what he chooses to do next. He's the victim in this little mess. But I don't think I want you talking to him about the situation or offering him advice." She was beginning to feel a little nervous talking about such a serious subject while he stood gazing at her from the shower. She tried to explain. "Julian, you promised this matter would be just between you and me."

"You're chewing on your lower lip again, which means you're getting very anxious about something. I think I'm beginning to get the drift." His voice hardened. "You're afraid I'll try to involve Keith in this bargain of yours?"

"Will you?"

"I gave you my word, Emmy. The only one I'll expect payment from is you." This time she could hear the thread of steel in his words.

"But if you go to Keith and he agrees to accept your help in finishing the matter," Emelina began breathlessly, "won't you—that is, will you consider him *involved?*"

"No. As far as I'm concerned it's all part of the same deal, Emmy."

She stared at him, eyes wide and anxious for a long moment, and then she nodded and turned away to finish her hair.

"Do you trust me, Emmy? Do you believe I'll keep this just between you and me?" he pressed, an underlying note of urgency in his question.

"Yes, Julian. I trust you." And she did. Given what she had read about Mafia dons, she didn't know why she should trust him, but she did. Emmy drew in a long breath and said conversationally, "When are you going to get out of the shower and fix us a pot of decent coffee?"

"I think we'll go into town for coffee this morning," he told her thoughtfully.

"Too lazy to make it yourself?"

"No, but I'm in the mood to watch you terrorize the townspeople."

"Julian!" She whipped around to stare at him as he ducked behind the plastic curtain.

"I love it when you get all protective in my defense," he drawled. "Makes me feel wanted. Between you and Xerxes I feel so *safe!*"

Emelina glowered ferociously at the shower curtain, but she couldn't think of anything to say. What really bothered her was that he was right. And it was all so ludicrous. The one thing this man definitely did not need from her was protection. He got all the protection he needed from men like Joe Cardellini who carried guns in shoulder holsters and looked at the world through grim eyes.

"We have to go into town anyway," Julian was saying conversationally. "I'll need to use the pay phone at the store to call Joe."

Forty minutes later Emelina dug at the dust in the street with one toe while Julian stood inside the phone booth making his call. The black Lincoln was pulling up in front of the cottage an hour after that.

"Where did you drive from this morning, Joe?" Emelina asked interestedly. "You got here so quickly."

"Portland," he said, his gaze softening as he looked down at her. Emelina knew that that softening was as far as the expression would ever go. It was clear that Joe Cardellini would never dream of poaching on his master's preserves. Not because he stood in fear of Julian, Emelina realized with sudden insight, but because he respected his boss far too much to trespass. This morning Julian appeared to realize the same thing because, although he was as casually possessive as ever, there were no more veiled warnings either for her or for Joe.

"Have you been staying in Portland all this time?" she queried.

"I've been assigned there for the past couple of years," he explained politely.

"Assigned? Oh, I see." Emelina nodded wisely, remembering that the modern Mob was run like a cross between a closely held family corporation and the military. Julian's interests must extend far, indeed, to warrant having a "security" person stationed in the Northwest. The thought was depressing.

Sooner or later Julian would go back to "business" and this romantic idyll would come to an end. The next time she heard from Julian after this episode had ended would be when he called in the tab. Emelina stifled a shudder of gloomy dismay. Sooner or later the piper would have to be paid.

"Emmy? Are you listening?" Julian interrupted her thoughts, frowning briefly at her inattentiveness. "Joe's going down to Leighton's house to collect the mikes and then we'll listen to the tapes."

Emelina nodded and straightened her shoulders. This was what she had come for.

In the end the tapes proved every bit as incriminating as she could have wished. They confirmed and clarified the smatterings of conversation she and Julian had heard on the beach that night, portraying Eric Leighton and the others as a crew of professional drug smugglers who had been operating with impunity along the West Coast for nearly two years.

"I wonder why he bothered with something like black-mail. He's making money hand over fist with this stuff," Joe noted curiously. "Why risk the other?"

"Jealousy," Emelina sighed regretfully. Both men looked at her and she explained. "I think Eric was simply jealous that my brother managed to make it in the establishment. Keith has acquired everything Eric wanted: respect, success, even a little power, and all legitimate. Eric was always envious of my brother, I think. Even when both were going through their radical stage it was Keith who had the respect and attention of their fellow radicals, not Eric. My brother is a natural leader," she concluded with a mild shrug.

Julian nodded slowly, accepting her explanation. Then he glanced at Joe. "Did you get everything out of the cottage?"

"There's not a sign of anything having been touched, boss. You ought to know I wouldn't leave any evidence." Joe fixed a reproachful expression on Julian's hard features.

Julian smiled. "I know. I'm just anxious to tie this thing up neatly."

Emelina hesitated, glancing from one man to the other as she chewed on her lower lip. "What we did by bugging the cottage—that was illegal, wasn't it?"

"Let's just say that I'm not going to turn that bit of evidence over to the Oregon police. That information was just for our own use to confirm your suspicions."

"The police!"

"Yes. If I can talk your brother into it, that's who we're going to turn this over to as soon as possible."

"But, Julian," she exclaimed, "you can't risk that. Neither can Keith!"

"Just let me handle it, okay, Emmy? Run along and get packed."

She argued with him in the back of the black Lincoln all the way to Portland. Joe was driving and he had Xerxes sitting up front with him. Emelina was still arguing when Joe and Xerxes put Julian and her on the shuttle to Seattle. Joe had said he would take care of the dog. Emelina was almost hoarse from her arguments by the time the shuttle landed at Sea-Tac airport and Julian commandeered a cab into town.

"I keep telling you this isn't the way Keith wants to handle it! The whole point is to try to keep his name out of this. That will be impossible if he goes to the cops!"

Julian smiled blandly. "You won't let me go to the police because you're afraid I'll be arrested, and you won't let your brother go because you're afraid his career will be ruined. Maybe we'll have to send *you* to the cops."

"Me!" That thought shut her up until the cab they were in reached the entrance to the high-rise office building where her brother worked. By the time she was asking the receptionist to notify Keith of her presence her mind was churning with various alternative explanations she could give the police. They were certainly going to want to know how she had discovered what was going on at Eric Leighton's beach house! She fashioned one tale after another, plotting furiously.

"Emmy!" Five minutes later Keith Stratton stepped off the elevator into the lobby. Emelina looked at him with a touch of pride. Her brother was the perfect image of the fast-track corporate male. His dark chestnut hair, so much like her own, had been cut with a conservative razor and the chalk-striped suit he wore had been hand-fashioned by a tailor. Keith wore an aura of quiet authority with natural grace, and everyone he passed in the lobby nodded politely. Her brother was definitely in his milieu, Emelina decided with fond satisfaction.

"Emmy, what's going on? I thought you were down in Oregon." Keith gave his sister a quick kiss on the cheek and stepped back to slant a considering glance at the man by her side.

"I'm Julian Colter," said Julian, extending his hand. "And I would like to invite you to share a cup of coffee with Emmy and me down in the cafeteria. There are some things that need to be discussed."

If Keith wore the look of budding authority with natural instinct, Emelina decided, Julian wore the aura of well-established power with the confidence of a man who has wielded it for years. He had dressed for the trip to Seattle in a charcoal suit which fit his lean figure with a hand-crafted look. The white shirt he wore also had a conservative, handmade appearance, and his subtly striped tie was of silk. Joe had brought the clothes along with him when he had been summoned from Portland. Dressed in her jeans and a button-down yellow preppy shirt, Emelina felt like an urchin next to these two masculine symbols of success.

It was funny, she thought as Keith nodded austerely at Julian and prepared to lead the way to the cafeteria, how success in the underworld looked a lot like success in the legitimate corporate field. If she hadn't known better, she would have guessed Julian to be a man at the top of the corporate ladder her brother was intent on climbing.

"So," Keith began conversationally as he got coffee for the three of them and found a booth, "how was your vacation, Emmy?" He shot his sister a shrewd glance.

"Julian knows all about my 'vacation,' Keith. You don't need to pretend around him," she sighed, sipping her coffee.

Keith said nothing, merely arching an inquiring brow at the older man. He wasn't going to commit himself until he learned just how much Julian knew, Emelina realized. Smart boy.

"Much to my everlasting astonishment," Julian drawled wryly, "your sister's crazy scheme worked. Your friend Leighton is using the beach house for less than legal purposes. He's running drugs down the coast. Once a month, to be exact. There will be another shipment the twenty-eighth of next month."

Keith stared from one to the other. "You're kidding!" His startled expression told Emelina all she had to know.

"I told you so!" she growled. "You didn't believe me when I told you he was up to something there, did you?"

"No," Keith retorted honestly. "I didn't." He turned to Julian. "That's why I let her go down there alone. But who the hell are you?" he demanded bluntly.

"Don't be rude, Keith. Julian helped me." Eagerly Emelina ran through the whole tale for her brother's sake. "It was Julian's idea to check the receipts in the grocery sacks. And he was with me on the beach the other night when Leighton and his crew arrived," she concluded. "We've got all the proof you need, Keith."

Keith absorbed the news, his eyes never leaving Julian's expressionless face. "I see. But that still doesn't answer my question, does it? Who are you, Julian?"

For the first time since he had arrived in Seattle, Julian's mouth curved slightly. "I'm the man who tried to save your sister from embarking on a career of breaking and entering and wound up doing the job myself. I was supposed to be taking a small vacation in the cottage down the street from the one your sister rented."

"But who *are* you?" Keith persisted doggedly.

"Never mind, Keith," Emelina interrupted firmly, unwilling to see Julian pinned down. Besides, she definitely did not want Keith to find out exactly who Julian really was. "Julian has business interests along the West Coast," she explained. "He lives in Arizona, though. He just had the misfortune of renting a cottage near mine, that's all."

Keith gave her a level stare and then apparently decided to let the matter drop temporarily. Julian's smile edged upward as if he were secretly amused. "Since my sister seems to have dragged you into this and you now know what's going on, what do you intend to do?"

"I was going to offer a little advice," Julian murmured.

"Such as?"

"How about giving what we know to the cops and finding out if they'd be interested in watching the Leighton house next month on the twenty-eighth? If they pick your blackmailer up in the middle of a dope transaction that should get him out of your hair. Leighton's unlikely to further incriminate himself by dragging your name into the picture. He'll have his hands full trying to get himself out of the smuggling charges."

"The police will ask a lot of questions, Julian," Emelina handled anxiously.

"I'll handle the police," he stated calmly.

"You will?" Keith watched him carefully.

"I will simply tip them off as to what I witnessed one night while vacationing on the Oregon coast. I'm sure the local cops will be happy enough to pursue it from there. Neither you nor Emelina will have to be involved."

Keith drew in his breath while Emelina stared. "That's very generous of you, Julian," he said quietly. "May I ask why you're choosing to be that generous?"

Julian's smile reached his eyes. "You're going to go far in the corporate world, Keith. You keep asking questions."

"Am I going to get some answers?"

Julian shrugged. "Isn't it obvious why I'm volunteering my help? I'm doing this for Emmy." He didn't look at her as he spoke, his whole attention on her brother. "She's become a close friend of mine."

"I see," Keith said quietly, ignoring the restless way his sister was moving in her seat. He assessed Julian coolly for a long moment and then nodded. "I see," he said again. Emelina felt suddenly closed out of the conversation.

"If you two have finished with your man-to-man communication," she snapped irritably, "could we get on with some concrete planning?"

Keith smiled wryly. "Watch out for her when she starts in with that funny little habit of chewing on her lower lip," he advised Julian. "That's when she's at her most dangerous."

"I thought she did that when she was nervous or anxious," Julian said, turning to give Emelina a considering glance.

"No, she does it when she's scheming. Her imagination is very vivid," Keith warned.

"So I've learned."

CHAPTER EIGHT

IT WAS THE SIGHT OF Joe Cardellini's grimmer than usual expression as he greeted them in Portland that night that made Emelina realize wistfully how much she had hoped the idyll with Julian could have continued. She did not welcome the return to reality and neither, apparently, did Julian.

"What's up, Joe?" he demanded as he slid Emelina into the back of the Lincoln and followed.

"I had word from the Arizona office this afternoon, boss," Joe said quietly as he guided the big car out of the airport. "They've got some problems back in Tucson. Tony wants to talk to you ASAP."

Emelina withdrew into the corner of the seat, staring out the window as the two men conversed. She didn't want to know about this side of Julian's life, she realized.

"Tell Tony I'll call him first thing in the morning, Joe. It'll wait that long at least?" Julian's gaze was on Emelina's profile.

"Yeah. Not much you could do tonight, anyway, is there?"

"No. Drop us off at Emmy's apartment. No point going back to the beach until I find out what's happening down in Tucson."

Emelina's head came around in mute question. Her apartment?

"Won't you give me a bed for the night, Emmy? Good friend of the family that I am?" he asked softly.

She flushed, aware that Joe could overhear everything. Not that he didn't already know exactly what sort of relationship existed between his boss and herself, she thought.

"Does giving you a bed for the night constitute the first installment payment on my debt?" she whispered with an attempt at flippancy.

"No," he shot back blandly. "I'm asking for the room purely on the basis of our, er, friendship."

She looked away from the gleam in his eyes and nodded. "Yes, you can come home with me," she told him gruffly. What else could she say?

"Thank you, Emmy."

Twenty minutes later she silently opened the door of her downtown apartment and switched on the hall light. Julian gazed at the surroundings with deep interest.

"Your vivid imagination extends to other things besides plotting and scheming, doesn't it?" He grinned, examining the colorful, eclectic decor.

"I'm not too fond of pastels," she noted dryly, following his eyes as he took in the bright yellow carpet, the green print furniture and the occasional touches of glossy black.

"No mauve?" he inquired blandly.

"I'm afraid not. Have a seat and I'll find us something to eat. I'm sure I left some stuff in the freezer." Emelina hurried into the crisp white kitchen and started opening cupboards and freezer doors. "How about some tuna fish on bagels?"

"Terrific." His voice sounded somewhat absent in tone, as if he were thinking of something else at the moment.

"Julian?" Curiously she went to the kitchen door and glanced into the living room. He was standing beside her typing table, looking down at a manuscript that she had left neatly stacked on one side. "Come away from there," she ordered huskily. "I've told you I don't let anyone read my work."

"Except faceless editors in New York?" he concluded, turning aside reluctantly. "Can't you make an exception for me, sweetheart? I already know so much about you and I want very badly to know even more."

"I'm sorry," she returned crisply. "I just don't make any exceptions to that particular rule."

"Not even for me, Emmy?" he coaxed gently, his eyes soft and searching.

"Not for anyone."

"Why not, honey?"

"It's too damn personal! That's why not. Now come in here and tell me how you like your tuna fish."

He sighed and came forward. "What are my options?"

"With onions or without," she told him stonily.

"Without."

Two hours later he tugged her into his arms on the couch and kissed her with lazy expectation. "That's why I chose to have my tuna fish without the onions," he told her when at last he freed her mouth.

"Oh," she said a little weakly. "You should have explained. Then I would have had mine without, too."

"It's all right, you taste delicious." He kissed her again, pulling her across his lap and cradling her close. "Emmy, I may have to leave in the morning," he whispered huskily, stroking the curve of her hip.

"Do you…do you think that whatever is going on down in Tucson will be that serious?" she asked, her brows drawing into a line of worry.

"Maybe. There were some things brewing before I left that may have erupted into a full-scale explosion."

"Oh, Julian," she breathed anxiously.

"Will you miss me if I have to go back in the morning?" he asked whimsically.

Emelina took a deep breath, aware of a deepening level of commitment. "Yes."

"Good," he retorted in satisfaction and leaned forward to find the line of her throat with his lips. A few minutes later when she began to twist restlessly under his hands Julian got to his feet with Emelina in his arms and headed for the bedroom.

There in the darkness Emelina surrendered with an urgency tinged with fear of what awaited her on the morrow. She knew she could not keep Julian with her forever, but she had longed with all her heart for even a few more days together down on the Oregon beach. Something was already warning her that such an extension of the idyll was not to be.

It was the ringing of the bedside phone that awakened Emelina the next morning. She stirred lazily, reorienting herself, and then she recognized the compelling weight of Julian's arm across her breasts. She struggled to blink the sleep out of her eyes.

"Julian! The phone!"

"I hear it," he growled. "Ignore it. It's probably one of your *former* boyfriends."

"No one knows I'm here in town. Only Joe knows we're here." Emelina elevated herself on her elbow and reached for the receiver, knowing with deep foreboding who would be on the other end. "Hello?"

"Emmy? Joe. Is the boss there? I've got to speak to him right away."

Sadly she handed the phone over to Julian, who propped himself back against the pillows and let the sheet slide down to his waist. "Okay, Joe what's up?" he asked in resignation. "Okay, okay. I'll call him right now." He watched Emelina as she edged toward the side of the bed. Then he hung up and dialed another number. "Don't rush off, Emmy," he whispered as he waited for the phone to be answered on the other end. "You haven't kissed me good morning yet."

"You're like Xerxes," she groaned, trying to maintain a cheerful tone. "You think you have a right to affection from me whenever you want it!"

"You better believe it. Come and kiss me, sweetheart."

Her lips had just touched his when she heard the receiver click on the other end of the line. Reluctantly Julian freed her mouth and prepared to talk to the person in Tucson. Emelina hurried to the shower. She didn't want to hear the conversation that would take him away from her.

When Julian stepped into the shower stall behind her ten minutes later she knew the worst had come to pass. Without a word he wrapped his arms around her waist and leaned down to nuzzle her ear.

"You have to go to Arizona, don't you?" she whispered, aware of the hard warmth of him as he dragged her close to his naked length.

"I have to be back there this afternoon. Emmy, I wish I didn't have to go. Not so soon." There was a savage honesty in the words, and she took some comfort from them. Emelina could think of nothing more to say. Wordlessly she turned in his arms and pressed her soap-slick breasts against his chest, her hands going to his shoulders. She lifted her mouth to his and he took the offering hungrily.

"Joe will see about getting your car back from Oregon," Julian said quietly over breakfast. "I don't want you going near that place again, Emmy. Not until this is all over."

"You're so damn bossy," she complained, but she couldn't be mad at him. She was too afraid of the coming parting. They took a walk after breakfast while Joe confirmed Julian's flight reservations. Neither Emelina nor Julian mentioned the departure, itself, however. Neither wanted to talk about the inevitable.

It wasn't until it was time to leave for the airport that Julian lifted her chin with his forefinger and smiled gently down into her upturned face. "This isn't the end, honey. You know that, don't you?"

"I know." But next time it would be different between them. Next time she would be paying off the debt. "Oh, Julian, I wish…" She let the sentence trail off hopelessly.

"I'll phone you tomorrow night," he interrupted roughly and bent to brush his mouth against her own. "Be home."

"I'll see if I can work it into my schedule," she teased, but her hazel eyes were a little misty, and for some reason it was getting hard to swallow.

"You'd better," he rasped, not showing any sign of amusement over her attempt at lightness. "Or the next time I see you, I really will beat you."

"Promises, promises. I'll be here, Julian," she added quickly as his eyes narrowed. Clearly that was one subject he did not wish to banter about.

There wasn't any time to say more. Joe appeared in the open doorway and politely picked up Julian's bag. Emelina saw the hesitation on her lover's face and knew he wanted to say something else but couldn't quite find the words. The same was true for her. There were things that probably should have been said, but the relationship was still too new and there was still that debt hanging over her head.

On impulse Emelina stepped quickly over to the typing

table and scooped up the manuscript lying there. "Here," she blurted, thrusting it into Julian's hand. "Take it. Something to read on the plane. Goodbye, Julian."

"Thank you, Emmy," he said quietly, glancing up from the manuscript to her face. He didn't say anything else. He kissed her a little roughly and then he was gone.

Emelina spent the next hour berating herself for having broken her own policy. What in the world had possessed her to give that manuscript to Julian?

By the time Emelina had finally grown philosophical about the matter, telling herself that there was nothing she could do to retrieve it now, Julian was settled into his seat on the jet to Tucson. The stewardess had just put a cup of coffee in his hand. Mindful of the ill effects of spilled coffee on white manuscript pages, Julian very carefully hauled out the precious package Emelina had given him. For a long moment he stared at the title page, aware of an absurd feeling of being on the verge of invading Emmy's privacy in an intensely personal manner.

Which was a totally ridiculous attitude, he told himself firmly. After all, she was hoping to get the thing published, wasn't she? It was meant to be read. And she had given it to him, herself. That last thought brought a wave of pure satisfaction, and Julian deliberately focused on the title of the manuscript: *Mindlink*. With rising eagerness he turned to the first chapter.

There he discovered a woman named Rana. She was a heroine with an unusual problem. Born a nontelepath in a world where telepathy and the ability to link one's mind with another were the norm, Rana had been an outsider from the start. Not for her was the special kind of communication that existed when two humans linked minds. And not for her was the special relationship that came into existence when a man and a woman in love shared the intangible togetherness of mind-linking.

In an effort to escape the knowledge that she was a misfit, Rana had accepted a position as companion to the eldest daughter of a powerful house. She was to accompany the young woman off-world and conduct her to a neighboring planet in the system where the woman would be married to the head of an equally elite family. The job would give Rana a chance to get off her planet and perhaps free herself from the local star system entirely. Somewhere out there in the rest of the galaxy there were worlds where people like her, nontelepaths, were the norm. She had made up her mind to find one.

But first she had a job to do, and the responsibility of escorting the beautiful telepathic bride to her equally telepathic betrothed became very complicated when the ship on which they were traveling came under assault from enemies of the bride's husband-to-be.

Flung free in a crippled lifeboat while the main ship was under attack, Rana and her companion drifted helplessly in space, awaiting rescue. The problem, of course, lay in worrying over who would comprise the rescue party. The possibility that it would be the groom's enemies bent on kidnapping the bride was a strong one. By chapter two, Rana and her employer, Kari, were waiting, stranded, in the drifting lifeboat as the "rescue" party arrived and began forcing open the jammed air lock.

"It's useless, Rana," Kari wailed softly as she stared, stricken, at her companion. "Their minds are as closed to me as yours is! I can't even tell how many of them there are out there!"

"We still have the needle gun," Rana pointed out. "If we turn off the lights, we'll have a small advantage as they come through the air lock. They can only enter one at a time. The lock's too narrow to allow more than that." Her fingers clenched nervously around the tapered handle of the petite weapon she had found in the lifeboat's emergency stores.

"What good will that do us?" Kari shook her head. "Whoever it is out there will be armed to the teeth."

"It's the only chance we've got. Get behind the computer console, Kari. I'll need a clear line of fire." Great Helios! She'd never even fired a gun before in her life. Would she be able to pull the trigger of the one in her hand if it proved necessary? She flipped off the light.

There was no time for further thought. With a hiss, the inner door of the air lock slid open revealing a man's figure in a heavy space suit. The helmet was unlatched and thrown back, exposing the harsh planes of a rugged face.

"Kari of the House of Toran," he began with great formality, "I am Chal. I have been sent by the House of Lanal to rescue you. Do not be afraid."

"She's not afraid, just nervous around strangers," Rana forced herself to drawl coolly. She must sound as though she was in command of the situation. Men like this wouldn't bluff easily. "It's been an upsetting day. Enough to give a new bride a real case of jitters. Now suppose you convince us you're who you say you are."

The man who called himself Chal swung his suit light around in an arc until he picked out her figure crouched behind the console chair. He stilled as he saw the steady aim of the needle gun in her hand. "Who in Helios are you?" The formal tone of his voice had disappeared completely.

"The lady's traveling companion."

A slow, appreciative grin slashed across the man's face

as he stood there regarding her. "Somehow I always thought of ladies' traveling companions as gentle, demure types."

"We've changed a bit over the years." Rana motioned with the needle gun. "Have one of your people set up a com link with the House of Lanal. I want to know who you really are before this goes any further."

"Yes, ma'am," he agreed mockingly, backing carefully toward the air lock. "Why don't you come and see me about employment when your present assignment is completed? I could use a traveling companion who takes her job seriously."

"Move!" Rana hissed, feeling a little desperate.

"I'm on my way. Just remember that when you're working for me I'll expect the same kind of service you're giving your present employer!"

Julian's mouth crooked gently as he read. There was something in Chal with which he could identify. And he wasn't at all surprised when the heroine wound up working for the space adventurer. There were thrills and excitement enough in Emmy's tale, but as he finished the last page Julian realized that what fascinated him the most was Emelina's handling of the fiery romance that developed between Rana and Chal.

Both were cursed with nontelepathic minds, minds that were forever closed to the magic of mind-linking. Living amid a society that depended on mind-linking as a means of assuring honesty and integrity, these two were forced to learn trust the old-fashioned way. For them, falling in love involved a risk that others never had to worry about. The telepaths around them knew exactly where they stood with one another, and when a telepathic man and woman fell in love there was never a question about the genuineness of their emotions. It could always be tested by mindlink. That certainty was denied Rana and Chal.

Yet through Emelina's imagination, a tender and deeply loving relationship grew between Rana and Chal. A relationship that seemed somehow all the stronger and more enduring because it had to be built carefully.

So much of his sweet Emmy was in that manuscript, Julian realized as the plane touched down in Tucson. A sense of integrity, a lively imagination, a romantic outlook; all were caught between the pages of *Mindlink*. He walked to the baggage area to collect a disgruntled Xerxes, telling himself that he'd eventually have it all. He had to have it all. Like the hero in Emelina's novel, he had been living in a partially sealed off world until his woman arrived on the scene.

EMELINA WAS STILL BERATING herself off and on over having given Julian a copy of the manuscript when the phone rang in Portland the next afternoon. She picked up the receiver to find the otherworldly voice of a New York editor saying she wanted to buy *Mindlink*.

As she set the phone back in its cradle with a shaking hand, Emelina no longer worried about the fact that Julian had read a copy of the manuscript. Instead she sat staring at the wall of her apartment with glazed eyes and wished with all her heart that Julian were there to help her celebrate. He was, she realized in a flash of blinding insight, the one man on the face of the earth with whom she wanted to celebrate the great event.

And she didn't even know his phone number in Tucson. There was, Directory Assistance informed her, no listing at all for Julian Colter.

By seven o'clock that evening Emelina had opened the fifteen-dollar bottle of Cabernet Sauvignon she had purchased earlier in the day. The small dish of caviar was prepared and the stereo had been fed a tape of Mozart concertos.

Just as she was sitting down to enjoy all three in lonely splendor, the phone rang.

"Emmy?" Julian's voice was deep and soft on the other end of the line.

"Julian!" she breathed. "Oh, Julian, I sold the book! An editor called this afternoon! I tried to phone you, but I didn't have your number. My brother is in L.A. on an overnight business trip and there was no one to tell!"

"You sold *Mindlink?* Congratulations, sweetheart. But I can't say I'm terribly surprised," he chuckled. "I liked the book. Very much."

"You did?" Somehow that was as important as the editor's having liked it, she thought.

"Umm. It was full of you. How could I not enjoy it when I could find something of you on every page?" he said simply.

"Oh," she managed a little weakly.

"What are you doing?" he asked.

"Right now? Celebrating."

Instantly the pleasantness faded from his voice. "With whom?"

"Myself." She waited.

He sighed. "Do I sound possessive?"

Emelina decided to ignore that. "What are *you* doing?"

"Watching the evening news and petting Xerxes. He misses you, I think."

"Uh huh," Emelina muttered skeptically. "Sounds very homey."

"What did you imagine I normally do in the evenings?" he baited gently.

"I wouldn't dream of speculating."

"Sure you would. With your vivid imagination how could you help but speculate?"

"Julian, are you teasing me?"

"Only because I wish I was there helping you celebrate instead of here, patting my dog," he drawled wryly.

"Julian, I'm so excited," she whispered. "I think I'll quit my job tomorrow."

He laughed. "On the basis of one sale?"

"The editor said her publishing house is looking for a lot of books to fill a new line of women's adventure and science fiction. She feels my writing style will fit right in. They wanted another book as soon as possible."

"Hmm." He sounded abruptly serious. "Then we'd better see about getting you an agent, hadn't we? I don't think I want you taking on the New York publishing world all by yourself." Then he relaxed again. "Are you going to put your own personal adventures into a book?"

"That depends. Would you like to see yourself in a book, Julian?"

"Good God, no!" he retorted with great feeling.

"Then you'd better be very nice to me, hadn't you?" she taunted lightly.

"I see you're not averse to a little blackmail, yourself, honey. But as it happens, I have no objection to being very nice to you. If I were there right now, I would show you exactly what I mean."

"That sounds like another sexual innuendo," she accused.

"Sexual innuendoes are the most interesting kind."

"I get the feeling this conversation is about to degenerate into an obscene phone call!"

"It's okay. We're lovers," he assured her.

Long after he hung up that night Emelina considered the word. Lovers. As she stared with unseeing eyes at the remains of her caviar, she realized that, for her, at least, the word was a truthful one.

She was in love with Julian Colter.

Combined with the fact that she had sold her first manuscript, the realization was enough to make that particular day far too memorable.

In love with Julian Colter.

How had it happened? She knew instinctively that it wasn't because of what he could make her feel in bed. In fact, what happened to her when she was in his arms probably occurred precisely because she was in love, not the other way around.

She couldn't even begin to pinpoint the exact moment when she had taken that dangerous step over the edge of desire into love. But it had happened. She knew that now with absolute certainty.

She was in love with a man she knew almost nothing about and who held a very expensive debt over her head. Emelina surged restlessly to her feet and began clearing away the remains of her small celebration. What was he going to do? What happened to a woman who fell in love with a man like Julian Colter?

A man who wasn't even in the phone book, for heaven's sake!

What did he truly feel about her? There could be no doubting his desire, not after the way he had made love to her. And he could be trusted, she reminded herself. He had kept his end of the bargain they'd made.

Which only served to remind her that he would be expecting her to keep her end. She stiffened her shoulders as she carried the dishes to the sink. Julian would have no cause for complaint on that score. She always paid her debts. But how long would he go on wanting her after the situation with the debt was resolved?

Damn it, there were simply too many unknowns. All she could do was take it one day at a time. She headed back toward the telephone and made another attempt to contact her brother. Keith would want to know about the sale of the manuscript.

This time she got lucky. He was staying at the hotel he generally used while in Los Angeles, and his reaction was all she could have asked for.

"So you're going to quit your job, huh? Just like that?" he finally chuckled into the phone.

"I want to write full time, Keith. And the editor assured me that she would be very interested in the next book," Emelina told him excitedly.

"Well, I guess there's no harm in it. Even if the editor changes her mind, you won't starve to death, will you?"

"You mean you'll come to my rescue with a sack of groceries now and then?" she retorted.

"I don't think I'll have to worry about you, Emmy," Keith said easily. "You'll have Julian to make sure you get fed, won't you?"

"Julian!" she gasped.

"I had the distinct impression the man had staked a claim on you, sister. I don't see him relinquishing it very easily."

"But he's not... I mean we aren't...aren't planning on anything like marriage or—or even living together!" The protest came out in a fumbled manner as Emelina tried to get the message across to her brother. "Julian and I don't have what you'd call a...a relationship," she explained, unaware of the wistful note in her words. "We, uh, just got to know each other at the beach, and he offered to help with my scheme to trap Leighton. That's it, Keith, really it is."

"Sure it is." She could almost see him grinning into the phone. "Emmy, you don't have to play games with me. I'm your brother, remember? I know damn good and well you're in love with the man."

"Oh, Keith, what am I going to do?"

"Julian Colter can take care of his own," Keith said succinctly. "And he wants you. He'll look after you, Emmy."

"I don't particularly want to be looked *after,* you idiot!"

"I know," he sighed. "You want the promise of flaming love and eternal, torrid passion. But men don't have that sort of romantic outlook on life. You ought to know that by now. At least not men like Colter. Take my word for it, his type thinks in much more fundamental terms."

"You mean in terms of sex?" she asked icily.

"Yeah, that's one of them. Now tell me exactly what the editor said about your manuscript. When will the contract arrive? How much is she willing to pay up front? How about the royalty figures?"

"To tell you the truth I was too excited to ask all those questions," Emelina grumbled.

"Then I think we had better look into an agent."

"That's what Julian said," she groaned.

"I'm not surprised. The publishing business is definitely not one to enter with a pair of rose-colored glasses. I have a hunch it would chew a little romantic like you to pieces."

"You and Julian are very cynical!"

"We think alike on some things. I have a hunch Colter will take a very level-headed approach to the matter."

Like intimidating the publishers into paying the royalties on time? Emelina wondered with a wry grimace. Then she made a stab at changing the subject. "Keith, have you heard anything yet about Leighton?"

"No. After he gave me the ultimatum last month he said he'd be around to collect sometime next month. Julian called yesterday to suggest that I make the first payoff so

Leighton wouldn't be suspicious. He's talked to the Oregon police, and they're going to watch the beach house on the twenty-eighth. If everything goes according to schedule, Eric should be out of my hair by the first of November. And that will be one hell of a relief," he added with a heartfelt sigh. "What a mess. I don't know what we would have done without Colter. Things could have gotten awfully sticky."

"Don't forget the whole thing was my idea!"

Keith laughed. "And to think I thought it was all a harebrained scheme which would come to absolutely nothing. Goes to show a man should never underestimate his older sister, doesn't it?"

"I'm glad you've learned something from this mess," she said sweetly.

"Good night, Emmy. Remember what I said about getting an agent." Keith hung up the phone.

Could an agent deal with Julian Colter? she wondered with interest. Perhaps that was who she should send to negotiate the final payment of her debt. Determinedly she put the fanciful notion out of her head. She had no grounds for "negotiating" at all. She'd accepted Julian's help, making an unqualified promise to pay him in whatever way he demanded.

She always kept her promises.

The days slipped by as the twenty-eighth of the month approached. Keith called her one afternoon to inform her that he'd made the first payment to Eric Leighton. "God, I'd like to see his face when the police pick him up with a suitcase full of dope next week!" he'd concluded.

Julian phoned nearly every night, and she gathered from what little he said about the matter that he had his hands full in Tucson. She was afraid to ask too many questions. But he kept her informed of his dealings with the Oregon police and assured her that everything was on schedule.

"It'll be all over with next week, honey," he said as the twenty-eighth approached. "And this mess here in Tucson should be cleared up by then, too. That will leave us time for ourselves," he finished in satisfaction.

Emelina drew a deep breath and then said deliberately, "Julian, I want to get the debt out of the way. I don't want it hanging over my head."

"Don't worry," he told her coolly, "that's the first item on my agenda."

Emelina didn't know whether to be relieved or terrified as she hung up the phone that night.

Somehow the twenty-eighth finally arrived. Emelina was half tempted to return to the cottage she had rented on the beach just so she could observe the conclusion of the matter, but something told her that Julian would be absolutely furious if she went anywhere near the action. The thought of facing his fury just now was more than she could handle. She went back to her writing.

The phone rang on the morning of the twenty-ninth.

"It's all over, Emmy." Julian's voice sounded grim and remotely satisfied.

She shut her eyes briefly. "The police have Leighton?"

"Yes. I told your brother about it a few minutes ago. Leighton won't be bothering him anymore with blackmail attempts. He's going to have his hands full fighting the drug-running charges. And from what the police said, he doesn't stand a chance of getting out of them."

Emelina let out the breath she had been holding. "Thank you, Julian."

"Don't thank me," he muttered. "You're going to *pay* me, remember?"

"Yes." She sat very still, holding the phone as if it were made of heavy lead. Ever since the night when she had re-

quested that the debt between them be cleared up as soon
as possible, he had been almost cool on the phone. There
had been no more teasing innuendoes or talk of being
lovers. The phone calls since then had been far more businesslike and this one was the worst yet. There was no
doubt that the warmth of their relationship was rapidly de-
teriorating, and Emelina didn't know how to salvage it.

"There are a few more things I have to clean up here in
Tucson and then I'll be free to settle matters between us,
Emmy," Julian went on in that cool, detached tone. "I'll call
you the first of next week."

"Say hello to Xerxes for me," she instructed softly and
gently replaced the receiver. She had to blink her lashes
several times in order to clear away the moisture that had
gathered behind her lids.

He was going to summon her next week to pay off the
debt. What would he require of her?

Money? Perhaps. What an irony if she had replaced one
blackmailer with another. She had no business contacts he
would find useful. Her brother would have been the one to
tap for that, and Julian had promised to keep her brother
out of it. What did men like Julian Colter ask of people like
her? Did power depend on having a bunch of little people
in debt? Was that how the big crime syndicates worked?
Or was it just instinctive for Julian to demand something
in return for his assistance?

More than anything else in the world, Emelina wanted to
pay off her debt to Julian Colter. Until she did, she would
never know if there was really a chance for their relationship.

CHAPTER NINE

HE HAD TO DO IT BEFORE he lost his nerve completely.

What the hell was the matter with him, anyway? Everything was going according to plan. He knew Emelina would come when he called. Julian had never been more certain of anything in his life. All he had to do was pick up the phone and tell her to come to Tucson.

No, he corrected himself mentally, not *tell,* ask. There was no need to give Emelina an order. She would come to him, no questions asked, if he simply requested her presence. She owed him.

Request. That sounded unbearably arrogant, too.

Julian sat very still in the padded leather chair behind his ebony-colored desk and stared at his hands as he spread them out on the blotter. It almost looked for a moment as if his fingers were trembling. Grimly he closed the offending hands into frustrated fists.

Slowly he swiveled the leather chair around so that he could stare broodingly out the window of his fourteenth-floor office. It was a beautiful day in the desert city. In the distance the majestic mountains clawed a cloudless sky. The city basked under the seventy-five-degree warmth of a late fall day. Just the sort of day the tourists dreamed about.

But all Julian could think about was a foggy night at the beach. The urge to follow the mystery lady down the street as she slipped past his cottage had been irresistible. Even if Xerxes had not scratched at the door and whimpered expectantly, he would have stepped out into the chilled night and gone after her. In his mind Julian had been speculating for days about the nature of her interest in that deserted cottage.

He had watched her go into town in the mornings and return alone and had wondered if she were awaiting the arrival of a man, a lover. But no one had appeared. He had felt a sense of relief when no male showed up to claim the woman in the cottage down the street, a relief he hadn't wanted to fully acknowledge.

That night when he had followed her and found her trying to break into the old beach house, he had known he wouldn't be able to get the strange, restless curiosity out of his system until he had all the answers about the lady who lived down the street.

Yet the answers had only increased the restlessness and made him more thoroughly aware of her than ever. He could identify the physical desire easily enough. If what he felt had amounted only to that he could have handled it. He was a healthy, adult male, but he was not at the mercy of his physical needs.

Just as Emmy wasn't at the mercy of her newly discovered desire, Julian reminded himself. There had been more in their coming together than sex, and he knew it.

So why the hell was he terrified of picking up the phone and making the call that would bring her to Tucson? he challenged himself grimly. Why was he afraid to call in the tab? Emelina would pay. He could trust her.

There was no point putting off the day of reckoning. With an effort of will, Julian reached for the phone. If he waited any longer, he might lose his nerve completely. God knew it had been getting harder and harder to communicate with her long-distance. He'd been fully aware of her reaction to his increasingly stilted conversations. She had been gently withdrawing from him. There was no choice but to get her down to Tucson before the distance between them grew too great.

With great precision, Julian dialed Emelina's number. His hand was really shaking by the time he finally realized she wasn't home. Hell, he didn't dare put this off a moment longer. He cut the connection and dialed another number, that of Western Union. It might be easier to do this with a telegram, anyway, he assured himself. What a coward. It had been a long time since he'd been this scared. But, then, he consoled himself, perhaps a man was entitled to a few jangled nerves over a creature like Emmy Stratton.

When he'd finished dictating the message to the Western Union operator, Julian called the Portland office and asked for Joe Cardellini. Joe came on the line immediately. No one kept Julian waiting.

"Yes, sir?"

Julian repressed a rueful smile as he heard the respectful tone in the younger man's voice. To think he'd once known a stab of jealousy when Joe had gently tried to soothe Emmy that morning in the cottage. Cardellini could be trusted, and even if he couldn't, Julian knew he could trust Emelina.

"Joe, I want you to make flight reservations for Emmy. She'll be coming down to Tucson on, let's see…" Julian broke off a moment, rubbing his temples as he tried to think. Better give her a couple of days to pack and make arrangements to be out of town. "On Thursday of this week. I'll have her call you to confirm."

"I'll arrange it," Joe said calmly.

"Yes, I know. Thank you, Joe. And thanks for the

bugging work at the beach. Everything went perfectly on the twenty-eighth."

"Anytime, sir."

Julian replaced the receiver and continued to sit staring across the room, his fingers drumming uselessly on the desktop. It was done. In two days Emmy would be arriving at the airport. Carefully, largely to take his mind off his jitters, Julian began to make plans. He'd take her out to dinner at that plush restaurant in the hills overlooking the city. He'd make sure the chef knew ahead of time that Julian was arriving with a very special guest. That way they were certain to get the *escalopes de veau* and the best of the wine selection. Thoughtfully Julian decided he'd use the Mercedes with the top down so that when he drove her back to his house after dinner the wind and the stars would be in Emelina's hair. She'd like that. At home he'd have the cognac ready and some Mozart on the stereo. He recalled seeing Mozart in her tape collection. Desperately he racked his brain for anything he'd overlooked. Flowers. He'd have to see about getting some flowers. What else? Jewelry? Something simple in that line. Emelina wouldn't want flashy jewelry. Perhaps a little gold collar of a necklace. Yes, that would look good on her.

And then, when he'd paved the way with as many inducements as he could find, he'd tell her what he wanted in exchange for helping her brother.

Emmy would pay. She always paid her debts. And from now on, Julian decided, she would be in debt to no one but him.

THE TELEGRAM WAS WAITING for Emelina at six o'clock that night when she returned from the public library. She tore it open with shaking fingers and scanned the message inside.

I CAN'T WAIT ANY LONGER. COME TO
TUCSON ON THURSDAY. CONTACT JOE FOR
RESERVATION INFORMATION. I'LL BE
WAITING AT AIRPORT.

JULIAN.

Slowly she crumpled the flimsy paper. So Julian had
summoned her at last.

In a way it was a relief. Emelina set down the groceries
she'd picked up on the way home that evening and sank into
the nearest chair, trying to collect herself. A *relief*. That's
what it was. Didn't she want to get the whole thing over
and done with? Of course she did. She would pay her debt
and then see what remained of her relationship with Julian.

Two days. According to the telegram she had to wait two
whole days. How could she possibly manage that? Her
nerves would never survive the wait now that a deadline
had been set! God! She had to get the whole thing over with
as quickly as possible!

Impulsively she picked up the phone and dialed one of
the airlines. There was no way in the world she could wait
until Thursday. She would leave for Tucson tomorrow.

The ease with which she got reservations was frightening. Had she been subconsciously hoping that the airline
would be booked? What was the matter with her? Emelina
wondered as she hung up the phone and glanced down at
her trembling fingers.

Nervously she got up and wandered into the kitchen to
find something to eat. But when she had the cheese and
sprout sandwich made she found it almost impossible to
get down. Her stomach felt as if it had become a perma-
nent residence for a flight of butterflies.

I'm turning into a nervous wreck, she realized grimly.

It was ridiculous. Or was it? Her whole future hinged on what happened in the next twenty-four hours. The man she loved had summoned her to pay off a debt.

What would he demand of her?

All the tales she had ever read of how the Mob operated came back to her as she stood with the uneaten sandwich in her hand. It could be anything. Perhaps Julian wanted her to embezzle for him? No, that was ridiculous. She no longer even had an employer from whom she could steal! She'd quit her job two weeks ago.

Perhaps he needed an unknown woman he could infil-trate into some organization in Tucson. Would she be asked to serve as a Mafia spy?

The various possibilities whirled through her mind in vivid, living color, keeping her awake most of the night. Emelina spent the time packing and repacking the one suitcase she intended to take to Tucson.

In the end the one suitcase became three large cases. A woman never knew what she might need in a situa-tion like this.

As soon as she thought Joe might be in the office the next morning, she phoned and asked for him. The phone was answered simply as "Colter & Co."

"Hello, Emmy. I've got your reservations all ready," he said easily as he came on the line. "I'm sure Xerxes will be looking forward to seeing you."

"Yes, uh, thank you, Joe. I was wondering if I could have Julian's home address just in case I miss him at the airport or something," she requested a little weakly.

"Huh? Oh, sure. Just a minute and I'll get it for you." Joe came back on the line shortly and read her off the address. "But I wouldn't worry about missing him. I get the feeling he'll be waiting at the airport with bells on his toes."

"An interesting image," Emelina smiled wryly.

"Yes, it is, isn't it?" She could sense Joe's slow smile. "Well, you can pick up your tickets at the airline counter on Thursday. Or would you rather I came by and took you to the airport?" he added quickly.

"Oh, no, that won't be necessary," Emelina said hurriedly, wishing she didn't have to deceive Joe. "A friend is going to take me."

"Okay. Call if you need anything else."

"Thank you, Joe," she murmured humbly.

"Anything for Julian's lady," he told her emphatically.

Emelina hung up the phone, turning the words over in her head. Julian's lady. No, she couldn't really be Julian Colter's woman until after they had cleared up the business between them. And by then the chasm between them might be far too wide to cross.

What if Julian asked something absolutely impossible of her? What would she do then? Emelina shuddered as she thought of such assignments as putting poison in a competitor's tea.

No, Julian wouldn't operate in that fashion, she assured herself in the next breath. She had the feeling from the way he communicated with Keith that he handled his business in a very modern corporate style. Julian was no back-alley thug or former killer. And everyone knew the modern Syndicate was into all sorts of legitimate businesses.

Yes, Julian would be in something that was reasonably legitimate, Emelina told herself as she hauled her three suitcases down to the basement garage. It might not do to inquire too carefully into his background, but surely his current operations would be relatively businesslike.

In which case the question of what he could want from her became even more confusing.

The flight to Tucson was uneventful, but Emelina arrived with nerves that felt as if they had just ridden out a thunderstorm. She managed to get herself and the three huge suitcases into a cab and from there into a modern motel, but shortly thereafter she felt as if she were going to collapse.

Action, that was what she needed. She would case the situation and make plans. Hastily she threw on a pair of jeans and button-down shirt and hurried out of the motel to find another cab.

"Could you please drive me past this address?" she requested, climbing into the backseat.

"Sure," the driver said equably. "You don't want to stop?"

"No, I just want to cruise past." She sat back in the seat and watched eagerly as the driver took her out to an expensive area of town. The houses were set wide apart on lots that were landscaped to blend in with the desert surroundings. They slowed as they went by a modern house done in stark white and built around an interior courtyard. Wrought-iron gates protected the inviting garden inside. There was no way of telling if anyone was at home.

"This is it, ma'am," the driver said. "You want to go by again?"

"No. Once is enough," she whispered, staring out the back window at the beautiful, expensive home. "Thanks."

"You bet." The driver shrugged. It wasn't his business.

So much for casing the joint, Emelina decided back in her motel room as she paced the floor. Now what? It was getting close to five o'clock. Perhaps a little food would settle her stomach before she called another cab.

What was she going to wear for the big reunion? After unpacking all three suitcases, Emelina decided that nothing she had brought along seemed appropriate for the occasion ahead of her. She wound up showering and putting on her jeans again.

Standing in front of the mirror she piled her hair into a loose knot on top of her head. The Oxford cloth shirt and jeans appeared very functional, she told herself. Then she headed downstairs toward the restaurant next to the motel.

Nothing on the menu, however, looked as though it would settle her stomach.

"I'll have a margarita," she finally announced to the hovering waitress. Perhaps a little alcohol would unjangle her nerves. Emelina glanced at her watch. It was going on six o'clock. What time did Julian get home from work?

Twenty minutes later she was so pleased with the effects of the first margarita she ordered another. The salt on the rim tasted especially good.

Twenty minutes after that she glanced at her watch again and told herself Julian might have been delayed in getting home from the office. No sense rushing out to his house.

"Another margarita?" the waitress inquired as she drifted past Emelina's table.

It was all the encouragement Emelina needed. "Yes, please."

"Perhaps some chips?" the woman suggested gently, surveying the rather strange gleam in her customer's eyes.

"That sounds lovely," Emelina decided, feeling much more cheerful.

When the chips arrived she downed them along with the third margarita. The drinks were working, she decided in satisfaction. Her stomach felt almost normal. It was too bad her head was beginning to feel slightly detached from her body. But it seemed to make it easier to think clearly.

"That was a lovely dinner," she confided to the waitress

as the woman came by a fourth time. "But I think I'd better be on my way. No sense putting this off any longer, is there?"

"Probably not," the waitress agreed, stifling a smile as Emelina very carefully extricated herself from behind the small table. "Are you driving, ma'am?" she added with a genuine touch of concern.

"Heavens no! I was going to call a cab. I don't know my way around Tucson, you see."

"I'll, uh, call it for you, ma'am," the woman volunteered.

"That's very kind of you." Emelina tipped lavishly and walked with great precision toward the door.

When the cab arrived she settled herself thankfully into the seat. It had been difficult standing up, she'd discovered. "I want to go to this address, please."

"Sure," the young man said, hiding a smile as he studied his inebriated fare. He made sure her door was closed securely and then headed for the exclusive suburb. "Looks like you got an early start on the party," he murmured as he pulled the cab to a halt in front of the modern home a short while later.

"Party? What party?" Emelina opened her eyes. They had been closed most of the way from the restaurant. She blinked owlishly.

"There seems to be a party here tonight," the driver explained as he glanced into his rearview mirror. "The cars are parked clear up to the next intersection."

"Oh, I see." Emelina decided the man was right. Julian's drive was filled with vehicles which poured out into the street and lined the block. "Well, that's just too bad. I'm going inside anyway! How much do I owe you?"

He told her the sum and Emelina added a five dollar bill to cover the tip. "I'm feeling quite generous tonight," she explained gravely as he started to protest.

"Well, thank you," the driver said uncertainly and then jumped out to help her open the door. She was having some trouble with it.

"Good night and thank you," Emelina said politely. With her chin high in a regal gesture, she started up the walk to the open wrought-iron gate. Somewhere in that house was Julian, and she wasn't going to turn around and leave now, even if he was giving a party. Deep in the foggy recesses of her brain Emelina knew that she would have great difficulty working up her present level of courage again tomorrow night.

No one stopped her as she walked through the gate into the beautifully landscaped courtyard. Soft lanterns lit the handsomely dressed men and women who filled the garden. The laughter and chatter carried easily into the night, and Emelina decided that it sounded genuine. Good. If everyone here was enjoying himself or herself, then Julian probably was, too. He would be in an excellent mood, she decided craftily. It would be an ideal time to hit him up about that stupid debt.

A few people turned to glance inquiringly at her as she came through the gate. When they realized they didn't recognize her they smiled and turned back to their conversations. A few cast interested glances at her jeans, but no one stared rudely.

Off to one side, near an open glass door, Emelina spotted the bar that had been set up to serve the guests. Instinctively now she headed for it.

"A margarita, please," she requested gently of the politely inquiring bartender. "I'm going to mingle."

"This will no doubt help," he agreed, fixing the drink. "Here you go."

"Thank you. Have you seen Julian?" Emelina licked the

salt off the rim of her glass and leaned back against the bar. The support was welcome. She scanned the cheerful throng.

"He came by a few minutes ago," the bartender said. "I think he was headed in that direction." He nodded vaguely toward the opposite corner of the garden.

Emelina braced herself with one elbow and followed the bartender's glance. There, in close conversation with two other men, stood Julian. He was sipping casually at a glass which appeared to contain scotch on the rocks and looking very much at ease in a conservatively cut evening jacket and slacks of near black. In the lantern light his dark hair gleamed, and harsh shadows fell on the rugged planes of his unhandsome face. He was deeply intent as he talked to the two men who stood with him.

"Isn't he beautiful?" Emelina whispered to the bartender.

The bartender arched one brow. "Well, to tell you the truth, I hadn't thought of him in quite that way," he hedged carefully, unwilling to engage in open argument with one of Colter's guests.

"He is, you know," Emelina confided helpfully. "Oh, I'll admit he's no movie star, but I was never the type to fall for movie stars, anyway. There's something else about Julian."

"Women are often attracted to power," the bartender observed with surprising insight.

Emelina shook her head emphatically. "No, that's not it. Many of my brother's friends have power and I've never fallen for them. No, the thing about Julian is that you can trust him, you see. He always upholds his end of a bargain." She took another sip of the margarita.

"You've got a point there," the bartender conceded thoughtfully. "He's got a reputation in this town. Always does what he sets out to do, or so I hear. Pays his hired bartenders well, too," he added with a grin.

"These people," she gestured at the assembled crowd. "They're all friends of his?"

"Friends and business acquaintances. Colter gives two parties like this a year to repay his social obligations. I don't think he particularly enjoys them, though."

"No," Emelina smiled sunnily. "He's really a quiet type at heart, isn't he?"

"Well, I wouldn't know too much about that," the man said hastily. "Nobody talks about him being a playboy, though. Keeps his love life quiet and out of the public eye. You a close friend of his?"

"I owe him," Emelina explained very seriously. "I'm here to pay off a debt."

"I see." The bartender sounded vaguely mystified and appeared to be on the verge of risking another question when a fierce, joyous barking shattered the civilized hum of conversation. "Oh, hell, that damn dog got loose! Colter will be furious. It was supposed to be locked up in the backyard!"

As if on cue the entire crowd turned to stare at the open gate as Xerxes came tearing around the corner and burst upon the scene. The sleek Doberman announced his presence with another loud *whoof* and then he bounded straight for Emelina.

"Xerxes!" Julian's voice rapped sharply in the sudden silence. "What the hell!… *Emelina!*"

Julian stared at the figure going down beneath the happy assault of the Doberman. Xerxes had managed to knock her completely off balance and was standing over her as she lay flat on her back on the grass. For an instant Julian felt absolutely frozen in astonishment and then he managed to unglue himself from where he was standing and stride quickly across the garden to the pair on the lawn.

"Nice dog, nice dog," Emelina was saying breathlessly,

pushing ineffectually at the happy dog. "Down boy. Let me up, Xerxes. I have to get up."

"Xerxes! Sit!" This time Julian's voice brooked no argument, and the dog responded obediently, sitting on his hind haunches beside Emelina.

"Oh, Julian," Emelina muttered trying to sit up and brush herself off. "There you are. Thank you for calling off your dog. I suppose he means well," she allowed grudgingly, "but he's so *aggressive!*"

Julian stared at the rumpled figure sitting on the ground beside his dog. Emelina's hair had come free of the clip that was supposed to be holding it back and cascaded in disarray around her shoulders. The jeans she wore were faded and had shrunk until they hugged her full hips. The maize-colored shirt was stained from the grass and as he took in the oddly bright expression in her hazel eyes Julian realized that his sweet Emmy was more than a little tipsy. The margarita she had been holding in one hand when Xerxes appeared had splashed on her jeans.

Julian realized that he was torn between a wave of affectionate amusement and sudden fear. She was here. Not precisely in the right place at the right time or in the right condition, but she was here. He reached down to lift her to her feet.

"Emmy, you sweet idiot. What the hell do you think you're doing?"

"Paying off my debt," she explained politely as she stood in the circle of his arms and stared up at him with a serious mien.

"Of course," he drawled very dryly. "What else would you be doing. Come inside, Emmy. George," he added brusquely, signaling to the bartender. "Take Xerxes back to the other yard and see he's properly chained this time."

"Right away, Mr. Colter," the man said obediently, reaching rather tentatively for Xerxes's collar. "Come on, dog."

Xerxes didn't move, his dark eyes on Emelina. The bartender tugged carefully. The dog ignored him.

"Let him come with us, Julian," Emelina sighed. "He's such a stubborn sort of dog. Rather like you."

Julian groaned, feeling as if the situation had exploded in his hands. He'd never felt so out of control in his life. "Forget it, George. Come on, Xerxes," he growled and turned to walk through the open door, his arm still around Emelina. The dog followed at a brisk pace, and the crowd settled back into amused conversation.

"Trust you not to follow the plan," Julian sighed as he eased Emelina into a large chair and went to the sideboard to pour himself another scotch. He needed it, he realized grimly.

"Could I have another margarita?" Emelina inquired blandly, watching him as he paced once across the room and back in front of her. It was a charming room, done in the Spanish style with heavy beams and whitewashed walls. The furniture was equally heavy and much of it looked hand carved.

"Sorry, I don't have the makings for a margarita here," he told her roughly and instantly regretted his tone of voice. What was the matter with him? He didn't want to get her upset by yelling at her! Why the devil did she have to arrive drunk? On the other hand, maybe that would make things easier. "Would you like a glass of wine?" he offered apologetically.

"That would be lovely." She smiled at him serenely.

"Emmy, you are bombed out of your charming little skull, aren't you?" he groaned as he poured the wine.

"I had a lovely meal at the restaurant next to my motel," she explained placidly.

"I'll bet. How many margaritas?" He handed her the wine and frowned. She had to use both hands to hold the glass upright.

"I don't remember. But there were chips. The waitress brought me some chips."

He listened to the overly careful emphasis on each word and shook his head ruefully. Then he took a sip of his own drink and lowered himself into the chair across from her. Xerxes sprawled between them, a happy dog. "I can't figure out whether your being drunk is going to make this easier or harder," Julian confessed, stretching out his feet and leaning back into his chair. He watched her from under narrowed lids.

"Oh, it makes it much easier," she told him cheerily, downing a swallow of wine. "It needs salt," she informed him, examining her glass.

"Which needs salt? The wine or our conversation?" he grumbled. Damn, he could feel his fingers trembling again. He clutched them more tightly around the glass.

"The wine. As far as our conversation goes, I'm not sure what it needs." Emelina frowned and shook her head. "No, that's not true. It needs to get over and done, I think."

"You're right," he agreed, trying to take a grip on himself. "But first tell me why you jumped the gun. Why are you here tonight instead of on Thursday?"

"I couldn't wait. I was getting very nervous, Julian." She regarded him with wide eyes. "I hate being in debt."

"Emmy, honey," he began softly, wanting more than anything else in the world to take that reproachful look out of her eyes. "Will it be so very difficult?"

"Paying the debt?" She blinked sleepily. "That rather depends on what you ask of me, doesn't it?"

"I suppose." And in spite of his determination, Julian found he still couldn't quite bring himself to tell her what it was he would be requiring of her. What if she turned him down? No, he reminded himself in the next second, she wouldn't refuse. She'd pay. His knuckles whitened around the cold glass in his hand. Of course she would pay. *Tell her what you want, you fool.* "Does Joe know you're here?" In disgust he heard himself ask the unimportant question instead of the important one.

"Nope." Emelina shook her head emphatically. "He thinks I'm going to be on the three-ten flight tomorrow. I tricked him," she declared proudly.

"So I see. I'll have to have a word with him," Julian said dryly. Instantly Emelina looked stricken.

"No! You mustn't be upset with him! It's not his fault. It's mine!"

"That doesn't surprise me."

"Julian," she began very firmly. "You're not to get angry at Joe. Promise me you won't be mad at him. He did as he was told!"

"Okay, I won't be mad at him," Julian capitulated, realizing that there was really no point in trying to conduct any kind of argument with Emelina tonight. And he didn't want to risk annoying her now. The discussion about Joe was only one more delaying tactic.

Another such tactic mercifully appeared from the direction of the garden as George the bartender traipsed embarrassedly through the room. "Sorry, boss. We're out of ice. I'll just be a minute."

There was dead silence in the living room as the young man hurried on through into the kitchen and then reappeared with several sacks of ice. He nodded quickly at Emelina, who smiled benignly back at him and then disappeared again into the garden.

"A very nice man," Emelina remarked to Julian. "I've met a lot of nice people today. Cab drivers, waitresses, bartenders. Everyone's been most kind." She raised her glass in a salute. "Here's to kind people everywhere."

Julian's mouth turned down wryly as he watched her drain the last of the wine. "Do you number me among the folks who have been kind to you, Emmy?" he asked softly.

"Oh, definitely," she assured him. "Could I have another glass of wine?"

"Honey, I think you've had enough."

She shook her head. "No, not enough. I can still think a little. Be kind to me, Julian, and fetch me another glass of wine. There's a good boy."

He rose reluctantly and took the wineglass. "You don't have to talk to me as if I'm Xerxes."

"You two are a lot alike," she countered firmly.

"Maybe we're both just hungry for affection?" he suggested as he handed her back the half-filled wineglass. Damn it! He was going to have to get this over with as soon as possible. His pulse was thudding heavily and the palms of his hands were damp. Julian felt like an idiot. Abruptly, he also felt a little incensed. Nothing was going according to plan! "Hell, Emmy, this wasn't the way I wanted to do it! I was going to take you out for a beautiful dinner and drive you through the desert night with the top down on the car and then bring you back here and serve you cognac…"

"And seduce me?" she concluded brightly.

"No! At least not right off," he amended in a flash of honesty. He lounged back in his chair and tried to muster his courage. "No, Emmy, I wasn't going to seduce you until after you had agreed to pay the debt," he ground out.

"Ah! Now we come to the heart of the matter. What, exactly, are you going to require of me, Julian? I warn you,

I'm not very good at spying or embezzling or various forms of mayhem. Also, I feel I should warn you that I no longer have a regular income. You will have to wait right along with me for the royalties to arrive if it's money you want." She faced him boldly, chewing on her lower lip.

Julian stared back at her, every fiber of his body taut and aware. "Emmy," he said gently. "I don't want your money. I don't want you to spy for me or embezzle for me. I want something only you can give me. I want you to come and live with me here in Tucson."

Emelina frowned at him. "Say that again?"

"You heard me," he growled, suddenly terrified. "Give me your word that you'll come and live with me, Emmy. I need you."

"*That's* what you want in payment of the debt?" she gasped.

"Yes." The single word came tightly through his teeth.

She stared at him a second longer and then slowly, emphatically shook her head. "No."

Julian felt the blood drain from his face as he absorbed the impact of the single word. It was like absorbing the impact of a body blow. A wave of helpless anguish washed over him. *He loved her!* He hadn't fully realized it; hadn't wanted to acknowledge the depth of his own emotion. He loved her and she was rejecting him. Julian felt as if the world around him had just crumbled.

There was a frozen silence in the living room as Emelina and Julian faced each other. Xerxes lifted his head questioningly, sensing the strained atmosphere and uncertain what to do about it.

From somewhere Julian managed to find the energy to speak. The effort seemed to take everything he had. "I thought," he rasped dully, "that you always paid your debts."

Emelina yawned and patted her mouth politely. "Oh, I do, Julian. But I would never come and live with you in order to uphold a *bargain*."

"I see." My God! What was he going to do now? Julian wanted to rage or accuse or condemn. She had promised him that she would pay her debt! She had given him her solemn word! And now she was reneging on it. Never had he felt so incredibly helpless or so incredibly desperate.

Emelina yawned again and set down her wineglass. She leaned comfortably back into the corner of the chair and curled her legs under her. Her lashes settled on her cheeks. "I will come and live with you, Julian," she murmured sleepily, "not because of the bargain, but because I love you. It's not fair to tease me, though. In the morning you must tell me what it is you really want in exchange for our deal at the beach."

Julian surged to his feet, nearly tripping over Xerxes as he took one long stride toward Emelina's chair.

But there was nothing more to be said that night. Emelina had passed out very comfortably in the padded leather chair.

CHAPTER TEN

EMELINA OPENED HER EYES the following morning to find an apparition sitting at the foot of the bed holding a cup of coffee.

"Good lord, Julian," she groaned, her hand going to her aching head, "you look worse than I feel." She surveyed his burning dark eyes, the rumpled pelt of his hair and his obviously slept-in shirt and slacks. "Must have been some party."

"It was," he rasped dryly. "Actually, it was a little dull until you arrived, but between you and Xerxes things managed to liven up considerably."

Xerxes, who was standing guard at the side of the bed, shoved his nose at Emelina's outflung hand and she automatically patted him. "Stupid dog," Emelina murmured affectionately. "Oh, God, my head hurts."

Julian moved forward with the coffee and held it out to her. "Here. This will help."

"I doubt it." But she struggled to a sitting position against the pillows and took the cup with unsteady hands. Julian's eyes never left her face. "I guess I look pretty bad, don't I?" she sighed.

"You look beautiful." He half smiled.

There was a tentative silence while Emelina sipped her coffee and considered the precarious state of her stomach. Then, in an effort to break the lengthening lull in the conversation she said very politely, "You have a lovely home, Julian."

He ignored that, his gaze still intent on her strained features. "Emmy," he whispered, "how much do you remember about last night?"

She frowned, trying to recall the details. "Why?" she demanded suspiciously. "Did you take advantage of me?"

"Of course not!" he denied gruffly.

"Too bad. Well, as long as I didn't miss anything, I guess I can't complain."

"Emmy, stop teasing me or I'll…" He broke off helplessly.

"Or you'll what? Beat me?" She smiled blandly. "There's no need to turn violent, Julian. I already feel as if I've been through a war."

"Damn it, Emmy, did you mean what you said last night?" he grated, his hands tightening in frustration.

"Could you be more specific?"

"About loving me!" he almost snarled and then he had the grace to look ashamed. Julian sucked in his breath, clearly striving for patience. "Emmy, did you mean it when you said you'd come and live with me not because you owed me but because you loved me?"

"Oh, that," she murmured with a breeziness she wasn't exactly feeling. "Of course I meant it." How blind a man could he be about a woman, she thought wonderingly. "Didn't you know I loved you?" she whispered gently.

He looked at her with raw hunger. "No." He shook his head dazedly. "That is, I didn't think of it in those terms. I only thought about tying you to me, making you mine. Seeing to it there were no escape clauses. I never thought about love."

"Probably because you don't believe in it," she retorted tartly. "But that's the only thing that would tie me down, Julian. Did you really think you could have me in exchange for doing me a favor?"

"You said you always paid your debts," he ground out carefully.

"Love isn't something one can bargain for. Even if I wanted to pay you that way, I couldn't have faked it. You forbade me to fake that sort of thing, remember?" she taunted softly.

"That was sex, Emmy. That had nothing to do with love."

"Didn't it?" she whispered. "Perhaps not for you, Julian, but it did for me. Somehow it all comes bound up in a single package when I'm with you. The love and the sex and you and your dog."

Reluctant amusement edged his hard mouth as Xerxes inched closer to Emelina. "You're determined to make a joke out of this, aren't you?"

She winced. "Surprisingly, I don't feel in much of a joking mood this morning. Did I make a terrible fool of myself last night?"

Julian put out a hand and pushed some of the straggling chestnut hair off her face. His eyes softened with infinite tenderness as he smiled down at her. "No, sweetheart. I'm the one who made a fool of myself. I didn't realize I'd fallen desperately in love until the moment you told me you wouldn't come and live with me. I felt as if my whole future had just been shattered like a mirror. Until that point I kept telling myself that if I could get you to agree to come to me as part of our deal, I would be guaranteeing myself a woman who was faithful, loyal and completely trustworthy."

"Sort of like a nice dog, hmmm?" But Emelina's mouth gentled as she waited for him to go on. A strange warmth moved through her as he confessed his love.

He grimaced. "I'll admit I've grown rather cynical about relationships based on attraction. That's about all my first marriage had going for it. I decided a relationship based on integrity might have a better chance."

"I think you're right as far as it goes. You just didn't think it all the way through," Emelina decided, trying another sip of coffee. "Real love seems to demand some risk taking, doesn't it?"

"Emmy, when did you realize you loved me? When did you decide to take the risk?" he asked tightly, thinking of the risk her characters in *Mindlink* had taken.

"I'm not sure," she replied honestly. "I kept feeling more and more *committed*." Emelina broke off, her brows drawing together accusingly. "Which was exactly what you wanted me to feel, wasn't it?"

Julian nodded slowly. "I wanted you to feel so bound to me you wouldn't be able to break free. No, don't say it. I already know I'm selfish, arrogant and ruthless."

"Well, you can't be all bad. Xerxes likes you."

"Emmy! Here I am trying to make a confession of love and you keep bringing my dog into the picture!"

"Didn't you once say, 'Love me, love my dog'?" she inquired.

"And you once said something about having to take your coffee along with you," he reminded her indulgently.

"Has it come to that? You're even willing to tolerate my coffee?" she breathed, her eyes shining in spite of the terrible way she felt.

"I think I can figure out something to do about the coffee. I *know* I can figure out something to do about it. As long as I know I can have you," he added bluntly. "Emmy, I love you. I think I must have loved you from the first. I've never wanted a woman the way I want you. I've never plotted and planned and coerced to get a woman before." He looked stricken by the lengths to which he had gone.

"I was so afraid at times during the past few weeks that you were withdrawing from me," she confessed, remembering the increasingly stilted phone conversations. "When you left Portland I thought we had some kind of understanding, at least. I thought there was hope for a relationship. But you kept getting more and more distant on the phone."

"Because I kept getting more and more terrified of what would happen when I finally demanded that you come to Tucson and live with me," he muttered. "On the one hand I kept telling myself you would do as I asked because you always paid your debts. But I was scared, Emmy. Scared in a way I've never been scared before in my life. I suppose I knew, deep down, that a man can't bargain for the kind of thing I wanted from you. I knew it amounted to so much more than physical attraction, but I was afraid to put a name to it until last night. Oh, Emmy, you ruined everything by arriving a day early, do you realize that?" he groaned. "I had everything planned."

"My nerves would never have survived another day," she pointed out.

His mouth crooked wryly. "Mine might not have either. Last night was hard enough on them!"

"What did happen last night?"

"After you passed out on me with that immortal exit line about loving me? I carried you off to bed and put Xerxes on guard. Then I spent the rest of the evening running back and forth between my guests and you. I was determined to be around when you finally woke up, you see. I wanted to make sure I'd heard correctly!"

"Didn't you go to bed?" She scanned his disheveled figure.

"I went to bed." He indicated the other side of the wide bed on which she lay. "I slept, sort of, over there. Mostly I just looked at the ceiling and wondered how long you were going to sleep. It was probably the longest night of my life, Emmy. I don't ever want to go through another one like it. Will you marry me, sweetheart?"

Emelina's reeling stomach stilled for just a moment. "The last offer I heard was to come and live with you."

"For the rest of our lives," he clarified a little huskily. "Which means you might as well marry me. Please, Emmy!"

Instead of answering, she merely searched his haggard face. "You're not really a gangster, are you?"

"You sound disappointed," he retorted wryly.

"Well, marrying a genuine Mafia chieftain would have given me some great research material for my next book," she pointed out thoughtfully.

"Emmy! For God's sake! Put me out of my misery!" he thundered.

"Yes, Julian. I'll marry you." She used her meekest tones.

He reached for the coffee cup in her hand, removed it and set it on the bedside table. Then he made to gather her close. "When," he growled, his face less than five inches away, "did you decide I might be a legitimate businessman?"

"When I started realizing that you and my brother shared a few traits in common. And then last night when I saw all those nice people who were your friends, I began to realize you were probably just an ordinary businessman."

"A rather dull sort for a writer to marry?" he queried grimly.

Emelina managed a smile. "Not at all. I have the feeling you will be a source of great inspiration, in fact. Julian, I love you so. And, frankly, although it might have been terribly exciting to be a Syndicate wife, I'm rather relieved that we'll be able to live a normal life."

"Honey, I don't see any life with you ever ranking as 'normal'!" he told her feelingly.

"Why did you let me and everyone else go on thinking you were an underworld figure hiding out?" she demanded.

He shrugged. "I didn't care what the townspeople thought. They probably got the idea from watching me arrive in the company limousine. And they saw Joe a couple of times. I guess that probably added to the impression."

"An impression you were too arrogant to correct!"

"Maybe," he agreed noncommittally. "I was there on the beach for a much needed rest. I kept to myself and I didn't want to be bothered."

"Uh, what exactly *is* your business, Julian?" Emelina asked cautiously.

"I run a chain of hotels in the Western states."

"And good old Joe really does look after 'security'?"

"Yes. Hotel security is very sophisticated stuff. Joe has quite a background in it. Not that he goes around bugging guest rooms," Julian hastened to add quickly.

"I should hope not!"

"Emmy, honey, I'm sorry I didn't tell you the whole truth, or at least straighten out your misconceptions about me," he said seriously. "But I wanted to give you the impression I really could help your brother and I suppose I thought you might believe I was capable of handling a man like Leighton if I had some underworld connections."

"You know what I think?" she retorted. "I think you let me go on believing you were a hood because in your arrogance you liked the notion of my falling for you even though I thought the worst!"

He looked pained. "Sweetheart! How could you imagine something that ruthless? Never mind," he added immediately. "I just answered my own question. You are capable of imagining a great deal! Which should give you a long and interesting career as a writer."

Julian leaned closer, his mouth hovering above hers, his intentions plain. "God, I love you, honey. I can't even imagine living without you now that I've found you."

"Julian," she asked deliberately, "I don't think now is a good time to kiss me."

He stilled. "Why the hell not?"

"Because I think I'm going to throw up."

THREE DAYS LATER EMELINA smiled down at the plain gold band on her left hand and studied it with pleasure as she sprawled languidly on the wide lounger in Julian's garden. "Do you know, darling," she drawled thoughtfully as her husband came through the sliding glass door with two glasses and a bottle of champagne in his hand, "I'm beginning to have some suspicions about why you married me."

He groaned, setting down the glasses and pouring champagne into each. "Let's hear what that overreactive imagination of yours has come up with this time!"

"Well, it occurred to me during the ceremony this morning that there are a lot of vows and promises made during the marriage service."

"Isn't that the truth, though?" Julian sounded as if the notion had only just occurred to him, too. He handed her a glass and sank down into the padded lounger beside her. Xerxes walked around in circles at the foot of the wide chair and then settled down peacefully.

"Did you decide to marry me because you realized that I'd be sure to honor my wedding vows?" Emelina nestled in the curve of her husband's arm, not particularly alarmed at the possibility of Julian's having ulterior motives.

"Nope, that was merely a fringe benefit," he assured her equably.

"Truthfully?" Her voice turned serious as she cautiously sipped the champagne. It was her first taste of alcohol since the fateful night of her arrival in Tucson.

"Well, I can't pretend the idea didn't cross my mind," he admitted slowly, a little roughly. "Knowing you're a woman who keeps her word, I suppose it's a temptation to keep trying to bind you with promises. But I would have married you, regardless of the wording in the marriage vows. I wanted you to know I was making a commitment to you, Emmy. I couldn't think of any other way to do it in this day and age. You never seemed to ask for promises from me, so I thought I'd give them to you in the form of a wedding service," he explained, sounding awkward all of a sudden.

"Oh, Julian," she whispered gently, touching the side of his face with her fingertips in a gesture of undisguised love. "I never asked for promises because I've always known on some level that I could trust you."

He caught her fingers in his hand, pulling her palm to his mouth and kissing her with exquisite intimacy on her wrist. "And I think I've known from the first that I could trust you. Emmy, I love you so much!"

He moved his mouth to her lips in a kiss of promise that would span a lifetime.

"I love you, Julian."

Unsteadily, Julian removed her glass from her hand and set it down beside his before turning back to place his palm on the curve of her breast. Emelina felt the tenderness and the urgency and the possession in his touch and her arms wound around his neck, pulling him to her. When she felt her nipple hardening beneath his palm and realized where the intimacy was leading, Emelina hesitated briefly.

"Julian, someone will see us!"

"No," he growled. "No one can see into this corner of the garden, and if anyone dares come to the gate, Xerxes will scare him off."

She relaxed with a moan of surrender as he fastened his mouth once more on hers. Slowly, with loving care they fed the passion between them. Emelina's clothing seemed to melt away from her body and somehow Julian's was quickly disposed of, too.

"I want you, wife," he muttered hoarsely as they lay naked together. His strong thigh touched hers, and he used one wide hand on her hips to draw her more firmly against him.

"And I want you, husband," Emelina breathed, glorying in the delicious sensations they produced so readily together. She moved her breasts gently against the cloud of curling hair on his chest and he groaned under the blatant provocation.

His hands moved over her with sure intimacy, rediscovering her with possessive satisfaction until Emelina was throbbing with the force of her desire. She touched him in turn, her fingertips sometimes gentle, sometimes wicked, but always loving.

Slowly they merged, coming closer and closer together on every level until, with an aching exclamation of need, Julian parted her legs with his hand and lowered himself into her pulsating warmth.

"Oh, God, Emmy," he grated as he filled her completely, losing himself in her even as he took possession. "Oh, my God!"

Together they rode out the gentle storm, each clinging to the other as if nothing in the universe could drive them apart, and when it was over, Julian continued to nestle into Emelina's welcoming embrace, his body never leaving hers.

"Do you know," he said in tones of wonder as he looked into her eyes, "that I never realized until I met you what this was all about?"

She smiled dreamily. "Sex?"

"No." He shook his head with grave certainty. "I knew what sex was all about. But I knew nothing of making love."

She saw the honesty in his eyes. "I understand, darling. It's the same for me. I never had an inkling about what it meant to really make love until I met you."

He grinned suddenly, his mood lightening as he regarded

his charmingly tousled wife. "I would have thought a born romantic like you would have had it all figured out long ago. Surely with your vivid imagination?…"

"Imagination," Emelina declared firmly, "can only take a woman so far." She shifted beneath his heaviness, luxuriating in the way his body meshed so perfectly with hers. "Julian?"

"Hmmm?" He was beginning to nibble experimentally at the lobe of her ear.

"Have you decided how I'm going to pay off my debt?"

"Yes, I have, as a matter of fact." He raised his head, dark eyes laughing with love. "I will consider the debt paid the day you finally learn to make respectable coffee. I came to that decision only this morning when you handed me your latest attempt."

Emelina winced. "That could take me the rest of my life! You can be very hard to please when it comes to your coffee!"

He bent to her earlobe once more. "Umm. That's the whole idea. I'll have you in my clutches for the rest of your life." There was a husky note in his voice.

Emelina became aware of the tightening of his body, and her softness began to react to the distinct hardening of him within her. The warm tingling sensation seeped into her veins, becoming liquid fire. Emelina's eyes widened questioningly. "Julian?" she breathed.

"Don't worry, sweetheart," he murmured with deep urgency. "It's not a figment of your imagination." And he proceeded to illustrate the reality of his love.

WIZARD

CHAPTER ONE

SHE PREFERRED COWBOYS.

She was like a brilliantly plumed bird who had accidentally invaded his serenely black-and-white world, bringing life and color and enthusiasm. And she preferred cowboys.

Maximilian Travers swallowed a sigh along with his wine and considered the vibrant young woman sitting across from him. Sophia Athena Bennet was making it very clear that she had no real interest in professors of mathematics, with or without tenure. She was sharing dinner with him tonight in this plush Dallas restaurant purely out of a sense of duty.

Didn't she understand that even staid professors of mathematics sometimes found themselves attracted to members of the opposite sex? Or would she care, he asked himself wryly, that something about her vivid, animated presence tugged at his awareness? Probably not. She preferred cowboys.

Max eyed her over the rim of his wineglass as she went into a long and, he suspected, deliberately boring discussion of the staggering growth of Dallas, Texas. Even when she was trying to be dull, Sophy Bennet seemed to glow with barely repressed energy. He had never met anyone quite like her, he realized.

It wasn't that she was particularly beautiful; she wasn't.

But she intrigued and tantalized him in a way he had never before experienced around a woman. She was the embodiment of warm, feminine energy, whereas he was accustomed to genteel, academic composure. She was slightly outrageous excitement, and he was used to well-bred civility.

"They're calling us the Third Coast, you know," Sophy said chattily in her low, faintly husky voice. "Lots of high-tech industry has moved in, and we've become a major financial center what with all the banking and brokerage firms. A real boomtown! Honestly, even those of us who live here have a hard time keeping track of the skyline. It changes so often." There was a subtle emphasis on "those of us who live here," and Max knew he was once again being delicately told that he did not belong. At least, not around her.

But he was getting accustomed to the not-so-subtle hints. He ignored this one in favor of studying Sophy's eyes. He really liked those eyes, he decided. A wonderful mixture of blue and green that kept a man guessing about the true color. Vivid. Everything about Sophy Bennet was vivid. Her amber brown hair was a mane of curls that fell to her shoulders in a frothy mass, framing strong, animated features. Actually, Max told himself, classical beauty would have been superfluous in Sophy's case. It would probably have detracted from the striking lines of her face. The expressive mouth, the firm angle of her nose, and the wide, slanting blue-green eyes somehow managed to be quite captivating all on their own. And they hinted at an inner strength.

The wild, scarcely controlled tangle of curls was a dramatic style that was more than echoed in her clothes. A blouse with a peplum and huge, puffy sleeves, done in glittering shades of vermilion and turquoise, was

belted over a narrow skirt of jonquil yellow and turquoise. The belt itself was a massive affair of what
appeared to be stainless-steel links and red leather. It
wrapped Sophy's slim waist very tightly, emphasizing
the slenderness of her small figure. She wore turquoise
pantyhose and high-heeled, strappy little turquoise
sandals. The overall effect, combined with the wide
yellow bracelet cuffs she had on each wrist, was enough
to make any head turn.

"Your parents will be pleased to hear you're happily
settled in Dallas," he murmured into the first conversational
pause. It hadn't been easy to find the pause. Sophy had kept
up a running monologue on Dallas since he had arrived at
her apartment earlier that evening in his rented Ford.

She gave him a repressive glance and took a large bite
of her roasted bell pepper salad. "No, they won't. Dr.
Travers, my parents haven't been happy with me since I
was three years old, when it became obvious that I was not
going to be a little child prodigy. I am now twenty-eight
and they're still hoping I'm a late bloomer." Suddenly she
smiled, a ravishing, brilliant smile that seemed to contain
all the mischief and promise of every woman who had
ever lived. "Haven't you guessed why Mom and Dad asked
you to look me up here in Dallas, Dr. Travers?"

"Please, call me Max." He had the feeling he was about
to be deliberately pushed off-stride, and he wasn't at all
sure how to deal with the coming taunt.

The glittering smile widened with amused warmth.
"They're hoping you'll fall madly in love with me, seduce
and, of course, marry me. They should know better, naturally.
After all, they're both certifiable geniuses themselves, so
you'd think they'd know that the chances of another genius,
especially a mathematical genius, falling head over heels in

love with a nongenius are pretty remote. But I imagine they're still praying for some alternative to the Disaster."

"An alternative?" Max heard himself ask blankly.

"Sure. They're undoubtedly hoping for another shot at a crop of little geniuses. They never got a second chance after me, you see. Mom was told she shouldn't have any more children. They were stuck with one chance at producing a wizard to follow in their footsteps, and they wound up with me. I don't think they will ever fully accept the situation, poor dears." She sounded affectionately regretful.

"I see." Did he sound as bewildered as he felt? Max wondered.

"About the only thing I can do to salvage the situation in their eyes is marry and hope their genes will combine through me with the genes of someone like you and produce the child I should have been," Sophy explained wryly.

"But you, uh, don't intend to carry out their wishes?" he hazarded warily.

"Marry a brilliant mathematician like yourself?" she scoffed. "Hardly. I spent all of my childhood and young adult years competing against geniuses. I'll be damned if I'll turn around now that I'm free and marry someone like you! No offense," she added quickly.

"No offense," he repeated slowly, thinking that the quick remorse in her eyes appeared to be genuine. "But you just happen to prefer cowboys?"

She grinned wickedly. "One particular cowboy."

"The one you had to explain me to this afternoon?" he pressed, remembering Sophy's dismay at having to break her date with Nick Savage.

"Nick understood. I told him you were a friend of my parents who had been asked to look me up when they learned you were going to be doing some consulting work for S & J Technology. He realized there wasn't much I could do under the circumstances except entertain you for an evening. But now you and I have discharged our duty and we can go our separate ways, hmmm? How long will you be in Dallas, Max?"

"A few weeks," he replied neutrally.

Sophy tilted her head to one side, her blue-green eyes narrowing in amused perception. She fully comprehended the deliberate neutrality of his tone. She'd heard her father complain about such "consulting" trips often enough in the past. "You're going to hate every minute of it, aren't you? The theoretical mathematician compelled to lower himself to the real world of applied mathematics. Such a boring state of affairs," she teased. "But don't fret. It will soon be over and you can scurry back to your ivory tower. Have you done much consulting work in the past?"

"I get out of my ivory tower a couple of times a year."

"You mean you're pushed out by the university, which likes the prestige it gains when it occasionally lends you to industry, right?"

"I'm hardly *loaned*," he stressed mildly.

"No, of course not," Sophy chuckled. "You go for a very high price, don't you? What's the going rate now for the services of brilliant theoretical mathematicians? A thousand a day?"

"I don't get to keep the whole fee," he pointed out in a low voice.

"Will they let you keep enough of this particular consulting fee to enable you to buy some new clothes when you return to North Carolina?" she asked interestedly. Then, immediately chagrined at her audacity, she flushed in sudden embarrassment and reached for her wine. "Never mind, that was very rude of me," she mumbled into the

Burgundy. "Besides, I know that styles among the academic elite don't change very frequently. Heavens, my father has an old tweed jacket he's worn for over twenty years. And my mother's wardrobe looks twenty years old, even if it isn't. I realize that you're quite suitably dressed for life on a university campus."

Lord, it was getting worse. Why hadn't she kept her mouth shut? She really hadn't intended to embarrass her parents' distinguished colleague, Dr. Maximilian Travers. She had set out with every intention of doing her duty tonight, even though she was well aware that both she and Max had been coerced into the untenable situation.

For just a moment she allowed herself to admit privately that under other circumstances this date wouldn't have been such a chore at all. Sophy knew she had been strangely, vitally aware of Max the moment he had entered her office to introduce himself. She had looked up from her typewriter and realized she was actually holding her breath as he approached her desk.

Then, of course, he had introduced himself and ruined everything. Yes, she should have kept her mouth shut.

"I will admit that we do tend to dress a bit more conservatively back in North Carolina," Max allowed politely. He slanted a meaningful glance around the elegant restaurant. Several of the other men were wearing obviously expensive jackets, many cut with a decidedly Western flair. There was more than one pair of masculine feet clad in beautifully etched leather boots. A certain good-natured extravagance marked the attire of most people in the room, making Max's tweed jacket and white shirt seem very quiet in comparison.

It wasn't just the plain white shirt, the too-narrow tie and the old tweed jacket that marked him, Sophy thought to herself. It was also the horn-rimmed glasses that framed his serious, smoky eyes and the plastic pack of pens and pencils in his left pocket. A "nerd pack" as it was amusingly called by her co-workers at S & J Technology. Such packs were carried by engineers and mathematicians the world over and had become a symbol of their dedication to numbers. Sophy shuddered delicately. She hated numbers. Hated math of any kind.

But even if Max Travers had not arrived equipped with the accoutrements of a typical mathematician cum university professor, she would have recognized him anywhere. After all, she had spent her formative years surrounded by his type.

Perhaps it was the intense, undeniable intelligence that flared in those smoke-colored eyes that identified him. Or it might have been the quiet, analytical air that was so much a part of him. Sophy had the feeling that Max Travers never did anything on impulse. He would carefully weigh all options, analyze all data and catalog every scrap of information before acting. He looked out of place here in this flashy restaurant, and he certainly looked out of place as her date. Max should have been sipping sherry at a faculty party and discussing his latest treatise on math with someone who could understand.

Too bad he had that faintly disapproving, wet-blanket attitude, Sophy found herself thinking. Too bad he was brilliant. Too bad he was from that other world, which she had avoided so carefully for the past few years. Too bad about a lot of things because there had been that breathless moment just before he had introduced himself. It was a moment that existed only in her imagination, she sternly told herself.

But all the same Sophy found herself wondering what it would be like to see passion in that remote, smoky gaze.

Instantly she stifled the dangerous question. She had to admit, however, that there was something about the fiercely carved masculine features that subtly invited her awareness. Almost absently Sophy pegged his age at thirty-five or thirty-six. For a man who had spent his entire life in the rarefied atmosphere of academia, he didn't appear soft or weak. But then, who knew better than she that there was nothing particularly soft about genius?

Maximilian Travers wasn't conventionally attractive. The austere line of his nose and the aggressive planes of cheek and jaw left little room for good looks. Instead his features revealed an inner power that wasn't diminished even by the severe white shirt, old-fashioned tie and well-worn jacket. Sophy decided she didn't care for the implication of masculine strength. Oh, she liked strong men well enough; she just didn't like strength allied to brilliance. It didn't seem fair.

It would have been reassuring to discover a paunch beneath the old jacket, but there was none. The narrow, scuffed leather belt Max wore clasped a lean waist, and Sophy had to admit that she had seen no other signs of physical weakness in him either. Very unfair, really.

"Your parents said you just recently moved to Dallas?"

"That's right. A few months ago," Sophy agreed easily as she buttered a chunk of French bread. "It took me a while to find a new job. I'm afraid Mom and Dad are still shuddering over the one I did find." She lowered the butter knife and leaned forward melodramatically. "I'm only a secretary, you know," she confided in a stage whisper. "The horror of it all. A Bennet working as a mere secretary." Then she sat back and smiled blandly. "But it's better than selling clothes in a department store, which is what I was doing in Los Angeles, don't you think?"

"I wouldn't know," Max mumbled a bit uneasily.

Sophy's smiled broadened. "Of course you wouldn't. I'll bet you've never had to do anything so mundane in your whole life, have you? Shall I take a stab at outlining your past?"

"You don't know me at all," he protested quietly.

"The hell I don't." She grinned. "I know your kind. How's this? Declared academically gifted at an early age, perhaps even before first grade. Immediately placed in advanced preschools, advanced kindergarten and then into classes for the mentally gifted. Probably skipped a couple of grades here and there. Finished high school a few years ahead of the rest of the plodders and entered college at a tender age. Zipped through college and went directly into a doctoral program. From there it was merely a hop, skip and a jump to the faculty of a fine university where your talents are appreciated and duly rewarded with a corner office and a light teaching load. Right so far?"

"Do you read tea leaves as a hobby?" There was a dry note to his voice, and his smoky eyes narrowed fractionally. It occurred to Sophy that there might be more than academic temperament buried in this man. There might be genuine male temper. And that implied passion. Sophy brushed the thought aside. Mathematicians were rarely passionate about anything except math.

"No tea leaves," she responded airily. "It's just that, as I said, I know your kind. I spent too many years desperately trying to keep up with your type and failing. I'm lucky I wasn't traumatized for life. Or perhaps I was," she added thoughtfully. She reached for her wineglass and smiled again.

"You don't appear terribly traumatized."

"Just ask my parents. They think I'm on the verge of

going off the deep end. Twenty-eight years old and still changing jobs regularly. And what terrible jobs! Cocktail waitress, department store clerk, secretary. So demeaning for someone who should have inherited brains." Sophy shuddered delicately.

"You don't appear any more demeaned than you do traumatized." Max paused while the waiter served the entrée, lamb with apricot sauce.

"Well, to tell you the truth," Sophy confided cheerfully, "I really don't suffer from either of those two conditions. Not anymore. Not since I discovered the real world. I do very well in the real world, Max."

"What did you mean, you spent a lot of years trying to keep up with 'my kind'?" Max frowned down at his lamb chop. He was accustomed to mint sauce, not apricot sauce, on lamb. Sophy had recommended the apricot but now he wasn't so sure.

"I'm afraid my parents were never reconciled to the fact that they had produced an ordinary little girl, not a brilliant little prodigy," Sophy explained equably. "It was very hard on them. Go ahead. Try the apricot sauce. It's delicious on lamb. Live a little, Max." She ignored his frown. "Where was I? Oh, yes. As I said, my not being brilliant was hard on my parents. They had been so sure that the mating of two highly intelligent people would produce intelligent offspring. They refused to believe otherwise and, of course, no one dared to tell them differently."

Max looked up, still frowning. "What do you mean?"

"Well, before he went into semiretirement, Dad was one of the leading mathematicians in the country—"

"He still is," Max interrupted.

"Yes, I know, but in those days he was wildly sought after by just about every university in the nation. They all

wanted him as a shining ornament for their math depart-
ments. The last thing anyone wanted to do was risk offending him. My mother, being such a prominent physicist, was
also considered a prize. The pair of them wrote their own
tickets as far as their careers were concerned. Naturally I
was pushed into advanced, avant-garde classes, the kind
they have on campuses for the children of the faculty.
Everyone knew who I was and none of the teachers wanted
the responsibility of informing my parents that I wasn't
exactly a genius. Mom and Dad kept thinking that I was
just late in developing my talent, whatever it was." She
leaned forward expectantly. "How's the lamb?"

"It's all right," Max allowed cautiously.

She sat back, smiling. "Of course it is. Geniuses tend to
be much too unadventurous. Back to my traumatic childhood. Well, Mom and Dad kept shoving me into the most
advanced classes they could find. Classrooms that were
filled with little boys and girls who, like you, really did
grow up to be geniuses. I consider my school years the
worst years of my life."

"Because you always found yourself competing with
people like me?"

"Exactly. Oh, I had my role in the grand scheme of things,
I suppose. I mean, with me around, the rest of you always
looked positively brilliant. I helped maintain the class curve,
as it were. The low end of the curve was my slot. The *very*
low end. Do you have any idea what it was like to always be
the dumbest kid in class?" Sophy shook her head once, answering her own question. The mane of amber curls bounced
in a lively manner and her eyes brimmed with laughter. "No,
of course you don't. What a silly question. You were always
the one bringing up the class average to levels that were impossible for people like me to even approach."

"Did you drop out of school?"

"Oh, no, I stuck it out through high school, and, although my grades were terrible, my father managed to convince a small college in the Midwest to accept me. College, I discovered, wasn't really bad at all. It was chock-full of real people, not just you gifted types. I held my own very nicely in college, but I was so soured on formal education by that time that I still disliked the work. To please my parents, though, I made it to graduation. Then I pronounced myself free, informed Mom and Dad that there was no help for it, I was doomed to be average, and went out to make my way in the world. It's a world they know very little about, however, so they worry constantly. They would feel far more content if I would just get married to a proper math wiz such as yourself and settle down to producing a bunch of little wizards."

"Something you have no intention of doing?" Max eyed her questioningly.

"Not on your Ph.D.! Don't worry, Dr. Travers," Sophy chuckled, "you're safe. I guarantee I have absolutely no matrimonial designs on your person."

"Only on the person of a certain cowboy?"

"Nick's not just any cowboy," Sophy drawled. "He's an ex-rodeo star with a sizable ranch outside of Dallas."

"Are you going to marry him?" Max persisted.

"We're considering the matter," she allowed loftily. "Nick and I lead very full lives and we're content to let our relationship develop naturally."

"And after things develop *naturally,* will you settle down and raise lots of little cowboys? I should think Texas already had enough of those," Max commented with a hint of irritation.

"Spoken with the true disdain of the intellectual elite for

the rest of us lowly mortals," she shot back, some of her amusement fading.

To her surprise, Max had the grace to redden slightly. "Sophy, I didn't mean to sound elitist about it."

"No, I expect it comes naturally. Don't worry, Max, I understand. Far better than you will ever know. When you go back to North Carolina, feel free to tell my parents that I am alive and thriving in Dallas and that I have no intention of becoming a broodmare for geniuses."

"I think you misunderstood their motives in asking me to look you up," Max said repressively.

"Dr. Travers," Sophy countered with rueful humor, "I may not understand differential equations or vector analysis, but I do understand my mother and father. Furthermore, I think it's safe to say that I understand people in general a good deal better than Mom and Dad and you ever will."

"Sophy," Max began in a severely pedantic tone, "when your parents learned that I was being sent to S & J Technology for a consulting trip, it was quite reasonable that they should ask me to introduce myself to their daughter. There was no ulterior motive."

Sophy shook her head. "Take it from me," she said with a grin. "There was. You've been tagged as good breeding stock, as we say here in Texas. They'd be absolutely thrilled if you got me pregnant."

"Sophy, I think you're being deliberately outrageous." The high bones of Max's cheeks were stained a dull red beneath the natural tan of his skin.

"We underachievers sometimes resort to such tactics to hold our own against people like you," Sophy admitted pleasantly. "But in this case, I'm only trying to give you fair warning. Not that you're in any genuine danger."

"Because you prefer cowboys," he concluded flatly.

"I prefer just about anyone to a genius. And if you're honest, you'll admit that you would be horrified at the idea of being tied to someone who wasn't as intelligent as yourself. No one likes to be mismatched. It's extraordinarily painful, believe me."

"People like me intimidate you?" he asked quietly.

"Not anymore! But your type did a hell of a good job of it all during my school years. It wasn't your fault. I was the misfit sparrow thrust in among the mental peacocks."

Max suddenly, unexpectedly, smiled. "I would have said it was just the opposite."

"What?" Sophy eyed him uncertainly.

"I would have said you were the peacock tossed in with us rather dull sparrows," he explained gently.

Sophy blinked, taken aback at the quiet sureness of his words. Hastily she recovered. "Well, that's all over now. I'm free and I intend to remain free. As much as I love my parents, I'm not going to live my life for them. They will just have to accept the Disaster."

"When did you start calling yourself their Disaster?" he queried.

"So long ago I can't even remember. I realized very early in life that I wasn't going to be the daughter they had dreamed of producing. I'll bet your parents were absolutely delighted with you, though, weren't they?" she asked.

He glanced down at his plate as if doing a quick mathematical analysis of the position of the lamb in relation to the peas. "They seem satisfied, yes."

"Where do they live?"

"In California. They're both retired now."

Sophy sensed the shutters coming down and wondered why. Instinctively she pressed a bit further, finding herself suddenly very curious about Dr. Maximilian Travers. "Are they both from the academic world?"

"Yes."

"Mathematicians?"

"My father is a mathematician. My mother is a biologist. They were both on the faculty of a West Coast university until they elected to retire a couple of years ago."

There was a stilted inflection in his words, but Sophy couldn't quite put her finger on what was wrong. Oh, well, she told herself firmly, it wasn't her problem. Geniuses didn't need someone ordinary like herself worrying about them. "Well, I'm sure they're very pleased at your success," she said bracingly. "Have they urged you to marry and carry on the tradition of academic excellence?"

"They, uh, mention marriage occasionally. I imagine they'd like a grandchild."

"Sound just like my parents." Sophy nodded wisely.

"Sophy, it's considered natural for parents to want grandchildren."

"Ah, but in our case they wouldn't want just any sort of grandchildren, would they? They'd want little wizards. Are you going to have dessert? They make a fabulous margarita pie here."

"That sounds awful." He looked genuinely appalled.

"Be daring. After all, you'll have to go back to your ivory tower in a couple of weeks, and you may never get another chance to sample margarita pie."

"I don't know. Maybe a slice of cheesecake...."

But Sophy was already signaling the waiter. There was something amusingly pleasant about pushing a wizard around a bit, even if it was only over something as trivial as margarita pie. "We'll have two margarita pies," she announced as the waiter hurried over to their table.

The man swept off with the order before Max could change it. Accepting the failure with good grace, he gave Sophy a rather hard smile. "It will be an experience, I suppose."

"You'll love it, Max. Where are you staying while you're in Dallas?"

"One of the downtown hotels." He told her the name and she raised her expressive brows.

"My, my. Nothing but the best for visiting genius mathematicians, hmmm? That's a very posh place."

"Perhaps you'd like to drop by for an afterdinner drink in the lounge before I take you home?" he suggested politely.

"Oh, I don't think so, thank you. It's getting rather late and I'm sure you've got better things to do than entertain your colleagues' daughter. Besides, I told Nick I'd meet him for a drink around ten. He's spending the evening with some fellow ranchers at one of the local clubs. When I told him I wasn't going to be free tonight, he decided to join his friends for a few hours and wait for me."

Max abruptly became aware that his fingers were curling very tightly around his knife as he set it down beside his plate. She'd set up another date for the evening. After she left him, Sophia Athena Bennet was planning on going straight to another man. The knowledge was strangely annoying.

"Your cowboy didn't mind your coming out with me this evening?" he asked deliberately as he finished the lamb and waited in resignation for the margarita pie.

"Oh, he wasn't thrilled, but he understood. After all, he's got family, too, and he knows they can make demands."

"It's not your family that made the demand, it was me," Max felt obliged to point out in a very even tone.

"Only because my family asked you to look me up."

"It doesn't occur to you that I might have wanted to have dinner with you?"

"In a word, no," she said, grinning.

He winced inwardly because in a sense she was absolutely right. He *had* looked her up as a favor to her parents. But the moment he'd seen her, he'd been grateful he'd had the excuse of knowing Paul and Anna Bennet. Without that he wouldn't have been at all certain how to approach such an alien creature. In the natural order of things, he simply didn't encounter women like Sophy very often. Dealing with her was going to be like dealing with a new and exotic math frontier.

"Sophy…"

"Oh, I realize you might be a bit lonely here in Dallas," she said quickly. "Maybe having dinner with me was better than sitting alone in a hotel room."

"It was," he agreed dryly.

"But not much, hmmm? You're probably bored already. We haven't even touched on the theory of relativity or Boolean logic."

"Believe it or not, I do find other things in life interesting besides mathematics!" he growled.

"I'm sure you do," she soothed in a condescending tone that irritated him even further. "But I don't know any more about those things than I do about math, so I'd make pretty poor company."

"I wasn't talking about academic interests," Max gritted as the margarita pie arrived. He eyed the dessert apprehensively.

"Really? What other things were you referring to, then?" Sophy asked idly, digging into her pie with obvious relish.

He seriously considered telling her that professors of

mathematics were just as capable as anyone else of being interested in sex, but almost immediately dismissed the idea. If he said anything that blunt, she'd probably fling the pie in his face and get up on the table to declare once and for all that she was not a broodmare for wizards. Seeing no acceptable alternative and mindful, as always, of his role as a gentleman and a scholar, Max shook his head. "Never mind. Where is your cowboy going to meet you? Should I drop you somewhere downtown?"

"No, you can take me home. He'll be meeting me there."

"I see. Will he be staying the night?" What the hell had made him ask that? Max wondered savagely.

Instantly the mischievous smile in her eyes disappeared. "That's really none of your business, is it, Dr. Travers?"

He was learning, Max thought. When she called him Dr. Travers, she was annoyed. "No," he admitted, "it isn't. I'm sorry I asked."

The smile reappeared. "I'm sure my parents are just as curious."

"Have they met him?"

"No," Sophy said carelessly. "How's the pie?"

"Not nearly as bad as I had feared."

"You shouldn't be so shy about new experiences, Max."

"In your own way, you can be quite condescending, did you know that?" he asked coolly.

She chuckled. "This is turning into a pretty horrible evening, isn't it? Sorry about that, but I could have warned you. People like you and me don't mix very well together. Don't fret about it. You've done your duty and you can report back to my parents that you did, indeed, look me up while you were in Dallas. That's all they can reasonably ask of you."

"Meaning they won't demand that I perform stud

services, too?" The words were out before he could stop them, and Max was shocked at his lack of control. What the hell was the matter with him? He never talked like this! Especially not to women. It was all wrapped up with the fact that Sophy was going straight home to that damned cowboy.

"I think you can rest assured that they won't embarrass everyone concerned by asking whether or not you managed to sleep with me while you were here in Dallas," she shot back. "Now if you don't mind, Max, I would like to leave. Nick will be expecting me."

Max nodded, not trusting himself to speak for a few seconds while he recovered his equilibrium. Mutely he pulled out his worn leather wallet and found his credit card. Then he signed the slip the waiter had prepared. He was getting up from the table, his mind on taking Sophy home to her cowboy, when she abruptly put a restraining hand on his arm and smiled pointedly.

"You forgot your copy of the credit slip."

"What? Oh." Unaccountably embarrassed at the small oversight, Max hastily reached out to tear off the slip.

"Don't worry, my father does that all the time. So does Mom, for that matter."

Max winced at the unspoken implications concerning absentminded professors. He had the sinking feeling the cowboy never had such lapses.

"Are you sure you don't want to stop by my hotel for a nightcap?" It was a halfhearted attempt that Max knew was doomed to failure. He had always been a little socially awkward simply because socializing had seemed relatively unimportant in the grand scheme of his life. But tonight he would have given a lot for some suave social polish. Tonight it would have been very pleasant to be the kind of man capable of sweeping a woman like Sophy off her feet.

"No, thanks," Sophy said predictably as she slipped into the front seat of the rented Ford. "It's almost ten."

"And you wouldn't want to keep the cowboy waiting, would you?" Max muttered under his breath as she shut the door. He wasn't sure whether or not she had heard him. If she had, she chose to ignore the hint of masculine disgust. Or worse, perhaps she found it amusing.

The drive into the north side of Dallas was accompanied by another running monologue on the city's growth and prospects. At several points along the way Max was sorely tempted to clamp a hand over Sophia Athena Bennet's sweet mouth to halt the flow of deliberately boring words.

And then what? Stop the car and drag her into the back seat? Hardly the sort of behavior expected of a tenured professor of mathematics. Also hardly the sort of behavior he was accustomed to indulging in around women. Max realized with a start of surprise that he'd never met a woman he wanted to treat in such an elementary fashion. Christ! If her father only knew what he was thinking at the moment. Dr. Paul Bennet was a gentleman and a scholar and assumed that Max was in the same league.

"Well, Max, thank you very much for dinner." Sophy sounded relieved as the Ford pulled into the driveway of her garden apartment complex. "I suppose I'll see you around the office off and on for the next few weeks."

"You don't sound terribly thrilled at the prospect."

Instantly an expression of genuine contrition swept over her face, and she lightly patted his arm with five carmine-tipped nails. In the shadowed interior of the car, her eyes seemed very wide and deep.

"I'm sorry if I've offended you, Max. Please believe me, I didn't intend to. I know this evening was just a duty date for both of us. But now we've met our obligations, so there's no need to worry about the matter further. You can go back to North Carolina in a few weeks and assure my parents I'm alive and well out here. I'm going to be seeing them myself weekend after next when I go back to Chapel Hill for an award ceremony honoring Mom. I'll give you some good press when I see them. We'll both be off the hook."

She was already sliding along the seat, her hand leaving his arm as she opened the car door. A sudden glare of headlights in the rearview mirror caught Max's attention, and he turned to glance out the back window in time to see a long white Lincoln purring to a halt behind the Ford.

The cowboy had arrived to claim his lady. As Max watched the vivid creature he had just taken to dinner fly into the arms of the tall man with the Stetson who had just alighted from the depths of the Lincoln, he felt a wave of grim resentment.

It was a resentment that had no logical basis, he told himself roughly, and put the Ford in gear.

No logical basis unless you counted the very primitive logic that Max wanted to be the man who spent the night in Sophia Athena's bed.

Damned cowboy.

CHAPTER TWO

She had told Max Travers that her relationship with Nick Savage was developing naturally, and Sophy was positive that was true. Even as she hurried from the Ford to meet Nick, Sophy told herself that it was a great relief to end the evening with Max.

But the relief she experienced was not precisely the right sort, she realized vaguely. She ought to feel as though she had just escaped a dull, boring evening with a man in whom she could never be even remotely interested, even as a friend.

Instead the feeling welling up inside was one of relief at having escaped a potentially dangerous situation. And there was absolutely no reason for the sensation. Deliberately she pushed the thought out of her mind as she lifted her face for Nick's kiss. Tall and rugged, with black, wavy hair and bedroom eyes, Nick Savage was the perfect antidote to an evening spent with a wizard.

"What are you smilin' at, darlin'?" Nick asked as he took her hand and walked toward the apartment door.

Sophy told herself that his Texas drawl was sensual and sexy. She wasn't about to admit that occasionally it got on her nerves. The good-ole-boy twang was as much a part of Nick as his Lincoln, she reminded herself.

"I was thinking how good an ex-rodeo cowboy looks

after an evening spent with a professor of math," Sophy teased, digging her key out of the tiny leather purse that was clipped to her wide belt. "Honestly, Nick, I thought the evening would never end."

"I can't say I'm sorry to hear your visitin' genius was a little dull." Nick took the key from her hand and used it on the front door. "Just don't expect me to give up any more evenings so that you can do your duty," he warned as he stepped into the hall behind her.

"Never again." With a happy sigh, Sophy turned and put her arms around his neck, standing on tiptoe to kiss him.

Nick wrapped one arm around her waist and used his free hand to remove the gray Stetson. With practiced skill he sent it sailing across the room to land on the coffee table. There it struck a pile of magazines and sent them slithering to the floor.

"You're getting awfully good at that," Sophy marveled, ignoring her scattered magazines.

"I intend to get a whole lot better, darlin'. Pretty soon I'm gonna make that hat land on the bedpost in your bedroom."

His meaning was clear and Sophy didn't demur. Surely it was only a matter of time before she went to bed with Nick Savage. After all, they were falling in love and they were both mature adults. If the truth were known, Sophy had already wondered silently at Nick's willingness to be put off this long. But he seemed to respect her desire to be sure of their emotions. It was one of the many things she liked about him.

The only thing that secretly bothered her on occasion was why she, herself, kept hesitating.

"I'll get the brandy," Sophy said after a moment, slipping from his arms to head for the kitchen. "I don't know about you, but I need something."

"Don't mind if I do a little celebratin' myself. Won a fair piece of change off Cal Henderson this evening."

"So that's what you spent the evening doing—playing poker. Shame on you." She sent him a laughingly reproachful glance across the counter that divided the living room from the sleek, modern kitchen.

"Honey, any Texan worth his salt plays poker on occasion. Be downright suspiciously unpatriotic and unneighborly to refuse a friendly game." With a satisfied grin, Nick threw himself down onto the melon-colored sofa and propped his booted feet on the Lucite coffee table.

Sophy smiled at the sight of him sprawled in her living room. Nick Savage was everything that had traditionally attracted women to cowboys. He had a handsome, suntanned face that was attractively open and rugged, and he was over six feet tall. He had the casual Western manners that thrived in Texas, and he wore the local style of clothing well. The feet on her coffee table were encased in handtooled gray leather, and the gray, Western-cut suit he wore was perfectly detailed from the yoked shoulders to the flare-legged pants.

As usual, Nick wore the huge, inlaid-silver belt buckle that proclaimed his past championship status as a rodeo star. It was a trifle unfortunate that a small paunch was beginning to appear over the edge of the buckle, but there was still enough masculine, Western-style arrogance about him to pique any woman's interest. Sophy felt quite lucky that he had taken to her at the party where they met.

Cradling a brandy glass in each palm, she walked out of the starkly done black-and-white kitchen and into the colorful living room. Sophy's love of exotic, eye-catching hues was evident not only in her apparel but throughout her home.

The melon-colored couch on which Nick lounged was

set off by vanilla walls and a jade-green carpet. The rainbow-hued easy chair by the fireplace had a mate on the opposite side of the room, and here and there dramatic touches of black underscored the vivid effect. It was a room that fit her personality and her lifestyle.

"Ah missed you this evenin', darlin'." Nick draped a casual arm around Sophy's shoulders as she sank down beside him and curled her feet under her. He smiled, fingering one of the huge sleeves of the blouse she wore. "This new?"

"Umm." Sophy swallowed a sip of brandy. "Just finished it yesterday. Like it?"

"Oh, I like it well enough. Just don't fancy you wearin' it for the first time with that visitin' nerd." Nick moved his fingers absently on her shoulder.

For some reason his use of the term "nerd" to describe Max bothered Sophy, although she admitted she might easily have used it herself. With a touch of restlessness, she put down her brandy glass and sat forward to restack the magazines that had been pushed onto the rug by the flying Stetson.

"You sure do subscribe to a lot of those business magazines," Nick observed, watching her idly.

"A woman who has plans to start her own business has to do a lot of groundwork." Sophy smiled, piling a government pamphlet profiling successful entrepreneurial women on top of a magazine describing women in business.

"All your plans still goin' along fine?"

"Oh, yes. In a few more months I should have the financial backing I need."

"Won't be no need for my woman to work, you know," Nick said softly.

Sophy ignored the comment about not needing to work and told herself that the possessive sound of "my woman" was very nice to hear. She gracefully yielded the brandy glass when he reached out to remove it from her hand, and then she allowed herself to be drawn close.

Nick's kiss was warm and pleasurable, his mouth moving on hers with undeniable expertise. Sophy gave herself up to it, wondering what it would be like when she and Nick finally went to bed together. Soon. The time would soon arrive. Nick had been so considerate, so patient, so respectful of her desire to be certain....

"I wish to hell I didn't have to get up at five tomorrow mornin'," Nick groaned a few minutes later.

"That trip to Phoenix?"

"Yeah. You'll be a good girl while I'm gone?" Nick nuzzled her neck.

"Of course."

"You'd better." He got reluctantly to his feet, collecting the Stetson. "Much as I hate to leave, I reckon I'll have to get goin'. Long drive back out to the ranch."

"When will you be back?" Sophy asked conversationally as she walked beside him to the Lincoln. There was very little of the long, white luxury automobile that wasn't decorated with chrome. The license plate was personalized with the brand of Nick's ranch, the Diamond S.

"Wednesday," Nick said as he stopped beside the car to light one of his long, dark cigarettes. He cupped his palm around the flame from the gold lighter, which was also embossed with a diamond and an S, and bent his head to light the cigarette. It was a delightfully masculine gesture that made Sophy smile. Too bad she didn't approve of smoking, she thought. It could be so damn sexy. She'd bet her new electronic sewing machine that Max Travers had never touched a cigarette in his life. He would have decided long ago that it was foolish to take the health risk.

"I'll be back in time to take you to the Everet shindig," Nick went on as he exhaled. He wrapped his arm around her shoulders and leaned back against the car.

"I'm looking forward to it. A real Texas barbecue, hmmm?"

"They pull out all the stops once a year. We'll have a good time. Bring your swimsuit. There's a pool that folks will be using." He took the cigarette out of his mouth and bent his head to kiss her goodbye.

Sophy steadfastly ignored the taste of smoke in his mouth, but she couldn't quite ignore the sudden jab of pain in her midsection.

"Ummph!"

"What's wrong, honey?"

"Nothing," she assured him quickly, adjusting her position. "I just came close to committing hari-kari on your belt buckle."

He chuckled, glancing down at the huge silver championship buckle with evident satisfaction. "A good year. Had some wild times on the circuit."

"Miss the rodeo?"

He shrugged. "It's a young man's game. Best to get out while you're on top. And after Dad died, the ranch needed attention, anyway. It's time I settled down." He smiled meaningfully. "With the right woman."

Sophy smiled up at him brilliantly and stood on tiptoe to brush his mouth with her own. "Good night, Nick. Drive carefully."

"I will. I'll call you on Wednesday when I get back from Phoenix."

Sophy stood in her doorway for a minute after Nick left, watching the big white barge of a car slip silently down the street and out of sight. At least she'd managed to spend a little time with Nick tonight. The duty date hadn't spoiled the entire evening.

Back inside she shook her head wryly as she began to undress for bed. If ever there were two men who were diametrical opposites, they were Nick Savage and Max Travers. One was exciting, the other quite dull. One was unintimidating intellectually; the other came from another world, the totally intimidating world of higher math. Nick would surely be a sexy, experienced lover. Max probably made love by the numbers. One would make a dynamic, successful husband, and the other would probably spend hours at a time so wrapped up in his math that he would forget he was married altogether. Sophy knew which man was right for her.

Didn't she?

"Getting married isn't like buying a bull," she advised herself as she climbed into bed wearing the plum-covered nightgown she had made the previous week. "I'm not looking for good breeding stock! I'm looking for love and passion and compatibility."

Tongue absently touching her lower lip, Sophy found herself wondering what would have happened if she'd accepted Max's offer of a drink at his hotel. Nothing, probably. Men like Max didn't lower themselves to making passes at women. Men like Max were gentlemen and scholars.

But if he had made a pass, attempted to take her in his arms, how would she have reacted? Why was she even asking herself the question? It was ridiculous! Annoyed, Sophy twisted onto her side and fluffed her pillow. Perhaps there had been too much tequila in that margarita pie. Something was making her imagination take some bizarre turns tonight!

She smiled wryly to herself in the darkness. Her parents would be disappointed that she and Max hadn't instantly fallen for each other. But they'd had twenty-eight years to adjust to the continuing disappointment of their only child. They'd handle this current matchmaking failure just as they'd handled all the other failures: with stoic bravery.

Deep down, in their own way, Sophy knew, they loved her, just as she loved them; but communication between parents and child had always been difficult. When she was younger, Sophy had felt as badly about the Disaster as Paul and Anna had. Guilt over her own lack of genius had kept her doggedly plodding her way through all those endless accelerated classes designed for the intellectually gifted.

As one despairing teacher after another had failed to find the courage to tell the Bennets that their daughter simply was not a genius, Sophy had begun to hate the role into which she had been cast.

"She simply doesn't apply herself," her fourth-grade teacher had explained to the Bennets at a conference. "I'm sure she has the ability, but she seems perpetually bored in class. It's like that sometimes with the truly gifted. It's hard to engage their attention, even in advanced classes such as this one, because they're so far ahead mentally."

"She'll come into her own in high school," the seventh-grade instructor had assured the Bennets. "In the meantime, all we can do is keep exposing her to as much intellectual stimulation as possible."

"She'll blossom in college," the high school teachers had insisted. "Some bright teenagers simply don't do well in high school, even in these academically accelerated classes."

And all along, the only one who had admitted the truth was Sophy. She wasn't bored in class; she was usually totally lost, desperately trying to comprehend what her fellow students picked up so easily. She wasn't failing to apply herself. She worked hard, driven by guilt and the fear of disappointing her parents.

But always there had been the wizards surrounding her. From the day she had been sent off to the carefully selected preschool for precocious children, Sophy had been trapped in the midst of the truly brilliant.

Sophy's only satisfaction during those formative years had been pursuits that involved color and fabric. In kindergarten she had latched on to the discovery of crayons with a vengeance, going through one coloring book after another until she was designing her own coloring books. Unfortunately, the rest of the class was working on the rudiments of mathematical set theory.

In grade school, art had been taught in the accelerated classes, usually in relation to mathematical perspective and the properties of light. Sophy hadn't been overly interested in the scientific side of the matter, but she'd happily played with the watercolor paints until they were gently but firmly taken from her.

Her parents had briefly considered the possibility that her true genius might lie in the realm of art, but when she showed no great interest in drawing anything other than doll clothes, they abandoned the idea.

When she discovered dressmaking, Paul and Anna Bennet steadfastly decided to treat it as a hobby. They were still treating it that way. In all honesty, they weren't the only ones who looked on her skills as a hobby. There were times when she suspected that Nick Savage did, too. That realization was vaguely annoying, but she told herself that in time he would realize how important her budding career as a designer was to her. Firmly she dismissed the concern. Nick would learn.

Someone like Max Travers would probably never understand, though. His academic elitism would always get in the way. Not that it mattered. She could care less what Max Travers thought of her future career. But why had she felt so wary around the man tonight? Hadn't she left those old feelings of intimidation behind for good? Of course she had. So why that primitive wariness? Why had she practically run from his car tonight? It made no sense.

SOPHY HAD PUT THE RESTLESS questions out of her head by the next morning when she walked into the downtown high-rise building that housed S & J Technology. She had a large box under one arm, and as soon as she stepped off the elevator on the fifteenth floor and into the section where most of the clerks and secretaries worked, a murmur of anticipation went up from the group standing around the coffee machine. A half dozen people came hurrying across the room.

"Is it finished?" Marcie Fremont, who had joined the staff shortly before Sophy and who had the desk next to hers, glanced expectantly at the box.

Sophy smiled at her and began unwrapping it. Marcie had paid well for what was inside, but Sophy was satisfied that she had delivered a dress worth the money.

Co-workers privately thought the two women offered an interesting contrast. Where Sophy was vivid and colorful and slightly outrageous at times, Marcie was cool and sophisticated. Her blond hair was always confined in a sleek, businesslike twist, and her beautiful, patrician features were always made up in subdued, refined tones.

Marcie Fremont dressed for success, as she herself put it, firmly convinced that the route out of the secretarial pool was going to be easier in the right clothes. Slim, tailored suits, silk blouses and restrained jewelry comprised her professional wardrobe. The overall effect was poised, efficient and rather distant. Sophy had kept that image in mind when she'd designed the after-hours dress.

"Remember, if you don't like it, you don't have to pay for it." Sophy smiled as she lifted the lid. Marcie smiled back quickly and Sophy was pleased to see the genuine anticipation in her eyes. Lately she had sensed a kind of quiet desperation about her new friend. Secretarial work was strictly a temporary situation for Sophy, but for Marcie it could prove to be a dead end.

"If Marcie doesn't want it, I'll take it, sight unseen," Karen Gibson announced. The others standing around nearby agreed.

"I'm sure I'll like it," Marcie said firmly. The gown came fluidly out of the box to murmured gasps of appreciation. A long, body-hugging line of black crepe with the dramatic impact of a swirling white organdy collar, it was obviously perfect for Marcie Fremont. It dipped low in the back to reveal an elegant length of spine, and it was slit up one side to the knee.

Marcie reached for it with real delight. "It's stunning, Sophy. Absolutely stunning! You're a genius." She held it to her while everyone else admired the effect.

"No doubt about it," Karen remarked, "it's absolutely right for you, Marcie."

The outer door opened at that moment and everyone swung around to see Max Travers standing just inside the room. There was a faint frown of curiosity on his face. He took in the sight of the women grouped around the sleek black gown and looked as if he were about to back out of the room. He held a sheaf of papers clutched in one hand as his eyes sought out Sophy.

Look at her, he thought as he found her instantly, so full of warmth and life and enthusiasm. She'd make any man happy. Any man who could hold her, that was. And she only let cowboys hold her. Damn it to hell, what's the matter with me? Grimly he took a grip on himself, unaware that his frown had intensified.

"Excuse me," Max began aloofly. "I was told I could get someone down here to type up these notes for me."

Feeling mildly chagrined at having been the one to create the decidedly unbusinesslike scene, Sophy stepped forward. "I'll take those, Dr. Travers."

Max's smoky eyes darkened behind the horn-rimmed glasses as he thrust the papers into her hand with an abrupt gesture. "What's all the fuss about over that dress?" he asked gruffly, nodding his head at the small group still hovering over the black gown.

"I just finished designing it for Marcie." Absently Sophy flipped through the sheaf of papers.

"Oh." Max glanced at the dress with more curiosity. "I didn't know you sewed."

"My parents have tried to keep it a deep, dark secret. We all pretend it's just a hobby." She nodded at the papers. "Anything unusual about these notes? Want them done in a standard format?"

Max brought his attention back to the papers. "It's company proprietary stuff, so don't make any copies. Your management probably would just as soon not have any duplicates floating around."

"Max, you can trust everyone here." Sophy smiled blandly. "We all work for the company. We wouldn't spill its little secrets. Besides, who here could understand all this complicated stuff about a mathematical model for a chemical processing system?"

Max cocked an eyebrow. "You apparently understand it enough to tell what it is just by glancing through a few notes."

Sophy shook her head indulgently. "I have a good mathematical and scientific vocabulary, thanks to all those years spent among wizards. I can translate what you're saying, but that doesn't mean I can comprehend it. It's like being a medical secretary. She might have the vocabulary for writing up the doctor's notes, but she couldn't perform the surgery. Get it?"

Max looked vaguely uncomfortable and his mouth firmed. "Was your cowboy glad to have you back safe and sound last night?"

"He seemed happy enough to see me."

"I'll bet. What would he have done if I'd been a little late getting you home?" There was a surprisingly belligerent tone to Max's query.

"Beaten you to a pulp, probably. Now aren't you grateful I didn't stop off to have that drink at your hotel?" Sophy asked sweetly.

"I would have been willing to take my chances," Max told her softly.

Sophy blinked, startled by the quiet conviction in his voice. For a split second their eyes met in complete understanding. In Max's smoky gaze Sophy saw the answer to the question she had asked herself the night before. Max Travers would most definitely have made a pass at her if she'd gone to his hotel with him. That question answered, she was faced with the remaining one. What would she have done in response?

In that moment of frighteningly honest communication, Sophy had a terrifying premonition about the answer to that question, too. And she didn't like the way her nerves seemed to thrill to it. What on earth was wrong with her?

It was impossible for her to be interested in Maximilian Travers. Desperately she tried to regain her composure, breaking off the intense eye contact.

"You might have been willing to take your chances, but I certainly wouldn't have been so willing," she said staunchly. "My parents would be furious if I sent you back to North Carolina in a pulped condition. They're already convinced I don't have enough respect for higher math as it is!"

"Maybe I could teach you a little respect for it," Max suggested whimsically. "Will you have dinner with me tonight?"

"Max, please…" Sophy felt suddenly very nervous, and it made her angry.

"The cowboy?"

"Nick is out of town. And I'd appreciate it if you'd stop calling him the cowboy!"

"You call me the wizard."

"So I do," she sighed. "Your logic is impeccable. Only to be expected from a professor of mathematics." Sophy waved the papers in her hand. "I'll see that these are ready by noon."

"Wednesday night?"

Sophy bit her lip. "Is that hotel room really so bad, Max?" Good heavens! Now what was she doing? Was she actually making excuses to see him again? Trying to convince herself that she felt sorry for him?

"Yes. The hotel room really is that bad."

"I'm busy Wednesday night," she heard herself say hesitantly. "But I might be able to make it for lunch sometime this week. Or…or a drink after work, perhaps." She must be feeling sorry for him. That was the only reason she could think of for agreeing to go out with him again now that her duty was done. But even as she made the uncertain suggestion, Sophy knew she was kidding herself.

"Thank you, Sophy, I'll look forward to lunch and a drink. Thursday for the lunch?" he asked calmly.

"Yes, well, I suppose…"

"Friday after work for the drink?"

"Max, I'm…" She broke off in annoyance. "Nick will be in town by then and we'll probably have plans for Friday evening."

"We'll discuss it Thursday at lunch," Max compromised smoothly. Then he turned around and walked out of the office without another word.

Sophy watched him go with a sense of foreboding. Then she slowly made her way back to her desk.

"You're going to type up Dr. Travers's notes, Sophy?" Marcie Fremont glanced at her co-worker. The dress was back in its box, safely stowed under Marcie's desk.

"Yes," Sophy mumbled, sitting down and arranging the work.

"Maybe you can learn something from them," Marcie observed. Marcie, in her efforts to climb the corporate ladder, was the kind of secretary who didn't just type up data, she studied what she typed. As a result she had an excellent working knowledge of the technical side of the company's business. So far, though, that knowledge hadn't done her much good in securing advancement.

"I doubt it," Sophy said. "It's very complicated. A lot of higher math. I'll be lucky to translate it. By the way, have you heard anything from Personnel yet?"

Marcie's mouth curved wryly. "Not a word. They're sure taking their time selecting someone for that position in Quality Control. I get the feeling they think it's a man's job."

"When the truth is, you could do it better than anyone else who's applied!"

"Thanks." Marcie smiled. "I needed that. What's with you and Dr. Travers, though? Did I hear you agreeing to have lunch with him?"

"He's a friend of my parents'. They all live back in North Carolina." Sophy busied herself with Max's notes.

"But he seems personally interested in you," Marcie persisted.

"He's just lonely. He's spending a few weeks here in Dallas, and I guess the hotel walls are closing in on him." And that was all it amounted to, she assured herself silently. That was all it could amount to. So why was she so damned aware of the man? Why was she anticipating, and yet nervous about, having lunch with him?

DURING THE NEXT TWO DAYS Max seemed to be nearby every time Sophy turned around. He dropped by to check on the progress of his notes. He made a point of being in the building lobby when Sophy was leaving work. He somehow managed to go through the cafeteria line behind her when she was on morning break.

And when he wasn't around, Sophy realized she was unconsciously watching for him. A hundred times she lectured herself about the dangers of letting Dr. Max Travers get too close, and a hundred times she assured herself that she was only treating him like a family friend.

Late Wednesday afternoon, however, Sophy had cause to wish she had heeded her own lecture. She glanced up at a quarter to five as Max came toward her desk with a stack of papers and an intense, preoccupied air.

"Sophy, I hate to ask this, but I've got to have these done by eight tomorrow morning." He wasn't looking at her, rather at the notes in his hand, so he missed Sophy's horrified expression.

"Max! It's almost five o'clock! I can't possibly get those typed up today!"

"It's okay," he assured her absently as he arranged the papers on her desk. "I'm allowed to authorize overtime for you."

Sophy felt a wave of panic. "Max, I don't want any overtime. Not tonight. I've got a date with Nick. You know that. Maybe someone else…"

Max met her eyes very steadily across the width of the desk, and Sophy was startled by the cool, calculating expression in the depths of his smoky gaze. "Sophy, you know none of the other secretaries can handle this tonight. You're the only one with the vocabulary and the scientific background to get through this in an evening. Besides, you're the one who's been working on this project all along. It will take any of the others a couple of days to get up to speed, and I haven't got that much time." He tapped the folder on her desk with a pen he had removed from the pack in his shirt pocket.

"Max, I'm going out tonight. I just don't have the time. Maybe I could come in early tomorrow," she tried desperately. She was feeling trapped. For some reason it seemed absolutely imperative that she see Nick tonight. She needed to reassure herself about her relationship with him.

Sophy realized in a blinding flash of perception that she badly needed Nick Savage tonight as an antidote to Dr. Maximilian Travers.

Max shook his head at her suggestion. "I need the report typed up first thing in the morning for a meeting with S & J management. Don't make me pull rank, Sophy."

Rage swept through her. Sophy's chin came up and her eyes flashed with warning. "Rank, Dr. Travers? Exactly what kind of threat are you making?" Damn him!

Max leaned forward with an aggressiveness Sophy had not yet seen in him. His palms were spread flat on the desk, and it struck her that he had rather large, strong hands for an academician. Dangerous hands.

"Miss Bennet, may I remind you of what it's costing your company per day to engage my services? Your boss would not be pleased to have to pay for even one unnecessary day. When he discovered that that delay had been caused by the intransigence of one of his secretaries, I think he would be downright furious, don't you?"

Sophy went very still, watching him with bitter eyes. Max was absolutely right about her boss's reaction. Frank Williams would be thoroughly angered if he thought her stubbornness had cost an extra day of Max's expensive time. He'd catch hell from his boss, and she'd probably wind up being the scapegoat.

And right at the moment, Sophy knew, she couldn't afford to lose her job. Too many of her future plans depended on the income.

But there was more involved here than her personal plans for the dress boutique and her association with Nick. Max was making it abundantly clear that on this level, at least, she was more or less in his power. And that thought alarmed her more than any other aspect of the situation. Instinctively she knew she should be putting as much distance between herself and Max as possible, not allowing herself to slip into such untenable situations as this one. But for the life of her, she couldn't see a way out. She took refuge in sarcasm.

"Ah, Dr. Travers, how quickly the facade of the gentle professor disappears. Give me your precious report. You'll have it by eight tomorrow."

Max's mouth twisted. "Sophy…"

"If that's an apology hovering on your lips, let's just forget about it, shall we, Dr. Travers? I'm not really all that surprised at the use of the threat, you know. I've known all my life that, in the pursuit of their goals, wizards have a way of not letting anyone or anything stand in their path. They have some notion that they are the elite and the rest of us should be only too happy to serve. My parents could be absolute tyrants when the occasion demanded."

"Sophy," Max tried again, "I'm sorry the occasion demanded I play the tyrant."

"I understand, Dr. Travers. And I'm sure you'll understand when I say that something has arisen which will make it impossible for me to have lunch with you tomorrow." It was a poor retaliation, but it was all she could manage on such short notice.

"What has arisen?" he shot back, eyes narrowing.

"Your academic arrogance. Excuse me, I'd better get started on these notes right away."

Damn it to hell, Sophy seethed as she began to work. Now she had to call Nick. He wasn't going to appreciate this. And she didn't want him mad at her. Not now. It was so important that he provide her with some reassuring evidence that she couldn't possibly have begun to fall for anyone as arrogant and as out of her world as Dr. Max Travers.

CHAPTER THREE

HE *HAD* BEEN ARROGANT, Max admitted to himself an hour later as he carried a paper sack full of hamburgers and french fries and coffee up in the elevator to Sophy's floor.

Incredibly arrogant.

Sophy herself didn't even appreciate the full extent of his arrogance! He had deliberately set out to sabotage her date with the cowboy, and if she ever learned the truth there would be hell to pay. Much better to have her thinking he was simply pulling rank in order to get his project done.

For all the good it had done him.

Look at the price he was paying, Max chided himself. She'd canceled their lunch date tomorrow! But the convenient necessity of needing those notes typed up into a full-fledged report had seemed too good an opportunity to pass up.

Would she condescend to share the hamburgers with him? Since he was out to lunch tomorrow, and since she had flatly refused to consider a break for dinner tonight, Max hadn't been able to think of any way to get a meal with her other than to bring in the fast food.

This evening was his one chance with Sophy, and he couldn't afford not to take advantage of it. He hoped the damned cowboy was frustrated as hell.

As he opened the door into the office, which was empty except for Sophy, Max braced himself for more of the ice treatment. He took a deep breath as she swung coldly accusing eyes on him for a fraction of a second and then returned to her work. She had been working with single-mindedness determination since she'd surrendered to his threat. Max's mouth hardened at the memory of how he had forced her to spend the evening with him. Then, for a moment, he simply drank in the sight of her, letting the pleasure of seeing her push out the uncertainties and feelings of guilt. What was it about Sophy that had attracted him from the first?

As usual, she made a vibrant splash of color against the subdued, neutral shades of the office decor. The curling mass of her hair was pulled back above her ears with wide yellow combs. Her outfit was a racy little yellow coatdress with lapels and cuffs in royal blue. Her narrow waist was cinched with a wide belt of blue leather trimmed with silver. As vivid as she was, Max was all too well aware that the attraction she held for him went far deeper than her appearance.

He was trained to see beneath the surface of things, but always before he had used that training in the realm of mathematics. With Sophy he wanted to use those skills in a new way. He wanted to know her completely. He wanted to secure her inner warmth and captivating *aliveness* for himself. Seeing her safely stuck behind the desk instead of dashing off to meet her cowboy gave him a feeling of untold satisfaction. Let tomorrow take care of itself. Tonight he had hours ahead with Sophy.

"I brought some hamburgers," he said on a determined note. She had to eat something, didn't she? "Since you insist on working through dinner, I feel obliged to make sure you get fed."

"Your consideration leaves me positively breathless, Dr. Travers." But she paused long enough to glance inside the sack. Then, to Max's relief, she withdrew a packet of french fries and began munching. Cautiously he sat down on the other side of her desk and reached for a burger.

"You can proofread the first section in a minute," she remarked shortly.

There was a long silence. "Was your cowboy very angry?" It was stupid to bring Nick Savage into the discussion, but Max suddenly had to know what the other man's reaction had been to the broken date.

"He wasn't thrilled."

Good, thought Max. Aloud he said, "I imagine he understands about the demands of your work."

There was another painful silence. When she failed to respond to the remark, Max decided to take the offensive. "Sophy, about our lunch date tomorrow…"

Her swivel chair swung around and she fixed him with a frozen glare. "Max, if you want this report done on time, you'll have to shut up and let me work. That was the whole point of the enforced overtime, wasn't it? To get this damn report out?"

He stifled a sigh and glanced down at what she had accomplished so far. "It looks like you're making good progress."

"I am." She swung the chair back around and returned to work.

"Well, in that case, we'll be able to knock off early and have a drink."

"My intention is to finish early and try to get to the party you forced me to miss this evening!"

Max froze. Damn it to hell. "Is your cowboy expecting you?"

"I'm going to surprise him. He said he was going to go anyway."

"I see. Sophy—"

"Shut up, Max, or you can damn well type this up yourself!"

"I don't know how to type," he retorted.

"Figures. I always thought they overlooked a few useful items in the education of wizards. I didn't get anything as useful as typing until I went off to college! Probably never let you waste much time playing with crayons, either, did they?"

"Well, no," Max replied bemusedly, "they didn't. I wasn't much interested in crayons, to tell you the truth. Why do you ask?"

"Never mind. Let me work."

Max hesitated a few minutes longer and then made his decision. It was time he met Nick Savage. "When you're done I'll drive you to the party," he stated gruffly. In that moment he couldn't have said exactly what made him want to see Sophy's lover. Max only knew that he had to find out what the other man was like. What did it take to attract Sophia Athena Bennet?

"That's not necessary, thank you," she said briskly.

"I don't want you taking the bus so late at night."

She glanced up in momentary surprise. "How did you know I took the bus this morning?"

"I, uh, just happened to see you come into work," he muttered, not meeting her eyes. Not for the world would he admit that when she came to work he was always standing at his office window, like a kid with his nose pressed to the candy store window.

"Well, don't worry. I've ridden the bus before at night," she assured him coolly.

"Sophy, I said I'll drive you to the party and that's final!" Was that him losing his temper? Good God!

She narrowed her eyes as if assessing his temper. "Oh,

all right, if it will make you happy. Anything to keep the expensive consultant in a good mood."

Max found himself torn between wanting to beat her and wanting to drag her down onto the floor and cover her body with his own. It was a bewildering and unfair tangle of emotions, and it clouded his normally very logical mind in an unfamiliar fashion.

By ten o'clock he could think of no further excuse to delay the inevitable. The report had been completed and proofed. It was perfect, and he knew Sophy was well aware of that fact. Time to meet the cowboy.

"I'll just freshen up in the ladies' room and then I'll be ready to go," Sophy said as she started for the door.

Max nodded bleakly behind her, watching as she disappeared down the hall. He did not want to turn her over to Nick Savage tonight, he realized. He wanted to take Sophy Bennet back to his hotel room and keep her there with him.

MAX'S MOOD BECAME increasingly grim as he followed Sophy's chatty directions to one of the exclusive homes in the northern area of Dallas. Her mood was lightening in an inverse ratio to his own heavy frame of mind, he realized in disgust. She was looking forward to being with her cowboy.

"I'd like to come in with you and meet this guy," Max announced as he parked the Ford at the end of a long line of Lincolns, Cadillacs and Mercedeses.

"I don't see why you should want to meet Nick," Sophy began as she stepped out of the car.

"Curiosity," he told her flatly. "Put it down to sheer curiosity. Besides, if I like him I can always mention that to your parents. It might help them adjust to the shock of having a cowboy for a son-in-law." There was no way on earth he was going to like Nick Savage, of course, but Max saw no reason to mention that fact to Sophy, who was already watching him a bit warily.

"Well, I suppose there's no harm, but Max, there must be nearly two hundred people at this party tonight. It's going to take a while to find him in the crowd."

"I'll help you look," Max said smoothly, resisting the urge to say that the search might be difficult for him due to the fact that all cowboys looked alike.

"Oh, all right, if you insist," she muttered, too eager to find Nick to waste time arguing.

The party had clearly progressed beyond dinner to the steady drinking stage. Max and Sophy were virtually ignored as they came through the door. Max glanced around uneasily. Stetson hats, flared trousers and leather boots were everywhere. The crowd was lively, raucous and well on its way to a hangover.

"He said he was going to be here," Sophy muttered above the din. "The Everets are good friends of his."

Max watch her expressive profile as she searched the room. It would be nice to have Sophy search that earnestly for him, he thought grimly. That fantasy led to other, more fundamental fantasies, and he found himself disliking all cowboys intensely.

"A lot of people seem to have drifted out onto the back patio," Sophy said abruptly. "Let's try there."

With a sense of mounting irritation, Max followed as she cut a bright swath through the crowd. By the time he caught up with her again she had reached the flagstoned area at the rear of the house. The soft glow of lights from artfully styled lanterns illuminated a scene that seemed as crowded as the living room had been. Sophy singled out an elderly-looking man and got his polite attention at once.

"Nick Savage?" Max heard him say. "Thought I saw

him a while ago with…" The elderly cowboy frowned and broke off hurriedly. "Uh, he was heading toward the pool, little lady. Yes, I do believe he was heading toward the pool." The man glanced up and sent Max a straight look. "You with this little lady here?"

"Yes I am," Max said firmly, ignoring Sophy's irritation.

"Well, then, I reckon that's okay, isn't it?" the other man said, clearly relaxing. "Yup, I think you might find Nick out by the pool." He winked at Max. "Might be a good idea to let him have a bit more time to himself, if you catch my drift."

Max heard the hint of warning in the stranger's voice, but Sophy appeared oblivious. She was already dragging him off toward the shadowy area round the huge, curving pool.

"Sophy…" Max started, and then stopped abruptly. A part of him instinctively wanted to urge caution, but another, more aggressive side wanted Sophy to push ahead and discover the possibly appalling truth. If he had understood what the older man had been trying to say, Max had a strong suspicion as to what Nick Savage was doing out by the pool. With a little luck the damn cowboy might obligingly condemn himself in Sophy's eyes.

"I don't see anyone," she complained as she hurried around the edge of the pool toward a row of shadowed cabanas. Then she stopped so suddenly Max nearly collided with her. An instant later he heard the soft sound. It was the unmistakable voice of a woman followed by the husky laughter of a man, and it emanated from the nearest cabana.

Before either of them could respond, the door of the cabana opened and Max looked up to see a man emerge, the same man who had emerged from the Lincoln the night he had taken Sophy home. Nick Savage had a pleased grin on his face, and he was just fastening his pants. In the moonlight the huge silver buckle of his belt gleamed obscenely.

"Nick." Sophy looked absolutely stricken. She stood staring at the man, who appeared nearly as startled. As they faced each other, a woman emerged from the cabana. She was blond and beautiful and still getting dressed.

The four people involved in the dramatic tableau simply stared at each other for an endless moment. Max knew a shattering, wholly elemental satisfaction as the full ramifications of the scene came home to him. Nick Savage had been making love to the blond.

But even as he realized just how thoroughly the cowboy had compromised himself, Max was aware of a fierce desire to protect Sophy. He caught her wrist and pulled her back toward him. "Let's get out of here, Sophy," he growled.

"No!"

He heard the feminine shock and fury that underlined the single word.

"You bastard, Nick! You lying, cheating *bastard!* How could you do this to me? How dare you?"

Nick finally moved, disengaging himself from the blond, who had caught hold of his arm with a possessive grip. "Sophy, wait!"

"Friends of yours, Nicky dear?" the blond inquired with commendable aplomb as she adjusted her blouse. She ran a hand through her long hair. "I thought this was a private party. Just you and me." Deliberately she smiled.

Nick swore furiously, striding forward as if he would catch hold of Sophy. Max moved, yanking Sophy out of reach. She turned to him with a pleading, desperate look on her face.

"Max, please," she whispered raggedly. "Please take me home."

He didn't hesitate. "This way, Sophy." With sudden decision he tugged her around the pool, leaving the cowboy and his friend behind. Sophy followed mutely, seemingly grateful to have him take charge. She was still in shock, Max thought worriedly. Gently he helped her into the front seat of the Ford and then he slid in beside her, switching on the ignition. Was she all right? She looked so pale and frozen in the moonlight.

He guided the car down the winding drive to the road and started back toward downtown Dallas. If Sophy noticed she wasn't being driven home, she didn't seem to care. Max glanced at her stark, set profile. Was she furious or overwhelmed with grief? He hoped to God it was fury she was feeling.

"Sophy, I'm sorry you had to go through that scene back there."

"I thought he loved me, Max." She sounded so stricken; so listless. Max decided he could cheerfully strangle the cowboy. And then he thought about how Nick Savage had just ruined himself in Sophy's eyes.

"Maybe he does love you, Sophy. In his own way. Some men aren't very good at being faithful." What a bunch of bull that was, he told himself wryly. But he felt obliged to say something.

Her small hand doubled into a fist in her lap. "I could kill him."

"That makes two of us," Max muttered half under his breath.

"I trusted him, Max. I believed him when he said there was no one else. He's been making a complete fool out of me. What a stupid little idiot I've been."

Max didn't know what to say to that. In a way, he decided, she was absolutely right. Damned cowboy. "You need a drink," he stated.

"Several of them, I think. Oh, God, Max, this has got to be one of the most humiliating moments of my entire life!"

She said nothing more as he completed the drive to the hotel. He saw her blank, uncaring glance take in the fact that he was taking her to a lounge and not to her own home, and then she seemed to lose interest completely in her surroundings. Max was torn. On the one hand, he wanted to comfort her, but on the other he found himself aching to seize the opportunity! *The cowboy was no longer in the way.*

The cowboy was no longer in the way, he repeated to himself as he gently guided Sophy into the darkened lounge and seated her in a private corner. There he ordered drinks and watched as Sophy took great gulps of her Manhattan.

Never again, he told himself, would he be given the chance of getting this close to Sophia Athena Bennet. When she recovered her normal poise, she would once again put leagues of distance between them. But tonight she seemed to need him. Max sipped his drink patiently and waited.

"I don't understand it," Sophy finally mumbled sadly. "How could he do that to me? I thought we were building something. Something important. Oh, Max, I thought he was falling in love with me. I thought he wanted me."

Careful, Max told himself, don't come on too strong, or she'll turn the anger on you. Just be supportive. "I don't know why he would do it, Sophy. He doesn't deserve you, that's obvious. Probably thought he could have his cake and eat it, too."

She took another swallow of the Manhattan and stared at him over the rim, blue-green eyes huge and vulnerable. Max wanted to pull her into his arms to comfort her but didn't quite dare. Not yet.

"I could kill him," she repeated a bit violently.

"The thing to do," Max found the daring to advise, "is

not waste another thought on him. There are other men, Sophy. Men who will appreciate you."

"All men are probably alike," she sniffed wretchedly.

"Sophy, you're smart enough to know that's not true."

"I don't feel smart at all at the moment. I feel as dumb as I used to feel back in school!"

"Feeling sorry for yourself?" he chided carefully.

"Yes, dammit!"

"Okay, okay," he soothed at once. "You're entitled, God knows. I hate to see you wasting any more emotion on that creep. You're too good for him. You deserve someone who appreciates you!"

"Such as?" she challenged morosely.

Max sucked in his breath, watching her intently. "Such as me, Sophy."

"You!" She drew back, eyes widening. For a moment Max could have sworn he saw genuine, feminine panic in that bottomless gaze. Panic? Over him?

"I think you're the most fascinating woman I've ever met, Sophy." And that was no less than the truth, he realized.

She eyed him across the table, her expressive face revealing an indefinable emotion. What the hell was she thinking? He shouldn't have pushed so fast, Max admonished himself.

"It's very kind of you to try to make me feel better," she finally said in a small voice.

"Sophy, I'm not…"

"Could I have another drink, please?" she inquired with what sounded suspiciously like a sniffle.

He ordered, and they sat in silence while she sipped the second Manhattan a little more slowly than the first.

"It's sweet of you to be concerned, Max," she said at last in a polite little voice, "but I'll be all right, really I will. I feel like a fool at the moment, but I'm quite capable of looking after myself."

"Are you?"

"Oh, yes. We average types are really much better at handling the day-to-day shocks of life than you sheltered, ivory-tower geniuses. It's because you spend all your time wrapped up in your intellectual pursuits. People like you never learn about the emotional side of life." She paused. "Maybe you're lucky."

"Because the emotional side of life can be painful?" he queried softly.

Her eyes glistened with unshed tears, and Max wanted to put his arms around her and let her cry out the pain she was clearly feeling.

"Yes," she whispered tightly. "Very painful. Oh, *Max...*"

He got to his feet at once and pulled her gently up beside him, holding her close with one arm while he signed the tab. "It's okay, Sophy," he murmured as he led her through the lobby. "It's okay, honey. Go ahead and cry. Get it out of your system. Then maybe you can start to forget him."

He kept up the soft monologue all during the ride in the elevator and the walk down the hall to his room. She clung to him and he took a strange, unfamiliar satisfaction in that. Sophy said nothing until he was turning the key in the door. Then she sniffed and moved restlessly within the curve of his arm.

"I should be getting home," she whispered a little dazedly, dashing the back of her hand across her eyes. "It's very nice of you to spend so much time with me, but..." The words trailed off on a small sob. "Maybe if I could wash my face?" She glanced up at him pleadingly.

"Right through there," Max said, inclining his head toward the bathroom door. God help him, his fingers were trembling. This was the first time he'd ever held her close, he thought. He watched her walk slowly across the room toward the bath. His hands were actually shaking!

She was here, right here in his hotel room. Now what?

Was she aware of where she was? Did she care? She couldn't be drunk, not after only two drinks. But she was, perhaps, a bit drunk on her own humiliation and anger, he told himself.

It wouldn't be fair to take advantage of her under the present circumstances.

Not fair at all. Not the act of a gentleman and a scholar.

She was feeling lost and hurt and miserable and she was very, very vulnerable, Max told himself grimly. Damn it to hell, what was he thinking of doing? Taking advantage of Sophia Athena? Daughter of Paul and Anna Bennet? God forbid.

He'd probably get no further than trying to kiss her, he told himself angrily as he stalked across the room to find the bottle of complimentary champagne that the hotel had sent up when he'd arrived. It was where he had stuck it, safely stored in the small refrigerator. Moodily he removed it and began to open it.

She'd probably turn all her fury and pain on him if he even so much as tried to take her in his arms and kiss her. He poured the champagne.

But she was so weak and vulnerable right now. She might not realize his intentions until it was far too late. The champagne tasted strange. He glared down at the bubbling stuff in the glass in his hand. Simultaneously he heard the sound of running water from the bath. How long would she be in there? Max wondered. He tried another sip of the drink and stared at his reflection in the mirror.

He didn't look anything like a cowboy, and Sophia preferred cowboys. Or she had until tonight, he reminded himself savagely. Then Max groaned. He wasn't likely ever to get another chance with Sophy Bennet and he knew it. Never again would he have her all to himself in a hotel room. Never again was he likely to find himself cast in the role of comforter.

What if he abused the unique position in which he found himself tonight? What if he actually managed to get her into bed? His palms went abruptly damp.

"She'd hate my guts in the morning," he told his reflection with grim certainty. *God help him, he wanted her.*

Max winced and turned away from the too-revealing mirror. She'd hate him even more than she hated that cowboy.

But he'd never get another chance like this. Max was so certain of that. If he didn't take advantage of the situation, he'd never know what it was like to make love to the most intriguing woman he'd ever met. He'd never wanted a woman so badly in his life. What in hell was the matter with him?

His fingers tightened around the stem of the champagne glass. How could he make himself walk away now from the glittering temptation that had been put in his path? God help him, he was only a man, regardless of how often she called him a wizard.

Was having Sophy tonight worth the risks of incurring her fury in the morning?

Damn it, the answer was yes. He downed the last of the champagne, staring out the window with unseeing eyes. What if he could make it so good for her that she wouldn't remember their time together with rage? What if he managed to show her just how much he needed her? There was a streak of compassion in her, a gentleness that might temper her anger. If she realized how much he needed her, perhaps she would be kind to him in the morning. Perhaps she would stay with him....

The door to the bathroom opened on that dangerously tantalizing thought. He turned abruptly to find Sophy framed in the doorway. She looked so miserable and bleak. And it was all that stupid cowboy's fault.

"I could kill him."

"What?" She glanced at him in confusion, and Max realized he'd spoken aloud. He shook his head and walked stiffly across the room to put a glass of champagne in her hand.

"I said I could kill him. Except that he's not worth the trouble. Sophy, you're better off without him. You'll realize that eventually."

"I suppose you're right." Wistfully she took the champagne and sat down on the edge of the bed, smiling wanly. "It's just so hard to admit how stupid I've been. I *trusted* him, Max."

"You weren't stupid." He sat down carefully beside her and put his arm around her. She accepted the proffered comfort, leaning her head against his shoulder. "You thought you were in love and you thought he loved you."

"It could have been worse," Sophy mumbled, sipping the champagne.

"Worse?"

"I think I would have felt even worse if...if Nick and I had been lovers," she mumbled into the glass.

Max stifled a surge of satisfaction, barely managing to keep his tone neutral. "You mean you weren't sleeping with him?"

She shook her head. "Maybe that's why he turned to that blond," she chastised herself. "Maybe I shouldn't have kept him waiting."

"Sophy, you mustn't blame yourself."

"But I…"

Max cut off the self-castigating flow of words with his fingers on her lips. "No. Sophy, he's the one who cheated on you. None of this is your fault. You're the wronged party in this mess. Remember that."

Her wide blue-green eyes stared at him as he continued to press her mouth gently with his hand. Was that a flicker of awareness he saw in her gaze? Was it possible she might want him just a little?

"Oh, God, Sophy…"

On a low groan of barely controlled need, he removed the glass from her hand.

"Max? Max, I'm not sure…"

"Hush, Sophy. Don't think about anything. Just relax and let me comfort you. Please, honey. It's all I want to do." It was the truth and it was a lie and Max didn't know how to explain it.

Slowly, half-afraid she might disappear in his grasp if he moved too quickly, Max lowered his mouth to feather her parted lips with his own. She didn't move as he made exquisitely exciting contact. He felt the tiny tremor that went through her, however, and somehow it fueled his own carefully contained desire. At least she wasn't totally indifferent to him, he thought exultantly.

"Relax, Sophy, just relax. Let me hold you until you forget him." He didn't know where the soothing words were coming from. They seemed half-instinctive, the calming, gentling words men had used from the beginning of time to tame nervous women.

She tensed as he drew her slowly backward onto the quilted bedspread. He sensed she was about to resist and he didn't know what else to do except chain her with another kiss. His mouth closed more deliberately over hers and he heard a faint moan from far back in her throat. The sound made the urgent longing in him all the more insistent. A part of her did want him, damn it!

"Max, no, I don't…" Her head shifted restlessly on the quilt as she freed her mouth.

"I always seem to find myself looking for ways to shut you up," he muttered hoarsely, yanking off his glasses and tossing them heedlessly onto the nightstand. For a second he stared down at her, glorying in the knowledge that there was a tiny, faltering flame in her now. She trembled again as she met his gaze, and with a rasping exclamation Max lowered his head to plunge his tongue deeply into her mouth.

Instinctively he used his weight to pin her more securely to the quilt. Her slender body was still stiff and uncertain beneath him, but he could feel the thrusting softness of her breasts. She felt so good lying there under him. He pushed his lower body strongly against her thighs, seeking to let her know the extent of his own arousal.

"Max!" It was a soft cry, torn from her when he freed her mouth temporarily to explore the sensitive place behind her ear.

"Hush, Sophy. Just relax and trust me tonight. I'll take care of you. I'll make you forget him. By morning you'll only think of me, I swear it."

CHAPTER FOUR

SOPHY'S SENSES SEEMED TO be spinning. Not in a mad, frightening whirl, but in a deliciously intriguing manner. Everything was suddenly right. The moment Max had taken her in his arms, everything had become right.

The restless uncertainty, the attraction she had been experiencing, the indefinable aura about Max that made her so totally aware of him were suddenly explained. Fully explained.

She wanted him.

The realization was too startling to deal with on an intellectual level tonight. Sophy wanted only to give herself up to the sweeping feelings of the moment. Her emotions felt raw, and Max's arms promised soothing safety. There would be time enough in the morning to consider what she was doing.

With a sigh of longing that had been suppressed since she had first set eyes on Max Travers, Sophy pushed aside all thoughts of the future and surrendered to the wonder of the moment.

This was what had been missing all along in her relationship with Nick Savage: this marvelous *rightness,* this sensation of need and the promise of shared satisfaction. This soft, sweet longing was a totally new and unexplored element in her life, and it was all bound up with Max Travers. In that moment Sophy was absolutely certain the emotions she was experiencing could not exist without Max as their focus.

It made no sense and yet it made all the sense in the world.

Sophy sighed against Max's mouth, a sensation of thrilling languor flowing through her. Her leg moved slightly on the bedspread, and Max's thigh covered it, pressing down firmly, trapping it.

"I want to be your lover tonight, Sophy. I want to hold you and make you forget that damned cowboy," Max growled against the skin of her throat.

"I don't want to think about him," she agreed fervently, sinking her fingertips into the dark brown depths of his hair. "You're the only one I seem to be able to think about at the moment." She heard him draw in his breath quite sharply and knew a distinct sense of satisfaction. He wanted her. Max wanted her as much as she wanted him.

"That cowboy is a fool!"

"Oh, Max…"

"Any man who would risk losing you just for the sake of a quickie at a party has got to be a fool."

"Please, Max. I don't want to talk about him."

Max cradled her in one arm as he stretched out slowly beside her on the bed. His other hand began to move with sureness and wonder on her body. The soothing words he murmured contained a tense urgency, a sense of demand that was at once wholly masculine and completely enthralling.

"Let me touch you, darling. Sophy, honey, you feel so good under my hands. So very good."

Sophy shifted restlessly, closing her eyes as her body warmed under his touch. When Max buried his lips in her throat, letting her feel the edge of his teeth, she shivered.

"Sophy! Sophy, I want you. I need you tonight. I have

to keep you here with me." He shaped her breast with exploring fingers and she whispered his name.

"Max...I feel so strange. I've never felt like this before. Oh, Max, what have you done to me?" Sophy asked wonderingly. Her arms went around him almost convulsively.

"Ah, sweetheart, you're so warm and soft and vibrant. You're all the colors of the rainbow. Did you know that? All the colors that have been missing in my life. I want to see you shimmer in my arms. I want to make you even more alive than you already are!" Max groaned again, his voice raw and husky. He found the buckle of the wide blue leather belt and undid it with deliberate movements.

Sophy could feel his body straining against hers as he slowly, carefully undressed her. The full, waiting male power of him was electrifying. As the yellow dress fell aside, he curved his hand around her buttocks and pulled her tightly against him. Sophy shuddered in helpless response.

"Feel how much I want you," he grated.

Her nails dug into the strongly contoured muscles of his back, and she found herself pressing closer, inhaling the satisfying scent of his body. The yellow dress seemed to have disappeared of its own accord, and a moment later the lacy little bra went the same route. All she wore now was a small triangle of satin.

"You're so incredibly exciting," Max growled in wonder as he bent his head to kiss her breast. "Just looking at you across a room is exciting. But having you here in my bed is almost unbelievable."

"Oh!" Sophy flinched in thrilling reaction as he drew her sensitized nipple into his mouth. Tiny shivers of pleasure pulsated through her, and she began to murmur his name over and over again. The nipple hardened at once beneath the compelling touch of his rasping tongue.

"So responsive," he breathed. "You must want me, Sophy. Please say you want me."

"Yes, Max," she whispered obediently. "I want you."

His palm was gliding down the warm skin of her stomach, and she writhed under the touch with the uninhibited pleasure of a cat being stroked. The prowling, tantalizing fingers slid down her thigh and up along the silken inside to the point where the satin underpanties barred his path. Sophy's knee flexed convulsively, her toes curling tightly.

"You're safe here with me, sweetheart," he murmured as he slipped his finger under the elasticized edge of the panties and began to touch her in the most thrilling manner. The patterns he wove at the center of her softness made her cry out in wonder and delight.

"Please, Max. Please…"

The urge to touch him more intimately came upon her in a rush, and suddenly Sophy was pulling at the knot of his narrow tie, yanking at the buttons of his shirt and fumbling with the buckle of his belt.

"Yes, darling, yes," he muttered, shrugging out of the shirt. He caught her fluttering hands when she would have paused to explore the expanse of his hair-roughened chest. "Finish undressing me, honey."

Sophy did as he demanded and a moment later he lay beside her, totally nude. She gasped with pleasure and flexed her fingers like tiny claws against the bronzed skin of his sleek body.

"God, Sophy, I feel like I'm burning up."

"Oh, Max, you're so…so…" She couldn't take her eyes off his aroused, utterly masculine body.

"So what?" he taunted softly with a shaky laugh. "So desperate for you? So full of aching desire that I hurt? I am, darling. Only you can give me any relief tonight. I've been wanting you since the first moment I saw you. I've never known such a hunger for a woman. You've got to satisfy me or I'll go out of my head. I can't wait any longer for you."

He sprawled suddenly across her with undeniable intent, forcing her thighs apart with his own. His hands closed over her shoulders, anchoring her firmly beneath him, and he lay looking down at her with a fire blazing in his eyes.

"Max, wait…" Too late Sophy realized it had all gone too far. Everything was spinning out of control. Her body was filled with sensual longing and her head was filled only with the desire to respond to Max's urgent demands.

"No, darling, I can't wait," he gritted with unexpected savagery as he covered her. "If I wait, I'll lose you." He blocked the words in her mouth with his lips and then he moved aggressively against her.

He was so heavy, Sophy thought. Heavy and hard and irresistible. God, how she wanted him. Her own body was shivering with reaction and desire.

"Put your arms around me and hold on to me," he ordered thickly. "I'll keep you safe, Sophy. Just hold on to me."

Blindly she obeyed, clinging to him as if he were her only source of security, even as a part of her dimly recognized that he was really the source of a threat unlike any she had ever known. Then he forged into her damp, heated softness, bringing a breathless cry of surrender into her throat. Greedily he swallowed the small sound. For a moment they both lay locked together in a kind of shock at the completeness of the union. Then slowly, powerfully, Max began to move.

Sophy was utterly lost. Never had she known such exquisite, almost terrifying passion. It captivated and compelled and controlled. She could no more have escaped it now than she could have stopped the earth in its orbit. Max held her, taking everything she had to give and rewarding her with the gift of himself. It was unbelievably primitive, an act of fire and passion, and it came to an end in a shivering culmination that had Sophy's nails leaving small wounds on Max's back. Her whole body tightened with the exploding release, and even as she gave herself up to it, Sophy heard Max's shout of heady satisfaction as he followed her over the edge.

For long, endless moments Sophy allowed herself to drift on the outgoing tide of passion. Vaguely aware of the warmth of Max's perspiration-damp body, she listened to the sound of his breathing as it settled back into a normal pattern. His thigh still sprawled across her legs, holding her immobile.

She didn't want to open her eyes, she realized. She wanted only to go on drifting forever in this pleasant, safe realm where reality could not reach her.

"Go to sleep, Sophy," Max drawled in her ear. "Just relax and go to sleep. We can talk it all out in the morning."

The command fit in very well with her own desire to avoid the reality of what had happened. Sophy closed her eyes and obeyed.

It was a faint sound in the hall outside the room that awakened her several hours later. For a moment Sophy lay perfectly still, trying to orient herself, and then she became violently aware of Max's hard thigh lying alongside her own soft one. Her head turned on the pillow to stare at his shadowed face. He was sound asleep.

The sound outside in the hallway registered. It was merely the scraping of a key in the lock of the room next door.

My God, Sophy thought, sitting up slowly. *What have I done?*

She stared down at herself as the sheet fell aside, and she knew a sense of shock at her own nakedness. How could she have been so weak? Nervously she looked down at Max's bare chest as he lay sprawled on his back.

He lay beside her like some ancient conquering hero. There was an arrogance in the lean, sleek lines of his body that she had never noticed before. But that was because she had always seen him in the camouflage of his academic uniform, Sophy thought on a note of hysteria. He had used the old-fashioned white shirt, the little nerd pack, the glasses and the corduroy trousers to get close to her the way a hunter stalks his prey in camouflaged clothing.

Maximilian Travers had promised comfort and given her passion instead.

Even with Nick Savage, Sophy thought grimly, she hadn't been so stupid.

But she had always lost out to wizards. All her life she had been unable to hold her own against them. This time was no different, except that a part of her had always felt that this was an area of life in which wizards would never be a threat.

Sophy's hands clenched in small fists as she continued to stare down at Max. She had to get out of there. Max was everything he had no right to be: strong, virile, dominant. And brilliant. She must get away from him as quickly as possible.

The damned wizard had deliberately taken advantage of her, Sophy told herself ruthlessly as she pushed aside the sheet and slid off the bed. Yes, that was what had happened. He had used her. Taken advantage of her emotional vulnerability last night. She was torn between a fierce desire to pound him with her hands and the equally strong desire to flee.

She elected flight.

With painful caution Sophy searched for her clothing, scrambling awkwardly into her underwear and the yellow coatdress. She found her shoes under the bed. In the end she couldn't find her belt, however, and she didn't want to waste any more time searching for it. She dressed hurriedly, her only goal to escape from the scene of her stupidity. No, damn it! Not stupidity. *Vulnerability.* It was her own vulnerability that had gotten her into this situation.

After running a hand through her heavy, tangled curls, Sophy checked for her small purse and then headed for the door. It was almost five o'clock according to the digital clock beside the bed. To her great relief, Max didn't stir as she let herself out into the hall. Cautiously, knowing she couldn't bear to face him at that moment, she shut the door behind her and hurried downstairs to find a cab.

Max watched her leave through slitted eyes. There was no point in calling out to her. She was running away from him.

"Hell," he muttered in the darkness as the door closed softly behind her. "Damn it to hell." She hadn't even waited until morning to leave him. She probably hated him.

With a groan, he sat up in bed and switched on the bedside lamp. Almost instantly his eyes fell on the familiar outline of her wide leather belt. Reaching down, he picked it up and then pushed his glasses onto his nose. For a long moment he simply sat staring at it. Cinderella had left her calling card, but he didn't need to be told that she didn't view him as a prince.

Such a slender little waist, he thought, fingering the belt. And such beautiful, flaring thighs below that tiny waist. Darn it, his body was hardening just at the memory! Max stood up with a muttered groan. He had about as much chance of getting Sophy Bennet back in his bed as he did of flying to the moon. Less. Then his hand tightened on the belt. Hadn't he been just as pessimistic about his chances with Sophy before that cowboy had been so obligingly dumb?

And she *had* responded to him last night, Max reminded himself resolutely as he headed toward the bathroom. Responded, hell. That was putting it mildly. She had been like molten gold in his arms. Would she try to deny it if he confronted her with that fact this morning? Probably. Reminding her of how she had surrendered in his arms would not be a gentlemanly thing to do. But he had to convince her that there was something between them, and he could think of no other way.

ON THE OPPOSITE SIDE of town, Sophy dressed for work with equally grim intent. In her mind she planned wildly different strategies for dealing with Max Travers. No sense pretending she could avoid him. The company wasn't that large and he would probably seek her out, anyway. Would he gloat about her surrender?

A part of her wanted to rail at him like a wronged woman, but another part wanted to maintain some sense of dignity. After all, she was twenty-eight years old. Dignity was crucial. It was about all she had left.

Half an hour early, she made her way into the office wearing a pin-striped dress trimmed with white collar and cuffs. It was the most severely styled dress in her wardrobe, designed primarily for weddings and funerals. It gave her a sense of aloof arrogance, however, and she badly needed that this morning. There was no one else around, so she occupied herself with brewing coffee. She was watching it drip into the pot when the door opened and Max walked into the room.

For an instant Sophy just stared at him, terribly unprepared for the confrontation. It was too soon. She needed more time, she thought nervously. Max was back in his familiar clothing but it didn't help. Sophy knew she would never forget the man underneath those unthreatening garments. All the camouflage in the world wouldn't serve to hide Max Travers from her eyes now.

"Good morning, Max. Come for a cup of coffee?" Sophy forced a breezy little smile from out of nowhere. Damn it, she would not let herself be intimidated. She had stopped being intimidated by wizards years ago, and Sophy told herself she had no intention of going back to those feelings of intimidation now.

He walked steadily across the room until he was standing beside her. His smoky eyes watched her intently behind the shield of his glasses. "I could use a cup, yes, thank you."

"Here you go," she said briskly, pouring out two cups and handing him one. "All set to discuss your preliminary report with management?"

He blinked warily. "What report?"

"Oh, you remember, Max," she said very sweetly. "The one you kept me working on until nearly ten last night."

A slow stain of red spread across his cheeks. "Uh, yes. I'm ready."

"Good. I wouldn't want to think the *entire* evening had been a waste. Heaven knows a good chunk of it certainly was. Nice to know something was salvaged." Darn it! She would not allow him to revel in her reactions to him last night. She would make him think it meant nothing. Absolutely nothing.

"Sophy…"

"Yes, Max?"

"Sophy, about last night," he began decisively.

"Max, you're supposed to be a very bright man. I should think you'd have enough intelligence not to discuss last night." Her tone was one of mild amusement, and Sophy was proud of it. But her blue-green eyes were swirling with chilled fury.

Max's face hardened. "You know as well as I do that we can't ignore last night."

"Why not? It seems like an excellent idea to me!"

"Damn it, Sophy. Stop acting like a brittle little creature whose emotions don't run any deeper than icing on a cake!"

"How do you know that's not exactly how deep my emotions run?" she challenged tightly.

"Because you showed me how deep the passion runs in you last night. And if the passion is that deep, so are the rest of your emotions!" he suddenly blazed.

"Your degrees are in mathematics! Not amateur psychology!" she stormed. "All you saw in me last night was desire!"

"The hell I did," he ground out coldly. "You gave yourself completely last night, Sophy Bennet. You gave yourself to me. Surrendered to me. I know the difference between temporary desire and real passion."

"How could you? You're only a mathematician!"

His mouth crooked in a strange little smile that faded almost instantly. "You taught me the difference, Sophy. You have only yourself to blame."

"Don't you dare blame last night on me!" she cried. "You took advantage of me! I was feeling emotionally weak and vulnerable. I'd had a great shock. You were supposed to be a friend. You said you wanted to comfort me. I trusted you."

"Sophy, all of that may have been true up to a point…"

"Nice of you to take a little responsibility for what happened!"

"I take fully responsibility for what happened," he returned gently. "But that doesn't change the basic fact that you surrendered last night, sweetheart. You came to me with no reservations and you gave yourself completely. I've never had a woman give herself to me like that. And now that I've had you, you can't expect me to let you just walk away saying it was only a case of temporary attraction."

"That's all it was! And you had no right to take advantage of me! Hardly the action of a gentleman and a scholar!" she seethed, grasping at the only insult available.

"I know." He offered no excuses, no explanations. He just admitted it.

"Damn you!" Sophy lost her frail temper completely and flung the rapidly cooling contents of her coffee cup all over his white shirt and narrow nerd tie.

For an instant they stared at each other in ominous, shocked silence, and into that frozen setting walked Marcie Fremont. Her blue eyes widened briefly in surprise as she took in the highly charged scene.

"I'm sorry. Excuse me, please." Politely she turned to walk back out the door through which she had just entered, but Sophy reached it ahead of her, flinging it open and racing madly down the hall towards the ladies' room.

She was vaguely aware of Marcie staring after her in concerned astonishment and she thought she heard Max angrily calling her name, but Sophy didn't stop until she was safely behind the door of one of the few refuges allowed modern woman.

Instantly she began to regret her lack of self-control. Hastily she dabbed at her eyes with a damp paper towel. How could she have made such a fool of herself in front of Marcie? Marcie was always so perfectly controlled. The scene would undoubtedly be all over the office within an hour.

No, perhaps not. Marcie Fremont was not a gossip. She was too conscious of her professional image to lower herself to common office gossip. Thank heavens it had been Marcie who had walked in on that horrible confrontation with Max. If it had been Karen or Sandy or Steve or Peter, the rumor mill would already be humming.

The door to the restroom opened and Sophy glanced up.

"Are you all right?" Marcie Fremont asked seriously.

"Yes. Yes, I'm fine."

"I'm awfully sorry about walking in on you and Dr. Travers like that."

"You could hardly have known what was going on." Sophy smiled shakily.

"Dr. Travers said you were a little upset about something that happened last night. Anything I can do? Does it involve you and your friend Nick Savage?"

"It's all tied up in one big mess, but no, there's nothing you can do, Marcie." Sophy sighed.

"Dr. Travers seemed very concerned."

"He should be! It's all his fault!"

"I see." Marcie hesitated a moment, watching as Sophy finished dabbing at her eyes. "Look, you don't have to worry about my saying anything, Sophy."

Sophy smiled her gratitude. "Thank you, Marcie. It's very kind of you to be so discreet."

"Dr. Travers asked me to have you call him when you've, uh, recovered," Marcie added gently.

"Dr. Travers can wait until the sixth dimension freezes over before I call him about anything," Sophy hissed, her temper flaring. "The bastard. I thought Nick was a bastard. He could take lessons from Dr. Maximilian Travers. God, Marcie, right now I don't care if I never date another man again!" Taking a deep breath, Sophy shook back her curling mane and fixed a grim little smile on her face. "I guess I'd better get back to work. Thanks," she mumbled again in helpless gratitude for the other woman's support and discretion.

"If you're sure you're all right?"

"I'm madder than hell, but I'm all right."

Marcie relaxed with a faint smile. "I guess today is going to be a traumatic day for both of us, one way or another."

Sophy arched an eyebrow inquiringly. "Personnel is going to make the decision?"

Marcie nodded, her excitement barely suppressed. "I heard they were going to announce the name of the person who's going to get that job in Quality Control. Oh, Sophy, I'm so nervous…"

"Marcie, you know you're the most qualified person for that job. You've got your business administration degree, and you've been assisting Quality Control on all those special tasks since you arrived. You've got a real working knowledge of what they're doing down there in QC!"

"Well, we'll find out today if Personnel sees things that way!"

Both women walked back to the office with determined resolve. Max had had the sense to depart.

When he made the mistake of calling at ten o'clock, Sophy didn't even bother to return his cautious greeting.

"Sorry, wrong number," she said sweetly, and replaced the receiver. "Arrogant wizard," she muttered as she hung up.

Max called again at eleven and she repeated the action. When he tried again at twelve it was Marcie who answered the phone, and as soon as she made eye contact with Sophy, the blond said, "I'm sorry, Dr. Travers, she just stepped out for a few minutes. I'll tell her you called."

Max showed up in person, however, right after lunch, advancing on Sophy's desk with a determined expression and a file of notes in his hand.

"Some revisions to that report you did for me last night," he stated without giving her a chance to react verbally to his unwanted presence. "They came out of this morning's meeting."

"Nice of you not to bring them by at five and order me to stay late to finish them," Sophy observed coldly.

"I had a feeling you might not be interested in working overtime this evening," he admitted dryly.

"You're quite right. I worked far too much of it last night."

He frowned and leaned forward, apparently conscious of Marcie sitting nearby where she could overhear the conversation. "I'd like to talk to you. Privately."

"Go to hell, Dr. Travers," Sophy gritted with an artificial smile.

"I'll take you out to dinner tonight," he continued roughly.

"I'm afraid that's impossible. I have other plans."

"Don't give me that. I know damn well you don't have a date tonight."

"You're wrong, Dr. Travers," Sophy retorted as inspiration struck. "I'm having a drink with Marcie after work. Aren't I, Marcie? We're going to celebrate Marcie's new promotion." She turned in her swivel chair and looked at her co-worker, eyes pleading for support.

"If the promotion comes through, we'll be celebrating it," Marcie said quickly. "If not we'll be having a consolation drink."

Max glared at Sophy and then at Marcie. Both women met his look with bland smiles. He was beaten for the moment and he was wise enough to know it. He turned on his heel and stalked out of the office without another word. A long, charged silence hovered in his wake. Then Marcie spoke.

"I'd really be quite happy to have a drink with you, Sophy."

"Thank you. I have a hunch we'll both need it."

"Yes."

THE NEWS ABOUT THE promotion arrived just before five o'clock. It came in the form of a brief call from Personnel to Marcie. Even as Sophy watched her friend's face become closed and withdrawn, she knew what the verdict was. Marcie thanked the caller with distant politeness and hung up the phone, her eyes glacier cold and filled with anger and disappointment.

"Oh, Marcie…" Sophy began sympathetically, knowing how much the job had meant to the other woman.

"They gave it to Steve Cameron," Marcie whispered. "Steve Cameron. He doesn't even have a business degree. He hasn't had the experience I've had working on QC projects. His only recommendation for that job is that he's a man."

"They're fools to give it to him. That man is all self-hype and no genuine ability!" Sophy said with sudden, fierce loyalty to Marcie. "God, if there's one thing I learned to recognize at a tender age, it's real ability. Believe me, Cameron doesn't have it. Idiots!"

"Oh, God, Sophy. I was counting on that job. When I took this position in the secretarial pool they more or less promised me that it would only be temporary. It was understood it was only to last until something better came up for which I was qualified! And I was qualified for that promotion, damn it!" Marcie's hand curled into a small fist.

Sophy bit her lip and then started shoving her unfinished work into drawers. "Come on, Marcie. Let's get out of here. Both of us have had enough for one day."

"It's not quite five," Marcie said automatically.

"Who the hell cares!"

The cocktail lounge they found nearby was just beginning to fill up with an after-work crowd. The hum of conversation provided a pleasant cover for Sophy and Marcie's grim discussion. Secluded at a small booth toward the back, they ordered margaritas and considered the circumstances in which they found themselves.

Under the influence of the bond cemented between them that day, Sophy found herself telling Marcie the whole sordid story of her night with Max. She explained the humiliating scene with Nick, the way Max had offered comfort and the way he had taken advantage of her emotional vulnerability.

Marcie listened compassionately, and then she poured out her own frustrations with trying to make it up the corporate ladder in what was still essentially a man's world.

"There are times when old-fashioned words like *revenge* sound very sweet," Sophy finally announced over the second margarita. "I've been having daydreams of revenge all day."

"I've been having them off and on for five years," Marcie admitted wryly. "Every time I got my fingers stepped on whenever I tried to climb the ladder. Damn it, I think this time I've had enough…."

She let the words trail off and Sophy looked at her curiously. "What are you talking about, Marcie?"

The other woman hesitated, and Sophy had the feeling she was carefully assessing her next words. Then she gave Sophy a very level glance. "Would you honestly like a chance at punishing Dr. Maximilian Travers?"

"I'd give anything to be able to teach him a lesson for what he did to me last night," Sophy heard herself whisper savagely. "But I don't see how that's possible. What could I possibly do to Max to repay him for what he did to me last night?"

"You could join me in what I have planned for S & J

Technology," Marcie said simply. Setting aside her drink, she leaned forward and told Sophy exactly what revenge could mean and how it could be taken.

CHAPTER FIVE

THE FOLLOWING EVENING SOPHY stood in the corridor outside Max's hotel room, her hand lifted to knock. At the last moment she almost changed her mind. In an agony of suspense she let her knuckles hover just above the door panel.

It would be simple to turn around and forget the whole thing. But deep down she knew what she had to do. With a sigh, she rapped her hand gently against the door.

"Who is it?" Max called impatiently from within.

"Room service," she muttered, not feeling like yelling out her name. There was the sound of a phone being dropped into its cradle, and a few seconds later the door was swung inward.

"I didn't order any... Sophy!" Max stared at her, his eyes narrowing in wary surprise. His tie was hanging loose and his dark hair looked as though he'd been running his fingers through it. "What the hell are you doing here? I've been trying to call you all evening!"

"Would you rather I turned around and went home to wait for your call?" she murmured sullenly.

"Don't be ridiculous. Come in." Max reached out to grasp her by the shoulder, tugging her into the room and slamming the door shut behind her as if afraid she might escape. Then he released her and leaned back against the door. His eyes roved hungrily over the narrow white skirt and safari-style shirt she wore, and Sophy could guess the memories he was recalling. She edged away from him, moving across the room toward a chair. She refused to glance at the bed.

"You must be wondering why I'm here," she began, feeling a wave of unease as she realized she was back at the scene of her debacle. Max must have seen the expression on her face, because he levered himself away from the door and motioned to the chair near the window.

"Please sit down," he invited gruffly. "I'll order something from room service." He picked up the phone.

"Make mine tea," she drawled, sinking into the chair with what she hoped was nonchalance. "I had a little problem handling my liquor the last time I was here, so I'd just as soon not take any chances."

One of Max's dark brows lifted tauntingly. "Going to blame everything on the fact that you had too much to drink? You weren't really drunk and you know it, Sophy."

"Tea," she repeated, disdaining to argue with him.

Max's mouth hardened but he ordered a pot of tea for two. Then he came slowly toward her to take the chair on the other side of the small oval table. "You've been ignoring my call all day. When I came to see you at lunch you claimed you were eating with your friend Marcie. When I asked you to have dinner with me last night you said you had plans with Marcie. When I tried to contact you this afternoon you had someone say you'd been sent across town on an errand. All that avoidance and now you show up on my doorstep." He ran a hand through his hair. "Why, Sophy?"

"Why have you been trying so hard to see me?" she countered coolly.

"You know damn well why."

"You're feeling guilty?"

"Guilt doesn't enter into it," he gritted. "I want you."

"You've had me," she reminded him gently.

"Stop trying to be so darn blasé about the whole thing."

"What exactly do you want from me, Max? Another toss in the hay? A few evenings in bed to help relieve the boredom while you're in Dallas?"

"Sophy, you're trying to twist everything."

"Shall I put a more sophisticated label on it? Do you want an *affair* with me, Max?"

"Yes, damn it, I do!" he exploded.

"Ah." She nodded. "Marcie was right." Sophy leaned back into her chair while Max eyed her warily.

"Marcie?" he finally asked cautiously.

"Ummm. She told me she thought you wanted a full-scale affair. Said she could tell by the way you watched me run out of the office the other morning when she walked in on us. Marcie, you'll be interested to know, is a very shrewd woman. Has her eye on the highest levels of corporate management. And she knows a lot about what motivates people. Probably going to be very successful someday."

"Stop playing with me, Sophy. Are you here because Marcie said I wanted to go on sleeping with you? Believe me, that analysis didn't take any great intelligence on her part. Any moron could tell I want you."

Sophy flushed in spite of her determination to remain serenely cool. "You weren't the only one Marcie Fremont analyzed. She had the astuteness to also realize that I was thirsting for revenge." Max looked startled at the matter-of-fact way Sophy announced the information. "But, then, she's a woman," Sophy continued coolly. "Probably only another woman could understand the wish for revenge in a situation such as this."

"Sophy..." Max began dangerously.

"Which brings us to my reason for being here tonight," she interrupted evenly.

"Revenge?" His smoky eyes were chilled.

"She suggested an interesting method, Max. Marcie proposed I continue with the affair. She thought I should show up on your doorstep tonight and admit that I simply couldn't stay away from your bed. She said I should imply I had been so overwhelmed by your virility and prowess in bed that I simply had no other choice but to surrender completely."

"Your friend Marcie seems to know her way around the male ego," Max drawled.

"Oh, yes. She's under the impression that as a staid, shy, humble professor of mathematics who's unaccustomed to dealing with situations such as this, you'd fall for it hook, line and sinker."

"May I ask what the point would be of leading on the staid, shy, humble professor?" Max's expression was one of unyielding granite.

"Now we come to the real beauty of Marcie's plan," Sophy said rather wearily. She had been up most of the previous night agonizing over Marcie's idea for revenge. The weariness she felt now was physical as well as mental. "While your male ego is thriving on my physical surrender, I am utilizing the opportunity to get close to you on every level."

"Marcie suggested some weird scheme whereby you allow me to think you're mine and then you betray me with another man, right?" he gritted.

"Nothing so primitive. Marcie Fremont is not a primitive sort of person. No, the idea was far more sophisticated than that. I'm to have my revenge on you by gaining access to the final version of the mathematical model you're doing for S & J Technology's new processing system. Once I have a copy of the model, I turn it over to Marcie."

Max looked blank. "Who will do what with it?"

"Who will then use it to exact her own revenge on S & J. She will use it to buy her way into a management position at a rival company. Marcie Fremont has given up waiting to have her abilities discovered and appreciated. She's going to find her own way to the top." Sophy closed her eyes and leaned her head back in the chair, remembering the incredible conversation with her friend. When she lifted her lashes again, she found Max staring at her in amazement.

"Oh, my God," he growled.

"Don't look so disgusted," Sophy advised. "Frankly, I think it might have worked."

"You're not making any of this up, are you?" he demanded incredulously.

"Nope. I have to admit my imagination is not that good."

There was a knock on the door, and with an irritated movement Max went to get the tray of tea. "Thanks," he muttered gruffly, hurriedly signing the tab and adding a tip. When he closed the door and turned back into the room, Sophy was reaching for her purse.

"Hold on, Sophy. You're not going anywhere just yet. Sit down." There was a new element of command in his voice, causing Sophy to blink warily. She hadn't heard that tone from him before.

"I've told you everything I know, Max."

"Why?"

"Why what?"

"Why did you tell me about Marcie's scheme? Why not simply go through with it?" He sat down again and watched her as if she were some infinitely complex formula he was trying to solve.

Sophy hesitated, unwilling to put into words the real reason she had been driven into coming to see Max. He was not to know that in the long hours of the preceding night she had battled with her own inability to exact a fitting revenge in such a manner. He was not to know that she had finally acknowledged at three o'clock in the morning that she could not bring herself to harm Max Travers in such a manner. If she stole the math model, he was bound to be implicated. He would be immediately suspect for having sold his work to a higher bidder. She had known with frightening clarity that she could not do that to Max Travers.

Her first loyalty had been to Max. But never would she admit that she was here tonight because she had discovered she felt strangely bound to this man.

"My parents might not have succeeded in drumming the principles of Einstein's theory of relativity into my head, but they did manage to teach me something about honorable conduct." It was as good an excuse as any.

"I see." Max appeared to be working out a problem. There was a preoccupied gleam in his eyes now.

"Look, Dr. Travers, I think this has gone far enough. I came here tonight to warn you because, frankly, I'm not sure I'm going to be able to stop Marcie. She's dead set on getting even with S & J Technology. To tell you the truth, I think she has a right to do exactly that. They treated her pretty shabbily. I think I can make her see reason eventually. She just needs a few days to cool down. In the meantime, I was afraid…I mean I thought she might…"

"You thought she might go through with the plan on her own somehow, right? So you decided to warn me, just in case." Max nodded, still looking thoughtful. "You're not interested in having your revenge, Sophy?" he finally asked.

She stiffened. "I'm not foolish enough to think there's much chance of real revenge in a situation like this. This sort of thing has been happening to women since the dawn of time, and the victims rarely get a crack at getting even. Not if the victims, unlike the victors, have a sense of honor!"

She knew she'd gone too far with that last sentence. Sophy saw the grim fury in Max's eyes as she voiced the insult, and she badly wished she could recall the appalling words. In the tense moment that followed she fully expected to reap a whirlwind in retaliation. Her fingers clenched on the arms of her chair and her chin lifted in unconscious pride and defiance.

The effort Max made to control his anger was visible. What astonished Sophy was that he managed the feat. But when he spoke again his words were measured. "If the corporate-espionage bit was a little too extreme for you, I'm surprised you didn't consider the other alternative."

"What alternative?" she asked cautiously.

"The one I suggested. That of having an affair with me—leading me on and then betraying me with another man."

"And thoroughly cheapen myself in the process!"

"Having an affair with me would make you feel cheap?" Slowly Max got to his feet.

"Yes." Sophy eyed him uncertainly. It was time to leave, she realized, getting to her feet as well. The atmosphere in this hotel room had gone several points above the danger level.

But even as the realization struck her, Max's hands were coming down on her shoulders. "You're determined to play the wronged woman in all this, aren't you?" he bit out, giving her a small shake.

"I was wronged!"

"The hell with it. Since I'm already a condemned man in your eyes, I haven't anything left to lose, have I?" He dragged her against him, forcing her head back over his arm as he lowered his mouth to plunder her lips.

Sophy struggled wildly as his kiss claimed her. It was the other night all over again, but she didn't have the excuse this time of being in a state of emotional shock or even of having had too much to drink. How can it be like this? she raged helplessly as she felt her body leap to life. *It isn't fair!*

She hadn't realized she'd spoken her last thoughts aloud until Max muttered his response against her mouth.

"What you do to me isn't fair either. Sophy, Sophy, please don't fight me. Just let me have you. I need you." His hands moved down her back to her hips, shaping the full curve with hungry familiarity. "You can't walk away from what we had the other night. You can't expect me to walk away from it either."

Sophy wrenched her head to one side, trying to avoid his seeking mouth. "Max, you don't understand. I don't want this. I don't want a relationship based on physical attraction. I want a whole lot more than that. Why do you think I wouldn't go to bed with Nick?"

"For God's sake, don't talk to me about that damned cowboy! Not now!"

"I'm trying to make a point, darn you! I didn't go to bed with Nick because I was trying to build a relationship with him first. I have no intention of leading a life full of one-night stands!"

"The other night wasn't a one-night stand and you know it," he gritted, and then fastened his mouth on hers so that her next words were caught in her throat.

"Max, no…" she gasped when he finally pulled away.

"If you want a relationship, build one with me!"

"In the few days you'll be here in Dallas?" she mocked furiously. "That's hardly likely, is it? You can't build a meaningful relationship in a few days, and even if it were possible, you and I couldn't do it in a lifetime!"

"Why not?" he demanded flatly, holding her still as he lifted his head to stare down at her taut features.

"Because a relationship has to be based on such things as mutual respect, and there's no way on earth a man of your intellectual caliber is ever going to be able to respect my abilities. The most I'd ever be for you, Max, is a toy," she snapped. "And I won't play that role for any man."

His mouth curved into a faint hint of amusement for the first time. "Are you trying to tell me you want to be loved for your mind?"

The humor in him pushed her over the edge. It severed the careful rein she had on her temper. How dare he laugh at her on top of everything else? "Even the thought of such a thing makes you laugh, doesn't it?" she blazed at him. "You insult me and then you have the nerve to wonder why I won't have an affair with you. Maybe you're not quite as bright as your academic achievements would indicate, Dr. Travers. Let me go!"

She stepped backward abruptly and his hands fell away, along with the amusement that had been edging his mouth. His eyes hardened.

"Sophy, stop it. You're behaving irrationally."

"Sometimes those of us at the lower end of the intelligence scale tend to function more on our emotions than on reason!"

"Then why don't you listen to your emotions?" he charged. "The way you did the other night when you gave yourself to me!"

"I'm not that big a fool!" she flung back harshly. Darn it, if she wasn't very careful she was going to burst into tears, and that must not be allowed to happen!

Yanking at the door handle, Sophy fled out into the hall. All she wanted to do now was escape. She needed to be free of the compelling influence this man had over her; needed to be free of the torment of her own emotions.

"Sophy, come back here. You can't go on running away from me!" He came after her, catching up to her at the elevators, his strong hands reaching out to halt her flight. She whirled angrily to face him.

"Let me go!"

"Not until you calm down."

"Someone's going to come along any minute and see you manhandling me in the hallway," she pointed out tautly. "Is that what you want?"

"What I want is a rational conversation!"

"Then you'll have to contact one of your academic colleagues. I don't have much talent in that area. Or any other area you're likely to be interested in either!"

At that his eyes became abruptly darker. "Now, that is an outright lie," he drawled. "You have a great deal of natural talent in bed."

She stared at him for an instant, utterly shattered by his wicked teasing, and then she lost her temper completely. Sophy slapped him. Not a ladylike tap on the cheek but a full-blown, arcing blow that had enough force behind it to snap his head to one side.

He didn't release her. When he looked back down at her there was warning in his gaze and his words were clipped. "I find your fiery temperament rather fascinating at times, but there are limits to how much of it I'll tolerate. Don't hit me again, Sophy."

"Or you'll hit me back?" she challenged. "I always said you were a real gentleman!"

Satisfied with the frustrated anger that leaped into his eyes, Sophy wrenched herself out of his grasp and stepped into the elevator as it arrived. Without a word she stared straight ahead as the doors closed. Only when she was safely out of sight and she realized she was alone in the elevator did Sophy relax her internal hold on her emotions. The tears began to trickle slowly down her cheeks.

Oh, God, what was the matter with her? How could she let him affect her this way? Half-blinded by the gleaming moisture in her eyes, she found her way through the huge lobby of the hotel and out into the parking lot. There, in the safety of her car, she gave way completely to the emotional storm that seemed to be raging inside her.

Eventually she managed to control the bout of tears and make her way home. It was Friday night. A week ago she would have looked forward to spending the evening with Nick Savage. Now every time she tried to think of Nick, the image of Max got in the way. She realized vaguely that she couldn't even summon up any anger toward Nick Savage now. All her emotions seemed to be focused on Max Travers.

Why a wizard? Why a man who lived in another world, an unreal world? A man who could never share her life, only her bed? Why did it have to be Max Travers who had succeeded in tapping the emotion that had lain dormant within her?

Sophy asked herself that question over and over again during the long drive home. She asked it as she morosely poured herself a glass of Chenin Blanc and settled down in her rainbow-hued chair to consider her life. She was still asking it an hour later when the telephone rang.

"Sophy? Don't hang up, this is important." Max's voice came across the wire with clipped command. "I've just been in touch with Graham Younger about what you told me this evening."

"Max! You didn't! I never meant for you to go to the

president of the company!" Shocked, Sophy pulled herself out of her dismal reverie, her anxiety taking a sudden new twist. "I told you I'd handle Marcie."

"Sophy, have you told Marcie you aren't interested in her little scheme?"

"Well, no, not yet…" No sense trying to explain that she had been reluctant to confess to Marcie that she couldn't go through with it. "But I will!"

"No you won't."

"Says who?" she shot back angrily.

"Says your upper management. They've got plans."

"The hell they have!"

"We're to be in conference room number eighteen-oh-nine at eight o'clock tomorrow morning. S & J Security will be there to discuss the situation."

"Max! What have you done? I only warned you to be on the safe side. I never meant for you to drag management and Security into this!"

"You could hardly expect me to let a thing like this ride on your assumption that you can talk Marcie out of it! From what you told me and from what I've seen of her, she seems quite likely to go through with some sort of corporate espionage on her own, whether or not you get involved. She has to be stopped. S & J wants her neutralized."

"Neutralized! For God's sake! You don't know her the way I do. There is no need to take this kind of action. Max, why didn't you call me before you contacted Graham Younger? Why are *you* getting involved? Neutralizing would-be corporate-espionage types is hardly your line of work. As long as you were warned, you could have taken a few precautions…"

"Just show up in the conference room on time, all right?" he asked wearily.

"Wait a minute. Tomorrow is Saturday!" Desperately Sophy tried to think. She could hardly refuse to show up. Not if she wanted to keep her own job at S & J secure.

"Exactly. Security figures there won't be too many people around."

She needed time to work this out. And she couldn't afford to jeopardize her job. Sophy chewed on her lip. "All right, Max. It doesn't look like I have much choice. I'll be in tomorrow at eight."

"I'll see you there." Max hung up the phone before she had a chance to beat him to it.

Sophy sat glaring at the instrument for a long time before she roused herself to fix something for dinner. She had gotten so wrapped up in her own dangerously emotional response to Max that she had neglected to think about the implications of this whole mess for poor Marcie. Somehow warning Max had taken precedence. She hadn't stopped to consider what might happen if he dragged S & J management into it.

NOT WANTING TO ANNOY the highest levels of corporate management, most of whom she had never met in person, Sophy arrived a little before eight the next morning and walked through the silent halls to the conference room. Though she was early, everyone else, it seemed, was there ahead of her.

Apparently S & J Technology had chosen to take the matter of Marcie Fremont very seriously. Sophy sighed and wondered what she'd unleashed as she greeted the president and his assistant very formally. Then she smiled at Sam Edison, the rather harried-looking man in the polyester suit who was in charge of S & J Security. She inclined her head very aloofly to Max, who had risen politely when she entered the room. Flustered by seeing someone in their midst rise to greet a mere secretary, the other males in the room had awkwardly done the same. Everyone sat down with relief.

"Miss Bennet," Graham Younger began pedantically, "we certainly appreciate your willingness to cooperate with us in this matter."

As if I had any choice, Sophy thought, sliding a glance at Max's impassive face.

"It was very good of you to go straight to Dr. Travers with a report of the Fremont incident," he went on pompously. "You have brought to our attention a serious threat to this firm, Miss Bennet. Industrial and corporate espionage are major problems these days. As a company involved in high technology we are especially vulnerable. Therefore we are most anxious to nip Marcie Fremont's larcenous tendencies in the bud. We intend to make an example of her."

Sophy stared at the older man's implacable face, feeling suddenly chilled. Poor Marcie.

"Miss Fremont is only a secretary, of course," the president's assistant put in mildly, "but we feel we must make it clear that this sort of thing will not be dealt with lightly."

Only a secretary. The words were vastly annoying. "If you'll excuse me, sir," Sophy said coolly, "I think too much is being made of all this. I seriously doubt that any corporate espionage attempt will actually be made. Miss Fremont is not the sort to involve herself in that kind of thing. Miss Fremont is very professional."

"I'm afraid we can't take the chance," Sam Edison put in quickly. "We don't know who she might be working for."

"That's right, Miss Bennet," Younger said evenly. "Frankly, we don't believe Miss Fremont is working alone. This sort of sophisticated plot requires planning at much higher levels. We don't just want to stop her. We want to find out who she's working with and stop the entire espionage ring."

"Espionage ring! I don't think…" Sophy began earnestly.

"We're not asking for your opinion, Miss Bennet," Younger interrupted coolly. "You will be expected to give your full cooperation to our plan."

Sophy bit back her annoyance. "What plan?"

"As I understand it, Marcie Fremont seems to feel you, ah, have reason to be rather upset with Dr. Travers. A lovers' quarrel or something. You're supposedly motivated by revenge," Edison said quickly, obviously uncomfortable with the delicate matter.

Sophy's mouth fell open in amazement. Then her head swung around and she pinned Max with an infuriated glare. "You told him about…about…" Words dried up in her throat. The tide of her fury threatened to stifle her. Max had told S & J management that she wanted revenge because of a lovers' quarrel? She'd kill him! She'd slice him apart with her pinking shears!

"Calm down, Sophy," Max cut in sharply. "I explained that Marcie apparently misunderstood the situation between us and is trying to capitalize on it."

She stared at him. Everyone else in the room was looking distinctly uncomfortable, including Graham Younger. *They know,* she thought. *Max is going to answer for this!* Exerting her willpower to the utmost, she managed to bring her shaking fingers under control and bury them in her lap.

"What, exactly, do you want me to do, Mr. Edison?" she asked far too softly.

"Well, we, er, that is, if you'd pretend to go through with Miss Fremont's plan, we might be able to trace the flow of information. Dr. Travers will supply you with a phony version of the math model he's working on. You will pass it along to Miss Fremont and we'll be watching to see who she gives it to."

"Pretend to go through with Marcie's plan?" Sophy's eyes went to Max. He met her glare unflinchingly, but she could read nothing in his expression.

"Sophy," he said coolly, "I have explained to everyone in this room that you and I are not, uh, romantically involved and that Marcie simply misunderstood the situation. What Sam is asking is that you pretend to be involved with me and that you tell Marcie you're going through with the espionage scheme."

"There will, of course, be a bonus in it for you if the plan works," Graham Younger put in.

"I see." So, on top of everything else, they intended to buy her cooperation. Sophy had never felt so disgusted in her whole life. They were trying to trap her just as they intended to trap Marcie. And with the unlimited ego of the ruling elite of the business world, they assumed it would be a snap to manipulate two dumb little secretaries. Sophy let the heavy silence reign for a few minutes, refusing to surrender to the pressure. All of these males needed a lesson.

"I suppose you won't believe me if I tell you that you're all overreacting?" she finally murmured quietly.

"I think we're the best judges of the sort of reaction required in this instance, Miss Bennet," the president's assistant declared politely. "If you just concentrate on the bonus and on your duty to S & J Technology, we'll do the rest."

The bonus. Sophy smiled coldly. Let them think she was going to do it for the money. Let them think they could push Marcie and herself around. "Very well," she finally agreed. "I'll cooperate." There was a collective sigh of relief from everyone except Max, who eyed her warily but said nothing.

Sam Edison leaned forward, his elbows planted on the table, and intently began to explain their plan. The more he talked, the less she thought of it, but she let him babble on because she was busy making a few plans of her own.

An hour later she and Max both left the offices of S & J Technology, but they left separately.

"Meet me at the hotel," he ordered brusquely as he said goodbye.

"No more orders, Max." She faced him in the building lobby. "Is that very clear? We're supposed to pretend to be lovers, but I won't go a step farther unless you agree to treat me as an equal partner in this stupid scheme."

"Sophy, I don't like this charade any better than you do, believe me!"

"I suppose there's nothing to do but make the best of it."

"Agreed. Now, how about lunch?" He sounded relieved.

"Lunch?"

"We are supposed to be spending the weekend together, remember? Part of the charade," he reminded her patiently. "I was wondering what plans you would like to make for lunch."

"Oh." She considered the matter and then said, "Actually, I did have some things to do today at home. Maybe dinner—"

"I'll bring some papers along and work on them while you're doing the things you wanted to do around your apartment," he interrupted. "We can have a sandwich or something for lunch. Doesn't have to be fancy."

For an instant Sophy thought she saw the jaws of a very lethal trap closing around her, and then she dismissed the image. She could handle Max Travers. As well as the management of S & J Technology.

Actually things might be easier if Max was busy working. She knew how totally involved people like him became when they were in the middle of a problem. She'd seen her parents disappear into their study for endless hours often enough. "All right, if that's what you would prefer."

"I'll get my briefcase from the hotel," he said before she could change her mind.

An hour later Sophy found that having Max in her kitchen was a strangely unsettling experience. He immediately adopted the kitchen table for a desk, appearing quite satisfied with the surroundings although they must have been much different from those in which he normally worked.

"What are you going to be doing this afternoon?" he asked as she opened the refrigerator to prepare sandwiches.

"I'm making a dress for one of the women at the office." Sophy found some cheese and a tomato and placed them on the counter. "Whole wheat bread or rye?"

"Rye please." He waited a moment and then said carefully, "That black dress you brought into the office the other morning looked rather nice."

She smiled cynically. "Thank you."

"Do you make your own clothes too?"

"Max, I know you're not really interested in discussing my sewing. Mustard or mayonnaise?"

"Both. What makes you say I'm not interested in your sewing?"

"Let me see if I can remember all the reasons why someone shouldn't take a hobby like sewing too seriously," she drawled, recalling her parents' lecture on the subject. "It's frivolous, takes up time that could better be spent on studying, and doesn't really engage the brain to any important extent."

"Whom are you quoting?" He half smiled, looking up from the table to watch her make the sandwiches.

"My mother and father. They were horrified when it became apparent that dress design wasn't going to be just a hobby for me but my main interest in life. They're going to be even more shocked when they find out I intend to open a design boutique here in Dallas." She slapped the cheese on the bread and sliced the tomatoes. When she turned to carry the sandwiches over to the table, she found Max smiling at her.

"It was hard on you, wasn't it, Sophy?" he asked quietly. "Growing up with two academically brilliant parents…?"

"Who couldn't bring themselves to admit that they hadn't produced an equally brilliant child. Yeah, it was a little tough at times." She smiled wryly. "But I survived. And so did they."

"They love you."

"I know."

"You're lucky," he murmured.

She glanced up, frowning. "What do you mean?"

"Only that through all the trauma and the frustration, at least you knew you were loved."

"Meaning you weren't?"

"My parents were a lot like yours, Sophy. They wanted a child in their own image. But they were far too involved in their own careers to waste any time on loving me. They simply saw to it that I was given the best possible education. They apparently thought that was all that was necessarily to raise a child."

She watched him uneasily. "You don't love your parents? They don't love you?"

"We can discuss higher math until three in the morning, and that's generally what we talk about when I visit. But that's about all we do together. When I was a kid I remember several Christmases when we didn't even have a tree because my parents were so busy with their studies and their research that they just forgot to get one. When they remembered presents they were always the educational variety."

"No crayons?" she asked with a smile.

"No crayons. Or anything else that was just plain fun."

Sophy felt a tide of compassion for the little boy who had been programmed to be a genius and who was never allowed to deviate from the program. Firmly she squelched the sensation. Damn it, she was not going to allow this man to play on her sympathy.

"You don't trust me, do you, Sophy?" he asked.

"Would you in my place?" she countered.

Unexpectedly he smiled. "You could try seducing me and we could find out what my reaction would be. I think I'd trust you afterward."

"Forget it." She got to her feet and picked up her dish. "Do you want ribs or a steak tonight? I'd better get them out of the freezer now so they'll be ready to barbecue later."

"A steak sounds fine."

"Okay." She reached into the freezer and dragged out a package. "I'll look forward to seeing you earn your keep tonight."

"What's that mean?"

She glanced up ingenuously. "I'll look forward to watching you grill the steak tonight," she clarified politely.

Max's mouth lifted wryly. "Sorry, you're out of luck. My domestic skills are limited to opening cans and sticking frozen dinners in microwave ovens."

Sophy's sense of humor rose to the surface. Exactly as she had suspected. "Another gap in your education. You can't type and you can't barbecue. Well, Max, prepare yourself. You're in Texas now, and here in Texas every real man knows how to grill a steak."

"Now, wait a minute, Sophy..."

"No excuses are necessary. Tonight, Max, you're going to cook a steak. Consider it an extension of your education."

CHAPTER SIX

WHEN SHE EMERGED FROM HER elaborately outfitted sewing room later that afternoon, Sophy smelled smoke. Curious, she followed the scent through the kitchen, where Max's paperwork was neatly stacked on the table, and out onto the patio. There she found Max, white shirt smudged with charcoal, eyeing the small flame he had produced in the pit of the barbecue grill.

"You look as if you're going to be forced to walk across the coals in your bare feet," she teased as he continued to stare at the charcoal with deep suspicion.

"Sophy, I told you I don't know much about this sort of thing," he growled.

"What good is a man who can't barbecue a steak?" she asked flippantly. "I'll go see about the salad. Women's work, you know." With a small sense of triumph that she knew was really very childish, Sophy went back inside the kitchen. He was going to ruin the steak, of course. It was a small thing, but he was going to make a fool out of himself in front of her and the thought brought some satisfaction. Well worth the price she had paid for the meat.

From time to time as she went about the business of preparing the salad and warming crusty rolls, she glanced surreptitiously out the window to watch Max. He was deep in concentration, intently studying the few instructions printed on the back of the package of charcoal briquettes. Sophy laughed to herself, relishing the moment when he would actually have to put the meat on the fire. She just hoped he realized that he was supposed to put it on the grill and not directly in the flames!

He was getting anxious, she thought as she came and went on the patio, setting the small, glass-topped wicker table and arranging the salad dishes.

"About ready for the steak?" she asked brightly.

Max looked up from his intent contemplation of the coals and started to say something. Whatever it was, he changed his mind at the last moment and nodded brusquely. Sophy smiled serenely and went back inside to get the meat.

"A pity to sacrifice a good piece of steak," she muttered to herself as she hoisted the tray and carried it out to Max with a flourish. "But it is going to be interesting to see just how burnt the offering is before he elects to serve it to me."

Max's gaze narrowed as he watched her approach with the meat. "Sophy, are you sure you don't want to take over?"

"Nonsense. Any man can grill a steak. It's an instinct, I believe. Every man I've ever known could handle a barbecue. Except my father, of course," she added blandly. "And I guess, now that I think about it, there were a few other exceptions. Mostly academic exceptions. Let me rephrase my original statement. Every man I've ever *dated* could handle a barbecue and a steak."

"In other words, you don't date men who can't project the machismo image, is that it?" he gritted, practically yanking the glass tray out of her hands. "Should I buy a horse and start wearing a six-gun?"

"I wouldn't bother going to the expense, if I were you.

After all, you'll only be in town a short while, remember? I'll fix you a drink. Men usually sip a whiskey or something while they're grilling a steak."

"Actually," he retorted, carefully unwrapping the steak from its plastic covering, "that sounds like one of your better ideas."

Sophy grinned again and went back inside to fix the drinks. After handing him his, she sank down onto the nearest patio chair, propped up her feet and prepared to witness the debacle. Max had already thrown the meat on the grill. Much too soon, she thought critically. It was going to be charred on the outside and raw on the inside.

"I'll tell Marcie that I'm going along with her big plan on Monday morning," Sophy said conversationally. "How long shall we wait before I turn over the fake information?" No sense telling Max she had other plans for S & J.

Max didn't look up from the burning steak. "A week, maybe. We can't rush it any more than that or she'll be suspicious."

"If she's as smart as I think she is she'll be suspicious anyway. Honestly, this has got to be the craziest scheme I've ever heard. Hard to believe it came from a man of Graham Younger's stature."

"Don't forget that the head of Security thinks it will work too."

Sophy shook her head in disgust. "Let's drop it, Max."

"What would you like to talk about?" he asked evenly.

She lifted one shoulder negligently. "Anything but higher mathematics."

"How about your plans to open a design boutique?" he surprised her by suggesting.

She watched him through half-concealing lashes. "Are you sure you're interested in my plans?"

"Sophy, anything that you're involved in interests me," he said simply.

She hesitated. "Okay, but don't blame me if you get bored quickly."

"The one thing I never am around you is bored." He gave her a fleeting smile. "I think you're my missing crayons."

"Your what?"

"The crayons I never had a chance to play with as a child. Life has always been rather black-and-white for me, Sophy. You're like a rainbow in it."

Sophy stared at him, uncertain how to take the gentle confession. He was doing it again, she thought, making her feel sorry for him, eliciting her compassion. She was going to have to be extremely careful around this man. He was proving to be dangerous in ways she would never have expected.

"Well, pay attention," she ordered gruffly. "My folks will want to know all the shocking details of my decision to make my dress designing into a career." And while he finished massacring the steak, she told him about her plans for the future.

"Designing and sewing for people has been a sideline for me since college, but it's only been during the past year that I've actually considered making a full-time career out of it," she concluded. "Dallas, with its optimistic, adventurous, anybody-can-get-rich-here atmosphere, seemed like a good place to try my luck. That bonus Younger promised me this morning might make the difference between my being able to take the plunge a few months from now or a year from now." Except that she never intended to collect that bonus!

"Is that the real reason you agreed to go along with the plan? The bonus?" Clearly he was remembering her comment about Marcie's threat to his career.

"Let's just say it was an excellent incentive," she murmured, not wanting to discuss the issue. The truth was, she realized unhappily, if Max hadn't been threatened along with S & J, she might have been tempted to let the company take its chances. It might teach management a good lesson if it got ripped off by a "mere" secretary! Now she had to concoct a more involved scheme to show Graham Younger the error of his ways.

Max stared down at the incinerated steak, and she sensed the wary anxiety he was feeling about the meat's condition. "I guess if we're ever going to eat, it might as well be now," he said.

"Lovely," she drawled smoothly, rising to her feet. "I'll get the wine."

The steak was charred almost beyond recognition. In a land where everyone preferred his meat rare, it was a total disaster. Oh, there was a rare, almost raw section left in the center, Sophy noted as she cut into her piece, but it looked quite unappetizing surrounded by the overdone part. There was little if any natural juice left in the meat. Max had stabbed the poor thing so many times with his cooking fork that it had all drained out. Dry, charred and tough, the steak was as thoroughly ruined as it was possible for a piece of meat to be. Sophy should have been feeling a sense of triumph.

After all, Max was clearly feeling as nervous and awkward about his failure at the barbecue as she would have felt trying to work a problem in one of his math classes. It was a small thing, but Sophy told herself she was giving him a taste of being a failure. Served him right. As she took the first bite she considered exactly how she would show her disdain for his inability to cope with such an elementary task.

Then she glanced up and found him watching her with nervous dread apparent in his gray eyes. He was waiting for the axe to fall, she realized abruptly. He knew as well as she did that the meat was terrible, and he undoubtedly knew exactly what she was going to say. There was a grim, stoically resigned expression on his hard features. He hadn't held his own against the men he was being measured against and he knew it. He'd probably known from the beginning that he didn't stand a chance. What hope did he have, never having grilled a steak before in his life?

Sophy read the reaction in him and told herself it was all she could have wished. Now was the time for a cold, cutting remark and a few choice, derogatory comments on his failure as a chef. It wasn't much, but it might be all the revenge she ever got. In some small way she had a chance to show Max Travers that as far as she was concerned, he was a nonstarter in her world.

"It's delicious," she heard herself say as she chewed with polite greed. "Exactly the way I like it. Honestly, everyone here in Texas insists on serving it so raw that it bleeds all over the plate. I've been too embarrassed to tell anyone that I like my meat well-done." ·

He stared at her, plainly astonished. He wasn't the only one, Sophy decided ruefully; she was equally startled at her words. But she knew she wasn't going to retract them. Instead she gave him a genuine smile and passed the glass salad bowl. What in the world was the matter with her?

Taking it automatically from her hands, Max continued to survey her intently. "You like it?" he finally managed.

"Ummm. I guess you have a natural talent for the barbecue, after all. Would you like some steak sauce?" She was pouring a lot over her own meat. It might help.

"Yes, thank you," he murmured humbly. Then he visibly

began to relax. "I was a little uncertain about the timing," he confessed, picking up his own knife and fork. "You're sure you like it well-done?"

"My favorite way," Sophy assured him cheerfully.

He took his first bite and chewed steadily for a long moment. "Don't you think it's a little tough?" he asked diffidently.

"That's the fault of the meat, not you." She smiled. "It was a cheap cut. They usually turn out tough on the grill." Actually, she'd paid a fortune for it.

"Oh." He nodded wisely, apparently relieved.

"I probably should have served the ribs, but I wanted to use up this beef. It's been in the freezer quite a while." Another lie. Why?

"It's not very juicy," he said tentatively, obviously appealing for more reassurance.

"That's because it spent so long in the freezer," she lied gamely. "Have a little more steak sauce on it."

Max appeared to relax even further. "Maybe we should have marinated this steak beforehand," he said very knowledgeably.

Sophy stifled a laugh. All the marinating in the world would not have compensated for the way it was treated on the grill. "You're probably right. Next time I have an old, cheap cut of beef, I'll try marinating it first. You did an excellent job with what you had to work with, Max. Delicious."

Why, she asked herself anxiously, was she bothering to pretend Max had acquitted himself well at the barbecue? Why hadn't she seized her small moment of triumph? What on earth had made her compliment him on the ruined meat just as though he were a man she really cared about, a male whose ego she wanted to soothe?

Damn it! This was the man who had deliberately taken

advantage of her, and here she was comforting and reassuring him! She must be out of her mind.

By the end of the meal, Max was showing signs of reacting to his success at the barbecue the way men always react to their triumphs. He was pleased with himself, jovial, willing to talk about anything and everything. A man on top of the world. Sophy didn't know whether to laugh or cry. It occurred to her that she might have created a monster.

"Next time I think I'll experiment a bit with the coals," he informed her seriously. "I think it might be a good idea to let them die down a little first before putting on the meat. What do you think?"

"Possibly," she agreed cautiously. "I'm really not much of an expert on barbecues."

"Because you always leave that side of things to the men in your life?" He smiled wryly. "Well, now that I'm the only man in your life, you won't have to worry about whether or not your next date can grill a steak, will you?"

Sophy looked at him helplessly. She *had* created a monster. "Are you as good at washing dishes as you are at barbecuing?"

"Better. I've had more practice in that department. Been a bachelor for thirty-six years, you know. I've washed a lot of dishes in my time."

"That may be more of an asset in the long run than being accomplished at the barbecue," she said lightly, rising to begin clearing the table. "A lot of women would value that talent more than barbecuing skill!"

"How about you, Sophy?"

"I've got a dishwasher," she informed him sweetly.

"Good thing I passed the test at the barbecue grill, then, isn't it?" he drawled softly behind her. "Since my other skills don't count with you?"

"Would you like some dessert, Max?" Determinedly, she started toward the kitchen with a stack of dishes. Damned if she was going to let him drag her any deeper into the quagmire that seemed to be stretching at her feet.

"Sure. What have you got?"

"Ice cream?"

"I can prepare ice cream even better than I can grill a steak," he confided cheerfully, opening the freezer and searching out the carton of chocolate ice cream she had inside.

What was she going to do with him this evening? Sophy wondered a little nervously. He was settling in very thoroughly. Very soon now she was going to have to make it quite clear that she had no intention of playing out Graham Younger's charade to the extent of allowing him to spend the night. Sophy began to feel trapped by the complex web of circumstances. She must perform this balancing act very carefully or face disaster.

She was lecturing herself on that point when the doorbell rang imperiously. "Now what? One more problem is all I need."

Max glanced up from his task of shoveling out huge scoops of chocolate ice cream. "What did you say?"

"I said, there's the doorbell," she lied politely, wiping her hands on a towel and walking into the living room to answer it. Who could it be on Saturday night? If it was Sam Edison or someone from S & J Technology checking up on her, she would be furious. On the other hand, what if it was Marcie Fremont?

Sophy opened the door with a frown and found all six feet, three inches of Nick Savage standing there. She stared at his handsome face in utter shock.

"You were the last person I expected to see here tonight," she informed him starkly. "What the hell do you want?"

"You," he said with devastating simplicity. He pushed the Stetson back on his head and his eyes gleamed down at her. "I figured I'd given you long enough to get over your little temper tantrum. I've missed you, darlin'."

Sophy was incredulous. "You've *missed* me! What an idiotic thing to say! The last time I saw you, you had plenty of company, as I recall. Go visit your blond girlfriend if you're lonely this evening."

Nick put out a hand and tousled her curls in the old, familiar manner. "You know, you're kinda cute when you're mad, honey. Now stop glaring at me and I'll explain all about Trisha."

"If Trisha is the blond, I'd just as soon not hear all the details."

"Honey," he drawled, "Trisha was just a way of fillin' time until you were willing to let me into your bed. She means nothin' to me. She's just a good-time girl."

"Well, go have a good time with her. You're not going to have one with me, I guarantee!" she hissed.

"Now, you don't mean that and you know it." He smiled confidently. "You're just a little upset because you caught me foolin' around with Trisha. I wouldn't have been, you know, if you'd kept our date that night."

"How dare you make it sound as if it were all my fault! You've probably been playing around with her all the time I've known you!"

"Like I said, honey, I was just fillin' in time—"

"Oh, shut up, Nick, and leave. I'm really not interested in discussing this further."

"Now, that's where you're wrong, darlin'. We both know you're very interested in discussing this. You're in love with me, remember?" His voice was smooth and assured. Nick was very sure of himself, Sophy realized.

"You really believe you can just walk back in like this and everything will be all right?" she whispered scathingly.

"I know you're a little upset about Trisha…"

Sophy shook her head. "Oh, Nick, you don't even have an inkling, do you?"

"I've got more than an inkling of how you feel about me," he murmured, stepping through the door. "You might be mad as hell about that little scene by the pool, but you'll get over it. With some help."

On the last words, he hauled her into his arms and lowered his head to find her mouth. Sophy stood perfectly still, deciding that the quickest way to discourage him was to show him that he couldn't influence her now with his casually expert lovemaking.

Even though she had no intention of betraying any reaction, it still came as something of a surprise to Sophy to find she *had* no reaction. Where was the pleasant warmth she had once experienced in Nick's arms? Why wasn't she responding even a little to the sensuous expertise he wielded so well?

Sophy was still working that one out when Max Travers's voice cut through the air like an uncoiling whip.

"Take your hands off her, Savage, or I'll stuff that Stetson hat down your throat!"

Sophy jumped, as much from the shock of hearing such violence in Max's tone as from his unexpected interruption. "Max!" She tried to push herself away from a grim-faced Nick, but he reached out to hold her, his arm gripping her shoulders. They both stared at Max, who was standing in the kitchen doorway with the carton of ice cream still in one hand.

"Who the hell is this?" Nick asked in astonishment, clearly not seeing any threat in the man who was challenging him.

"I'm the man who took her to bed the night you had your private little poolside party with the blond. Remember me? I was standing right behind Sophy when you came out of the cabana. I took her to my hotel after the show."

"Max! Please!" Sophy felt anger and fear rising up and twisting together in her stomach. She was angry at Max for his blatant claim on her, and she was afraid for him—afraid that Nick Savage would tear him apart. Already she could feel the fighting tension in Nick's body. The arm locked around her shoulders tightened.

"I don't believe you," Nick said dangerously. He sent a disdainful glance over Max. "You're not exactly her type."

"Maybe not," Max agreed easily. "But she's my type. Ask her. Ask her if she didn't spend the night with me. Ask her if she didn't give herself to me completely that night. *Go ahead! Ask her!*"

"What the hell's he talkin' about, Sophy?" Nick didn't look down at her, his whole attention on Max, whom he clearly couldn't imagine as real competition.

"He's just trying to be protective," Sophy said hurriedly, pulling free of Nick's grip. "He saw you that night by the pool and he's trying to protect me from you!" It was all she could think of at the moment. Damned if she was going to stand there and admit Max was telling the truth! The bastard! When this was over she'd give him a piece of her mind.

"I see," Nick said coolly. "Well, there's no call to play Sir Galahad. The little lady and I can work this out for ourselves. We don't need your interference. Why don't you run along and finish eating your ice cream? On second thought, why don't you just leave altogether? I don't much like the idea of Sophy here entertaining other men in the evening, even if they do let her cry on their shoulders."

Sophy caught her breath as Max slowly put down the

carton of ice cream and removed his glasses. Automatically he began polishing them on his shirt. "I'm not going anywhere, Savage. You're the one who will have to leave." He held the frames up to the light, squinting to check the polishing job. "Tell him, Sophy."

"Tell him what?" she snapped, enraged and genuinely frightened now. If Max didn't stop goading Nick there would be hell to pay. On the other hand, she told herself a little violently, maybe Max deserved to find himself flat on the floor.

"Tell him you're mine now. That you've spent a night in my bed and that you'll probably spend tonight with me too." He replaced the glasses with great care.

"Not tonight, too!" she shouted, and realized too late it was the wrong thing to deny. She should have denied spending the first night with him. Nick's narrowed eyes swung to her instantly.

"Sophy?" he began with soft menace, and for the first time Sophy realized just how dangerous the situation really was. She summoned her poise and faced him as coolly as possible.

"I think you'd better leave, Nick."

"Why, you little bitch!" he snarled. "It's true, isn't it? You actually went to bed with this little nerd, didn't you? Of all the cheatin', lyin', little bitches!" His hand came around so fast, so unexpectedly, that Sophy didn't even have a chance to avoid it. Nick struck the side of her face in a flat, vicious slap that sent her sprawling to the floor. She was too stunned even to cry out.

Before she could gather her senses, the room seemed to explode around her. She saw Max's nearly silent rush across the jade-green carpet and cried out. "Max, no! He'll kill you!"

But neither man paid her the slightest attention. The atmosphere in the room had gone very primitive in a hurry, Sophy realized, terrified. She struggled to a sitting position, her palm on her sore cheek, and watched in horror as Nick closed with Max.

The police! If she could just get to the phone… Sophy tried to rise to her knees and succeeded in doing so just as Nick landed with a thud on the carpet beside her. Eyes wide with shock, she knelt, looking down at him. Then she glanced up at Max, who was calmly brushing off his sleeve.

"Are you ready to leave yet, Savage?" Max asked quietly.

"I'm gonna kill you, you bastard!" Nick gritted, getting to his feet and launching himself at Max in a low, powerful rush.

The results were the same as before. Max did something very economical and smooth with his hands and Nick landed once again flat on his back. This time he didn't get up quite so quickly. Max stood calmly waiting for him.

"You think 'cause you got lucky a couple of times I can't take you?" Nick muttered furiously. "Well, you're wrong. I'm gonna take you apart limb from limb!"

Max easily sidestepped the next bull-like rush, slicing down with his hand as Nick flew past. Like a matador in a ring, he toppled the other man with a seemingly casual display of skill. This time Nick didn't rise at all. He simply lay groaning on the floor. Sophy watched, half-numb with shock, as Max went over to his fallen victim and crouched beside him.

"Come near her again, Savage, and I'll do a lot more damage. She's mine now and she stays mine. You don't want her, anyway, remember? You threw away your chances with Sophy the night you screwed that little blond by the pool. You're a fool, but that's not my problem. Go find yourself another little blond."

Nick glowered up at him, massaging his arm. "I'll get you for this!"

Max raised one eyebrow. "Why bother? Would you

really want her back? Knowing she gave herself to me so easily after refusing you for months?"

Nick's angry glare swung back to where Sophy still knelt on the carpet. "Cheatin' little bitch. Nah, I don't want her," he spat. "You can have her!" He rolled to his feet and lurched furiously for the door. Max rose slowly, his eyes never leaving his opponent. On the threshold, Nick turned to stare briefly at him. "I guess you won her fair and square, nerd, but take some advice. Don't let her string you along the way she did me. Made a damn fool out of me, puttin' me off while she decided how she really felt! Led me a real dance, she did."

"While you were busy dancing with someone else?" Max half smiled.

"Man's got a right to some action on the side," Nick grunted huffily.

"Goodbye, Savage." Max waited for the other man to leave. Neither male glanced at Sophy, who was beginning to feel like a doe during mating season. Never in her life had she had a fight conducted over her, and the experience was the most primitive and unpleasant she had ever been through.

Without another word Nick slammed the door behind him and stalked down the path toward the waiting Lincoln. It wasn't until they heard the muted roar of the powerful engine that Max turned slowly to confront Sophy.

In absolute silence they regarded each other across the room. Sophy felt a combination of wariness and relief that left her trembling. Slowly she staggered to her feet, clutching at the nearest chair for support. She didn't like the glinting, fundamentally male expression in Max's smoky gray eyes.

"Max?" she began uneasily.

"I think," Max said slowly, "that the dumb cowboy may have had a point." He started toward her with an even, purposeful pace. "I did win you fair and square, didn't I? And I would be a fool to let you string me along, wouldn't I? You belong to me now."

"Max, stop it!" she whispered, backing away carefully as he approached. "I mean it. Stop it."

"I just fought a knock-down, drag-out battle for you, lady. I've never fought over a woman in my life."

"Max, this has gone far enough. I won't have any more violence in this house!" She backed away another step, chilled at the implacable look on his face.

"No," he agreed. "No violence."

"I'll call the police!"

"Not just now." He spoke almost absently as he came to a halt a foot away from her and lifted a hand to touch the cheek Nick had struck. "If he ever tries to hit you again I'll kill him."

Sophy shivered as he possessively smoothed her cheek. Her eyes never left his face. She could feel the male aggression flowing from him, a by-product of the fight, no doubt. And she knew before he said another word that she was going to be the target of that aggression.

"You belong to me," he repeated in a soft, rasping voice. "I just won you fair and square." He pulled her into his arms.

CHAPTER SEVEN

THE UNFATHOMABLE, UNNERVING, incomprehensible part was
that a part of Sophy agreed with him. She was shaken, overwhelmed by the violence that had just taken place. She was
equally unsettled by the knowledge that, having lain once
in Max Travers's arms, she no longer felt anything when
Nick Savage kissed her. What had this wizard done to her?

She couldn't seem to think logically as his mouth de-
scended to claim hers. Sophy tried to tell herself that she
shouldn't be responding so unreservedly to Max's compelling hold, but her lips parted in surrender beneath his and
she knew the truth. She was deeply attracted to this man
and she wanted him. In some distant corner of her mind
she even acknowledged that the attraction went far beyond
anything she had ever known—perilously close to love.
Oh, no! She must not be in love with him!

He was all wrong for her! But even as the lecture rang
through her brain, Sophy heard a soft moan and knew it
came from her own throat.

"I want you, sweetheart," Max grated as he teased her
mouth with his own.

"Oh, Max…"

"I'm going to take you tonight," he muttered, pulling
away to look down at her flushed face with burning eyes.
His hands moved compellingly along the length of her

spine, finding the nerves at the bottom of it and kneading sensually. "I'm going to strip all these bright clothes from your beautiful body and find the rainbow underneath. And then I'm going to make love to the rainbow. Oh, God, Sophy, don't try to stop me. Nothing could stop me now. I need you too much."

She trembled in his embrace, knowing that she wouldn't stop him even if she could. "Wizard," she whispered, burying her face against his shoulder.

She knew he sensed the surrender in her. She could feel the triumph and satisfaction in him, yet at the same time his hands on her were tender. Locked against the length of his body by one of his arms, Sophy felt him fumbling with the fastenings of her clothes. His fingers trembled slightly with the force of his desire, but they didn't hesitate. The colorful cotton knit skirt and top were lying in a pool at her feet before Sophy was fully aware of what had happened.

"You have skin like silk." Max brushed his lips along her shoulder while he undid the clasp of her small bra. When the garment fell away, he groaned and curved his palms wonderingly around her breasts. "I love the feel of your nipples when they get hard under my hands. Like small, ripe berries."

His hands slid to her waist, lifting her up with an easy strength. When her breasts were level with his mouth, he nipped erotically at both before lowering her down along the length of his body. Sophy shivered and whispered his name.

"Put your arms around my neck and hold on to me while I get undressed," he ordered thickly. Obediently she did as she was told, twining her arms around him. She met his steady, fiercely glowing gaze as he unbuttoned his shirt and unfastened his belt buckle. A moment later his clothes, too, lay on the floor, and he stood fully naked in front of her.

Deliberately he reached up to catch hold of her wrists, drawing her hands down over his shoulders, across his chest and along the firm, taut line of his stomach. Then he bent his head and plunged his tongue deeply into her mouth as he pushed her hands down farther to the throbbing evidence of his desire.

Sophy gasped at the bold demand, but the masculine aggression in him brooked no denial. With delicate fingers she found the waiting hardness and gently caressed.

"Sophy," he groaned into her mouth, "Sophy, your touch is enough to send me out of my mind!" He deepened the kiss and slid his hand around to clench the curve of her buttocks. When Sophy gasped again, he slipped his palms inside the nylon panties she still wore and found the secret hidden in the triangle of tightly curling hair. Impatiently he pushed the panties off altogether.

"Oh, Max!"

"I can feel the heat in you, sweetheart," he groaned as he began to stroke magic patterns on the heart of her desire. "So warm and welcoming. Put your arms back around my neck."

"But, Max..." She wanted to go on touching him, exciting him. Arousing a wizard was heady business.

"Do as I say, my sweet love," he urged. When she once again had her hands locked around his neck, he pushed his bare foot between her legs, gently forcing her to stand with her feet apart.

Sophy was suddenly aware of feeling incredibly, sensuously vulnerable. Too vulnerable. Instinctively she started to lower her hands, but he stopped her with a muttered word and a reassuring kiss. She trembled as he began to caress her more intimately, his fingers boldly invading her body.

"I want to know I can make you want me," he growled

huskily as his hand stroked the fire in her. "I want to feel
you trembling and hear the soft sounds you make when
you're aroused. I want you to know just how much you
want me, too. Tell me, Sophy. Tell me with words as well
as with your body!"

Her head fell back as she looked up into his passion-
carved face. How could she deny this wizard anything he
asked tonight? She belonged to him. He had fought for her
and now he seemed to have every right to seduce her. God
help her, she was feeling every bit as primitive as he was.

"Max, I want you. You must know I want you," she got
out in a throaty little voice.

"Did you ever want that damn cowboy this much? Did
your body become hot and damp and did you tremble when
he touched you?"

"No," she gasped as he did something unbelievable to
the center of her. "No, never like this. It was never like this
with him…. It's never been like this with anyone," she
added helplessly as she moved against his hand. "Please,
Max, please make love to me…."

"I am making love to you," he drawled gently.

"You know what I mean." Urgently she writhed, forcing
her hips closer to his.

"What do you mean, Sophy?" he growled. "Tell me
exactly what you mean."

"Take me," she begged. "Here. Now. Please take me."
She used her hands on his neck, trying to make him sink
to the carpet with her. Slowly he followed her as she went
down to her knees.

"You're sure this is what you want?" he taunted.

"Don't tease me, Max!" Sophy went down onto her
back, pulling him urgently across her body.

"I only take what's mine," he warned deeply.

"I am yours," she cried, opening her thighs for him. "Oh, Max, I *am* yours. I belong to you."

"Fair and square," he murmured hoarsely, and then he was completing the union with a rush of power and strength that momentarily deprived her of breath.

Sophy gave herself up joyously to the passionate wizardry of the man who was claiming her body so completely. There might be a price to pay later, but tonight everything seemed right. There was no alternative tonight other than to succumb to this thrilling torture.

The overwhelming excitement seemed to twist tighter and tighter within her until Sophy thought she would break apart into a thousand glittering pieces. Max seemed to understand every nuance of the sensations that assaulted her, and he capitalized on each one. His body drove relentlessly into hers, mastering, taking, leading and guiding. She could do nothing but cling to him, her legs wrapped around his waist, her arms clutching at his shoulders.

Higher and higher they raced until the final twisting convulsion claimed Sophy completely.

"Oh, my God, *Max!*"

"Yes, darling, yes," he ground in her ear, nipping savagely. "Hold on to me and let yourself go."

Her throat arched and her eyes were tightly shut as Sophy let the tide of passion sweep through her. She was dimly aware of an exultant masculine cry and felt Max's body go rigid in the final response. Then she was drifting, catching her breath and marveling at the utter relaxation of her body.

When she gradually surfaced a long time later it was to find Max still lying along the length of her, his legs tangled with her own. She opened her eyes to find him balanced on his elbows, looking down into her face. For a moment they stared at each other.

It was Max who broke the spell of bemusement. "If someone had told me two weeks ago that I would take advantage of a woman and seduce her and then fight some cigarette-ad cowboy for her and follow that up with another seduction, I would have told him to go play with an abacus. Sophy, you bring out a side of me I never knew existed." He looked dazzled and stunned by his own actions.

She lifted a hand to play with the hair at the back of his damp neck. "And if anyone had told me I'd be seduced by a wizard, I would have said he was crazy. Max, what have you done to me?" she whispered, dazed.

"Made you mine." He dipped his head and feathered a kiss along the top of her breast. Then he licked the glistening perspiration that had collected in the hollow between the two soft globes. "And I'm going to go on making you mine again and again until you finally believe it yourself. I want you to know it for a fact, not just when I've got you lying under me like this, but every waking moment of your life."

She didn't know what to say—didn't really want to say anything. It was all too frightening and dangerous to consider closely. Her instincts bid her flee and her body said that was impossible. When she stayed silent, her blue-green eyes wide and eloquent, his mouth kicked upward in wry amusement and he kissed her gently. "Don't fight me, Sophy. I want you so, and I can't resist reaching out to take you."

Her lashes lowered as Sophy realized she couldn't maintain direct contact with his eyes. She licked her lips tentatively, aware of the swollen feel of them. Her whole body felt the vivid aftermath of passion. "Max, why didn't Nick beat you to a pulp?"

"You thought he was going to, didn't you?" he retorted whimsically. "You were afraid for me, weren't you?"

"Yes." It was the truth. She had been terrified that Nick would hurt him badly.

"I like having you worried about me," Max decided.

"But how did you handle him so easily? It was like watching a matador and a rather awkward bull. You didn't even get your shirt rumpled."

He grinned, a wicked, utterly masculine grin that told her just how pleased he was with himself. The triumphant male. "Right," he stated categorically, "was on my side."

"Uh-huh. Along with a little scientific judo?"

"Hapkido," he corrected. "I work out with a colleague of mine who's an expert." He lost interest in the matter, beginning to toy with the crown of her breast. "You make me feel so unbelievably fantastic, Sophy. I would have fought ten clones of that cowboy tonight for the right to possess you." Before she could say anything he suddenly came alert.

"What's wrong?"

"The ice cream! I just remembered I left it sitting on the table over there. It's going to be melting all over the place." He got to his feet in a lithe movement and strode across the room to collect the rapidly softening ice cream. At the doorway into the kitchen he turned and glared at her. "Don't move. I'll be right back."

Sophy stayed where she was, not at all certain she could move. Her body felt boneless, utterly satiated. Her mind was in a shifting, dreamy state that was new to her. She had no will to look beyond the present. It was far easier to focus only on this moment. Sophy was still telling herself that when she realized Max was standing beside her.

"Now you can get up," he murmured, reaching down to lift her to her feet.

She opened her eyes and drew in her breath at the arrogant maleness of him. Every inch of his body seemed to tug at her senses. The musky scent of him was intoxicating. When she came to her feet in front of him, she stumbled as her legs refused to function properly.

"Poor Sophy," he whispered, sounding quite satisfied with her unsteady condition. "You're not sure yet what's happened to you, are you?" He bent and lifted her easily into his arms and smiled as the curling mane of her hair tumbled across his shoulder.

"Where…where are we going?" Not that she would be able to protest if she didn't like the destination, Sophy decided with an inner smile. She was too enthralled by Max's wizardry tonight to do anything else except stay with him.

"To bed."

She leaned her head against his shoulder, her fingers playing idly with the fascinating cloud of hair on his chest, and let herself be carried down the hall to the bedroom. There in the darkness he settled her gently onto turned-down sheets. Then he stood for a moment, drinking in the sight of her lying in the center of the bed, waiting for him. Sophy could read the exultant arousal that was beginning anew in his eyes. Wordlessly she opened her arms.

"Sophy, you make my blood sing." Then he was lowering himself to her once more, gathering her close. All through the endless night Sophy stayed safely locked in the wizard's possessive embrace. She refused to think about the coming dawn.

Ultimately, it wasn't the dawn that awakened her the next morning. It was the ringing of the telephone. Sophy came drowsily to her senses, aware that the bed was empty beside her and aware, too, of the fragrance of freshly made coffee.

The phone rang again. There was something about the phone in the mornings, she reminded herself vaguely. Something about the phone ringing on Sunday mornings.

Was it Sunday? Her mother always called on Sunday mornings. With a start, Sophy struggled to a sitting position and reached for the extension beside the bed.

Before she could pick it up she heard Max answer on the living room extension. Helplessly Sophy listened to his greeting. She prayed that it was not her mother.

"Hello? No, you've got the right number. This is Sophy Bennet's apartment. What? Who's this? This is Max Travers speaking. Why, hello, Dr. Bennet. Good to talk to you again. How's the weather back there? Hotter 'n' hell down here in Texas. You were right about Dallas, by the way, all chrome and glass and Western atmosphere. Did you know they've still got real live cowboys left down here? Not as tough as they used to be. Then again, maybe they never really were all that tough to begin with. Maybe we've all just been fed a romanticized image of the Western folk hero."

Her worst fears confirmed, Sophy quickly lifted the bedside receiver. "Max, wait. Mother? This is Sophy. That's Max on the other extension. He, uh, came by early this morning. I'm taking him to see some of the local sights." Frantically Sophy rushed into the conversation, desperate to correct the impression her mother must have gotten when Max answered her daughter's phone so early in the morning.

"I see," Anna Bennet began, only to be interrupted by Max again.

"Sophy's been very gracious to me, Dr. Bennet," he drawled easily. Where the hell had he picked up that faint Texas drawl? "She and I grilled steaks last night and this morning we're going to have breakfast together. Then we'll have to see about making some plans for the rest of the day."

"You're having breakfast together?" Anna Bennet inquired with a mother's deep interest. "It's rather early for Sophy."

"You can say that again. She's still in bed. I was just about to take her some coffee, in fact, to help her get her eyes open," Max chuckled fondly.

"Max just arrived, Mother," Sophy put in abruptly. "He caught me a bit unprepared." Shut up, Max, she begged silently. For God's sake, just shut up!

"How's your husband?" Max was saying cheerfully. "Good. Tell him I got a chance to read that paper he gave me on Jordan curves. Fascinating."

"He'll be looking forward to discussing it with you when you get back to Chapel Hill," Anna Bennet said. "And I'm so glad you and Sophy are hitting it off well. You know, Sophy was hanging around with some cowboy, last we heard, and her father and I were a trifle nervous about the relationship, to say the least."

"Mother!"

"No need to worry about the cowboy," Max assured Dr. Bennet a little too smoothly. "He's not in the picture any longer. Rode his horse off into the sunset."

"Max!"

"Well, that's reassuring," Dr. Bennet said happily. "Sophy, dear, you know how I felt about that cowboy. When you lived in California I used to dread your getting involved with some long-haired surfer type. Then when you moved to Texas I had to worry about cowboys. Such a relief to know you're seeing a nice young man like Max. Why don't you talk Max into coming back to Chapel Hill with you next weekend?"

"Excellent idea," Max put in swiftly before Sophy could hedge.

"I'm sure he's much too busy…" Sophy tried valiantly.

"I can manage the time."

Sophy could practically see her mother's beaming

smile. "Fine. What time does the flight arrive at the Raleigh-Durham airport, Sophy dear? Your father and I will meet the plane."

"The flight gets in at ten-thirty," Sophy sighed, knowing she was beaten.

"Wonderful. We'll be there. Can't wait to see both of you. Oh, and Max, thank you so much for looking Sophy up down there in Dallas."

"Believe me," Max drawled, "it's been my pleasure. You don't have to worry about Sophy anymore, Dr. Bennet. I'll be looking after her here in Dallas."

"Well, of course, Max," Dr. Bennet said, sounding vaguely surprised he should even bother to mention the subject. "Paul and I both know you're a gentleman as well as an outstanding scholar. See you next weekend!"

"With pleasure," Max laughed. "I could use a couple of days back in an academic environment. You know what a thrill it is to get out into the real world and lend industry a hand," he added derisively. "Actually, the only thing that has made this trip worthwhile is Sophy."

"Goodbye, Mother!" Sophy tried to infuse a certain amount of command into her voice, and fortunately the other two seemed to sense it.

"Goodbye, Sophy, dear. And goodbye to you, Max. See you soon."

Max and Sophy put down their separate extensions simultaneously, but Sophy's came down a good deal harder. "Damn it! Max, how could you!" she shouted.

He appeared in the doorway of her bedroom, coffee in hand, a charmingly bland expression of inquiry on his face. "How could I what?"

Hastily Sophy yanked the sheet up to her throat, blushing at the possessive gleam in his eyes as he surveyed her in bed. "What on earth were you thinking of, answering the phone at this hour? Do you have any notion at all of what my mother must be thinking? She'll be weaving all sorts of marriage plans around the two of us, if I know her. She's probably already planning on enrolling him at Harvard!"

"Enrolling who?" Max looked at her blankly.

"Their grandchild!"

"Oh, him. I was thinking of Princeton, myself. That's where I went to school. Best math department in the country…" He broke off to dodge the pillow Sophy hurled at him and managed the feat without spilling the coffee.

For some reason the casual masculine grace of the movement stirred memories of his lovemaking during the night, and Sophy grabbed another pillow in blind self-defense.

"Sophy, honey, wait a minute." Max grinned, coming forward with the coffee in a gesture of appeasement. "Just listen to me."

She ignored him but dropped the pillow back on the bed as she got to her feet and grabbed for her robe. "No, you listen to me, Dr. Travers. You can play all the male games you want and my parents can dream all the dreams they want, but I am not going to be the ball you big cats bat around for fun, is that clear? I'm going to live my own life. I will not be your mistress, in spite of what happened last night. I will not settle down to producing little wizards for my parents to educate. I am going to open my own business here in Dallas and I'm going to date all the cowboys I want to date. And if and when I ever decide to marry, I'll send you all an invitation."

"Sophy!" As Max set down the coffee cup, his voice lost its teasing tone. Suddenly it held ice and steel. "To begin with, I don't recall mentioning marriage."

"Then you shouldn't have answered that telephone and implied to my mother that we're sleeping together!" she stormed, inexplicably hurt by the way he brushed off the word *marriage*. What was the matter with her, anyway? Of course she had no intention of marrying him. Why should she want him to be thinking of it?

"But now that the subject of marriage has arisen," Max put in deliberately, "I think it should be discussed."

That made her even angrier. "It sounds like much too academic a subject for me. I'm going to take a shower!" She whirled. How dare he treat it so deliberately and...and *academically?*

"Now hold on just one damn minute, Sophy Bennet." Max reached for her and yanked her around to face him. His gray eyes glittered with sudden male dominance. It occurred to Sophy that Max had undergone a dangerous transformation in the few days she had known him. That first night, when he had taken her out to dinner, he had been far more diffident and unassertive. She would never have guessed that in such a short time she would find herself not only seduced by him but intimidated on something other than an intellectual level.

"Let me go, Dr. Travers!"

"In a moment, Miss Bennet. There are a few things we should get settled first. What happened last night doesn't just get wiped out by a phone call from your mother, or because you're having second thoughts this morning. You're mine now. I told you that last night, and what's more important, you admitted it."

"I was...was caught up in an emotional, highly charged situation and I...I..."

"Are you going to claim I took advantage of you again? That you were emotionally vulnerable and I pushed you into bed? Don't bother, Sophy. It won't wash. You and I are definitely, undeniably *involved,* whether you like it or not. We're having an affair—"

"Two nights in bed together doesn't constitute an affair!"

"It does in our case," he retorted coldly. "Furthermore, I have some surprisingly primitive feelings on the subject of fidelity. Don't threaten me with cowboys ever again, because if I ever catch you with another cowboy or any other man, I'll beat you so thoroughly you'll think studying differential calculus was a treat by comparison!"

Sophy couldn't believe her ears. "And to think I once considered possessiveness in a man rather quaintly attractive, a sign of affection. But it's nothing but the basic male ego at work, isn't it? You think that because you've made love to me a couple of times you can set down all kinds of rules!"

"I haven't just made love to you a couple of times, Sophy Bennet," he gritted. "I have also fought another man for you and I have had you surrender completely in my arms. That gives me all kinds of rights, and I'm sorry if you don't like the possessiveness. It's a little new to me, too. I haven't ever felt quite this way about a woman before. But I'm damn well not going to go back to the stage where you walk all over me."

"I never tried to walk all over you! I simply tried to put as much distance as possible between us!" she cried wretchedly.

"Well, we're not going back to that stage either," he vowed, hauling her against his half-nude body. "I've worked too hard to get close to you!" He crushed her mouth under his, ignoring Sophy's impotent attempts at freeing herself.

She was terribly vulnerable, trying to battle him while she stood nearly naked in his arms, Sophy realized hysterically. All the memories of last night's passion were still too strong, especially in these surroundings—the rumpled bed; the memory of the way his shoulders had blocked out the moonlight when he'd lowered himself to her in the middle of the night. Even the scent of their lovemaking seemed to hover in the air. And they all contrived to leave her without any weapons when he forced his kiss on her lips.

God help her, Sophy thought agonizingly as she felt her body's reaction to Max's embrace, she was falling in love with the man. This wasn't mere sexual attraction, and it wasn't anything like what she had known with Nick Savage. She would be fooling herself terribly if she pretended she wasn't falling in love with Max Travers. And it was all so hopeless. He was so very wrong for her. Just as wrong as she would be for him. She would not be his crayons!

"Sophy," Max groaned huskily, "don't be afraid of me or of what we have together."

She shivered in his grasp, but whatever she would have said was lost in his deep kiss. When he lifted his head, they both knew the fight had gone out of her. Wordlessly she freed herself and headed for the shower.

Over breakfast forty minutes later she tried the rational approach. Pouring herself another cup of coffee, she took a deep breath and plunged in. "Max, have you given any real thought at all to what everyone's going to think if you go back to Chapel Hill with me next weekend?"

"Sure. They'll think we're passionately in love." His smile was very bland and very dangerous.

She must never forget for one moment that the intelligence behind those smoky eyes was formidable, Sophy reminded herself. Men like this had always been intimidating, but since she had left the academic world behind they had never posed a real threat to her. Now this man had moved into a sphere in which she should have been more than able to hold her own. And he was outmaneuvering her. He was ably assisted by her own traitorous emotions.

She had to fight or go under the tidal wave that threatened to engulf her.

"Well, we'll just have to make very sure that folks back in North Carolina don't accidentally get the wrong impression, won't we?" she said with a smile every bit as bland as his own. But she could still hear the satisfaction in her mother's voice.

And I'll have to make damn sure I learn how to stay out of Max Travers's bed, she added with grim conviction.

CHAPTER EIGHT

ON MONDAY MORNING SOPHY walked into the offices of S & J Technology with a briefcase full of business-oriented magazines lifted off her coffee table and a profound thankfulness that Max had displayed a certain forbearance the night before. He had allowed himself to be sent home after dinner, much to Sophy's astonishment.

She hadn't questioned her luck, but she did question the emptiness of her apartment after he'd gone. Briskly she thrust aside the thought and walked toward Marcie's desk with firm purpose.

The blond looked up expectantly, a bit surprised.

"Marcie, we need to talk."

Warily Marcie bit her lip. "I know. It was a stupid idea, wasn't it? Of course you don't want to go through with it. And now that I've had the weekend to think it over, I don't either." She sighed. "I want to make it to the top, and I'm willing to be a little ruthless to get there, but I guess the truth is I'm not willing to compromise myself."

Sophy smiled. "I had a hunch you'd feel this way. But there's something else we need to talk about. Let's go down to the cafeteria and get some coffee."

"But it's too early to take a break," Marcie noted uneasily.

"Believe me, taking an early break is the last thing we should spend time worrying about. Marcie, this is important."

"All right."

Fifteen minutes later they secluded themselves at a corner table with two cups of hot coffee. A few members of junior management cast displeased glances at the pair of secretaries who had dared to take an unofficial break, but nothing was said.

"I don't know what got into me on Thursday," Marcie began unhappily. "I was so damned furious over being rejected for that promotion. I let my temper get the better of me."

"And I was just as angry over the fool I made of myself with Max Travers." Sophy couldn't bring herself to explain about the manner in which she'd run to Max to warn him and how everything had blown up in her face. There was no point, she told herself. This was a time for action. "Both of us let our anger get the best of us for a while. But when all is said and done, we really were rather justified, don't you think?"

Marcie smiled wryly. "Oh, yes. I think we both had justification."

"When dealing with a large corporation, a certain amount of subtlety is necessary," Sophy murmured thoughtfully as she stirred cream into her coffee. "And that applies to the fine art of teaching a lesson."

Marcie stared at her. "What are you talking about, Sophy?"

"I think the management of S & J needs a lesson."

"What kind of lesson?"

"It needs to learn that mere secretaries should be taken a bit more seriously in the future."

"Sophy, you look very dangerous right at this moment," Marcie observed.

"I'm feeling a little dangerous. And a little reckless. We're going to find you a job, Marcie."

"A job!"

"Ummm. Oh, not here at S & J. We're just going to make sure that S & J appreciates what it lost when it loses you."

Marcie grinned. "A pleasant thought, but I don't see how we can manage that."

Sophy opened her briefcase and drew out a handful of booklets. Automatically Marcie leaned over to read the titles. "*Women in Business? Successful Women? Profiles of Successful Women and their Corporations?* Sophy, what are you going to do?"

"Find you a job at management level in one of the female-run technology firms profiled in these pamphlets. Oh, there aren't a lot of them because most such firms are run by men. But there are a couple, and all we need is one good one." She fanned out the pamphlets and grinned. "Pick a company, Marcie. Any company."

"And then what?"

"Then we convince that company they can't survive without you," Sophy said simply.

"What if the company doesn't happen to have any job openings?"

"It will. A good company always has openings for brilliant managers."

"And how are we going to make me look brilliant? The only jobs I have on my résumé are secretarial positions!"

"We start by rewriting your résumé," Sophy said. "And we go from there."

"Sophy, I get the feeling I'm seeing a new side of you."

"Not really. I just haven't had much chance to display this side before now," Sophy laughed.

Throughout the rest of the day Marcie snatched every spare moment to study the magazines and pamphlets Sophy had given her. While she did so, Sophy concealed a copy of her friend's résumé among the pile of papers on her desk and surreptitiously made notes.

"It's too bad no one realizes just how much a good secretary really learns in the process of her work," Sophy noted at one point.

"I'm tired of waiting for recognition. You know the first thing I'm going to do when I get a high-level position, Sophy? Hire a male secretary."

"One with good legs?"

"Go ahead and laugh. I'm going to do it. It will be a symbolic action."

"I'd rather like to see Max Travers working as someone's secretary," Sophy decided wistfully. "The man can't even type."

As if the thought of him had conjured him up, the phone on Sophy's desk rang. Before she even said hello, she had an instinctive knowledge of who would be on the other end of the line.

"Sophy? I'm going to have to stay late with the programmer and work on this processing model this evening. I was planning to take you out to dinner tonight, but it looks like we'll have to postpone it. I'll call you later this evening."

Sophy heard the preoccupied note in his voice and almost found it endearing. The wizard at work. It was amazing, actually, that he'd even remembered to call. She knew a sense of relief mixed with a very real disappointment at the information that she would be spending the evening alone. "That will be fine, Max."

Her sense of disappointment had become anxiety by that evening, when she analyzed the situation. She was aware of feeling pressured, trapped and terrified at the prospect of being in love with a man who was totally wrong for her.

How could Dr. Maximilian Travers ever really love and

respect a woman who wasn't his intellectual equal? And how could she love a man who was destined to spend his life in an ivory tower?

"What I want is a man who can laugh with me as well as make love to me," she muttered aloud as she lay stretched out under the kitchen sink, preparing to fix the leaking fitting. "I want a man who lives life down here on my ordinary, humdrum level, not in the rarefied atmosphere of an academic tower. Damn sink. I want a man who can respect my abilities. A man who really thinks I'm his equal, not a toy he can play with. I'm not a pack of crayons, for crying out loud!"

The doorbell cut into the monologue.

"Oh, for pity's sake!" she exclaimed, as a box of soap nearby fell over when she scrambled out from under the sink. Sophy glared at it and at the evidence of the leak she had set out to fix. Then, grumbling, she headed for the door. Max Travers was on the threshold.

"What I really want," she gritted, waving the wrench at him, "is a man who knows how to fix a sink, unclog a toilet and grill a steak!"

Max's gaze went from the menacing wrench to the yellow T-shirt and orange trousers Sophy was wearing. Then his eyes went to the smudge on her nose and he smiled. "You want a plumber who can cook?"

"This is not funny!" She glared at him and then thrust the wrench into his hand. "Here. Show me you can do something useful in the world. We don't need more people who can think in five dimensions at the same time; we need people who can fix leaky plumbing. Cheap. What good is a man who can't fix a faucet?"

His eyes slitted as he looked down at the wrench. "You're in a swell mood, aren't you?"

"I mean it, Max. If you can't fix my faucet, just get in your car and go back to your hotel!"

"Sophy, I came here tonight to talk to you, not to fix your sink," he began reasonably, stepping inside the door and shutting it firmly behind him.

"Well, I don't have time to talk."

"Listen, honey, why don't you just call a plumber? Or the apartment manager?"

"At this hour of the night? It's nearly ten o'clock," she exploded. "One doesn't call managers or plumbers at ten o'clock at night unless it's a real emergency!"

He frowned. "Well, isn't it?"

"Max, all that is necessary is to use this wrench to tighten up a loose fitting on the pipe under the sink," Sophy retorted with exaggerated patience. She spun around on her heel and stalked back to the kitchen. "I realize that someone with a Ph.D. in mathematics might find such simple household repairs beyond his ability, but the rest of us have learned to take care of the little problems in life."

"Sophy…"

She heard the incipient irritation in his voice and ignored it. "Go away, Max. Tonight I need a man who knows and understands the real world, not a mathematician."

"Damn it, Sophy, give me the wrench!" He yanked it out of her hand just as she was about to lower herself back under the sink.

Sophy looked at him in astonishment. He was scowling rather fiercely. "Forget it, Max. I don't want a bigger leak than the one I've already got."

"I'll fix your damned sink!"

"You don't know how to fix a sink!"

"I learned how to grill a steak, didn't I? You said yourself there are some things men are supposed to know instinctively. Well, I'm a man and I've got instincts like every other man. I'll put my instincts up against those of any dumb cowboy you can find in Texas! Now, get out of my way, woman. I'm going to fix the plumbing."

Sophy blinked and found herself stepping aside. She thought about telling him he'd cooked a lousy steak, but for some reason she couldn't do it. He looked so determined to fix the sink that she didn't have the courage to refuse him the opportunity. He was already examining the unique shape of the wrench in his hand. The next thing she knew he was crouching under the sink, eyeing the shape of the fittings. She watched him check the position of the leak, and then his hand tentatively went to the fitting above it.

"That's the one," she grudgingly admitted, kneeling beside him and peering at the piping.

"Geometry," he muttered. "Simple geometry."

"You fix plumbing your way and I'll fix it mine. I don't use geometry!"

He leaned down and turned over on his back, sliding under the curved pipe. "This," he said in satisfaction, "is going to be a snap compared to grilling a steak."

Sophy got to her feet with a muffled groan. What was she going to do if he succeeded in actually fixing the damn fitting? "As long as you're down there…" she began.

"If you're going to make me spend the whole evening working on your plumbing, you can darn well think again. One fitting is all I'm going to do tonight."

"What I was going to say," she shot back far too sweetly, "is that as long as you're down there, I thought I could give you some advice."

"Wonderful."

"Don't waste any more time working up a fake

computer math model of that processing system. I can tell you right now that Marcie isn't going to steal it."

He paused and she wondered at the sudden stillness in him. "You're sure?"

"I'm sure."

Another pause. "What about, uh, Younger's big charade?" he finally asked carefully. "Our posing as lovers and all."

"Oh, that can stand as it is," Sophy said airily.

Another pause. Longer this time. "Mind telling me why?"

"I've got plans of my own. Besides, we'll never be able to convince Younger that his scheme won't work. For the time being I want to act as though I'm still following orders."

"Sophy…" He sounded abruptly worried.

"Don't fret, Max. I'll explain everything when it's all over. I'm just telling you a bit now so you won't waste your time dummying up a fake printout. You can let Younger think you're still working on it, though."

"Sophy, I don't know what you're up to, but I don't like it."

"Don't worry about it, Max. This is my world. I know what I'm doing."

"I do not want you getting into any trouble," he began adamantly.

"The only trouble I have at the moment is a leaking faucet. How are you doing down there?"

"I don't know yet."

"There was one other thing I wanted to mention."

"I knew it," he groaned. "What is it?"

Sophy took hold of all the fortitude she possessed. "Max, I am not going to sleep with you again. Is that very, very clear?"

There was a sudden loud clang as something metallic

scraped harshly along something else that was also metallic and then fell on the floor of the cupboard.

"Max! Are you all right?"

"Damn it to hell," Max growled.

"What's wrong?" she asked anxiously, going down on her knees to glance inside the cupboard.

"Nothing." The single word came out sounding like a curse. It was followed by another four-letter word that was definitely out of the "expletive deleted" variety. "I'm just fixing the darned sink."

Sophy climbed back to her feet, frowning worriedly. "Oh. Well, did you hear what I said, Max?" Somehow it was easier having this very necessary conversation with him trapped under the sink. Sophy realized that the last thing she wanted to do was to have to look him in the eye while she told him she wouldn't go to bed with him.

"I heard you. Would you please hand me a rag?" One strong arm extended itself from the confines of the cupboard. Wordlessly Sophy stuffed a rag into the waiting fingers. "Thank you," Max said very politely, and went back to work. Several moments passed. Sophy began to grow restless.

"Max?"

"Hmmm?"

She cleared her throat. "Max, I mean it. I know I haven't given you any reason to think I have willpower, but I assure you—"

"What I'd really like at the moment, Sophy, is a drink. I think the fitting is going to stay tight now." He began to inch his way out of the cupboard. Then he was crouching in front, surveying his handiwork while he wiped his hands on the rag. He looked rather pleased with himself, Sophy thought, and squelched an inner groan of dismay. "You know," he announced, "that wasn't really too hard. It's just a matter of analyzing the situation and then applying the wrench in the proper manner. Take a look."

Sophy slanted him a long glance and then obediently bent down to check his workmanship. "It looks like it's stopped leaking," she agreed cautiously, and realized almost at once that wasn't enough. He was hovering beside her like a proud artist showing off his masterpiece. Max wanted some genuine applause, and for some damn fool reason she couldn't resist giving his ego the stroking it wanted. "You did a terrific job." She could have kicked herself for saying the words he wanted to hear. "It's definitely stopped leaking." What else could one say about a fixed pipe? She leaned into the cabinet and tested the once-loose fitting. "Oh, that's on a lot more securely than I could have managed," she added brightly. Idiot. What was the matter with her? But Sophy couldn't bring herself to denigrate his first attempt at fixing plumbing. "You're very useful around the house, Max. I really appreciate your help tonight. That leak has been pestering me for days."

"No problem," he declared smoothly, getting to his feet. "Now, about that drink?"

"Actually," she said carefully, "I was going to pop some popcorn and watch an old movie on television this evening." Best to scare him out of the house before things got dangerous, Sophy told herself firmly. And she *had* been planning to watch the film.

He looked closely at her. "What old movie?"

"Nothing you'd be interested in, I'm sure," she said quickly. "It's one of those old science-fiction thrillers from the early fifties. You know, *The Eggplant That Ate Seattle* or something. You wouldn't like it at all."

"Why are you going to watch it?" he asked, leaning back against the counter.

"Because those old science-fiction flicks are hilarious," she said without thinking.

"I could use a good laugh after working on that damn program all evening and coming home to fix broken plumbing." Max rubbed the back of his neck in a gesture of weariness.

Sophy flinched at his use of the word *home* and narrowed her eyes. "It will keep you up rather late, Max. If you're tired, you should go back to the hotel and get some rest."

"I can rest sitting on your couch watching the film. Where's the popcorn? I haven't had popcorn in ages." He glanced around the kitchen in anticipation.

"Max…"

"There's the corn popper. Up on top of your refrigerator. I'll get it down for you." He reached up to lift the machine down before she could find any words of protest. "Now, where's the oil?"

She grimaced. "It *has* been a long time since you had popcorn, hasn't it? That's one of the new air poppers. It doesn't use oil."

"Oh, yeah?" He glanced down at the machine in his hands. "How does it work?"

"You mean the physics of it?" she drawled, rummaging around in the small pantry for the popcorn. "I wouldn't have the vaguest idea. All I know is that you dump the corn in here and turn the sucker on. Presto! Popcorn."

"Fascinating."

"Uh-huh. Something tells me you're not going to be equally fascinated by this movie, Max," Sophy warned above the roar of the popping machine. "Are you sure you shouldn't be heading back to the hotel? You must be tired."

He gave her a level glance. "I'll survive."

She sucked in her breath. "I meant it, you know. You can't spend the night here, Max." She studied the growing pile of fluffy popcorn in the bowl on the counter.

"Are you afraid of me, Sophy?" His voice was low and gentle.

"I've behaved like a fool with you. I suppose we're all a little afraid of people who can make fools out of us."

"Look at me, honey."

Her head lifted warily. There was a curiously earnest gleam in his smoky eyes. It made her even more uneasy. "Max, please, I…"

"Don't be afraid of me, Sophy. Just relax. Treat me like a man, not a mathematician," he said with a faint edge of humor curving his mouth. "Give me a chance, honey. I told you I've got all the normal instincts."

"I've already encountered your normal instincts!" she snapped, switching off the popper. "On at least two different occasions. And as far as I'm concerned, that's twice too often. I meant what I said, Max. There will be no more sex between us! Now, if you're going to stay and watch this movie and eat my popcorn, you'll have to give me your word of honor as a gentleman that you won't force yourself on me."

He sighed, folding his arms across his chest. "Sophy, listen to me."

"Your word, Max."

"All right, all right. My word as a gentleman and a scholar. You can eat your popcorn in peace."

She chewed her lip and then nodded, accepting his promise. "Okay. You can stay. But you won't like it."

"Not being able to make love to you? I know I won't like it, but I'll live."

"I meant the film! You won't like the film!" she corrected waspishly as she carried the popcorn out into the living room and set the bowl down on the coffee table. Then she switched on the television.

"How can you be so sure of what I'll like and not like?" he demanded, following her into the front room.

"Believe me, this is not going to be your kind of film. The science in it is shoddy in the extreme. Mostly, it's completely lacking. Lots of bug-eyed monsters and mad scientists."

"I know a few of those, myself," he retorted equably.

"Monsters or mad scientists?"

"Mad scientists. Hey, the film's in black-and-white."

"I told you it was old. These were pretty low-budget flicks." She sat down beside him on the couch and reached for the popcorn. "Just let me know when you get bored and want to leave."

"I'll let you know," he promised sardonically.

But he didn't get bored. Much to Sophy's surprise, he joined with her in cheering for the monster and booing the newspaper reporter and the good scientist who were trying to stop him. The corny dialogue and ridiculously old-fashioned special effects sent Sophy off into gales of laughter, and Max was not far behind. Together they wolfed down the entire bowl of popcorn and gave the monster a lot of advice on how to survive. But at last the creature went down, drawn under the sea in a whirlpool created by the scientist.

"Gone but not forgotten," Sophy pronounced. "He'll return, mark my words. You can't keep a good monster down."

"I hope not. I'd like to see him return. He was a fairly decent sort of monster. Not his fault the humans kept getting in his way. All he wanted was to feed off the energy in those bombs." Max leaned his head back against the couch, his legs stretched out in front of him. He glanced at Sophy. "Thanks."

"For what? The popcorn?" she asked lightly.

"And the film. I've never seen anything quite like it."

"Obviously you had a deprived childhood." She smiled. "Personally, I would have had a deprived one, too, if I hadn't snuck downstairs late at night to watch television. I also nourished myself during my formative years with a pile of superhero comics I kept stashed under my mattress. I read them with a flashlight under the covers."

"I didn't get to read a comic until I was in college," Max said quietly. "Not even the funny pages from the newspaper. My parents thought they were silly and frivolous. To tell you the truth, I agreed with them."

"They are silly and frivolous. That's why they're good for you."

Max smiled. "You're good for me," he said softly, reaching out to gather her into his arms.

Instantly Sophy was on her feet, scooping up the empty bowl of popcorn. "I think it's time you went home, Max." Turning her back on him, she headed for the kitchen. Behind her she heard him slowly get to his feet.

"It's a long drive back downtown…"

"Then you should have left earlier."

"Before I found out whether the monster or the scientist won?" he protested, ambling into the kitchen behind her.

She swung around, her chin lifted proudly. "I meant what I said, Max. You're not staying the night." There was almost a pleading note in her words.

He looked down at her for a long moment, and she could read nothing in the depths of his eyes. Then he lifted his hand to toy with the curls that fell on her shoulders. "Such wonderful hair," he breathed, leaning forward to inhale the scent of it.

"Good night, Max," she whispered huskily. Already she

could feel the flickering sensual tension beginning to flare between them. But this time she would not succumb.

"Sophy, at least let me kiss you," he murmured in that low, persuasive voice that he always seemed to use when he got close to her. It played havoc with her senses. Sophy's fingernails bit into the softness of her palm, but she held fast to her resolve.

"No, Max."

"I want you, sweetheart."

"No, Max."

He groaned and abruptly hauled her into his arms, the flash of desire in his eyes burning strongly for a moment. "You can keep me out of your bed tonight, but you owe me this kiss, damn it!"

"Why?" she challenged, bringing up her hands to push against his chest.

"Because I fixed your leaky plumbing!" Then he was drinking his fill from her lips as if he anticipated dying of thirst in the near future. His mouth moved on hers with the sensual, plundering provocation she had already learned was her nemesis. But before she could summon the will to resist, he freed her, stepping away with an annoyed, frustrated and dangerously male expression on his hard features. "If you'll excuse me, I'll get my coat and be on my way," he drawled far too politely.

Sophy waited restlessly in the kitchen for him to collect the old tweed jacket from the hall closet. She heard the closet door open and close, and then she heard nothing more. There was no sound of his footsteps coming back down the hall. Damn that man! If he thought he could get away with forcing his way into her bedroom, he had a few things to learn about her!

"Max?" she called menacingly as she went down the

hall. There was no answer. "Max, where are you?" The light was off in the bedroom. If that man was playing games with her, she would be furious!

"I'm in here, Sophy," his answer finally came, sounding distant and vague, as if he were only half-aware of her call. The sound of his voice was emanating from her sewing room.

"Max? What in the world are you doing in here?" she demanded, pushing open the door.

"Just looking." He was bent over the large worktable, examining the pattern pieces lying on top of a length of material. He seemed as intent and curious as if he were looking at an oversized math problem. "How does all this work, Sophy?" he asked, glancing up briefly as she came into the room. "These lines on the pattern—they're very precise."

"Well, of course they're precise. Start out with a sloppy pattern and you'd wind up with a sloppy garment," she muttered, moving to stand on the opposite side of the table.

"The angles here—"

"Those are called darts. You use them to create shape in a piece of flat fabric, to help shape material to the human body. People have a lot of odd curves and angles on them, you know." A touch of humor laced her voice. "The wider the angle of the dart—"

"The greater the curving shape that will be created." He nodded at once, looking very serious.

"Well, yes," she agreed, momentarily surprised.

"What are these parallel lines for?"

"Pleats. They give fullness where I want it but with a sense of control."

He traced another line with the tip of his finger. "And this?"

"Just a seam line."

"And this curved section?"

"A collar. I want it to roll a bit, so I'm adding extra width at the outside edge." She leaned across the table to show the point where she had adjusted the outer curve of the pattern piece. "The more the neckline curve flattens, the greater the roll I'll get in the finished collar."

Max nodded again, looking surprisingly intrigued. Then he walked across the room and stood before a large sketch of a deceptively simple dress. "I think I can visualize how you get from the pattern to the finished garment," he said after a moment. "But there's no way on earth I could do it. And I can't even begin to figure out how you get from the sketch to the basic pattern. The original design is art. The pattern is a mathematical procedure. The final construction is art again. Amazing."

Sophy stood staring at him, equally amazed. No one from Max's world, not even her parents, had ever shown any interest in her work. The designing and construction of a garment were loosely labeled "sewing" and relegated to a pile of topics deemed mundane or frivolous. For a moment Sophy experienced a bond of communication, an understanding, that she rarely knew when dealing with someone from Max's world. He understood enough of her work to appreciate it. Her heart warmed.

She was still staring when Max turned around, swung his coat over his shoulder and walked back across the room to brush her mouth gently with his. "I'll go now, Sophy. But there's one other thing…"

"Yes, Max?" What was she hoping for. That he might insist on staying?

"I think you should call off whatever little scheme you've got going with Marcie Fremont. The woman suggested corporate espionage to you once. No telling what she might involve you in now."

The warmth that had crept into her began to fade. "I know what I'm doing, Max. And the scheme isn't Marcie's idea. It's all mine."

He frowned. "Sophy…"

"Don't worry. This won't affect you. All I'm going to do is find Marcie another job," she said too easily.

"Sophy, I…" He broke off on a sigh of resignation. "You're not going to tell me what's going on, are you?"

"Last time I did that, you ran straight to Graham Younger."

He winced. "I thought it was for the best."

"And look what you got us involved in."

"I can see this conversation is going nowhere. Good night, Sophy. I'll see you at work."

And then he was gone, leaving her with a new uncertainty and a new sense of ambivalence to add to her already unmanageable list of problems concerning Dr. Max Travers.

CHAPTER NINE

THE FOLLOWING MORNING Sophy put the next step of her plan into action. Marcie had selected her ideal company, a California firm run by a woman. It was a high-technology company competing in many of the same areas as S & J.

"I could really make a contribution there," Marcie said earnestly over coffee. "And there seems to be a fairly equal spread of men and women in management. It's an aggressive young firm, but it seems well-founded financially. From what I can tell, though, the staff seem to be pretty heavy on technological skills and rather light on business experience. Maybe they could use someone like me who has a slightly different background."

"If that's the one you want, that's the one we'll go for," Sophy said firmly. "Oh, by the way, here's your new résumé." She handed the paper to Marcie.

"But, Sophy, this doesn't even sound like me," Marcie gasped after a moment's close concentration. "This makes me sound…well, fabulous. Like I've been practically running S & J since I got here!"

"What we're going to do next," Sophy announced smugly, "is get some letters from S & J management testifying to that."

"What?" Marcie looked startled.

"Let's go back to work, Marcie. I have some letters to write."

The letters eulogizing the contributions of one Marcie Fremont to S & J Technology went out to be signed by appropriate members of management that afternoon. Sophy judged it wise not to allow Marcie to see them before they went out. The blond was liable to be somewhat appalled by the liberties Sophy had taken.

"Actually, it's just a bit of creative writing," Sophy had explained when Marcie anxiously tried to read one. "Now go back to work. You've got your hands full doing my tasks as well as your own today."

The first letter was slipped into a pile of correspondence waiting to be signed by the vice-president in charge of planning. It graphically detailed Marcie's expertise in that area. The second letter went into a stack sitting on the desk of the president's assistant. In each case Sophy waited until the executive's personal secretary was out of the office. Then she waylaid the secretaries and chatted with them while their bosses signed the letters while hurriedly pausing by the secretaries' desks. It was an easy matter to remove the letters from the piles of legitimate correspondence when the secretaries turned their backs.

A few more such letters from important people in the company joined the first two. And then Sophy wrote the cover letter that was to accompany Marcie's résumé and letters of recommendation. This she let Marcie see.

"But, Sophy, it says here I'm sending this packet of information at the request of their manager in charge of executive recruiting! I didn't get any such request."

"Details."

"Sophy, you're sending the letter to the vice-president instead of Personnel."

"The first rule in dealing with a corporation is to ignore Personnel," Sophy assured her blithely, stuffing the packet into a large envelope. "No one ever got a really high-level position by going through Personnel."

Marcie stared at her in wondering admiration. "You seem to know your way around corporations."

Sophy grinned. "I should. I've been studying them very carefully for several years. When I start my own business, I want to know as much as possible. Believe me, the vice-president who receives this packet will never figure out that his recruiting officer knows nothing about it."

"I'm fascinated. What's next?"

"A phone call later on in the week after we know this envelope has had a chance to reach its destination."

"Phone call? From whom?"

"From Graham Younger's office, of course, complaining loudly that the other firm is attempting to pirate you away. A few threats and requests to please not tempt you. That sort of thing."

"From Younger's office?" Marcie gasped.

"That's what the other company will think."

"Who's really going to make the call, Sophy?" Marcie demanded with an arched brow.

"Me."

"Oh, my."

"Believe me, hype is everything. Once they learn that S & J is frantic not to let you go, nothing will keep that California company from hiring you."

"Sophy, something tells me I should stick around here a little longer and learn from you!"

Sophy laughed. "I won't be here much longer myself."

The phone call went as planned. By the time Sophy hung up the receiver she was feeling very pleased with herself. Now it was all a matter of time.

"But something tells me they won't take long beating a path to your door, Wonder Woman," she told Marcie with a laughing smile.

MAX WAS AWARE OF AN ODDLY possessive sense of pride as he escorted Sophy off the plane and into the waiting lounge of the Raleigh-Durham airport. She was as vivid and colorful as ever today, he thought. Her expressive face was full of anticipation and pleasure at the prospect of seeing her parents. Even without the added effect of the racy turquoise jumpsuit she was wearing and the tumble of thick curls cascading down to her shoulders, that face caught and held one's attention. It held his at any rate, he amended wryly. She certainly wasn't trying to hold him with sex!

He still had no clear idea of what she was up to with Marcie Fremont, but he had made a conscious decision not to question his luck. She was still playing out the charade demanded of her by Graham Younger and his associates. Right now that seemed to be all that mattered. He'd keep an eye on her and make sure she didn't get into any real trouble. In the meantime, he'd told Younger's assistant that the plan was going well. They had agreed to let him manage things by himself until the crucial juncture.

The fact that there wasn't going to be a "crucial juncture" didn't particularly worry him. All he cared about was keeping Sophy within reach.

Until this past week Dr. Max Travers hadn't realized that he could actually lie alone in bed and hunger physically for a particular woman. The knowledge left him unsettled and restless, but it didn't affect him as badly as knowing that what he felt was not just a craving of the body. He found himself making every excuse imaginable just to be around

Sophy. The time that he wasted running back and forth to her office to check up on the various reports she typed for him was appalling!

"Mom! Dad!" Sophy was running ahead, leaving Max to bring her small under-the-seat bag. He had a momentary wish that the obviously feminine case weren't such an eye-catching shade of magenta. Then he grinned to himself. If a man was going to hang around Sophy Bennet very long, he would have to get used to being seen amid a lot of color.

Max watched a little wistfully as Sophy threw herself into her parents' arms. Then he took a firm grip on himself. One of these days, he vowed, Sophy would learn to greet him that enthusiastically.

"Sophy, dear, it's so good to see you again." Anna Bennet smiled warmly as she hugged her daughter. The older woman was something of a contrast to Sophy, and Max had to look closely to see the faint traces of resemblance. They were there in the curling hair that Anna Bennet kept severely trimmed, and in the gentle shape of the nose, but they weren't startlingly obvious. Dr. Bennet wore a conservatively cut tweed skirt, a sweater and a pair of sensible shoes.

Sophy's eyes, Max decided, came from her father, although his blue-green gaze seemed slightly faded compared to his daughter's vivid one. Paul Bennet was taller than his wife and daughter, his gray hair cut much like Max's. The realization made Max wince. Maybe he should think about getting his dark hair trimmed in a slightly less conservative style. Sophy might like it better. Paul Bennet was still a handsome man, his strong features revealing the intelligence and character that had shaped his career. He was dressed in a slightly rumpled tweed jacket, and in his shirt pocket there was a plastic pack of pencils and implements. The horn-rimmed glasses reminded Max uncomfortably of his own pair.

Watching Sophy flutter energetically among the three of them as greetings were accomplished, Max realized just how different she was from himself and her parents. She was colorful and outrageous, whereas the other three were bland and conservative. She was lively and full of laughter while he and the Bennets were reserved and far quieter in their demeanor. Watching the Bennets interact with their daughter, Max had a flash of insight into just how difficult things must have been for Sophy at times. It had undoubtedly worked both ways, he decided. Paul and Anna Bennet must have had moments when they wondered whether or not their daughter had been a changeling, a mischievous elf substituted at birth for the quiet, serenely brilliant daughter who should have been theirs.

But there was love in the family, even if the three people concerned sometimes wondered how Paul and Anna Bennet had managed to produce such an unexpected sort of daughter. Max's sense of wistfulness grew. He had been everything his parents had wanted and more, and yet he'd never known this kind of family affection.

"Max! Glad you could make it," Paul Bennet said genially, extending his hand. There was genuine pleasure in the eyes that so resembled Sophy's, and Max relaxed. Sophy might not appreciate his interest in her, but her parents were quite content with him, he thought on a note of humor.

"Thank you, sir. To tell you the truth, I was glad of the excuse to take a break from Dallas." *And I'd have followed your daughter to the North Pole.*

"Miss North Carolina, do you?" Paul chuckled as he shepherded everyone to the baggage-claim area.

Max cast an appreciative glance out at the rich green countryside. "Let's just say Dallas is a little different," he murmured dryly.

"Poor Max has been suffering greatly," Sophy informed everyone melodramatically. "Nearly three weeks of the real world and he's about to pine away."

"Sophy has done a great deal to cheer me up during the course of my exile," Max shot back smoothly, catching her eye and daring her to push the topic further. He received a speculative glance in return and then, much to his surprise, she moved on to another subject.

"What time is the ceremony and reception, Mom?" she asked brightly.

"Seven o'clock tonight. Did you bring something to wear?"

"What a silly question," Paul Bennet murmured as three huge magenta suitcases came trundling around the baggage belt.

Max grinned at the older man. "Sophy claims she likes to travel prepared."

Paul shook his head in wry affection. "She always did have a thing about clothes."

"I'll have you know that at least one of those suitcases is full of presents," Sophy tossed out indignantly as the two men picked up the colorful baggage. "After all, one can't go visiting an award-winning physicist without a few gifts!"

Max slid her a sidelong glance as he picked up the two heaviest cases and led the way out to the parking lot. She really was quite proud of her mother, he thought, in spite of her comments about academicians.

"Sophy's presents are always interesting, to say the least," Anna Bennet said with a knowing smile. She glanced at Max as the magenta cases were stowed in the back of the Bennets' car. "Has she had occasion to give you anything yet, Max?"

Max smiled as he slammed the trunk lid. "Yes, Sophy's given me some very special gifts," he said softly. He saw the sudden wariness in Sophy's eyes, and his smile broadened as he took her arm and guided her into the back seat of the car. "But I'm having a hard time finding out what she wants in return. Would you like me to drive, Dr. Bennet?"

"Thank you, Max." He handed over the keys. "It will give me a chance to talk to Sophy." He assisted his wife onto the seat alongside Sophy and then climbed into the front seat as Max started the car. "I understand the two of you have been seeing a lot of each other lately. Any surprises in the offing?"

There was a moment of electric silence during which Max considered a hundred different ways of saying he wanted Paul Bennet's daughter. But it was Sophy who rushed in to fill the breach.

"How did you know?" she demanded cheerfully. Max glanced quickly into the rearview mirror and caught the look of determination on her face. One thing was certain, she wasn't going to announce any engagement. "I've decided to open my own design boutique down in Dallas. I'm really very excited about it, aren't I, Max? Of course, I'll have to take out a loan, but I think I can get that. I made a dress for the woman who manages the loan department of my bank, and I'm sure she'll back me now that she's seen my work."

Another tense silence followed the exuberant announcement. It was Anna Bennet who broke it this time. "Oh, Sophy, dear, are you sure that's what you want to do? Have you given any more thought to going back for your master's degree? You know your father and I would love to have you get at least one more degree and we'd be more than happy to finance your educational costs."

Sophy took a deep breath. "Mom, I don't care if I never set foot on a campus again. Wasting time getting another degree is just about the last thing in the world I want to do. I'm going to open the boutique."

Her father coughed meaningfully. "But what about you and Max? I understood the two of you were hitting it off rather well. If the two of you decide to…that is, why would you want to open a little clothing shop if you're going to be getting—"

"Dad, I think this is an appropriate moment to say quite clearly that Max and I have absolutely no plans for marriage, do we, Max?" Sophy challenged him from the back seat.

Max heard the defiant taunting in her voice and simultaneously sensed the questioning glances he was getting from both of the Doctors Bennet. Trust Sophy to find a way of putting him on the spot. Maybe the Bennets should have spent more time applying their palms to Sophy's sweet backside rather than force-feeding her quadratic equations.

"Your daughter, sir," he said coolly to Paul Bennet, "seems to have a certain aversion to marrying anyone with a Ph.D. after his name."

"Oh, is that the problem?" Anna Bennet chuckled from the back seat, patting Sophy's hand affectionately. "I'm sure you'll overcome her prejudice, Max. She always claimed she'd never marry a professor, but we've told her time and time again that when the right man comes along, she'll change her mind."

"Well, since I haven't changed my mind," Sophy muttered forcefully, "we have to conclude that the right man hasn't yet come along."

There was a painful pause as everyone in the car

absorbed the full implications of her words. There was no doubt but that her statement hovered on being an outright insult. Sophy, herself, bit her lip in sudden anxiety, wishing she'd kept her mouth shut. But, damn it, she wasn't going to be pushed into anything, regardless of what her parents wanted! Max had created this mess by answering the phone last Sunday morning. Let him figure a way out of it.

Guiding the car along the stretch of freeway leading toward the town of Chapel Hill, Max could almost read her thoughts. She was feeling pressured again and she was going to fight the pressure, just as she had been doing for so many years.

"I get the feeling that Sophy would rather, er, live in sin than compromise her principles where professors are concerned," he drawled.

"I think it should be noted at this juncture," Sophy began dryly, "that I haven't been given a choice where Max is concerned."

Paul Bennet turned in the seat to stare quizzically at his daughter. "What are you talking about, Sophy? For heaven's sake, girl, make sense!"

"Okay, I'll lay it on the line," Sophy retorted with obvious relish. "Max has not asked me to marry him. Therefore, this whole discussion is absolutely pointless, isn't it, Max?"

He flicked another glance in the rearview mirror, and this time it was Anna Bennet's questioning gaze he found there. His hands tightened on the wheel.

"I have learned," Max said evenly, in response to the uncomfortable silence in the car, "that if one wants the best results from Sophy, one doesn't *ask* her anything. One tells her."

Suddenly Paul Bennet laughed out loud and a moment later his wife joined him. "I think you may have the right approach, Travers. She's an independent little thing, isn't she?"

"Probably gets it from her parents," Max said gently.

Anna Bennet smiled contentedly. "Oh, we tried to make a proper daughter out of her, Max. Don't think we didn't try. But Sophy always went off on her own tangents. She brought home stray kittens instead of straight A's on her report cards. She read Nancy Drew stories when she should have been reading her Boolean algebra, and she was forever playing with scraps of fabric when she should have been playing with physics. Every time I turned around, the child had a crayon in her hand instead of a pencil and a calculator. When she was five, my entire kitchen was decorated with designs for doll clothes."

And your house was filled with color and the unexpected, Max added silently.

"Mind you," Paul Bennet inserted quickly, "she has the basic ability; it's just that her interests have never been, well, properly focused. That's why we keep hoping she'll go back to school."

"Dad, you don't have to sell me to Max," Sophy drawled from the back seat. "He knows perfectly well that I'm not a wizard. No point trying to fool him."

Paul shifted uncomfortably in the front seat, and suddenly Max found himself grinning conspiratorially at the older man. "Sassy, rebellious and undisciplined," Max said, "but I would say that the genes are undoubtedly quite sound. Couldn't be anything else coming from you and Anna."

"Max Travers!" Sophy nearly choked on her outrage, but everyone else was laughing and a moment later she succumbed to the humor of the situation. Max was getting a little too fast on his feet, she decided wryly. He was starting to hold his own in areas that had been exclusively hers, like taunting wizards.

BY SEVEN O'CLOCK THAT EVENING equilibrium had been restored to the Bennet household. Max had walked from the Bennets' to his own home a few tree-shaded blocks away, saying he would return in time to walk with them to the campus where the ceremonies were being held.

"I'm going to see if I can dig out a new nerd pack for the occasion," he'd murmured to Sophy on the way out.

"Good idea," she retorted. "Why don't you fill it with crayons instead of pens and pencils? Might set a whole new style on campus." She smiled saucily as he gave her a strange glance.

When he returned at seven, wearing his best tweed jacket and his newest tie—which was still about an inch too narrow—Sophy and her parents were ready to go.

"You look very charming tonight, Anna," Max said politely, meaning it. She was dressed more fashionably than usual in a striking black-and-white suit that complemented her refined, academic air.

"Sophy made this for me." Anna smiled, gesturing at the skirt and jacket. "It was one of the presents in the suitcase."

Max looked at Sophy. "I've heard people say she's a genius with clothing design," he said softly. Sophy herself was wearing one of her typically flashy outfits, a tiny, pencil-slim suit with a nipped-in jacket trimmed with broad lapels. The suit was white, the lapels shocking pink. "What was your present, Dr. Bennet?" he asked, nodding at Paul.

"A smoking jacket." Paul Bennet chuckled. "Never had one before. Sophy says it will go nicely with the image. I'm supposed to sit in front of the fire and smoke my pipe in it. Really, my boy, I think it's time you started calling me Paul," he added firmly as he pulled his wife's coat out of the closet.

"Thank you," Max murmured politely, his eyes on Sophy. "Are we ready?"

"Not quite," Sophy said abruptly, turning away to head down the hall toward the bedrooms. Her impossibly high heels made tantalizingly tapping sounds on the parquet floor, and Max watched until she disappeared.

In the bedroom she used whenever she visited her parents, Sophy opened one of the magenta suitcases and removed the last gift. Up until now she had been of two minds about whether or not to give it, but for some reason the decision had been made. Clutching it firmly in her left hand, she went back into the paneled living room where Max and her parents waited.

"Here," she said brusquely. "This one's for you, Max."

Behind the lenses of his glasses Max's smoky eyes flared for an instant before he lowered his gaze to the long, narrow box in her hand. "For me?" He looked as if he didn't know what to do with it, and Sophy found herself remembering all the Christmases and birthdays when his parents had forgotten to give him presents or had given him "learning" toys.

"Don't worry," Sophy murmured, "it's not an educational toy."

He grinned suddenly, taking the box with an eagerness that left her nonplussed. Wasting no time on the outer wrapping, Max tore off the paper and the small strip of ribbon and yanked open the box.

"A tie!" He lifted the length of silk fabric out of the tissue paper. For a long moment he simply stared at it, and then he looked at Sophy. "You made this?"

"Ummm." She nodded, feeling a little uncertain about her decision to give it to him. It wasn't really Max's style at all. Then again, could anyone truthfully say that Max had a style? "If you don't like it, I can always palm it off on Dad, here." The words were defensive and she knew it. Was she afraid of his rejecting the gift? What nonsense. How could it matter one way or the other? But it did. It mattered terribly.

"Sophy, it's beautiful. I've never seen anything like it." Max was turning it over in his hand, examining the delicate handwork on the other side, noting the way it had been cut on the bias. The silk was not a loud pattern, rather an unusually refined and conservative one, considering Sophy's basic tastes. It looked rich and elegant.

"You can make me one like that anytime," Paul Bennet said to his daughter.

Anna Bennet looked bemusedly at the new clothes and the tie, and then at her daughter. "You really do have a certain talent, don't you, darling?"

Paul Bennet nodded agreement. "I hadn't quite realized…" He broke off as he peered over Max's shoulder. "Going to wear it tonight, Max?"

"You bet I am!" Max was already tearing free the old-fashioned narrow tie he was wearing, tossing it carelessly on a nearby chair. Then, collar flipped up, he stood in front of the living room mirror and knotted the new tie with careful precision. When the task was done, he stepped back and eyed his reflection with obvious satisfaction. "Thank you, Sophy. Thank you very much."

Before she realized his intention, he strode the three paces that separated them and kissed her soundly. As she stood there, blinking in wide-eyed surprise over her own actions, Max took her arm and guided her out the door. "Shall we go?" he asked. "Dr. Anna Bennet's fans will be waiting."

Anna Bennet laughed gently, her pleased eyes on the way Max was holding her daughter's arm. With her own arm linked in that of her husband, she traded a knowing glance with her mate. Then the four of them walked through the brisk evening toward the university campus.

Sophy watched the award ceremony with deep pride. Anna Bennet's accomplishments in the field of physics were known by many in the academic world, and the honors she received that evening were well deserved. No one knew that better than Sophy, and no one could have been prouder, unless it was Anna's husband, who glowed with pride and happiness.

The reception that followed the short ceremony was crowded with friends and colleagues of the Bennets' and of Max's. In fact, most of the academic community had turned out for the event. Sophy felt as if she had been plunged back into the world she had fought so long to escape. If it hadn't been for the fact that it was her mother who was being honored, she told herself as she hovered near the small hors d'oeuvre table, she would leave immediately. She'd always dreaded academic receptions. Lousy food and pompous people.

"Are you Sophy Bennet?" A somewhat rumpled-looking young man with wire-rimmed glasses, a corduroy jacket and curling hair that badly needed a cut smiled tentatively from the other side of the table.

Sophy smiled back, labeling him instantly and accurately as a graduate student. "Yes, I am."

The young man nodded in quick relief and adjusted his tie—a tie that was too narrow. "I'm Hal Anderson. A student of your mother's. She suggested I might like to meet you." His eyes darted curiously over her outrageously stylish appearance.

"I'm pleased to know you, Hal," Sophy said easily, helping herself to a pile of little cucumber sandwiches. "Was there some special reason you wanted to meet me?"

He turned a dull red. "Oh, no, well…that is, I, er, saw you standing over here and I sort of wondered aloud who you were, and your mother heard me and said you were her daughter and why didn't I come over and say hello."

Sophy nearly choked on her bite of cucumber sandwich and then recovered nicely. An academic pickup! She seemed to be rather popular with the academic community these days. Still, this was a student of her mother's and he really was rather sweet. "I'm glad you came on over, Hal." The young man relaxed slightly and smiled faintly. "What area are you specializing in?"

That was all the opening Hal Anderson needed. He plunged into a rousing discussion of solid-state physics that enabled Sophy to smile encouragingly a lot and munch cucumber sandwiches to her heart's content.

"Don't let Hal bore you to death," another man warned, wandering over to join in the discussion. "I'm Dick Santini. I'm in the math department."

"Oh, I'm quite fascinated with Hal's area of expertise. I'm sure he's going to make some outstanding contributions to his field," Sophy said smoothly. "And what about you, Dr. Santini? What area of research are you engaged in?"

Santini was well into a discussion of his work in spherical trigonometry, and Hal Anderson was putting in several more comments on physics, when two or three other graduate students and faculty members wandered up to join the discussion. Sophy found herself surrounded by earnest academicians, each eager to tell her about his line of work.

Across the room she briefly caught Max's eye and saw that he was beginning to frown as the group around Sophy grew. Cheerfully she smiled back, silently assuring him that she was quite content, and then she went back to orchestrating the discussion.

They followed her lead readily enough, and somehow her pile of cucumber sandwiches grew rather than shrank as eager hands sought to make her comfortable. Somewhere along the line Sophy realized just how well she was doing juggling all the different academic disciplines. Where had she picked up this marvelous social skill? Heretofore at such receptions, she'd always wound up standing alone, unable to maintain any kind of conversation.

It came from juggling members of corporate management, she decided in a flash of perception. The thought made her smile broaden. Some skills were useful in both worlds.

"Excuse me, gentlemen." Max's deep voice cut through the lively discussion like a hot knife through Jell-O. Sophy glanced up at him and found that there was a certain amount of fire behind the smoke of his eyes. Max was looking a bit dangerous. "Sophy, I came to take you outside for a breath of fresh air," he began determinedly, moving to stand possessively close.

"Oh, I'm doing fine, Max. Dr. Mortenson here has been keeping my glass full of sherry and I don't feel the heat at all. We were just having the most interesting discussion on the applications of probability theory in various disciplines. Dr. Santini has done some fascinating work on the subject of—"

"I'm aware of Dr. Santini's work," Max drawled dryly.

Good grief, Sophy thought in astonishment, Max *was* starting to exhibit a certain Southwestern accent. Strangely enough, although it had annoyed her faintly in Nick Savage, it seemed rather attractive in Max.

Dr. Santini was looking vaguely uncomfortable under

Max's assessing glance and hastened to fill in the conversational lapse. "Miss Bennet is very interested in quite a variety of topics, Max."

"Is she?"

Sophy moved to intercept. "Oh, yes, Max! After all, occasionally one should check up on investments, don't you think?"

Everyone in the group, including Max, stared at her blankly. "Investments?" Dr. Mortenson asked.

"Well, of course," Sophy laughed gently. "You, all of you—" she waved a graceful hand to include the entire academic campus "—represent a considerable investment on the part of the business world. Sizable investments should occasionally be monitored."

"I'm not quite sure what you mean," Hal Anderson said carefully.

Sophy grinned. "Gentlemen, where do you think the money for research and education comes from? It comes from business. Funding universities and colleges represents a long-range investment in the future. The corporate world, the *working* world, has its faults, but you have to admit that it has the guts to put its money where its mouth is, even when it isn't always sure of what the final outcome will be. If there's one thing the business world believes in, it's the future."

There was a pause while the group digested that. Finally Hal Anderson chuckled. "Not the most flattering way of looking at the matter, but I suppose it contains a good deal of truth. I guess academic elitism sometimes sets in around a campus."

Sophy nodded wisely. "And corporate elitism sometimes sets in around a large company. People are people. But the reality is that the academic world and the business world are interdependent. We need the education and skills and research done on campuses to further practical development in the business world. And you need the continuing financial investment and support of the business world to continue your education and research. We all benefit in the end."

In her own way, perhaps, Sophy realized, she had been just as guilty of elitism as any academician. With that realization came another: She was no longer intimidated by the academic world.

"I just hope," Dr. Santini said wistfully, "that you'll continue to check up on your investments occasionally. A bit of interaction between the academic and business worlds is always useful…"

"Definitely," Hal Anderson declared. "Would you like some more cucumber sandwiches, Sophy?"

"Or some more sherry, Miss Bennet?" Dr. Mortenson asked anxiously.

Max made a firm bid for Sophy's arm, wrapping it protectively around his own. "I promised Anna Bennet I would rescue her daughter and return her to her parents," he said smoothly. "Come along, Sophy. You've done enough investment counseling for the evening."

Sophy slid him a sidelong glance as he coolly led her away. Her lips curved with inner laughter. "I think you may have spent too much time in Texas, Max. I'm seeing glimpses of lean, mean cowboy in you lately. Complete with accent."

He arched one brow over the rim of his glasses and there was a faintly sardonic twist to his mouth. "A good academician is always willing to learn, honey. I intend to get as good at handling you as you've gotten at handling members of a university faculty."

Sophy thought about that. "I did all right tonight, didn't I?"

"Sophy, honey, I've never seen you when you didn't do all right. Sometimes you scare the hell out of me!"

"You sound serious!"

"Professors of mathematics are always serious," he informed her. "And I will seriously consider beating you if I find you doing too many impromptu lectures on the interdependence of the academic world and the business world in front of an all-male audience!"

"Yes, Max, I do believe you've been a little too long in Texas." But in her heart Sophy was thinking about serious professors of mathematics. Was it possible she could be more to Dr. Max Travers than a pack of crayons? Would a serious academician like Max waste time pursuing a mere pack of crayons?

Together with that question came a pleasant feeling of having held her own very comfortably in a world that had always been distinctly uncomfortable.

Perhaps, as she had just lectured several members of the university faculty and staff, the two worlds were intertwined. More than she had realized, herself.

CHAPTER TEN

MAX FOUND HIMSELF UNABLE to take his eyes off Sophy's profile as she sat beside him, staring out the jet's window. In another hour they would be back in Dallas. Back to where they started? The time in Chapel Hill seemed like a kind of truce that could be shattered again at any moment now that they were on their way back to Texas. There were so many questions. What was she up to with Marcie? How much longer would she be willing to play out the charade of having an affair with him for Graham Younger's benefit? How much time did he have?

Does she need me at all? Max wondered. *The way I need her?* Damn it to hell. What did you do with a woman who melted in your arms in bed but who kept you at arm's length outside it?

"I haven't thanked you for defending my boutique plans to my parents," Sophy said quietly, interrupting his thoughts. "It was very gracious of you to tell them you thought the idea was a good idea and that you believe I have real talent in business as well as design."

Max leaned his head back against his seat. "I meant it, Sophy. Every word. You do have real talents as a designer and a businesswoman. Even I can tell that." He fingered the tie she had made. He was wearing it again today. "I think your parents appreciate your abilities. They just don't understand the business world enough to see how you could ever make a career out of what they've always considered a hobby."

"The academic world is their whole life," Sophy sighed. "It's the only meaningful sort of career they can imagine. Your defense of my plans gave me some credibility because you have credibility in their eyes. Knowing you respected my ideas made them think twice."

"Sophy…"

"I'm rather grateful, Max."

"I don't want your gratitude," he half snarled.

"I didn't think I'd ever have reason to be grateful to a professor of mathematics, but it just goes to show, you never can tell," she went on, sounding vaguely surprised.

"Consider it a dividend on your investment!"

Something told Sophy it might be time to shut up. Max's temper these days had grown somewhat unpredictable. A woman in love learned to read the signs, she told herself wisely.

And then she realized exactly what she'd said. A woman in love.

She was in love with Max Travers. In love with a wizard. How could it have happened? Two hours later, as she threw her magenta suitcases onto the bed and began to unpack, Sophy was still turning the question over in her mind.

Could she really be more than a pack of crayons for Max Travers? Maybe the urge to play with them was simply a momentary diversion for him. But people like Max Travers, she reminded herself, rarely allowed themselves momentary diversions. They were too intent on the important things in life, like mathematics.

Max had been very silent tonight when he'd dropped her

off at her apartment after the flight. He hadn't even attempted to kiss her good night. All he'd said as she got out of the car was that he'd see her at work in the morning. What had he been thinking? That he was tired of pursuing a pack of crayons who continually made life difficult for him? With a groan of apprehension and gloom, Sophy got undressed and went to bed.

For someone who had prided herself on her ability to deal with the real world, she seemed to have gotten herself into one heck of a mess.

IT WASN'T MAX WHOM SHE saw first at work the next morning, however, it was Marcie Fremont. The other woman was already at work when Sophy entered the office. Marcie was always hard at work, Sophy thought with a rueful smile.

"How was the weekend?" Marcie poured coffee for both of them, eyeing Sophy curiously.

"Confusing. Interesting. Strange. I'm not sure how the weekend was, Marcie. My major accomplishment was surviving an academic reception without finding myself all alone in a corner."

"I can't imagine you ever finding yourself all alone in a corner at a party."

"I used to. Regularly. At least at academic parties. But it was different this time. It's been a while. I didn't realize how much I'd changed."

"A good feeling?"

"Yes." Sophy considered that further. "Yes, it was. I actually felt relaxed. Definitely a change for the better," she concluded firmly.

Two hours later the phone on Marcie's desk rang imperiously. Sophy, who had been just about to leave with her friend for coffee, paused and waited as Marcie picked up the receiver. And then intuition made her lunge forward to grab the instrument from her friend's hand before she had even spoken a greeting.

"S & J Technology, Miss Bennet speaking," Sophy said crisply, waving off Marcie. "Yes, this is Miss Fremont's office. She's busy at the moment. May I take a message…? Oh, I see. Well, perhaps I could slip a message into the conference room where she's conducting the meeting. Would you care to hold?" Regally Sophy put the call on hold and turned to an astonished Marcie.

"It's them! It's that company in California. The vice-president we contacted!"

Marcie's eyes widened as she reached for the phone. Sophy saw that her fingers trembled slightly.

"Oh, Sophy. This is it!"

"Not yet. You mustn't sound to eager. You're an executive they're trying to pirate away, remember? You're only vaguely interested in the position."

"Vaguely interested!" But Marcie dropped her hand and smiled reluctantly. "What now?"

"We let them wait on hold for a few minutes, and then you come to the phone, a bit irritable but aloofly polite."

"Oh, my God!"

"You can do it."

And Marcie did do it. Beautifully. When they finally rescued the unfortunate caller from several minutes on hold, Marcie was in perfect command of herself. Cool, in charge, full of executive presence. And when she eventually hung up the phone, she stared at Sophy with eyes that shone.

"They're begging me to come to work for them. I've been offered my choice of two management positions. One reports directly to the president!"

"That's the one you'll take." Sophy grinned decisively.

"We'll let them stew a couple of days and then you'll accept."

"And in the meantime?"

"In the meantime, we'll go have that coffee we were heading for when we were so rudely interrupted."

The two women walked to the elevators, drawing stares, as usual, because of the contrast they presented. They were unaware of the attention, however. Coffee break this morning was going to be a celebration.

Two days later Marcie made her phone call to California, and the excited, grateful company in California promised everything including a first-class airplane seat for the interview, which would be "merely a formality."

"You'll do beautifully," Sophy assured her, and then she reached for the phone on her own desk.

Max answered a bit brusquely and she knew she'd caught him in the middle of something. He softened immediately when he realized who was on the other end.

"I have to talk to you, Max," Sophy told him without preamble.

He didn't hesitate. "I'll be right down. The cafeteria?"

"Fine." She'd been spending a lot of time discussing business in the cafeteria lately, Sophy thought wryly.

Five minutes later she walked into the nearly empty room and found that Max had already obtained two cups of coffee and a private table. He looked up a bit warily as she came striding briskly toward him, and then his expression became impassive.

"It's over, Max." Sophy sat down and reached for her coffee. There was a deadly silence from the other side of the table. When she raised her eyes from her cup, she found Max looking at her with such intensity that she swallowed awkwardly and nearly choked.

"No."

That was all he said. She blinked in confusion. "But, Max, it is. There's nothing you can do. It's over."

"The hell it is!" He leaned forward, his palms flat on the table, eyes glittering icily behind the lenses of his glasses. "You're not going to just calmly phone me up and invite me for coffee and then tell me it's over. Not after all I've been through!"

Sophy edged back in her seat, shocked by the rough vehemence in his words. "Max, I'm sorry I started this whole thing by telling you what Marcie had planned, but at the time I sort of…well, panicked. I never wanted you to go to management with the information. But now everything's changed. Marcie has a new job and she'll be leaving the company soon. There's no way Graham Younger can ever implicate her in corporate espionage. You never even completed the phony model. There was no espionage."

"Marcie!" Max looked dumbfounded. "We're talking about Marcie? About your mysterious plans?"

"Well, of course. My plans to get Marcie a job in management. What did you think we were talking about?"

"You and me."

"Oh." Nonplussed, Sophy eyed him cautiously. He looked vastly relieved and at the same time thoroughly annoyed. "Well, uh, we're not. We're talking about the end of Younger's idiotic little scheme to trap Marcie and her 'web of conspirators.' Now we're going to have to tell Younger his brilliant plan didn't work, and I'm going to take great pleasure in doing so, if you want the truth."

She stood decisively and Max followed more reluctantly. "Uh…Sophy, there's something I have to tell you. You know this brilliant plan you've been criticizing from the beginning?" He ushered her into the elevator.

"What about it?"

"Well, it wasn't exactly Graham Younger's idea."

"Edison's? The head of Security?"

"Nope. It was all mine," he sighed.

"Yours!" Sophy stared up at him, her mouth falling open in astonishment. "It was *your* idea to play out this silly farce just for the sake of trapping poor Marcie Fremont? But, Max…!"

"I'm afraid so. Younger and Edison and I agreed before the meeting with you that you'd be more likely to go along with it if you thought it was a request from your boss. Besides, Younger thought it was a pretty good scheme. One that would work. He was willing enough to take credit for it."

"But, Max…!" She swallowed. "Why?"

"Not because I give a damn about Marcie Fremont and her potential as a corporate espionage agent, that's for sure!" The elevator doors slid open on the executive suite floor. "You can bet I normally don't get involved in such mundane things as corporate security," he growled.

"So why did you become involved?"

"The single merit of this asinine scheme was that it ensured that you had to keep seeing me. Think about it."

"But, Max," Sophy couldn't help but say, "it was such a silly idea."

"I know. You'd think I'd have enough sense to stick to mathematics, wouldn't you?"

CHAPTER ELEVEN

"YOU WERE MARVELOUSLY arrogant with Younger and Edison, Max." Sophy gave him a mischievous smile as she sat across from him at dinner that night. "Thanks."

The scene in Graham Younger's office had not been pleasant, Max reflected as he munched the taco salad Sophy had insisted he sample. Younger and Edison were both angry at having had their potential prey snatched from their grasp.

They had been even more furious to learn they'd been outmaneuvered by a mere secretary. And word of Marcie's new management position had made Younger positively livid, especially when Sophy explained just how much Marcie's undervalued knowledge of S & J's Quality Control would benefit her new employer.

Sophy had seemed rather unconcerned about her boss's attempt to make mincemeat out of her, although Max had caught a flash of appreciative gratitude in her eyes when he'd stepped in and restored a certain civility to the proceedings.

And now she was thanking him. No, she wasn't actually *thanking* him, Max decided unhappily, she was merely complimenting him on having put the other two men in their place. She hadn't really needed him to defend her, he realized. Sophy didn't seem to *need* him for anything.

Therein lay the crux of his whole problem.

Max picked up his wine. "You were a little arrogant yourself."

She shrugged, the frilly, flounced sleeve of her red dinner dress shifting intriguingly. "I can afford to be a bit uppity." She grinned. "I'll be quitting soon."

"To open your boutique?"

"Ummm. How do you like the taco salad, Max?"

"I'm not sure I like hamburger and corn chips in my salads."

"You'll get used to it."

"I doubt it. I'm going back to North Carolina on Wednesday." He delivered the statement with a deliberate lack of intonation. How would she react? Probably be thrilled.

There was a beat of hesitation, and for the life of him he couldn't begin to imagine what she was thinking. "Where you can eat hush puppies all day long and work on math equations? Are you sure you can readapt? What about that Texas drawl you're working on?"

Max was suddenly tired of the flippancy. "Why don't you come back with me and find out what happens to it?"

Sophy flushed. "Sorry. I keep my visits to Chapel Hill to a minimum. I love my parents, but I knew a long time ago I couldn't live too close to them or spend too much time with them. I don't have to be in their company five minutes before they're giving such useful advice as telling me to go back for my master's."

"They aren't fighting your boutique idea," he pointed out carefully. She was avoiding the point, but he let her for the moment.

"Only because you defended it. People back down when you come to the rescue. Have you noticed that, Max? Younger, Edison, my parents, poor Nick. They all either respect your opinion or are intimidated by you now. Quite a track record."

"Except you."

"Except me. Would you like me to be intimidated by you, Max?"

"No. I'd like you to need me," he said flatly. She went very still. "The way I need you."

"Max," Sophy said. "You don't need me. Not really. I don't fit in your world. I never have. You'd be bored with me in two months!"

"Come back with me for two months and find out."

"No!"

"I think the truth of the matter is that you're the one who's afraid she'll be bored. Bored with a staid, sober, dull professor of mathematics." He looked straight into her eyes. "Sophy, I've given this a lot of thought. The only way things will ever really work between us is if you discover on some level that you need me. You have to decide that you really need me in your life." He spoke slowly, setting everything out in the open. He had nothing left to lose. "And there may come a time when you do decide that, Sophy."

"Max, I don't know what you're trying to say, but…"

"But I think you need a little time. You're basically a very bright young woman, just as your parents have claimed all along," he noted whimsically. "And now I believe you need some time to think."

"About what, Dr. Travers?"

"About such matters as why I kept wanting to see you, be with you, whenever possible, even though you had sworn you wouldn't go to bed with me again. About why I stepped outside my area of expertise to concoct that ridiculous scheme and then convinced Graham Younger to involve you in it. About a lot of things."

"Oh, Max…!" she wailed softly. "I don't know. I can't seem to think. It's all so confusing."

"That's why I'm going back to North Carolina on Wednesday. Sophy, when you've thought it all out and made your decision, I'll be waiting." He leaned forward to catch her agitated fingers and squeeze them gently. "Come back to Chapel Hill anytime, sweetheart. You'll find me there, waiting for you."

MAX SAT IN HIS THIRD-FLOOR corner office, oblivious to the lush green grounds of the campus outside his window, and wondered if he was going out of his mind.

He hadn't been able to concentrate on anything since he had returned from Dallas. Oh, he'd gotten through the work on his desk and occasionally he'd picked up an article in one of the many esoteric journals he read. But the intense concentration that had always characterized him seemed to have disappeared. He had to struggle to think of anything at all except Sophy.

It had only been five days since he'd left Dallas. Monday morning. He had a graduate seminar in half an hour. He hoped he could fake his way through it. Shouldn't be too difficult. The students were studying the work of Evariste Galois, the brilliant French mathematician who, because of his fiery temper, had managed to get himself killed in a duel at the age of twenty. People had wondered for years just how much Galois might have gone on to contribute to the world of mathematics if his temper hadn't been quite so passionate. Before his death he had already established himself as one of the most original thinkers who ever lived.

For the first time in his life Max thought he understood Evariste Galois. Never before had he been able to comprehend a man as brilliant as Galois letting himself get sidetracked from his real work long enough to become involved in such an idiotic thing as a duel over a woman. Now he could.

He'd skip the graduate seminar altogether if it meant he could fight another cowboy for Sophy. Some things were more important than math.

He *must* be going out of his mind to think that!

Max crumpled the piece of paper he'd idly been twisting into a Möbius strip, a shape with the curious property of having only one side, and listened to the staccato tap of a pair of high heels out in the hall.

The sound reminded him of Sophy. Bright, energetic, alive. He wondered who on the third floor had worn high heels today. Usually the women in his department wore more sensible shoes.

The aggressive tap of the heels came to a halt outside his door and he glanced up automatically, aware that his body was tense with anticipation, just because of the sound of a pair of high heels that reminded him of Sophy. Things were getting worse. He really was going to go slowly out of his mind if he didn't do something drastic.

The knock on the door made him frown. "Come in." Simultaneously he realized that the sound of the high heels in the corridor had stopped. Whoever was knocking on his door was wearing the shoes. It was going to be painful to have the door open and find another woman besides Sophy standing there.

But the door opened and it wasn't another woman.

"Sophy!" Max surged to his feet. He felt dazed. "Sophy," he repeated far more softly. He realized he was staring, but he couldn't help himself. It was almost impossible to believe she was here in his office, bringing light and color and confusion to his orderly surroundings. Her mane of curls seemed more delightfully frizzy than ever.

The high heels he had heard tapping out the exciting rhythm in the hall were purple. Max thought vaguely that he'd never seen purple shoes. They went wonderfully with the purple-and-red dress she was wearing. Nobody else he knew could successfully wear purple and red. But the best color of all was the strange blue-green shade of her eyes. And right now those eyes were smiling at him.

"Hello, Max," she said softly. "I brought you something." She came toward him, carrying a small package in her right hand.

Feeling as if he were moving under the force of a spell, Max extended his hand for the gift. It wasn't what he wanted to do. What he really wanted to do was grab Sophy and hold her close to make certain she was real and not a bright illusion. She put the package in his fingers and he looked down at it.

"Sophy." He wasn't certain what to say next, so he tried to concentrate on unwrapping the package. The paper fell away beneath his unusually clumsy attempts, and he stared at the box of crayons, a slow smile edging the corner of his mouth. "Thank you." Damn it, couldn't he think of anything more intelligent?

"Do you still want me, Max?"

He heard the uncertainty and the wistful hope in her voice and groaned, dropping the crayons on his desk to walk around the front and pull her into his arms. "Sophy, honey, I've been sitting here for five days thinking about what I was going to do if you didn't come to me." He buried his face in the cascading curls and inhaled deeply. "My God, Sophy, I can't believe you're really here."

He held her close, and when her arms went around his waist he muttered her name again and searched out her mouth. For a long moment they clung together, mouths joined in heated dampness, their bodies touching intimately. Max let the tension seep out of his body, felt the happiness welling up inside. She was here. He couldn't believe his luck.

"Sophy, honey, I know I'm no macho cowboy..."

"No," she laughed into his shirt, "you're a macho university professor. Until you came along, I didn't know they existed. You've got a foot in both worlds now."

"So do you. How can you doubt it after the way you handled yourself at that faculty reception? And the way you handle yourself in the corporate world is a bit frightening! Someday I want to hear the whole story of how you got Marcie Fremont that job in California."

"Someday I'll tell you. You'll probably be shocked, though."

"Nothing you can do would shock me anymore," he murmured.

"Then maybe you really have come out of your ivory tower!" She lifted her head abruptly. "What would you have done, Max, if I hadn't come to Chapel Hill?" she asked, her eyes wide and inviting.

"I told myself I'd give you a month or so and then I'd find some excuse to fly back to Dallas. I was making lists of reasons I could give S & J Technology for having to update that math model I did for them."

"Your creativity outside the realm of math leaves me breathless," Sophy laughed gently.

"Don't worry. When creativity fails me I can always fall back on my new macho mentality."

"The direct approach?"

"Umm. Like carrying you off over my shoulder."

"Max, you wouldn't! Imagine what your colleagues would think."

"That's their problem. I learned a few things down in Texas."

"Yes, I know." Sophy grinned ruefully. "Like how to fix plumbing, and grill steaks, and wear stylish ties." She let her hand trail lightly down his shoulder to the tie he was wearing. She smoothed it affectionately. "You're going to wear out your new tie, Max."

"You can make me another one."

"I will."

"A wedding gift?" he suggested tenderly.

"You want to marry me?" He saw the flutter of hope and joy in her eyes and gathered her close again.

"That's the logical conclusion when two people are in love."

"Love? You love me, Max? Are you sure?"

"I'm very, very sure." He wrapped her close, his voice husky and low. "Only love could have made me go crazy that night after you discovered that dumb cowboy was cheating on you. I've never taken advantage of a woman before in my life! A whole lifetime of being a gentleman went up in smoke. And the worst part was that I didn't regret it afterward. That was just the beginning. When I found myself concocting ridiculous schemes so that I could have an excuse to go on seeing you, I knew I was in over my head."

"Oh, Max, I've always been so careful to steer clear of people in your world. I was intimidated by wizards for so long. I couldn't bear the thought of loving a man who couldn't possibly respect me as an equal."

"Sophy, you have your own kind of wizardry. You're an artist and a businesswoman. Do you realize what a rare combination that is? Few people have the ability to be both. I have a tremendous respect for your abilities."

"But my parents always thought—"

"Darling, I'm very fond of your parents. They've been wonderful to me. But I'm aware they're a little blind where you're concerned. They love you deeply, but they don't quite understand you. That's why they've always tried to push you back into their world—a world they do understand."

Sophy slanted a wondering glance at his loving eyes. "You're a bridge between my world and theirs, aren't you, Max?"

He gave her a strange half smile and shook his head. "No, you're the bridge, Sophy. For all of us. If it wasn't for you in their lives, occasionally turning it upside down and filling it with confusion, your mother and father undoubtedly would have turned out a lot like my parents. Cold and unemotional and completely secluded in their academic world. I probably would have wound up like my parents, too, if it hadn't been for you. I was well on my way! But I looked out of my ivory tower one day and saw what I'd been missing."

"The fun of brawling with cowboys?" she taunted gently.

"And the joy of eating popcorn while watching old sci-fi flicks, and of seducing you. Most of all seducing you. I need you. You make my life complete. But I can't help wondering why you love me, although I'm not about to question my luck!"

She saw the anxious hope in his eyes and lifted her fingers to smooth the harsh brackets around his mouth. "Much to my astonishment, I found myself loving you for some of the same reasons you say you love me," she admitted softly. "When you left Dallas all the color went out of my life. But it's so much more than that. I realized I had to take the chance of going to you. Our worlds may be different, but they complement each other. You make me feel complete. I love you."

He was watching her face with raw hunger now in his eyes. There was a longing in him that was a combination of love and desire and need, and Sophy felt herself responding to the potent mixture.

"I never thought wizards were capable of real passion for anything except their work until I met you," she breathed.

"You bring out the passionate side of me, along with a few other sides I didn't know existed."

"And you bring out some sides of me I didn't know existed, either. I've taken risks with you I've never even thought of taking with any other man. I can't imagine being willing to come back to Chapel Hill for any other man. But with you I was willing to take the chance. And I can't imagine letting myself get seduced by a man I hardly even knew the way I did with you. Oh, Max, we've both done some crazy things around each other, haven't we?"

"We should have realized it was love right from the beginning," he drawled.

"But I thought I had nothing worthwhile to give a wizard," she said wistfully.

"And I thought I had nothing worthwhile to offer someone like you, who seemed to have everything and who seemed to prefer cowboys. Sophy, will you marry me and live with me for the rest of our lives?"

She linked her arms around his neck and smiled dreamily. "Yes," she whispered, touching her lips to his. "Yes, yes, yes." A teasing light came into her eyes. "But do you suppose North Carolina is ready for my style of clothing design?"

She felt Max's warm chuckle as it moved through his chest. "Possibly not. But even if it is, I'm rather inclined to agree with your feeling that you should live some distance from your parents. It's true that you now have me to run interference with them when they start worrying overmuch about your lifestyle, but I think, all things considered, we'd be better off in Texas."

"Texas!" Startled, she stared up at him. He ruffled the curling halo of her hair and smiled.

"Umm. I hate to sound arrogant about this, knowing as I do how you feel about arrogant math wizards, but frankly, I can write my own ticket to any school in the country. How does Austin sound? I know it's not Dallas, but…"

"Austin. You're going to get a job at the University of Texas?"

"Why not? I had an offer from them last year, which I put on ice as I usually do. But if I were to change my mind, I don't think there would be any problem."

"But, Max, you've got tenure here."

"Tenure isn't particularly important to me. Your career is a lot more important. And I think you could pursue it better in a wide-open state like Texas than you could in North Carolina. And in Texas you won't have to worry about your charming parents gazing over your shoulder all the time."

"You really mean that, don't you? You're willing to take another position in another state for my sake? Max, I don't know what to say. I'm stunned."

"The expression is very becoming on you. Don't worry, honey, it's all going to work out perfectly."

"But will you be happy in Texas?"

"Sweetheart, I've begun to think lately that I was born in Texas," he drawled in his new accent. "I fit right in down there. Didn't you notice? I spent all my spare time brawling and grilling steaks and taking you to bed. A classic Texan. First thing I'm going to do when we get there is buy a pair of hand-tooled cowboy boots suitable for squashing rattlesnakes."

"Max, I love you."

"I love you." He feathered her mouth lightly with his own and then suddenly remembered something.

"Sweetheart, I'm supposed to be teaching a graduate seminar in about two minutes…"

She noticed that he didn't sound too concerned. "Really?"

"But I think my students will understand that mathematics can't always come first," he murmured, reaching behind him to punch an intercom button. Quickly, he arranged for an associate to take his place, then beckoned her. "Right now I've got other things on my mind besides teaching class. We Texans keep our priorities straight, you know."

"Ah, the marvelous, multidimensional, eminently logical mind of a wizard," she murmured, going back into his arms. "As a matter of fact, I was thinking about keeping the same priorities straight."

"Must be a case of great minds traveling on the same path."

"Could be. You know, I've come to the conclusion you're going to be very useful around the house, Max. I've got this checkbook that hasn't been balanced in six months, for starters."

"It's so nice to feel needed." He grinned wickedly. "Honey, I will be happy to barbecue your meals, fix your plumbing, fight off cowboys and balance your checkbook. But there is a price for a wizard's services. I believe I once pointed out that I don't come cheap."

"What's the price?"

"Let me show you." His mouth came down on hers, and Sophy gave herself up to the wizardry of love.

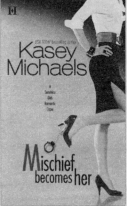

REQUEST YOUR FREE BOOKS!

2 FREE NOVELS FROM THE ROMANCE/SUSPENSE COLLECTION PLUS 2 FREE GIFTS!

YES! Please send me 2 FREE novels from the Romance/Suspense Collection and my 2 FREE gifts (gifts are worth about $10). After receiving them, if I don't wish to receive any more books, I can return the shipping statement marked "cancel." If I don't cancel, I will receive 4 brand-new novels every month and be billed just $5.49 per book in the U.S. or $5.99 per book in Canada, plus 25¢ shipping and handling per book plus applicable taxes, if any*. That's a savings of at least 20% off the cover price! I understand that accepting the 2 free books and gifts places me under no obligation to buy anything. I can always return a shipment and cancel at any time. Even if I never buy another book from the Reader Service, the two free books and gifts are mine to keep forever.

185 MDN EF5Y   385 MDN EF6C

Name _____ (PLEASE PRINT) _____

Address _____ Apt. # _____

City _____ State/Prov. _____ Zip/Postal Code _____

Signature (if under 18, a parent or guardian must sign)

Mail to **The Reader Service:**
IN U.S.A.: P.O. Box 1867, Buffalo, NY 14240-1867
IN CANADA: P.O. Box 609, Fort Erie, Ontario L2A 5X3

Not valid to current subscribers to the Romance Collection,
the Suspense Collection or the Romance/Suspense Collection.

Want to try two free books from another line?
Call 1-800-873-8635 or visit www.morefreebooks.com.

* Terms and prices subject to change without notice. N.Y. residents add applicable sales tax. Canadian residents will be charged applicable provincial taxes and GST. Offer not valid in Quebec. This offer is limited to one order per household. All orders subject to approval. Credit or debit balances in a customer's account(s) may be offset by any other outstanding balance owed by or to the customer. Please allow 4 to 6 weeks for delivery. Offer available while quantities last.

Your Privacy: Harlequin is committed to protecting your privacy. Our Privacy Policy is available online at www.eHarlequin.com or upon request from the Reader Service. From time to time we make our lists of customers available to reputable third parties who may have a product or service of interest to you. If you would prefer we not share your name and address, please check here. ☐

BOB08R

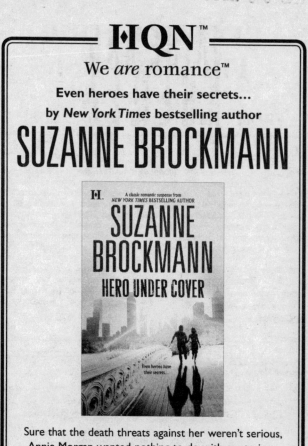

FEB 0 5 2009

JAYNE ANN
KRENTZ

77144   GAMBLER'S WOMAN   ___ $6.99 U.S. ___ $8.50 CAN.

(limited quantities available)

TOTAL AMOUNT $ _____
POSTAGE & HANDLING $ _____
($1.00 FOR 1 BOOK, 50¢ for each additional)
APPLICABLE TAXES* $ _____
TOTAL PAYABLE $ _____

(check or money order—please do not send cash)

To order, complete this form and send it, along with a check or money
order for the total above, payable to HQN Books, to: **In the U.S.:**
-3010 Walden Avenue, P.O. Box 9077, Buffalo, NY 14269-9077;
In Canada: P.O. Box 636, Fort Erie, Ontario, L2A 5X3.

Name: _____
Address: _____ City: _____ ·
State/Prov.: _____ Zip/Postal Code: _____
Account Number (if applicable): _____

075 CSAS

*New York residents remit applicable sales taxes.
*Canadian residents remit applicable GST and provincial taxes.

HQN™

We *are* romance™

www.HQNBooks.com   PHJAK1108BL